FIRST IMPRESSIONS

I stuck my eye to the peephole, but all I could see was a warped, unrecognizable face.

"Who is it?" I shouted.

"Detective Flynn. Duivel Police. Open up."

Police? Did I do something really awful last night?

"Show me your badge."

He held what looked like a badge up to the hole. He'd made enough noise that all my neighbors were probably peeking out their doors to see if the cops hauled me away in handcuffs—again. Living vicariously through my troubles brightened their ordinary lives.

I opened the door a few inches. Whoa! This was a nice one. He appeared around thirty, maybe a little older. His jet-black hair gently curled around his ears and he needed a shave, but he still looked yummy. He wore a rumpled jacket, a T-shirt and blue jeans that fit a fine, strong body. Detective Flynn. Too bad he was a cop. I kept one hand on the door, but I doubted I could close it fast enough if he wanted to force his way through. "What do you want?"

"I want to come in."

"And I should let you because . . . ?"

"Because I'm a nice person."

Funny, he didn't look nice. Sexy as hell—but not nice.

Viper Moon

A NOVEL OF THE EARTH WITCHES

LEE ROLAND

A SIGNET ECLIPSE BOOK

SIGNET ECLIPSE
Published by New American Library, a division of
Penguin Group (USA) Inc., 375 Hudson Street,
New York, New York 10014, USA
Penguin Group (Canada), 90 Eglinton Avenue East, Suite 700, Toronto,
Ontario M4P 2Y3, Canada (a division of Pearson Penguin Canada Inc.)
Penguin Books Ltd., 80 Strand, London WC2R 0RL, England
Penguin Ireland, 25 St. Stephen's Green, Dublin 2,
Ireland (a division of Penguin Books Ltd.)
Penguin Group (Australia), 250 Camberwell Road, Camberwell, Victoria 3124,
Australia (a division of Pearson Australia Group Pty. Ltd.)
Penguin Books India Pvt. Ltd., 11 Community Centre, Panchsheel Park,
New Delhi - 110 017, India
Penguin Group (NZ), 67 Apollo Drive, Rosedale, Auckland 0632,
New Zealand (a division of Pearson New Zealand Ltd.)
Penguin Books (South Africa) (Pty.) Ltd., 24 Sturdee Avenue,
Rosebank, Johannesburg 2196, South Africa

Penguin Books Ltd., Registered Offices:
80 Strand, London WC2R 0RL, England

First published by Signet Eclipse, an imprint of New American Library,
a division of Penguin Group (USA) Inc.

First Printing, July 2011
10   9   8   7   6   5   4   3   2   1

For my husband, who is the center of my life

ACKNOWLEDGMENTS

I need to be alone when I write. No music, no coffee shops—only blessed silence will allow my creativity to come out of hiding so I can maneuver it onto a page.

Getting those pages published, however, was not a solitary endeavor. This book would not be possible without professional and personal aid from many individuals. A few, but certainly not all, are listed below. There is no particular order of listing. Each was the "most important" at certain times.

My editor, Jhanteigh Kupihea, who so professionally and graciously guided me through the editing and publishing process.

Kerry Donovan, who believed in *Viper Moon*.

My agent, Caren Johnson Estesen, who had faith that my stories were good and never gave up on me.

My fellow writers and critique partners—present and past—whose critical feedback and encouragement was, and will continue to be, invaluable.

chapter 1

The Barrows
July 21—Full Moon

Mama wanted me to be a veterinarian. She'd probably have settled for a nurse, teacher, or grocery store clerk. She never came right out and said, "Cassandra, you disappointed me" or "Cassandra, you have so much potential," but I knew I'd let her down.

The idea of me running down a slimy storm sewer in the desolate, abandoned ruins of the Barrows section of Duivel, Missouri, probably never crossed her mind. The unconscious five-year-old boy strapped to my back and the angry monster with fangs and claws snapping at my heels were just part of my job. Maybe Mama was right— I'd made the wrong career choice.

I'm in good shape, but I'd run, crawled, and slogged through the sewer for over an hour. My chest heaved in the moldy, moisture-laden air by the time I finally reached my escape hatch. The glow from phosphorescent lichen gave me enough light to see the manhole shaft leading out of this little section of hell. Claws clattered right behind me and the tunnel echoed with slobbering grunts. This particular monster was an apelike brute with porcupine quills running down its spine and glowing green eyes.

Up into the manhole cylinder, two rungs, three . . . Roars bounced off the tight walls . . . Almost there—a claw snagged my slime-covered boot.

I jerked away and heaved myself out onto the deserted street.

Not good.

Clouds covered the full moon's silver face, so my vile pursuer might actually take a chance and follow me. The Earth Mother has no power here in the Barrows, save her daughter's light in the midnight sky. Maiden, mother, and crone, signifying the progression of life from cradle to grave, that ancient pagan female entity had called me to her service years ago. Now, in her name, I ran for my life. In her name, I carried this innocent child away from evil.

I'd managed to get off two shots and my bronze bullets hurt the ugly sucker, but a kill required a hit in a critical area like an eye. I could stop and aim or run like hell. I ran.

Its claws gouged out the asphalt as it dragged itself after me.

Under usual circumstances, I wouldn't have gone below the street. I'm good at kick the door down, grab the kid, and run. This time a bit of stealth was required since the door guards carried significant firepower. I was definitely outgunned.

Most things living in the storm sewers were prey. The small creatures ran from me. This time I'd crossed paths with a larger predator determined to make me a midnight snack.

I'd parked my car on the next block, so I sprinted toward a dark, shadowed alley that cut between the three-story brick buildings. Derelict vehicles and broken furniture made my path an obstacle course as I threaded my way through the debris toward the pitiful yellow light of a rare streetlamp at the alley's far end.

A coughlike snarl came from behind. The creature

would leap over things I had to go around. I wouldn't make it, and if I did, those claws would tear the metal off my little car like I would peel an orange. I'd have to turn and fight soon. I hoped I could take the thing down before it overwhelmed me.

Halfway down the alley, a door suddenly opened in the building to my left. A Bastinado in full gang regalia, including weapons, stepped out. Though technically human, Bastinados are filthy, sadistic bastards whose myriad hobbies include rape, robbery, and murder.

I had nothing to lose as terror nipped at my heels and gave me momentum. I rammed the Bastinado with my shoulder, knocked him down, and rushed inside. Drug paraphernalia and naked gang members lay scattered around the room. I'd crashed their party and brought a monster as my date. The Bastinado at the door certainly hadn't stopped it.

The creature roared louder than the boom box thumping the walls with teeth-rattling bass. The Bastinados grabbed their weapons. They barely glanced at me as I crossed the room at a dead run. Two guards stood at the front door, but they had their eyes on the monster, too. I shoved my way past the guards. Screams and gunshots filled the night. Throw the door bolt and I emerged onto the sidewalk.

I raced down the street. I hadn't gone far when the ground suddenly heaved and shuddered under my feet. The whole block thundered with a massive explosion. A vast wind howled, furious and red, and surged down the street in battering waves.

Tornados of brilliant orange fire blasted out the windows of the building I'd escaped, and washed over the street like an outrageous, misguided sunrise. A hot hand of air picked me up and slammed me to the broken concrete. I twisted and landed face-first to protect the boy strapped to my back, then rolled to my side with my body between him and the inferno. I covered my face with my arms. More explosions followed and the doomed building's front facade crumbled into the street while burning debris rained from the sky.

What in the Earth Mother's name had been in there?

When the fury abated a bit, I forced myself to my feet and headed for the car. Was the pavement moving or was it me staggering?

The sound of the explosion still hammered my eardrums. I opened the back door, peeled away the straps and protective covering holding the boy secure against my body. I laid him across the backseat. He didn't seem injured, and he still slept from the sedative I'd given him to keep him calm.

It wasn't until I climbed in the driver's seat and fumbled for my key that I noticed the blood—my blood—too much blood. Slick wet crimson streaked down the side of my face and soaked half my shirt. Shards of glass protruded like rough diamonds from my forearm's blistered skin. It didn't hurt—yet. Pain would come soon enough.

I turned the key in the ignition. Nothing happened.

Another deeper blast rumbled under the street, shaking the car.

Sirens sounded in the distance, police, fire trucks, ambulances, rushing to the scene. They rarely entered the Barrows, but the magnitude of the blast I'd lived through couldn't be ignored.

I turned the key again. And again.

Last month I'd had to make a choice. Fix the car's starter or buy special hand-loaded bronze bullets. I'd chosen bullets.

The fourth time I twisted the key, the engine jerked to life. It sputtered twice, then smoothed. I popped it into gear and rolled forward, away from the fiery beast still raging behind.

Symptoms of shock crept in and pain found me. It rose by increments, increasing in intensity with every passing moment. My heart raced at a frantic pace and my arms shook so I could barely hold the wheel. Sweat formed an icy second skin as my body temperature took a nosedive. Sweet Mother, it hurt. The street blurred and shifted in my vision. Worse, though, was the feeling of pursuit. My little car chased through the deserted streets by some invisible, unimaginable horror. With considerable will, I kept my foot from mashing down the gas pedal.

Clouds drifted away from the cold, exquisite full moon.

"Follow," a soft voice whispered and urged me on. The white orb in the sky suddenly filled the windshield, rising to a brilliant mass of pure, clear light. I drove toward the radiance, navigating well-known streets as if dreaming of driving. North, keep moving north. A stop sign? Okay. Don't run that red light. If a cop stopped me, they'd call an ambulance, take me to the hospital, and I'd die. I was already beyond the skill of modern medicine's healing.

The child in the backseat moaned, as if in a nightmare. I had to stay conscious long enough to get him to safety. I wouldn't go down for nothing.

The guiding brilliance faded as I reached my destination. Control of the automobile eluded me, however, and the mailbox loomed. Before I could hit the brakes, I'd rolled over the box and the small sign that marked the home and business of Madam Abigail. The sign offered psychic readings, but gave not a hint of the true power and grace of the woman who dwelled and worked there.

I plowed through the flowered yard. Abby was going to be seriously pissed at me. Two feet from the front porch, the car jerked to a halt. Abby would find me. Abby would care for me as she always had. Luminous moonlight filled the night again, then faded, leaving only sweet-smelling flowers that lured me into painless darkness.

chapter 2

The pounding wouldn't go away and I figured someone was beating on the apartment door and not my head. It couldn't be the landlord because I was only a week late with the rent. The soulless bastard knew me by now and usually didn't start harassing me until the third week. The utility company didn't pound; they flipped a switch downtown, like the cell phone people had three days earlier.

The air conditioner in the window hummed constantly, fighting to keep up with record heat washing in abundant thermal waves against the glass, even at the disagreeable hour of eight in the morning.

"Come on, I know you're there!" a male voice shouted through the door.

Now what?

I climbed out of bed, staggered to the door, then stopped. My long mustard yellow T-shirt had DOES THIS SHIRT MAKE MY TITS LOOK TOO BIG? printed across the front. Of course, it would take a lot more than a T-shirt to make *my* tits look too big. It smelled like a two-hour workout, but it covered my panties. I didn't plan to let the door basher in anyway.

He pounded harder and I winced. Each thud bounced around my skull and set my constricted blood vessels screaming.

Hell of a party last night. I'd gone out to celebrate my recovery from the injuries sustained at the last full moon. When did I get home? *How* did I get home? Something about my car . . . Damn.

I stuck my eye to the peephole, but all I could see was a warped, unrecognizable face.

"Who is it?" I shouted.

"Detective Flynn. Duivel Police. Open up."

Police? Did I do something really awful last night?

"Show me your badge."

He held what looked like a badge up to the hole. He'd made enough noise that all my neighbors were probably peeking out their doors to see if the cops were hauling me away in handcuffs—again. Living vicariously through my troubles brightened their ordinary lives.

I opened the door a few inches. Whoa! This was a nice one. He appeared around thirty, maybe a little older. His jet-black hair gently curled around his ears and he needed a shave, but he still looked yummy. He wore a rumpled jacket, a T-shirt, and blue jeans that fit a fine, strong body. Detective Flynn. Too bad he was a cop. I kept one hand on the door, but I doubted I could close it fast enough if he wanted to force his way through. "What do you want?"

"I want to come in."

"And I should let you because . . . ?"

"Because I'm a nice person. I had your piece of shit car towed off the sidewalk in front of Zeke's Deli this morning. It's downstairs. It could be at the impound lot."

Zeke's Deli was three blocks down the street. Funny, he didn't look nice. Sexy as hell—but not nice.

I opened the door wider and he stalked into the single room that made up my kitchen, living, and dining area. He stared around the apartment like a health inspector surveying a roach motel. Then he stared at me the same way. "You look like shit."

"Thank you. Glad you noticed. Hello. I'm Cassandra Archer and I'm delighted to meet you, too, Detective Flynn."

I went to the fridge, grabbed the bag of coffee, and tossed it on the counter beside the coffeepot and pack of filters. "Make some coffee. Did you bring donuts?"

"Fuck!"

Oh, my goodness. I must have pissed him off. I gave him what I hoped was an evil smile. "I'll take that as a no. I'm going to shower. If you're not here when I get back, I'll understand."

I headed for the bedroom. I really didn't want him to arrest me in a T-shirt and underwear. Arrest wasn't what he had in mind, though, or he'd have locked the cuffs on me as soon as he stepped in the door. He muttered something unintelligible behind me.

I went into the tiny, windowless bathroom with its depressing, anemic, industrial gray tile and turned on the shower. Five minutes later, a thin stream of warm water made its way up from the basement. I stripped off my shirt and panties, climbed in, and washed the lumps out of my hair. A couple of twigs, some leaves, and a few pieces of— That smell . . . was there a dog at the party? I washed my hair again, this time with a bar of citrus-scented soap my mother had sent me.

The situation was a first for me. I'd had only two beers last night—I think. I'd *never* been so drunk that I couldn't remember what I did. Now I'd lost everything past nine p.m. Entirely my fault, though. I hadn't followed orders.

Dear Madam Abigail said no beer for at least a month. The medicine, the foul-tasting potions and slimy oils that magically brought relief to my seriously burned skin did not peacefully coexist with even minute amounts of alcohol.

My laundry basket produced a reasonably clean pair of jeans and I found a tank top and panties in the drawer. My body is lean, muscular, and athletic. A few freckles dot my nose and cheeks, and my eyes are a dull brownish green, not the emerald so prized in redheads. I have great hair. I dried and brushed it to a copper sheen.

Now to see what the sexy yet abrasive Detective Flynn wanted.

Flynn sat at the table drinking coffee. My ancient appliance gurgled and gasped through its long cycle, but made a great brew. The nutty odor filling the room made my mouth water.

He'd removed the jacket that covered his gun and the badge he'd clipped to his belt, and hung it on the back of the chair. Not that it mattered. He could wear a tux but savvy people watchers would mark him as a cop by the way he moved. Tough, confident, ready to face whatever came his way.

I poured myself a cup and sat at the table across from him. He didn't smile. Intense weariness settled in eyes as dark and deep as the liquid in the cups. How long since he'd slept?

Flynn reached in the pocket of his jacket and tossed a picture, a four-by-six snapshot, on the table. He watched me with narrowed eyes. His grim mouth betrayed nothing.

I glanced at the photo of a little boy. Five years old, brown hair, wide innocent eyes, with his mouth turned up in a gap-toothed smile.

I shrugged. "Maxie Fountain. Picture in the *Duivel Chronicle*, maybe a month ago. Kidnapped. Snatched off his bicycle."

He produced another photo.

I picked it up. "Abandoned store. Exeter Street, near the docks. Blew up and burned, oh, two weeks ago. Bastinados stashed arms and ammo. Or so the *Chronicle* said."

The Bastinado gangs—the Exeter Street Slashers, Pythons, Blood Beasts, Butcher Boys, and Slum Devils—had recently found a source of heavy weaponry, something that greatly concerned me, given my last spectacular encounter. It probably unsettled cops like Flynn, too. I laid the picture down on the table. It reminded me of the pain I'd endured because of that blast.

Bitter frustration echoed in Flynn's voice. "That building blew, and the next morning Maxie Fountain was back in Mommy's loving arms."

"Good." I grinned at him, but wondered if—and how—he'd made a connection between me and the boy. "Happy ending."

Flynn scooped the photos up and stuck them back in his jacket. "When *we* couldn't find Maxie, Maxie's mother started seeing psychics."

I stayed calm, sipped my coffee, and let caffeine race through my nervous system, hot on the trail of any lingering alcohol residue.

"So what do you want?" I asked.

"I want you to tell me what happened. Tell me about Maxie."

"Why don't you ask his mother? Or Maxie."

"Mom says she found him on the doorstep, wrapped in a blanket, sound asleep. All Maxie remembers is falling off his bike." Flynn leaned back in his chair and studied me. "The last psychic Maxie's mother saw was *your* good friend Madam Abigail."

"Kidnappers are usually runaway parents or perverts, not psychics. Why were you watching the mother?"

"Because parents are always the first suspects. Maxie's mother is a hotel maid. The day he came home, she went to the bank and withdrew all her savings. A total of three thousand nine hundred and twelve dollars. She went straight to Madam Abigail, stayed ten minutes, then went back to the bank and redeposited all but four hundred dollars."

Of course she did. Poor woman had suffered enough without me and Abby taking her last dime.

He stood, went to the coffeepot, and poured himself another cup. He held the pot out for me, but I shook my head. He returned to his chair.

"And what did Madam Abigail say?"

"Not a damned thing. In fact, we sent two detectives to talk to her. They don't remember anything after going inside her house."

Many people sensed Abby's strength, and while they couldn't define its source, they walked a wide path around her. Abby's loving care and magic medicines had saved me many times before my most recent injury.

I sighed. "Are you going to believe me if I say I don't know anything?"

"No." Flynn stared at me with those dark, searching eyes, as if his unwavering resolve alone would draw a confession of evil acts from me. Criminals, beware!

He laid another photo on the table, this one of an adolescent girl.

"This is my sister, Selene."

Okay, now I knew why he'd come.

"How old is she?" The girl had Flynn's dark hair and eyes.

"Thirteen next month."

"Runaway?" Experience taught me the most likely scenario.

"Some of her clothes were gone. She left a note. It's not her handwriting, though." He handed me a piece of paper, a photocopy of a handwritten note. It said she was grown up enough to make her own decisions and she wanted a different life. A twelve-year-old preteen didn't write those words. I'd read many genuine farewell notes. Desperate parents searching for a child would shove them in my face, begging me to tell them what I couldn't. Was their child safe? What did they do wrong? The young authors usually spilled out their souls in cries for help or howls of rage.

"How long has she been gone?" I asked.

"Three weeks." He spoke with the uncompromising voice of a man holding his emotions under strict control. He believed she was dead. "She went to the mall and didn't come home. Someone stole the security videos before we got them."

"You filed a report?"

Flynn nodded. "She's one of ours. Half the force is working on the case."

"So why come to me?" I knew the answer to the question, but wanted to know what he knew. I had a reputation for finding kids, usually runaways. That I sometimes used methods beyond the law was supposed to be a secret.

"I'm told you're the person who finds kids lost in the Barrows. I went to the Barrows. I heard wild stories, most pure bullshit. Crazy even. But they have one common thread. You. And the kids."

"What makes you think Selene is in the Barrows?"

He handed me a small business-card-sized admission pass to the Goblin Den, a nightclub near the river. No place in Duivel could be worse for a young girl.

"I took her bedroom apart an inch at a time," he said. "She'd taped the card to the bottom of one of her jewelry box drawers."

I laid the card down. "Problem is, *if* she is in the Barrows, and *if* she went of her own free will—" I held up my hand to stifle his protest. "Laws that say she's a child don't mean shit down there. I find her, she doesn't want to come with me, I probably can't force her. I usually rescue by stealth. At twelve, almost thirteen, if I take her by force, she'll go back."

"So you won't . . ." He had both hands on the table, clenched into fists.

"I didn't say that. I'll try. I can't make promises."

"If you screw this up, I'll—"

"And I *don't* operate on threats. Just leave me the photo."

His mouth softened and his shoulders relaxed. Relief that I'd accepted the task. Curious, since he so obviously disliked me.

"I'm a little mystified as to why you're here. Your faith in my ability to find your sister is touching, but I detect an undercurrent of antagonism."

Flynn gritted his teeth. "*My mother* went to your precious Madam Abigail. *My mother* told me if I didn't come to you, she'd leave and I would never see her again. It's idiotic, but I don't want to lose her, too."

I've had mothers come to me and offer me their lives and everything they owned if I would bring their child back. I judged him—and his mother—to be that desperate. Flynn carried the substantial burden of being the cop, helpless in the face of a crime against himself and those he loved.

"I'll find her, Flynn. If she's *there*, I'll find her." I had to prepare him. "Or at least find out what happened to her."

"You think she's . . . ?"

"I don't think anything. Is she a fighter?"

Flynn nodded. The faintest touch of pride appeared on his face. "Oh, yes. She'll fight."

"Fighters last longer in the Barrows." I could give him that assurance.

He stood to go. The weariness in his eyes spread to his body and I could see how slow he moved. Maybe he wouldn't meet a bad guy on the way home.

"How did you know that was my car at Zeke's?" I asked.

"Easy. There's a photo in your file. Which, by the way, is three inches thick. Hell, I don't know how you stay out of jail."

"Lies. All lies. Do you have anything of Selene's? Some unwashed clothing? Or has Mom done all the laundry?"

He frowned. "There's a stuffed rabbit she slept with."

"Put it in a plastic bag. Try not to touch it."

"What? You're going to use a bloodhound or something?"

"Or something."

Flynn nodded. "Ms. Archer—"

"Just Cass."

"Cass." His face relaxed, smoothing the creases. "That blast in the Barrows two weeks ago took out the entire membership of the Exeter Street Slashers."

"Bastinados?" I laid a hand over my heart. "How dreadful. To whom should I address the sympathy card?"

Flynn's mouth twitched in a faint smile. "Don't know. So far, all we've found is three arms and two feet."

Fresh meat wouldn't lie around long that deep in the Barrows.

"What blew?" I asked. "No gas down there."

"Guns, ammo, maybe some plastic. A lot of plastic."

"I heard that. Where'd it come from?"

He sighed. "We don't know. Yet. Do you . . . ?"

I shook my head. "I don't deal in that. I find lost kids."

He offered me a business card. "Call the cell anytime."

Flynn stopped at the door. He gazed at me and his eyes softened. "You clean up pretty good. Like the hair."

He left and I sat back to enjoy the rest of my coffee.

So he liked my hair. Attractive man, Flynn, even if he did classify me and Abby as frauds. Not that there could be anything between Flynn and me. I had enough problems on the rare occasions I had a regular boyfriend. A cop? No way.

The hinge on the wall heating grate creaked and popped open and Horus leaped into the room. Horus is a cat who graciously consents to hang out with me. He's rather disreputable-looking with his scarred, chewed ears and half tail. His hair is short, marbled gray and black, and he has the longest, sharpest claws I've ever seen on a cat. Horus uses the now defunct central heating and air ducts as a superhighway around the apartment house. He carried two twitching mice in his mouth. "Look, ladies," I said. "Breakfast has arrived."

Nefertiti lay quiet in the sizable glass aquarium that covered the coffee table in front of the lumpy second-hand couch. I'd draped the couch with a sheet to cover the worn upholstery. She coiled her slender, four-foot-long beige-and-brown-mottled body into a tight ball. Her forked tongue flicked in and out, scenting the world around her.

In a smaller aquarium, perched on a bookshelf made of old boards stacked on concrete blocks, eighteen-inch red-and-black-striped Nirah stretched out on her favorite rock. Both snakes could crawl out anytime they wanted, but the glass defined their personal space.

Horus dropped the mice on the floor. I picked them up by the tails and deposited one in each aquarium, then went to the kitchen and opened a can of expensive cat food from the gourmet section of Athena's Prestigious Pet Emporium. The kitchen filled with the pungent aroma of prime tuna, laced with a bit of aromatic liver.

It's a good deal, I guess. I buy tuna and Horus feeds the girls. I suspect that the arrangement has more to do with his love of tracking and killing things than with altruism or his connoisseur tastes.

I'm an independent soul, and I approach life with graceless enthusiasm. The nine-to-five thing isn't for me, so I'm often impoverished, especially since I had to give up official private investigator work. I lost that thanks to one of Flynn's fellow officers, a religious zealot who declared war on psychics and what he called their minions. A minion, that's me.

When the Earth Mother called me to her service, she gave me special gifts. Unfortunately, money wasn't among them. Abby says she's never received material aid, either; hence her psychic business. Abby offers me money and I always refuse. My parents raised me with the idea that I had to take care of myself. I do have a few hundred dollars a month from my grandfather's trust fund, but I often have to choose between rent and other necessities—like bronze bullets.

I don't know the Earth Mother's true nature. I don't know the true nature of most of the world around me. If I had to use words to describe the Mother, I'd call her a demigod. Not *the* God, the all-powerful Master of the Universe, but a powerful being like the Darkness, who dwells in the Barrows.

Nirah had ignored her breakfast offering and crawled out of her aquarium to play a game of cat and mouse with Horus, though she whipped her slender body along faster than any rodent. They'd race across the floor, over and under furniture, and Nirah would let Horus catch her every now and then to keep him interested. Nefertiti came out, too. Her mouse made a small lump four inches behind her head. She went to the windowsill and stretched out in the sun. She liked to save her energy for a swift, deadly strike.

I went to the window, where I had a good view of the Barrows. My apartment house sits on a hill, and the land dipped lower to the south, toward river and marsh.

Duivel, Missouri, sits on the banks of the Sullen River, a deepwater channel that eventually empties into the mighty Mississippi. Local legend among the area's original Dutch settlers said that the devil pushed the land up out of hell. They named the city for him, the Father of Lies. Duivel—literally, the devil.

A hundred thousand people live in and around Duivel, a city surrounded on three sides by a wet marshlike area called the Bog. The Bog is the fountain, the headwaters of the Sullen River. The ruins of the Barrows sit on a ten-square-mile hard-rock area across the river and between the Bog and uptown.

When Detective Flynn and others refer to the Barrows, they are referring to the line of viable, if somewhat dubious, businesses that line River Street. While a few legitimate businesses struggle along the street, the tawdry, eclectic collection of flashy bars, pawnshops, cheap-rent apartment buildings, and dark stinking alleys hides all manner of evil. Behind that line on the south, two to three blocks in, begins the true Barrows. The abandoned buildings and storm sewers make a perfect home for human criminals and other monsters. More important, the deeper Barrows stand as a prison for the malicious specter called the Darkness, whose will controls so many within its domain. It's a prison with invisible bars, a prison of powerful magic.

See but don't see: The cloak of the invisible, one of the oldest spells in the world, holds the deeper reaches of the Barrows in a viselike grip. It's a strange and erratic thing, that particular spell. Those who live in the greater part of the city know the Barrows exists, but they ignore it. Those who live along River Street don't ignore the place, but neither do they speak of it, even to each other. They don't go into the ruins, either. I know a lot about the Barrows. What I *don't know* could fill an encyclopedia. Did it appear suddenly or was it created when the earth was formed? Every time I go there, I see and learn something new. Things that should be fixed in time and place often change. People change. The Barrows epitomizes the bizarre.

According to Abby, there is a place in the Barrows where the distance between worlds is thin. It is a doorway to the universe. A doorway to multiple worlds. I see science programs on TV speculating about the existence of other worlds, other universes. Abby says they need to keep on speculating. The Barrows is a seething cauldron of forces that do not belong in this world. All it takes is the right time, the right place, and something or someone can walk through into our world. In the Barrows, I'm usually the one who gets to deal with those *walkers*.

The worst thing about the Barrows is the windows where dark power seeps in. Windows where intelligent evil creatures can watch and influence this world. It is from one of these windows that the Darkness spreads his influence, and has been spreading for some time. The Earth Mother holds her ring of power around the Barrows, a ring upon which he constantly pushes. That ring is the only protection we have against those who do not belong here. Abby says *See but don't see* is the Mother's doing. She wants to keep people away as much as possible. Once inside, they make an easy transition into the service of evil.

Unlike the sewer monsters, who are nothing more than animals, the Darkness has no physical form in the Barrows, at least none that I know of. There are a lot of things I don't know. I keep myself honed in on the moment and on my job—on what I can change. I try to leave the big questions to those with bigger brains. I do know that the Darkness's power is real. It's like being in an empty room, but knowing in your gut you aren't alone. Sometimes it's watchful; sometimes it's filled with rage. It terrifies me. But I don't let it control me.

Ten years ago, when I first came to Duivel, Abby told me I had to rescue special children, get them out of the Barrows. To me, all children, then and now, are special. To Abby and the Mother, all are precious, too, but apparently some are . . . different. I keep looking for the why. Why are these special and others ordinary? No one, neither Abby nor the Mother, has ever enlightened me. I have, over the years, learned to feel a difference in some of them, though. It's as if some carry a link to the Darkness that makes them powerful in some way. Sometimes this power leads to evil, especially if they lead troubled lives. I don't believe any kid is a hopeless case, though. If you remove a child from an evil place and raise that child with kindness, love, and good discipline, he or she can usually be saved.

Detective Flynn, like most people in Duivel, gaze across the deeper Barrows without seeing it. His Barrows consists of only the businesses that line River Street and the docks. The spell holds him, so he doesn't believe the multitude of wild stories about me. Or he believes they're a cover for criminal acts—which they sometimes are. Apparently it's against the law to beat the hell out someone abusing a kid when you catch him in the act.

If Selene is in the Barrows, I'll find her. Getting her out might be a little harder.

I needed to talk to Abby. I could probably mooch supper, too, if I hung out long enough. In deference to the heat, I pulled my hair up in a ponytail and dug out shorts and a pair of sandals.

Now that booze-free blood surged through my veins, I rationalized a bit. I'd probably realized I was too drunk to get home safely, so I parked the car before I hurt someone, including myself. The car keys lay on the kitchen counter where I usually dropped them. Horus, Nirah, and Nefertiti would keep each other company until I returned.

I headed down the stairs, out the side door, and into the parking lot. Dry sauna heat made me gasp for breath, and the skin over my recently healed burns prickled. My apartment building is a concrete clone of the others on the block. Four-story square boxes painted a hideous, institutional green.

The garbage truck conveniently forgot to empty the Dumpster at least once a week, and my nose wrinkled at the intense odor of decay. Bare asphalt lots provided insufficient parking spaces and remained a constant source of friction among tenants.

My six-year-old POS, a dirty gray four-door sedan, was indeed in the parking lot. I could see no major dents added to the considerable collection already sculpted on the fenders, hood, and trunk. I'd patched all the claw holes in critical areas with that miracle of the civilized world, duct tape. I had a grudging respect for my wheels. The POS had carried me through and out of many a volatile situation. When it would start, that is.

I had my hand on the door handle when a tank of an SUV rolled up and stopped behind my car, blocking me in. If I'd been more alert, I'd have raced away before the SUV's tires stopped turning. Two muscle-bound steroid junkies jumped out and grabbed me by the arms.

"Come on," the one on my right snarled. He jerked me toward the SUV. The behemoth's dark-tinted windows revealed nothing inside. I jerked back and opened my mouth to yell and a thick, leather-gloved hand clamped over it. I'm strong, very strong, but I was way outmuscled on this one. It took only seconds for them to push, drag, and lift me into the SUV's backseat, in spite of my flailing legs. The one with the glove released my mouth.

"You can scream now," he said cordially.

"No, she can't," snapped the driver.

The guy riding shotgun turned and grinned at me.

The two brutes sitting on either side of me released my arms. Things were looking up.

"You stop this thing and let me out. Now!" I made a useless demand. They didn't reply. The SUV headed up Northwest Sixty-second Street, toward uptown Duivel.

I launched myself forward between the front bucket seats and grabbed the steering wheel. The shift lever jabbed into my stomach, but I held on tight and let my body's weight tear the wheel from the driver's hands. Better to wreck the car than go with these goons. The SUV lurched and tires squealed. The guy riding shotgun grabbed my wrists, tried to tear me loose, but I had a good grip. Then one of the assholes in the back leaned over me and grabbed a fistful of my hair. He slammed my face into the console. White light and pain flashed across my nose and cheek where they hit a couple of knobs, so I barely felt anything when they dragged me to the backseat. Something hit my head and everything went away.

chapter 3

I woke up with a sandpaper mouth and a cool rag on my forehead. I choked in a vain attempt to work up saliva. Someone came to my rescue, pressing a water-soaked sponge against my lips. I sucked the water and tried to clear my vision.

My abused head throbbed and protested the infliction of a hangover and blunt trauma, all in one day. My abdomen felt like someone had tried to flatten my stomach against my spine with a hammer.

"Try not to move too fast," a soft feminine voice said.

My eyes focused and I risked turning my head toward her. A nurse, complete with white uniform and wire-rimmed glasses. She lifted me up, propped pillows behind me, and offered me more water, this time from a glass.

Someone had dressed me in a man's white dress shirt, presumably because I'd bled on my T-shirt. I rubbed my hands across my aching face. The swelling wasn't too bad, and my nose wasn't broken, but they'd bandaged a cut high on my cheekbone. A man stood at the foot of the bed staring at me.

Carlos Dacardi, Duivel's premier organized-crime boss. Dacardi's picture graced the *Chronicle* on a regular basis, usually in association with some *Let's pretend*

I'm a good-guy philanthropist fund-raising benefit. His wife, a plain woman who liked designer gowns and sparkling jewelry, always stood beside him. The Duivel mafia wannabe clique stood as bantamweights compared to the big boys in New York and Chicago, but Dacardi was dangerous nonetheless.

Dacardi appeared powerful. Not like the muscled jerks who'd kidnapped me—more like a sturdy, resilient construction worker, with thick, callused hands, ready to pick up a hammer or shovel. He watched me with dark, vigilant eyes.

The nurse handed me a mirror. "The cut's small," she said.

I lifted the mirror and surveyed the damage. Red bloodshot eyes sharply contrasted the blue-black half-moons under them. A swollen lower lip complemented a long, raw scrape on my right jaw. The bandage added an interesting touch. The nurse went through a litany of questions, all designed to ascertain the condition of my brain. Like, *Do you have a concussion?*

I lied.

If Dacardi thought I was really injured, he might be tempted to get rid of me permanently rather than deal with someone asking questions about how I got hurt in the first place.

"You want to go to the hospital?" Dacardi asked.

The question carried a reluctant tone.

"No." I was sure of that. Definitely the right answer.

Dacardi nodded and the nurse left the room. I was lying in a real canopy bed, covered with a rose satin bedspread. Sheer white drapes hung from the framework above, and sun from the windows cast an anemic pall on my skin. Pretty, but not a room meant for people to live in. More like a tacky showroom with heavy furniture and ankle-deep pink carpet.

Dacardi walked over and sat on the bed beside me.

Not close enough to touch, but close enough to reach out and try to strangle me if he wanted to.

"You know who I am?" Dacardi cocked his head and gave me a cold smile.

"I know. Where am I?"

"Riverside."

Dacardi's Riverside house was Duivel legend, the constant subject of rumors of stolen antiques and fabulous treasures fit for a palace.

He cleared his throat. "Sorry you got hurt. Told the boys to bring you—"

"And you didn't think I'd object?"

Dacardi laughed. "Good thing I sent four of them. Tough bitch, ain't you? I like that."

Wonderful. He liked me because his goons hadn't managed to kill me.

"Okay, Dacardi, what do you want?" I wasn't completely surprised when he handed me a photograph. An adolescent boy, with his features, but lighter hair and blue eyes.

"My son, Richard. He's thirteen. He went to the mall. The fucking mall, for Christ's sake."

I had to rule out the most likely causes.

"Kidnap? Ransom? Have they contacted you?"

Dacardi shook his head. "No. Not that. I got a note. In the mail." He drew a piece of paper out of his pocket and handed it to me. Same handwriting, and virtually the same words as the note Flynn's sister left. Grown up, going to find a new life.

A vague sense of unease stirred in me. I suppose, to other people, the note would seem like a link, a clue, but to me it signaled convenient coincidence—too convenient. Nothing I do is that easy.

I didn't ask if he'd called the police. I didn't ask about neighborhood pals, either. Riverside reeked of luxury and security, where people kept their secrets safe inside high-walled estates; you didn't go next door and borrow a cup of sugar. Your housekeeper sent *her* servants to the store with money.

"I got the surveillance tapes from the mall," Dacardi offered. "Paid big money for them. They don't show nothing."

Hence the police did not see them when looking for Selene. Dacardi got there first. I doubted that they would show Flynn anything, even if I could persuade Dacardi to turn them over.

"Did you talk to his friends at school?"

"No." Dacardi's eyes narrowed like Nefertiti's. Dacardi grabbed my wrist. "Told them he's out of the country. With his mother in England."

"If he ran away—"

"He didn't run away." Dacardi's fingers tightened. I winced and he released me. "Me and that boy were— are—tight. He didn't tell me everything, but . . . I searched for him, bitch. I screwed this town upside down. You don't want to know what I did trying to find him. The only thing I got was the name of a woman who could find kids. Your name."

I closed my eyes.

"Every time I heard your name, I heard the name of the witch you hang out with. Madam Abigail."

No surprises there. My association with Abby was well known.

"A hundred thousand," Dacardi said.

"What?" My eyes popped open.

"I'll give you a hundred thousand dollars to find him."

"Money doesn't guarantee results."

"You found others." Dacardi's voice had taken on a serrated-knife edge.

"I've found kids, Dacardi. But sometimes I can't find anything at all."

"You *will* find him." Dacardi's eyes and voice went

flat and cold. "Or you might find yourself crying over your personal witch's grave."

I gave him my sweetest smile. "Okay."

A suspicious look crossed his face.

Mr. Crime Boss Dacardi's threats meant nothing to me at that moment, but I'd certainly deal with them later. Abby? I'd like to see him try to hurt her. What a show. She'd tear him apart.

Coincidence or not, the two notes linked Flynn's sister and Dacardi's son, and my priorities are all in order when it comes to the kids. That is the great tragedy and joy of my life. But I can't save them all. At least with twelve- and thirteen-year-olds, if I couldn't find them, I hoped that they'd hold on to their sense of morality and find a way to escape.

"Dacardi, I look for lost kids. I don't do it for money."

"What do you do it for?"

"That's my business. But I will tell you—warn you. Don't mess with Abby. Go to New York and spit in the big boss's eye. It's safer."

He balled up his fists, but he didn't say anything.

"Take me to Richard's room," I said. "I need to look around."

Dacardi didn't speak for a moment, then stood and offered me his hand. I didn't want to touch him, but I wasn't sure I could stand by myself, so I let him steady me. A roaring sound whirred in my ears and the room swayed when I stood, then righted itself. I stifled a whimper. By the time we reached Richard's room, I could walk on my own.

The kid's room was three times larger than my apartment. It nested in a tower overlooking the main house and the river. A panoramic view spread from massive windows on the south side. Someone, probably his mother, made an attempt to soften the walls with pale blue paint, but rock band posters tacked on the walls and ceiling successfully negated that.

Dacardi pointed to drums, guitars, and amplifiers sitting in the corner. "Had to move him up here on account of the noise."

One wall held a TV screen the size of my bed, surrounded by excellent, expensive-looking electronic equipment. "You search the room?" It looked too tidy for a teenage boy.

"Yeah."

"Why is it so neat and clean?"

Dacardi shrugged. "Maid."

"Finding Richard depends on information. Clues. You're going to have to help me out a little. Your son didn't live in a vacuum." I pointed at the guitar and drums. "Did he play with someone?"

"He met a couple of boys at a concert. They came here and made noise with him. Didn't like them. Both a couple of years older. Don't know their names."

"Okay, get a couple of your gorillas in here." I sat on the bed. "They can do my kind of search."

Dacardi nodded.

"Is anything missing?" I asked.

"No. Don't think so. I sent his computer to a geek. Nothing."

"Did the geek know what he was looking for?"

Dacardi's eyes widened a bit. "I doubt it. I don't even know what I'm looking for."

His men came and they followed my orders, even when I made them leave everything as they found it. They glared at me, but kept one eye on Dacardi. A rough-and-tumble, tear-out-the-walls search missed more clues than it found. I'd bet that's what they did last time—and left the mess for the maid to clean. I made them leaf through each book page by page, pull out all the dresser and chest drawers, and turn over the mattress.

While they finished searching, I scanned the pushpin board. Richard had tacked entertainment ads from four heavy metal nightclubs around town, including the Goblin Den.

"You let him go to these places?" I asked Dacardi.

"No. I kept a close watch on him."

"You watched? Or one of your . . . employees . . . watched?"

He glared at me.

The search revealed nothing else except a pair of obviously worn Jockey shorts behind a dresser. Dacardi laughed when I made them stuff the shorts in a plastic bag. "What? You got a bloodhound or something?"

"Or something."

The search revealed nothing new, but at least I wasn't the one moving furniture.

Dacardi led me downstairs into a room with plush, brown leather furniture and walls of books I'd bet *he'd* never read. "Sit down," he ordered, and pointed at a chair.

No problem. My head hurt like hell.

Dacardi picked up an envelope from a desk. He slipped out a handful of enlarged photographs and tossed them on my lap.

Shit! I bit my lip hard. Someone had taken them in my apartment last night while I lay in a drunken coma.

"What do you do with those snakes?" Dacardi asked.

"They're my pets."

"Yeah. You're lucky. We could've shot 'em. You wouldn't have known until this morning."

I tasted blood where I'd bitten my lip. I'd screwed up big-time and placed my friends and myself in danger. But if Nirah, Nefertiti, or Horus sensed danger, why hadn't they warned me? Once, when a burglar picked my lock and came in, Horus had jumped up and down on my bed. I had grabbed my gun, gone into the living room, turned on the light, and found the would-be thief, frozen, with his tiny flashlight pointed at a coiled and ready-to-strike Nefertiti.

Dacardi went to a small bar and poured a drink. The smell of whiskey nauseated me. He lifted a glass. "You want a Coke or something?"

I shook my head, an action I immediately regretted. I wanted to leave this place.

He sat on the couch and downed the liquor in one gulp. "He's in the Barrows, isn't he?"

"I don't know. What makes *you* think he's there?"

"It's the only place I can't get to. Don't think I didn't try." He stared at me. "You, now, you go in the Barrows and you come back with kids. Don't need to know how, but you tell me why so many disappear down there."

"No more kids disappear than anywhere else, in any city or town. The Barrows is my territory, though. I'm the one who hunts those streets."

"Why? You get lost when you were a kid?"

"No. Happy childhood here. Kids don't belong in the Barrows." That didn't answer his question, but it was all he'd get from me.

Dacardi nodded. He leaned back and relaxed, probably a result of the liquor. Rich man with no scruples who loved his son. Maybe I could use him.

"I might need some backup." I really was tired of things chasing me through the sewers.

"Backup? Like what?" Dacardi leaned forward with the hard-jawed intensity of a man challenged to show his prowess. I spoke his language, something he understood.

"Guns. Heavy-caliber automatics. Couple of reasonably smart men, trained to use them." His eyes widened. "You going to fucking war?"

"If I have to."

Dacardi chuckled. "You know, my granny, she was a

bruja. Crazy witch. She had snakes, too. Your pets don't bother me. Granny gave me a snake of my own when I was ten. My bastard daddy killed it."

"Granny make a believer of you?"

Dacardi spoke with the slight accent of a first- or second-generation immigrant. *Bruja* is the Spanish word for witch. It wouldn't hurt my hunt if he understood that there were indefinable things outside the narrow boundaries of the ordinary.

Dacardi stood. "Come on. I'll have someone take you home."

He led me downstairs into a garage that held a dozen cars. The bastard who had slammed my face into the console sat behind the SUV's wheel as my chauffeur.

Dacardi tried to give me a wad of hundred-dollar bills. I refused all but three for my time and suffering. I needed money, but not his. Finding kids gave me a personal satisfaction I doubt words could express. While nobility didn't pay the rent or ease hunger, I wasn't that hungry—yet. I did ask him to have my cell phone service restored. I also had him promise to take Richard's computer to Thor, my computer specialist buddy.

Dacardi balked a little when I told him he had to find bronze bullets, or at least bronze-coated bullets, for the weapons, but I actually stared him down and he agreed. An expensive proposition, since such things were usually handmade. I gave the sociopath driver Abby's address, and neither of us spoke as the SUV rolled out of Dacardi's gated and guarded Riverside estate.

A small wooden sign hung on the post below Abby's new mailbox: MADAM ABIGAIL—PSYCHIC READINGS. She devoted the house's front rooms to her business, a lucrative business since she wasn't a phony scamming money from desperate people. Her clients loved her.

Abby met us at the curb, opened the SUV's door, and helped me out. She smiled at my driver. He didn't see the tiny bag she slipped under the front seat when she eased me to the ground and closed the door. The SUV accelerated, rolled two hundred feet, suddenly swerved, and slammed into a telephone pole. The driver's door opened and Dacardi's man staggered out, followed by a rapidly dissipating cloud of . . . something.

He wasn't really injured—air bags and seat belts worked—but he fell to his hands and knees and started spewing the contents of his stomach on the sidewalk. I wondered what else the gassy potion would do to him, but I didn't really care.

Like I told Dacardi, you don't mess with Abby—or anyone she considers hers. I didn't ask how she knew he was the one who'd hurt me. Abby held me by the shoulders. "Come on. Let's go fix that concussion."

chapter 4

Abby is a soft woman, with rounded shoulders and plump cheeks, but not fat by any means. Neither young nor old, she keeps her iron gray hair pinned in a bun at the nape of her neck. That hair provides a contrast to her smooth, unlined face. Men usually smile with appreciation, but rarely approach her. It's a good facade. Madam Abigail is the Earth Mother's high priestess in Duivel, and a witch of incredible power. She can take things from her garden, from the earth, and make amazing potions—potions to heal, to remember, to forget. I'm quite certain she has powers I don't know about, probably shouldn't know about. While she can't see the future, she makes a good living as a psychic because she can read auras.

Abby kept a firm grip on me as she led me around the side of the modest bungalow she calls home. The Mother blessed Abby's yard and garden with a riot of flowers and other living things. The heady aroma of late-blooming honeysuckle made me smile, and daisies winked in a breeze from the river. She owns twenty acres of forest and gardens along the river, and uptown real estate brokers regularly offer her millions. She won't sell. Abby's garden serves as a temple to the Earth Mother, one of the few left in the world. We entered her kitchen by way of a back porch filled with pots of herbs that love the shade.

In a few minutes, I had a clean T-shirt, salve on my cut cheek, and my head over a steaming bowl of water generously laced with the foulest-smelling weeds imaginable. I didn't complain. By the time the water cooled, my head was clear and pain free. While I breathed the disgusting steam, I told her of Flynn's sister and Dacardi's son. She fixed me a sandwich and a cup of tea and placed them on the table in front of me.

Laughter usually fills her conversations, but she'd barely spoken since I'd come in. She sat in a chair across from me. One look at her eyes and I knew Abby wasn't there anymore. I swallowed hard. The Earth Mother had taken control.

The Earth Mother is powerful, contradictory, often ill-tempered, moving through her world, possibly with a purpose, possibly not. At times she seems absolutely archaic, as if dumbfounded by the changes time has brought. The Mother rarely explains anything to me. I suspect Abby gets a little vexed with her, too.

Like the Darkness, she has no physical presence—at least as far as I know. But I'm not an expert on that, either. The Mother did occasionally speak to me through Abby, or even directly into my mind, but it was rare, and only happened around the time of traumatic events. Such an event was probably bearing down on me like a herd of Saturday morning garage sale bargain hunters.

"Two children," the Mother said. "One belongs to the Warlord and the other to the Guardian. You must find them before the dark moon."

Though she spoke with Abby's voice, the power made me shiver. However, I was long past the much younger Cassandra's fear and awe of my mysterious and powerful patroness.

"Why?" I leaned back and gave her an expression I would never give to Abby herself.

Her mouth, Abby's mouth, twisted and exasperation marked her face. "Don't ask why—just do it!"

I shrugged, light-headed from breathing Abby's healing drugs. Though irritable at times, my attitude now bordered on outright defiance. Not that she'd ever force me to do anything. That's not her way. She never requires worship, either.

The Mother's breath hissed through Abby's teeth. "Do you wish to be released from your vows, Huntress?"

I threw up my hands. "What else would I do with my life? Do I have a life? I had a rough day—and night. That's all."

"If you'd listen to me and Abigail occasionally—"

"What? You're still pissed at me for getting a gun, aren't you?"

She drew herself, or Abby's body, up, mouth tight. "Those weapons are not the way—"

"You sent me into the Barrows ten years ago with a bronze knife. Eighteen years old. 'Go forth, Cassandra, and do great works,' you said. You spout cryptic nonsense—Warlord, Guardian. Why can't you just tell me what you want? You've never given me a dime to support myself—and, hell, I ran out of gas on the way out of the Barrows once. Do you know how hard it is to hitch a ride when you're covered in monster blood and shit?"

"I am not omnipotent, Cassandra." She spoke softly. "I've given you everything I am permitted."

Permitted by whom? But I didn't want to know. Absolutely not. I had enough trouble dealing with her, let alone someone—or something—more powerful.

But she sounded as if I'd hurt her feelings. How was that possible? At times I'd swear she was human. I leaned back and scowled. "Oh, I'm yours, Mother. *Your* Huntress. But I live in the twenty-first century. I love you, and Abby, but I'm going to use modern weapons if I need them."

Abby jerked as the Mother left her. She blinked and frowned. "What happened?"

"Mom was here. I pissed her off—again."

Abby sighed. "Did she lecture you on the gun?"

"Whined a little."

Abby's face scrunched in a rare grimace. She didn't understand my lack of awe for the being who stood at the center of her life. I didn't understand, either, but day by day it grew into a larger ball of insubordination in my guts.

"I'm not happy about the gun, either, Cass. Why do you insist on having it?"

Why couldn't she—or the Mother—understand?

"I'm tired of running, Abby. I'm so *damned* tired of running. I want to face the fucking perverts and murderers. Not to mention the monsters. I sneak around the Barrows, snatch a kid, and the son of a bitch who had him goes out and gets another one."

"And how many of those perverts have you killed?"

"With the gun? Three."

A deep sense of satisfaction crept into my heart. I didn't like that feeling. The Barrows had cut me to naked bone over the years, and I carried a deep-seated fear that its pervading evil would invade my soul and make me a callous killer.

"I've discouraged seven or eight from chasing me," I said, trying to soothe her.

The gun carries .45 bullets, ten to a magazine, but doesn't have a manufacturer's name, serial number, or any other identification. It's fast and accurate unless the shooter is incompetent—like the gun's former owner. Handguns are probably useless in hell, and the stupid Bastinado couldn't take it with him anyway. I confiscated it as a reward for having survived his poor aim.

"Why does the gun bother you so much?" I asked. Defensiveness crept into my words. "You just busted some bastard's guts because he hurt me."

Abby reached out and grabbed my hand. She squeezed so hard I thought she'd dislocate my finger joints. "What if they shoot back?"

"I guess I have to shoot first."

Abby released me. She held her hand across her mouth as if to stifle words she didn't dare speak.

"I'm not a Wild West gunslinger," I said. "I use bronze for the monsters. It's not good for shooting people. Not accurate, not much distance." I lied to Abby to reassure her of—what? That I wasn't a cold-blooded killer?

"Abby, I need to find Flynn's sister and Dacardi's boy now, before the dark moon—"

"What's the dark moon have to do with finding those children?" Abby snapped to attention.

"The Mother said— Wait. What's happening?"

Abby didn't answer. Her face had that inward-looking expression of a witch in search of a powerful omen. When she gazed back at me, I shivered. Whatever she'd seen had left her as cold as the Sullen in midwinter, and that same chill weighed her voice. "The coming dark moon is part of a special conjunction of stars, Cass. One star is dying and another will be born."

The term *dark moon* was familiar. Our neighbors at the farm next door were pagans and occasionally invited us to a dark moon feast. Because I'm an earth witch, it didn't surprise me that Abby used it, too. "Abby, the dark moon is just the new moon. I learned that in school. It's still there."

Abby smiled. "There is more to the dark moon than science. The ancients built their lives on the cycles of the moon and the connection to the Great Mother. Occasionally, there are two cycles of a dark moon in a single calendar month. That is the nature of the coming event— and it coincides with the conjunction of stars. Earth magic will grow more powerful and the connections to other worlds will grow stronger. Regardless of the Earth

Mother's gifts to me, I am still human and there is much I don't know. There is much I see and feel that terrifies me because it is incomprehensible."

"It's all pretty much incomprehensible to me. If I have to fight, I prefer things I can shoot or knife."

"Yes, that is your purview, Huntress. We live in the Earth Mother's domain. Humans are her children." Abby sighed. "I don't understand, but for some reason she won't touch, won't control any humans save us, you and I, and her other chosen servants."

"Us? Define 'us,' Abby. Define 'chosen'!" My voice carried a demand, something I'd never done with her.

She threw up her hands, a gesture so un-Abby-like it frightened me. "Surely you know that you and I are not her only servants."

"I suppose . . . I mean, it seems likely. I guess I never thought much about it."

Had I been arrogant enough to think I was the only Huntress? That I was special? Well, yes. I had.

"Cass, you live in the moment." Her voice warmed. Abby knew me well. I was special to Abby. She smiled. "You don't need to speculate on the nature of the realm of the occult, or those who dwell there."

"Do you have . . . contact. With others?" A bit of jealousy seeped in.

"No, not often. The Mother asked me not to. We are each assigned, if you will, to specific tasks when she requires our service. As far as I know, there is no special cadre of Huntresses like you. Or people like me."

"How long have you done this?"

"All my life. My own mother was a priestess before me."

"Why are you just now telling me this? I've served her—and you—for ten years."

"Because this is the first dark moon conjunction in forty years. The Mother won't tell me exactly what happened during the last one. She ordered me not to go into the Barrows. I obeyed. But I think it involved a thinning of the barriers between worlds, all worlds. And that thinning includes the barrier she holds around the Barrows. I believe . . ."

"What? Don't leave it there, Abby."

"I believe Duivel, in this century, is the epicenter of the Mother's power. She has spoken with me more in the last ten years than in a very long time."

"Why doesn't the Mother just go in and root the Darkness out? It is certainly not human."

"Because the very thing that keeps *it* imprisoned is the thing that keeps *her* out. If she goes in, she will break the walls she herself created and it will be free. I'm not sure . . . I'm afraid . . . she might not be able to defeat it if it were free." Abby stood and gathered my untouched teacup and saucer. "You need to leave now." The china tinkled as her hands shook. "Detective Flynn will be driving by in a few minutes. He's looking for you." I know Abby is psychic, but sometimes her sudden pronouncements make me uneasy. Mostly because they are always true.

"You know Flynn?"

"I know his mother. She came to me for help. The Earth Mother directed me to send him to you."

She set the plate and cup in the sink and headed for the front of the house, then stopped. She came to me, grasped my cheeks in her hands, and kissed me on the forehead. "You've been the Huntress too long. I love the Mother, but . . ." She released me and wiped at her eyes. "Does she think I don't see what's happening? You're the best Huntress in my lifetime. And because you're so good, she's using you up like a disposable tool. A weapon. Then she objects when you do what's necessary to stay alive." She shook her head and left the room.

Abby had always been the sanctuary in my haphazard life, and I couldn't remember a time when I'd seen her so distressed. I suspected she was right. The Mother was using me, but it was up to me to call a halt. *I should probably do that before someone—or something—kills me. Maybe this should be my last hunt. I could get a regular job, and . . .* What? Give up all the excitement, the death-defying feats of valor? The pain, the broken bones? I shivered at the memory of the burns. Who was I kidding? I'd become an action junkie, living on the edge, and it would probably kill me.

I let myself out the back door, strolled around the house, and, sure enough, a shiny red pickup truck rolled down the street toward me like a scarlet tank. It stopped at the curb beside me, and the passenger window slid down. I leaned against the door. Flynn appeared only a little less weary than he had this morning.

"I need a ride home," I said.

He nodded. "Get in."

I opened the door and pulled myself up into the full-sized truck cab.

Flynn stared at me. "You look like shit again. Only worse. Who did that?"

"I'm okay."

"Bullshit." He flipped my windshield visor down to expose a mirror.

My face looked like someone had slapped it with a brush of purple and black paint under my eyes and slashed a line along my jaw.

"A professional disagreement. That's all." I drew the seat belt over my shoulder and fastened it.

"Who won?" he asked.

"Won what?"

"The professional disagreement."

I shrugged. "It was sort of a draw."

"Then you won't mind going to the station and filling out a report."

"It wasn't *that* much of a draw." The seat belt clicked

when I pushed the button to release it. "I'll catch the bus."

Flynn grabbed my arm when I reached for the door handle. "No. I brought you Selene's rabbit."

He reached across me to take my arm. The weariness that slowed him earlier remained, but he'd showered and shaved. He smelled faintly of citrus and his dark hair still needed a trim. It fascinated me and I forced myself not to run my fingers through it. Professional distance, Cassandra. Keep it cool and under control.

He released me and leaned back.

"I don't like to be forced into things," I said.

"Neither do I. And here I am, forced by my mother to rely on the accomplice of a psychic fraud." He sounded resigned to the situation.

"The accomplishments of the psychic fraud and said accomplice don't impress you, I suppose." I tried to sound arrogant, but the words came out angry instead.

"They might if I knew a few details. Results are fine. It's how you get them that concerns me. I read your file, remember?"

Flynn the cop believed in law and order. The Guardian, the Earth Mother called him. I dealt with chaos and tried to make some order of things. Mostly I shied away from, or totally ignored, the law. At least his rules-on-paper version of the law.

Rush hour traffic had come and gone, so we rode easily through the streets. The sun had dropped below the horizon, taking some of the unbearable heat with it.

"What were you doing driving by Abby's house?" I asked.

His mouth tightened. "I don't know. I went home to get the damned rabbit. Then . . ." He shrugged.

I'd long since stopped believing in coincidence and

luck. Everything in my life seemed to have a purpose, even if I didn't recognize the reason at the time.

"What's that?" Flynn pointed at the bag I'd carried from Dacardi's house.

"Dirty jocks. Where's Selene's toy?"

"Under your seat."

I reached down and grabbed the plastic bag containing a well-worn, probably well-loved stuffed rabbit.

We rode in silence back to my apartment building.

When we arrived, he asked, "Do you need some aspirin? I'll go get some for you."

His sudden compassion touched me. "I need a new face. But thanks anyway."

"Your face is okay," he said. "Kind of pretty. Even if it is purple."

"Thanks for that, too."

Well, well, the man liked my face—and my hair. I smiled, and drew one from him in return. My, what a luscious mouth. Bad for me, bad for him. I can't be involved with a cop. So why did I feel a sudden surge of pleasure when he called me pretty? I made a ruthless effort to squash the feeling and forced it down.

I climbed out and he waited in the parking lot until I went inside.

Nefertiti, Nirah, and Horus waited for me. Nefertiti stretched across the back of the couch and Horus crouched on a cushion with Nirah draped around his neck like a red and black necklace. I sat on the couch and Nefertiti slid down and over my shoulders. She lifted her head to look me in the eye. I rubbed her under her lower jaw with my thumb.

"Okay, guys. I'm sorry. I let you down last night. Dangerous strangers invaded our home. Abby warned me. No alcohol for at least another month until I'm finished with the meds."

I didn't ask why they didn't warn me. They couldn't communicate on that level. Maybe they instinctively understood that I had been truly unconscious and lacked the ability to respond.

Horus jumped on my lap and I knew that meant he forgave me. I guess the girls did, too, because they wanted to cuddle. While we did, I let myself examine my life and why I lived in such a haphazard manner.

I grew up on a farm in north Arkansas with the best parents in the world. We lived with the seasons, worked hard, and enjoyed life in general. We weren't religious, but we weren't atheists. We believed in God, considered the land a sacred trust, and tried to be good stewards. Neither Mom nor Dad ever mentioned the Earth Mother, but I suspect they wouldn't be surprised to know she existed.

My world changed on my eighteenth birthday.

Mom had smiled hopefully when she gave me the details of Grandpa's trust fund for his only granddaughter. She reminded me that my good grades almost guaranteed me a scholarship, too. Go to vet school since I had such a strong affinity for animals. Horse whisperer? Cow whisperer? Pig, dog, cat—I understood them all, not in words but in feelings, and they listened to me when I spoke. When that facet of my personality appeared, my wonderful parents became vegetarians for my sake. No animal died around us except of natural causes.

I don't know if it was auspicious to turn eighteen on the full moon, or if something predetermined my life before my birth. I went to bed late that night, fell right to sleep, and woke up lying in the middle of the farm's pear orchard. Silver light misted the world around me to soft gray and black sculptures and the moon herself floated high against the black ceiling of the sky. I stood, not frightened, thinking I'd been sleepwalking, when a woman's voice spoke softly behind me.

"Will you accept the call, Huntress?"

I turned and faced a shadowy figure cloaked in white. Instinct, intuition told me the figure was female. She hid her face in the folds of her cowl.

"Who are you?" I asked. *Dreaming, I had to be dreaming.*

"I am the guardian of this earth. This is no dream, daughter; you are the Huntress. The little ones, the lost, call you. Will you find them?"

That's when I became afraid. I became a lost child, terrified, alone.

"Danger waits, Huntress. But I will give you strength and you will stand for me." The woman's voice grew inside my head—and the child's terror grew in my heart. "You were born on this night. I heard your first cries, saw your strength and courage. You were raised by good parents, taught right from wrong and respect for my lands. Now *you* must choose how you spend your life. I offer you pain, fear, and danger, but in turn you will be compensated."

I suddenly knew the joy of a child found, and the relief of a parent prepared for the worst. I swore I'd do what she wanted. In hindsight, it's always struck me as a little unfair to give a naive eighteen-year-old girl such a choice—a decision between an ordinary life and the opportunity to be an extraordinary heroine. Guess what she's going to choose.

When I woke in my bed the next morning, an address came immediately to my mind. Missouri, two hundred miles north and another state away. Abby's address. On my nightstand, underneath the lamp, was a significant bronze knife. The knife I carry today. To my mother's dismay, I emptied my savings account and left the next day.

Abby taught me about the Earth Mother, the Darkness, and the Barrows. I met Nefertiti in the Barrows one night when she generously bit a monster that had me pinned down. She followed me home. Not long after that, Horus arrived with Nirah. I knew, of course, they weren't animals or reptiles in the truest sense. I consider them precious gifts. I guess the Mother sent them, though she never said. All three have a limited ability to reason and override animal instinct. That was ten years ago.

I wish I could say the Mother gave me superpowers like a movie character. The old X-ray vision and a nifty fang-and-claw-proof suit would be nice. She did, however, give me physical strength, endurance, and rapid reaction times. Not fantastic, but I'd put myself up against an exceptionally strong weight lifter or distance runner any day. She has never given me anything of a material nature; hence my poverty. Unless you count her occasional nagging, she rarely interferes with my life.

I don't regret the decision to become the Huntress; the search fits my nature and feels right. But I sure wish I had read the small print in the contract before I signed on. At nine o'clock, I showered and dressed in jeans and a sky blue T-shirt. Back when I had money, I'd purchased a bottle of expensive concealing makeup. Since I now had a little funding courtesy of Carlos Dacardi, I applied the cream liberally to my face. It covered most of the bruising. Then I cleaned my gun and sharpened my knives.

The gun, the source of Abby and the Mother's irritation, was black and heavy in my hands. Would my patroness and guide be more comfortable if I carried a broadsword and shield? Maybe. My ammo dealer makes my bronze bullets by hand. He calls it his magic formula and charges twenty times the cost of regular ammo. I pay his price and ask no questions. I don't know why the Mother hates the gun so much, unless it symbolizes what men have done to her lands and she longs for the old days.

I slid the gun into a shoulder holster under my arm near my waist. The belt that held the holster in place also carried extra clips of ammo. One bronze knife went in a sheath on my left forearm and a smaller one slipped into a pouch on the side of my lace-up boots. Once I twisted, adjusted and readjusted, and everything fit right, I covered my arsenal with a light sand-colored jacket and headed out.

A pervert with a video camera and kiddie porn aspirations had kidnapped Maxie Fountain. The pervert gave me the details as I convinced him of the error of his ways and adjusted his attitude.

I'd also found kids snatched by a noncustodial parent who thought the Barrows made the perfect hiding place. But these were isolated incidences. The majority of children were taken for a far darker purpose. They became what Abby called acolytes, little soldiers of shadow, taken and trained to grow into service of the Darkness. She made it sound like some great conspiracy, some evil underground movement.

I found serious crime in the Barrows, but no major criminal organization—or any special evil underground movement—yet. Potential was there, though, and only lacked a leader. With the sudden infusion of a massive amount of arms and explosives, anything could happen. Someone may already be making plans.

Kids Selene and Richard's age were usually runaways, but it didn't take long for them to fall in with the others. The common thread of the notes and the Goblin Den, and the warning about the dark moon, didn't change the odds they were runaways. Many of my lost sheep were not lost at all. They were where they wanted to be. They were drawn by the thought that no one would find them among the derelicts along River Street. If they lived on the coasts, they would be drawn to New York or LA. Not much I could do except try to talk them into going home.

Usually I hunted those in the cheap diners and cafés

where kids hang out trying to bum a meal, and in the three street missions that ministered to the dregs. Tonight, I'd start my search at the top.

My POS was running well for a change, and the day's steaming heat had partially drained away. I stopped at a drugstore with a photocopier and made copies of the two pictures. I'd probably need to hand them out. Cooler air slid over the rolled-down windows as I crossed Copper Creek and drove down River Street and into the Barrows.

The inhabited Barrows spread on both sides of River Street, the main road that led to the prosperous docks along the deep channel. A thin line of businesses, no more than two blocks deep, lined the roadway. Beyond that, it fell into a twilight zone of partially abandoned ruins that the Bastinados used as home base for their operations. Their turf boundaries changed often as they continuously battled one another for supremacy over the square miles of urban ruins.

After that, you entered—if you dared—the Barrows' relentless, evil heart: the completely deserted Zombie Zone.

The Zombie Zone. Thirty square blocks of empty, crumbling buildings steeped in the rancid odor of dead industry. Deep in the center of the ruins, old articles in the *Chronicle* hinted that a total infrastructure collapse created the Zombie in 1929 and again in 1948, but it's hard to determine exactly when bad things happened there. I've found so little history. It's as if someone went in and erased the place. No one, not even the Bastinados, spend much time in the ruins, especially not at night.

The police do patrol River Street leading to the docks, but none venture deeper unless they are exceptionally well armed or exceptionally crazy. They fear the Bastinados, though, not the true danger that lies there. Some Barrows businesses with their own security force are safe enough and popular—like the Archangel. It's in a bad section of town, but the Archangel has first-rate guards, unobtrusive but well trained and well armed. A tacky, out-of-place neon sign on the building's facade spells out the name, along with a flashing representation of an angel, wings flapping with an erratic electric rhythm. Interesting name since it's an exercise studio and health food restaurant. Mercedes, BMWs, Jags, and other high-end cars fill the parking lot, watched over by vigilant guards.

The uptown young professional crowd keeps their bodies in shape at places like the Archangel, because most of them sit on their asses all day and make money. They have to have lots of money to join the exclusive club of the Archangel.

I cruised the parking lot until I spotted someone pulling out. Of course, others were doing the same thing, and I had to face off with a Mercedes. I gunned the engine on my POS, which sounded particularly powerful thanks to a hole in the muffler. The Mercedes backed down. I guess he figured from the looks of my car I didn't give a shit and would happily ram him and scratch his shiny paint job. Then I'd hire a lawyer and sue him. I smiled and waved as I climbed out of the car.

At times, people come to the Archangel in such throngs that they have to keep nightclub-style bouncers, discreetly referred to as attendants, to manage the line at the door. Tonight was one of those times. I ignored the glares of those in line as I entered. The attendants always let me in because Mr. Michael has given them strict orders.

Handsome, rich Michael owns the Archangel, and he has a thing for me. I've never figured that one out. He's the star, the golden boy, the one the ritzy crowd comes to see—and worship. While I like him a lot, I have some standards. I'm one of the Earth Mother's children. Michael is different. He belongs to the Barrows, and I'm not quite sure he's entirely human.

chapter 5

The Archangel occupied a renovated brick warehouse, filled with all those machines, wires, pulleys, and weights that I'm sure belonged in a torture chamber in another life. Yoga and aerobics classes had their own special floor cut out and a health food restaurant stretched across the back wall. The modern decor featured light oak wood and brown carpet, with splashes of bright green plants in pretty pots. Lively music and laughter filled the air, covering the incessant whir and clank of machines. It was all a little too neat, clean, and contemporary for me, but my opinion doesn't count for much because I'm a slob.

The Archangel's small restaurant sat on a low balcony overlooking the area where people were twisting their bodies in rather peculiar positions. Michael tells me yoga is great. He regularly offers me private lessons, which I regularly decline. The restaurant has good tea, but the food menu consists of various mixes of grassy stuff and grains we let the cows eat back at the farm. The place even smelled like a pasture.

In a few minutes, as usual, one of the Archangel's staff approached me. I recognized him as an employee by his lean, muscular physique, handsome face, and the little angel embroidered on his T-shirt.

"Mr. Michael would like you to join him upstairs," he said. His fake smile reminded me of a doll with a painted face. I followed the staff member's tight, shorts-clad butt up the stairs and into the elegant office with large one-way glass windows looking over the exercise area.

The office was a copy of the rooms below, clean modern lines broken only by a few potted plants and trees. The desk had a glass top and a cordless phone—period. No paper, no pens; only a spare mesh office chair, perfectly positioned, defined a possible work space. The room did contain a small bar with stools and a saffron leather couch stretched along one wall.

I went inside and the attendant closed the door behind me—reluctantly. He kept his adoring gaze on Michael as long as he could.

Beautiful, perfect Michael.

White blond hair flowed like liquid pearl across his shoulders and framed his flawless, symmetrical face. A tall man, built like a classical Greek statue, he wore a silk shirt that clung to his golden-skinned body. A body that made me clench my fists to resist the urge to run my hands over it. A godlike body.

I'd decided that Michael could not be completely human because of the way he manipulates people, the way he draws them. It's not just the looks. His voice, his gestures, his very presence demand adoration and worship. I realize that some movie and rock stars are adored, but when you meet them in person, it fades. Not so with Michael. He remains angelic and compelling in person.

Since I spent so much time in the Barrows, it was inevitable that I'd meet Michael. Five years ago, I'd found one of my runaways working in his kitchen. We'd had a small altercation. I beat the shit out of one of his bouncers. When Michael objected, I took him down, too. I surprised him. I wouldn't be able to do it again. Another reason for doubting Michael's humanity? He's super-strong. Stronger than me, even with the enhancement from the Mother.

Michael had sworn he didn't know the girl was a runaway, and very effectively persuaded her to go home. He invited me for a drink and I accepted. We talked. I told him I was a private detective—I still had my license then—and I found lost children. He seemed vaguely interested, but when he pushed me about why I was so strong, I left. Since then, I'd drop by occasionally and show him pictures of runaways; some of my biggest clues came from his staff. He has a fearsome reputation on the streets. People get nervous when they talk about him—but they won't tell me why.

I'm not exactly sure when he became obsessed with seducing me. Or why. I figured it was a challenge because I was partially immune to his powerful charisma. I don't know why I was immune, but he grabbed me and kissed me one night. I responded to his kiss for a moment, then shoved him away. Nobody grabs me like that. He immediately apologized. Since then, I've kept my distance.

Michael gazed at me with glacial blue eyes. He smiled and I broke into a sweat.

"The Huntress stalks her prey," he said. "She hasn't come to enjoy my company." He spoke in a smooth, lyrical tone that made women and some men lean forward, desperate to hear more.

I edged away from him. "I have an idea where enjoying your company might lead." My body reacted as it always did in his presence. It was purely physical. My skin tingled as desire rose. My body didn't care that he might not be human.

"Would that be so bad?" Michael moved closer. Too close.

"No. Not bad. That's the problem. And we've been through this before."

"Indeed we have." He brushed a finger over my cheek, a caress soft as a sparrow's wing. "Who hurt you?"

His powerful body emanated possession. He would avenge any wrong against me. *He has no right to that. I belong to no man.* I didn't answer his question.

"Tell me about the Goblin Den, Michael."

"The Goblin Den is a dangerous place for you, Huntress."

"The Barrows is a dangerous place for me, Michael."

He still spoke softly, but I caught an edge of caution. Was I actually beginning to know him that well? Well enough to hear nuances in his voice? I drew the pictures of Selene and Richard out of my jacket pocket and offered them to him. "I have a thread leading to the Den."

"You will not find these children at the Den. I will, however, inquire for you. I'll keep the photos and pass them around."

It was as much as I expected. "I don't have that much time. I have to go. The Den is my only lead."

"Then I'll take you there."

I stood silent, surprised, a rare thing for me.

Michael picked up the phone and ordered someone to bring his car to the front. He suddenly turned to me and, in a single swift motion, snatched me off my feet, removed my gun, and tossed it aside. Then he had me on the floor, on the soft carpet, my body pinned tight.

I stared into his face. His eyes burned with bright, savage intensity and he drew deep breaths like a man going into a life-or-death struggle. He crushed his mouth to mine and sent shock waves of desire racing through my body. My fingers locked in his silky hair. Great Mother, what would it feel like brushed across my bare skin? He released my mouth, but his hands caressed my breasts and I trembled under his touch. I spread my legs and felt him hard against me. Great Mother. I wanted ... but I would not. I twisted under Michael. "Let me go!"

Michael instantly released me.

He rolled over and lay beside me, with one arm draped across my waist. "Why not?"

"You're addictive." The words came out harder than I'd intended. "You're like a drug. Smooth as silk. If I get a taste, I'll only want more . . . and more. I won't let anything, or anyone, own me like that."

I truly feared that kind of relationship. My deepest fear and the thing of nightmares: I refused to be overwhelmed by anyone. I'd seen men and women give up their souls to keep another with them. I'd seen men and women use love as a weapon to bend their partners to their selfish will. Surely Michael would tire of me eventually. Then what would I do?

Michael rolled away from me. He was on his feet in a single graceful movement. He offered me his hand. I refused to touch him. I hoisted myself to my feet with the grace and elegance of a giraffe. He watched silently as I straightened my clothes, then found and holstered my gun.

Michael came close, but the sexual tension was missing. No, not missing. Only buried deep inside him, along with other desires I didn't want to know. He grasped my shoulders in gentle fingers. "What can I do to make you want me?" His voice brushed me like fine fur and I swallowed hard, desperate not to give in.

"Why do you want me?"

"Because you are brave and beautiful. I have watched you. You defy evil with courage and—"

"Stop it." That was too much. It was not an answer. "You are desirable. I am not totally immune. If you've watched me, you know I do things in my own way at my own time."

His hands slid down my arms, caught my wrists, and lifted my hands to his lips. I balled them into fists. He brushed a soft kiss on each one. "No, you are not one to give in to the shallow commitment of physical desire, Huntress. I'll be patient."

I pulled my hands from his. He could be as patient as he wanted. Michael, the Archangel, had something wild in him. He had secrets. Instinct told me his secrets could kill me. Once I finished this assignment, I'd never place myself in such a precarious position with him again.

chapter 6

A line had formed at the front door while I was upstairs wrestling with Michael. His admirers exhaled a few gasps and a collective sigh when he appeared. He recognized them with a regal, impersonal smile. After that, he ignored them. They paid lots of money, hoping to get a glimpse of the man. Exercise was the consolation prize if he didn't bless them with his presence.

A delicate silver-painted angel shimmered on the midnight hood of Michael's Jaguar. One of the bouncers opened the passenger door for me, and I slipped into a slate-colored leather seat so comfortable I'd fall asleep if I closed my eyes. It had a showroom kind of new-car smell. The Jag's engine barely made a sound when Michael climbed in and touched a keypad on the dash.

Euphoric confidence overwhelmed me and I stretched out to enjoy the rare freedom of power and money. The windows silently glided down. Some prefer not to use the AC. I do if it's available, but this was his car, his choice.

The light breeze coming through the windows fanned Michael's silky white blond hair. When a few strands drifted across his face, I laid my hands on my thighs and squeezed tight to crush the urge to reach over and brush them away. His heavy, magnetic presence still tugged at me, and if I touched him, he might draw me in again.

"Why are you doing this?" I asked. "The only help you've ever offered before was a few names and addresses. Good information, but some of those places were probably as dangerous as the Goblin Den."

"It amuses me to help you. What else would I do on this fine evening?"

"May I ask you a personal question?" Sitting in luxury, my confidence level soared.

"Please, be as personal as you like." Laughter sparkled in his musical voice.

"Are you human?"

Michael's eyes widened and he seemed locked in an astonished silence. I'd never asked him that before. Much as I feared his domination, I did like him and genuinely wanted to know. His stillness broke as he laughed softly. "What makes you believe I'm not?"

"Nothing I can define, but I bet you know what I mean."

"I belong to the Barrows, Cassandra. It makes me different, not necessarily a monster." A bit of anger threaded its way through his voice like a needle stitching cloth. "I'll show you something. Maybe you can find an answer to your question."

I hadn't called him a monster, but obviously he thought I had. I desperately wished I hadn't said anything at all. The more interaction I had with him, the more he would draw me into his life.

Michael didn't drive fast. The Goblin Den sits near the river, so we stayed on River Street. Since the roadway leads to the docks, the city of Duivel keeps it in good condition. All semblance of other civic responsibility ends on the sidewalks. This far south, the few operating storefronts have steel bars on windows and doors, and after dark, when decent folk leave, the street slips into anarchy. Prostitutes, male and female, stood on the street corners outside the bars, some of them so young they made my heart ache. They watched the Jag with hungry eyes and hunched their shoulders as if they knew deep in their hearts such precious possessions would never be theirs.

The falling moon had disappeared behind river fog that dropped low like the roof of a somber cave. Where taller lights fought it back, the hanging vapor stirred to a sluggish, poisonous-looking brown.

Michael suddenly turned the car down a side street and we rolled through a block of abandoned apartment houses. Nothing stirred here, at least nothing human. Only the Jag's headlights running before us cut the darkness. The Jag's engine sounded like a kitten's gentle purr. It barely disturbed the silence that filled these grim ruins. A musty smell, like wet towels dumped into a hamper and forgotten, filled the air. I shivered. As I finished a prayer to the Mother that Michael knew what he was doing, he stopped the car.

"You see that building?" He nodded to his right.

The bare outline of a three-story apartment house stood out against the nebulous fog. Great holes gaped in its facade, a testament to a time when windows and doors once secured people's homes and lives.

"I was born there," Michael said softly. "There was a health clinic on the corner then, and a nurse ran up three flights of stairs to catch me when I popped out. Her name was Katharine Lester. My mother tried to kill me, but Kathy fought her and stole me away. She persuaded the courts to let her raise me. I grew up in Katharine's apartment—and on these streets."

"Nurse Kathy? From the Fourteenth Street Clinic."

"The same."

I'd heard of Kathy. Her clinic still served the indigent in the Barrows, even though she'd died a few years ago. I'd gone a few times, but no one would tell me anything, so I gave up.

"Were there . . . things . . . here when you were a kid?"

Michael laughed softly. "You mean the creatures in the sewers? Yes, but not as many as now. There seems to have been a sudden population explosion over the last few years. We neighborhood boys learned how to avoid them as we grew up, or we became lunch. The Bastinados weren't as bad, either. Things grew far worse fifteen years ago when the sewers stopped working and the electricity went down. No one would come in and repair things. Kathy went down to city hall many times to complain, but they did nothing."

I wondered if the Mother had some grand plan to drive people out, but it didn't seem likely since she didn't go there. "Where do the monsters come from? You know?"

"No."

I wanted to ask why his mother had tried to kill him and what became of her. I didn't. I suspected I'd already asked one personal question too many.

"So, you're a survivor." I stared hard at him, at those lovely long-fingered hands that casually gripped the steering wheel. "What's it got to do with being human?"

"I survived because I was born with certain extrasensory abilities. Like some other people I know." The dim light from the dash painted his face with shadows.

"So are you saying that you're as human as I am?"

"Yes."

"You belong to the Barrows, so do you also belong to the—?"

"Don't speak of it. Not here. Not so close." He reached out and clutched my shoulder for a moment. "Let's not call too much attention to our presence."

It didn't comfort me to know he feared the Darkness. Many good servants fear their masters. Michael drove on, carefully steering around debris and holes in the street.

Once in my life I stood in the actual presence of the Earth Mother. She accepted my vow and I became her servant. Had the malicious Darkness touched Michael in the same way, and did contact with such powerful beings make us something less or more than human? My life could depend on the answer to that question by the time the dark moon rose. I knew from experience that such answers wouldn't come without a struggle.

Michael continued down the littered street and into the completely abandoned section of the Barrows. The Zombie Zone.

I cleared my throat. "Um, this is the Zombie, Michael."

"Yes." Michael silently laughed. He reached over, caught the back of my neck, and gave me a gentle shake. Like Horus when he plays with the mice he's half killed, then brings to the girls. "Don't worry, Huntress. You're always safe with me."

I shivered. The Darkness lay close here. Its presence filled the air and shimmered along my skin. Cold, so cold. I glanced over at Michael. His classic profile betrayed nothing. In spite of his caution not to *speak* of evil, he drove through the harrowing night as if he were driving in uptown Duivel, without a care in the world. I kept my eyes straight ahead. I didn't search the shadows and I didn't dwell on what threat might be pacing along the slow-moving Jag, right outside my open window.

We exited the Zombie Zone and soon arrived at the Goblin Den parking lot. Like the Archangel, the Goblin Den operates in a converted warehouse. Michael parked near the front door, where four rough-looking men stood guard. Michael's uniformed bouncers were polished and acted tough and competent. These guys looked like some idiot released them from a maximum-security prison yesterday. One walked to the driver's side and another approached me. My hand slid under my jacket for my gun.

"Good evening, Mr. Michael," said the man at the driver's door.

What? Mr. Michael?

Michael nodded his head like an emperor receiving a servant. The one on my side courteously opened my door. When I climbed out, I found Michael had come around to stand close to me. He put his mouth to my ear and spoke softly. "Leave your gun in the car." His lips trailed along my cheek and, may the Mother forgive me, I leaned into the solid mass of his chest.

"Michael, I—"

"You chose to come here with me, Huntress. Now you have to trust me to protect you."

My voice shook when I said, "I should trust a man who says he belongs to the Barrows?"

Michael shrugged. "We can leave."

Right. My choice. Could there be anything more fearful in the Goblin Den than I had faced before? I crouched by the open car door, drew the pistol, and stuck it under the passenger seat. When I stood and closed the door, I noticed the windows were still open.

"You're not going to lock it?"

"No one will touch it." Michael's hand closed on my arm with a firm, steady grip, and he led me to the Goblin Den's front door.

This appeared to be a night for revelations. "You'll excuse me while I reassess my opinion of you."

He released my arm and slid his hand around my waist. "That's my intention. Perhaps I should have brought you here sooner."

"I still have my knives, Michael, and human or not, I'll bet bronze will cut your ass."

Michael laughed.

I'd tried to sound mean, but it felt good being so near him in such a dangerous place. Just good. Not safe. More like hugging a tiger. A delicious tension radiated from his perfect body, but beneath that, I could sense power and energy that went beyond what the eyes could see. How could I not desire him? How could I not also fear him?

I'd been to the Goblin Den only once before. I snuck in the back door in broad daylight to steal a thin, pitiful four-year-old from his drug-addicted and fortunately unconscious mother.

Big barrel lights hung from the ceiling and illuminated an eardrum-busting heavy metal band as they shouted with youthful vigor from the stage. People of indefinable gender gyrated on the crowded floor while the band did a good imitation of Metallica. Sweaty bodies, bad beer, and other less classifiable odors oozed through the cloud of cigarette smoke laced with the more exotic aroma of marijuana.

I'd often wondered what called people to such a place. It didn't speak to me, but the expressions of ecstasy on the dancers' faces made me wonder if I should try it.

Michael led me around the room's edge. The stairs we climbed to the upper reaches of the building vibrated under our feet and smoke thickened and swirled around us. I drew shallow breaths, hoping I could draw in enough oxygen to stay conscious while sucking in a minimum of carcinogens. At the top, Michael opened a door and we entered a room with large windows that, like the office at the Archangel, overlooked the floor below. The noise level dropped to a heavy bass grumble. The room was cleaner and brighter than downstairs, and smelled infinitely better.

Not that it mattered, of course. Because when I saw who waited for me, I knew I was in deep shit. If Carlos Dacardi was a bad guy, then Pericles Theron was evil incarnate. And I didn't have my gun.

chapter 7

Theron's fierce dark eyes locked on me and I gave thanks to the Mother—and Michael—that I hadn't come here alone. Theron and I knew each other by sight and reputation. He sat on the corner of a fine oak desk, glaring at me like a predator that had captured something to kill.

"You got balls, Michael, bringing that bitch here." Theron's body was ferret slim, but his voice sounded deep and heavy with hatred. His two bodyguards, muscular bruisers worthy of Dacardi, stood behind him. Both had guns in shoulder holsters.

Carlos Dacardi might control the Duivel underworld, but he had no hold in the Barrows. Theron ruled human vice in the Barrows. A venomous man, his primary business ventures included prostitution and porno movies with money laundered through the Den. A buyer and worldwide distributor of kiddie porn, he paid hard cash for anything that starred children.

Theron stood and stalked toward me. I tried to step away so I could at least draw my knife, but Michael clutched me tight and I couldn't move.

"Fucking bitch," Theron snarled at me. "You crippled my best cameraman."

"Yeah, you should have been there, asshole." I stuffed

all my contempt into my voice. "He cried like a little kid when I broke his . . . camera." I had seriously damaged his filthy, pedophile cameraman when I rescued Maxie Fountain a few weeks ago. I'd interrupted a filming session, and hearing Maxie beg the son of a bitch not to hurt him again was more than I could stand.

I twisted, but tenacious Michael drew me tighter. A sliver of fear crawled up my spine. What was he doing? Holding me so Theron could attack me?

Theron drew a knife. "I'm going to cut you, bitch. Hurt you bad."

Michael released me, spun me away. By the time I twisted around, he had Theron by his wrist. The snap of bone sounded above Theron's single cry of pain. The knife fell to the carpet. The bodyguards reacted—seconds too late. Michael shoved Theron into one guard and the two men crashed to the floor. The second managed to get off a single silencer-muted shot. Michael snarled like a wolf. The bullet grazed his arm near the shoulder and slammed into a picture on the wall. Shattered glass tinkled as it hit the floor.

Michael caught the shooter by his shirt and belt, lifted him like a child's toy, and threw him at the glass window overlooking the dance floor. Only the window wasn't glass and it didn't break. The man slammed into the clear Plexiglas wall with a meaty thump, hung suspended for a fraction of a second, then slid to the floor and didn't move.

When Michael released the goon for his flying lesson, he immediately turned back to Theron and the other guard. The guard's gun lay a few feet from his hand, but Theron's struggling body pinned him down. Michael kicked the gun away, then kicked the guard in the head. The man drew one sharp breath, released it, and his body went limp.

Michael grabbed Theron by his shirt and hair and

hauled him to his feet. Theron screamed once, a single shrill cry that cut off midbreath.

"Cassandra." I jumped when Michael spoke my name. "Pericles looks a little tired. Why don't you find him a chair?"

I hurried over and dragged a chair from behind the desk. This scene went against all my training and the concept that I was the one who controlled the violence in my life. I didn't complain, though.

Michael sat Theron in the chair with surprising gentleness. Theron seemed physically shrunken. Other than drawing fast, deep breaths, he didn't make any noise. His arm hung down, but when Michael released him, he drew it up and cradled it with the uninjured one. The swelling lump on his wrist had to be extremely painful. Since I've had more than my share of broken bones, I could feel some empathy, but I didn't have any true compassion for a man who brutalized children. I studied Michael for a brief moment. He had suddenly shown an aptitude for violence I'd never seen. Maybe some of those rumors were true.

Michael stood in front of Theron. "Cassandra needs to ask you questions. I think you should answer them." His voice sounded pleasant, but it had a biting, deadly edge. I damn sure didn't want Michael the Archangel as an enemy.

Theron nodded. He ignored me now, opting to keep his eyes on the real danger standing in front of him.

"Show him the pictures, Cass," Michael said.

I fished Richard's and Selene's photos out of my jacket pocket and held them in front of Theron's face. He glanced at them for a second, then back at Michael. He stared at Michael for a long time, then said, "Hammer had them. I asked, but he said they were for a special buyer and I didn't have enough money."

I knew Hammer, a minor drug peddler and pimp. Not

known for kidnapping, but I supposed he could be expanding his business.

I've seriously injured a few Bastinados and perverts who got in my way, even killed a couple in self-defense. I drew my knife and decided I'd make my first true murder a man who prostituted children. Michael caught my wrist.

"Don't bother. Someone will take his place. Better a familiar evil than someone new."

I pulled against Michael's unyielding hand. Finally, I relaxed.

True, I knew how Theron operated, and that knowledge helped me find Maxie Fountain. But I still wanted to risk it all and kill him anyway. "You get a pass for now," I snarled at Theron. "Courtesy of the Archangel. Next time you might not be so lucky."

"Who is Hammer's buyer?" Michael demanded of Theron.

"I don't know. I don't know." Theron's head drooped.

I sheathed my knife and pointed at the blood on Michael's sleeve. "Is that bad?"

He stared at the blood as if seeing it for the first time. "No. Come on. He doesn't know anything else."

We left Theron sitting in the chair. Michael led me down the stairs and through the eardrum-bruising turmoil of the Goblin. He didn't exactly hurry, but he made a steady-moving beeline toward the door. In minutes, we were outside, in the Jag, and rolling back into the relatively blessed silence on River Street.

I laid my fingers on his wounded arm. What little blood remained came off to reveal smooth skin. I sat back and stared straight ahead. Human? Sure he was. Violent? Yes. Evil? I didn't know—yet.

Michael had lifted a man who had to weigh two hundred fifty pounds or more off his feet and tossed him across a room with less effort than a child throwing a doll. I could do it, but not that easily, not even with the strength the Mother gave me when I agreed to serve her. He'd also cowed Pericles Theron like a puppy scolded for shitting on the carpet, then rubbed his nose in it.

"What's your place in the Barrows hierarchy, Michael?"

"I'm a businessman." His soft laughter rippled the air.

"And Theron? How do you know him?"

"He's a businessman, too. He's nowhere near as powerful as people believe. I took you to him because I didn't want you to waste time—or get killed for nothing. The two you're looking for are too old for him."

If Michael belonged to the Barrows, how deep did the roots go? I had to ask the question then. "Why did your mother try to kill you?"

"Why don't you go ask her? Her name is Elise Ramekin. She's a patient at Avondale Manor."

Avondale Manor was a high-class private hospital for the criminally insane. Like the Archangel, the asylum catered to the wealthy. And Michael? Mystery upon mystery.

Who was he? He'd invited me to investigate his past. He wanted me to know something, but for some reason he wouldn't say it outright. I'd have to follow the trail he'd marked for me, but I'd be damn sure to keep one eye over my shoulder.

"Okay. I'll visit her. I owe you that. More than that."

Michael laughed, smooth as the fur of a black cat. "How should I collect on that debt?"

"What? You mean I have to fuck you to be even, Archangel? You have a scorecard somewhere? What's the going rate? How many pieces of ass for how many pieces of information?"

"You misunderstand. You don't owe me sex, no matter how much I desire you. You owe me the courtesy of remembering my answer to your question. I'm just as human as you are. Look to yourself, Cassandra. Look deep inside."

Michael stopped the car at a red light. He reached over and stroked a hand over my hair, then ran it down my arm and twined his fingers in mine. I didn't resist. With only a few words, he had touched on my fear. One that had haunted me from the day I accepted the Earth Mother's call. Would anyone ever love me if they truly knew what I was? If they knew what I did?

Michael squeezed my hand. "We're different, Cass. You and I aren't the same as those people uptown, living orderly lives. We belong together."

I had no answer to that, no smart remark. He had effectively gouged through one of my fears and thrown it in my face. The light changed, he released my hand, and he drove on in silence. We arrived at the Archangel's parking lot, where an irritated-looking Detective Flynn stood scowling at the front-door bouncers. I might not remember much of last night, but this one should be unforgettable.

chapter 8

When the car stopped at the entrance, I opened the door and went to Flynn. He stood straight with his arms at his sides and his jacket slightly open, badge and gun clearly visible. Not exactly threatening, but formidable none-theless. Two of Michael's hefty bouncers barred his way.

"Now what?" I said to him. He really pissed me off. "I said I'd find her. You have to let me do my job."

"I can see you're working hard." Flynn stared at Michael with that grim, hard-jawed cop expression. His voice had a sharper edge now.

Michael approached, nodded at Flynn, and gave him a smug smile. He handed me the gun I'd left under the car seat. "Don't forget this."

Damn him! The last thing I needed was for Flynn to question me about my illegal gun. Michael stood far enough away for me to have to make an obvious reach for my weapon. I grabbed it and shoved it into the holster under my jacket.

I did a quick introduction. What a joy. Conceited Michael meets hard-ass Flynn.

Michael extended his hand to Flynn. "Good evening, Detective."

In an automatic gesture, Flynn grasped the hand.

Michael frowned. "Does Cassandra require a lawyer?"

Flynn shook his head. "I only want to talk to her." He glared at me. "For now."

Michael nodded as if to say he understood the situation. Then the arrogant bastard stepped close, caught my arm, and gave me a velvet-soft kiss on the cheek.

"Don't say anything you'll regret, darling," he said gently, as if to a lover. Which I was not! He released me and walked into the building. The two muscle-boy bouncers followed. One grinned and winked at me.

Darling? Was Michael, perfect Michael, jealous? Or did he just want to fry my ass in front of a cop?

"How'd you find me?" I asked Flynn.

"I put out the word for anyone who saw your car to call me." His tone of voice said he didn't give a shit if such an action upset me. "Your pretty Michael had blood on his sleeve."

This cop didn't miss much.

"An accident. And he's not *my* Michael. What do you want?"

Flynn didn't say anything. He walked toward my car, leaving me to follow. When I got there, I saw a duffel bag and rolled-up sleeping bag on the backseat.

"What's that?" I asked.

"My clothes. I have some vacation time. I'd planned to use it hunting for Selene, but now I'm going to stay with you."

"What? You can't—"

"Oh, yes, I can." He scowled at me across the top of the car. "It's not my decision. If I don't, you'd better be prepared to face your Madam Abigail *and* my mother. Of the three of you, I don't know who scares me the most."

I opened my phone, walked three cars down. The evening actually felt warmer, not cooler. Sweat beaded on my forehead. I dialed Abby.

"Yes, Cassandra." Abby answered on the first ring. Only it wasn't Abby.

"I want to talk to Abby, not you."

The Earth Mother laughed. "No, Huntress, it is I to whom you must complain regarding Detective Flynn. He is to stay at your side until you find the children. If you serve me, Huntress, in this instance you *will* obey me."

"He can't stay with me. How do I explain the Barrows to him?"

"You show him, of course. Do I sense a bit of hostility, dear?"

"Hostility doesn't even begin to cover what I feel right now." I cut the phone off.

I am her servant. I'd made that vow and I'd kept it. I would continue to serve, but, damn, she made it hard at times. She'd never done anything like this before. I am a solitary lone hunter and now she'd forced me to accept someone in my hunt—and forced him into my life. I shoved the phone in my pocket and marched back to Flynn. He sat in the passenger seat and gave me an evil look when I climbed in.

"Where's your truck?" I stuck the key in the ignition.

"With my mother. Her car is in the shop. How'd you get the shit beat out of you if you carry a piece?"

"I only carry it in the Barrows."

"You have a license? The Barrows is part of the city."

"You think so?"

"That Michael. He's your boyfriend?"

"No. A friend." An arrogant ass of a friend.

"Your *friend* has a serious criminal record. You know that, don't you? They talk about him a lot at the station. Nailing him is something of a mission. He and Carlos Dacardi are the big badasses in crime in Duivel."

Oh, great! The two big badasses in town and I was now involved with both. This would not end well. I had children to think of, though. They came first. Oh, I'd heard the stories about Michael, but they were always vague, with no details. Nobody ever said, *Michael com-*

mitted this crime or *Michael committed this act of violence.* I figured it was like the rumors about me. Kill a few monsters, kick a few criminal asses, and you get to be a heroine—or a rogue vigilante, depending on who's talking. And yet, this very evening, I'd watched him take out two thugs and snap Pericles Theron's arm. He broke the bone without mercy and forced Theron to talk, for no greater reason than to please me.

"Just shut up and let me drive, Flynn." I did not want to talk about Michael.

I started the car and drove out of the Archangel's parking lot, leaving a Lexus and a Porsche to fight over my parking spot.

If, as the Mother insisted, Flynn had to stay with me, he had to know some of my secrets—and accept them without slapping me in handcuffs and hauling me to jail. For him, I'd have to break the veil of obscurity that cloaked the Barrows. He'd be initiated into a new world. Unlike the general uptown populace, he wouldn't be able to turn away and pretend he hadn't seen the weird and bizarre. Bigger problem? I didn't know how I'd conceal some of my more devious retrieval methods from him.

I pulled into the apartment house parking lot and switched off the car. "Are you a *shoot first, ask questions later* kind of cop?"

"No." He sounded offended.

"Good. If you shoot my friends, I will be *very* unhappy." Not to mention he'd have to shoot me because I'd stand in front of them. "Come upstairs and I'll welcome you to my world." When we entered the apartment, I told him to sit at the table. I sat in a chair across from him. "Pretend you're dreaming. It might help. Nefertiti? Nirah?"

Horus dashed across the room and leaped onto the table. Nirah coiled around his neck with her head between his ears. Her tiny forked tongue flicked in and out at lightning speed.

Nefertiti lowered her slender body from a cheap and gaudy chandelier with burned-out bulbs hanging directly over my table until her head was eye level with Flynn. I don't know how she made it up there. I hadn't noticed her when we came in. Neither had Flynn.

Flynn sat with his eyes wide and his mouth open. His hand was halfway to his gun.

"No shooting!" My muscles tightened as I prepared to throw myself at him. "They won't hurt you and you won't hurt them."

His hand moved away from the gun, but his eyes never left Nefertiti, Horus, and Nirah.

I reached out and stroked Nefertiti's head with my finger. She let go and her body hit the table with a solid thump. She coiled herself into a ball.

"Nefertiti, let's start with you." I held out my hand and she laid her head on my palm. For her, that signified trust. "This is Flynn. He's going to be staying with us for a few days. I want you to learn his scent so you can recognize him. Now, he's going to be nervous, so you be easy."

Nefertiti slid toward Flynn. He had his hands on the table in front of him, both clenched into fists.

"I went to school, Cass." His voice had an odd tone I didn't understand. "That reptile has a brain the size of a pea. She could strike at any minute."

"Maybe she isn't a snake."

He gave me a *You've got to be kidding* look.

Nefertiti's head reached his hands. Her tongue flicked, identifying his scent and body temperature, memorizing him as I would memorize the photo of a child I was hunting.

With impressive courage, Flynn sat still, frozen as someone facing a fearful unknown, determined to hold his ground. Nefertiti inched her way forward until she reached his arm, then stopped.

"She wants to crawl on you." I gave him a smile I hoped was reassuring. "Can you take that?"

Flynn nodded. A resilient man, facing an uncomfortable situation.

Nefertiti worked her way up his arm and shoulder, the only sound the faint rasp of her body across his shirt. For some reason, her brown markings had deepened to a near black. His jaw clenched when she slid across the bare skin of his neck. She didn't wrap herself around him, but she laid her head on top of his, mimicking Horus and Nirah.

Flynn's eyes were wide, but now more in shock than fear.

"Wait." I held up a finger. "Horus, your turn."

Horus marched up to Flynn with a cat's graceful, arrogant dignity, deigning to introduce himself.

"Nirah is small," I told Flynn. "You need to watch out for her."

It wasn't likely he would step on her—she is too fast for that—but unlike Nefertiti, Flynn would need to be aware of her at all times. Nirah isn't particularly aggressive, but she doesn't like strangers. Of the three of them, it was Horus's shitty attitude that really worried me the most.

Horus reached out a paw and flexed his incredible claws.

Oops. Horus the badass tyrant wasn't a team player. Nirah opened her mouth and hissed, flashing her fangs. Nefertiti darted forward across Flynn's head to meet Nirah. Her fangs dripped venom and her head swayed back and forth like a clock pendulum, matching Nirah's moves.

Flynn sat frozen. Formidable control. He might deal well with the Barrows, after all. An unbidden thought jumped forward in my mind. He might deal well with me, too. Did I want that?

"Hey!" I slapped my hand on the table. "You three, stop showing off. I'm ashamed of you."

Horus turned to me, and by default, so did Nirah.

I shook my head. "Okay, he's one of us now. Understood?"

Nefertiti slid off Flynn and joined Horus and Nirah, waiting for the next move.

"They're venomous." Flynn's voice was flat and cold. "It's illegal to keep venomous—"

"They only bite when necessary," I explained, but I doubt it comforted him. "A little kid could walk in here and pick up all three of them and be safe."

"You're saying these animals, reptiles, have the ability to reason?" He gestured at them, but quickly drew his hand back. "Choose who they bite?"

"Yes."

"I don't believe you. Where did they come from?"

"I don't know. I found Nefertiti in the Barrows. She crawled in the car and came home with me. Horus and Nirah were at the front door the next day. I consider them gifts."

"You communicate with them. How?" Flynn drilled me as if this were a criminal interrogation, a demand for facts. At least he'd actually accepted my gift for animal communication.

"Intuition. A psychic bond, if you can understand that. The way I've always been able to communicate with animals. Only, they're not exactly animals. At least I don't think they're animals. Or reptiles. You're on the fringe of reality here. Accept or reject. Your choice."

Flynn drew a deep, shuddering breath and rubbed a hand across his face. "People keep telling me you're . . . a lot of things. Downtown, River Street. I went down there. I asked everyone who would actually talk to me. I paid for information. Any clue, just a hint. They call you a witch. Or a demon. But they all say you find children."

I'd bet Flynn had an analytical mind, full of right angles, mixed with the gut instinct cops develop over time. My snakes and cat, only a brief glimpse into my world, created an unpleasant paradox for him. I wondered what would tip the balance toward acceptance or rejection.

"Let me see that gun." Flynn held out his hand.

Ah, something tangible to hold on to. Like Dacardi, this man understood weapons. After what he had just seen, he required the familiar, to balance things in his mind. I removed the magazine and gave him the pistol. While he inspected it, I used a paper towel to clean up the drops of venom Nefertiti had dripped on the table.

"Nice piece." He held the gun up. "Where'd you get it?" His calm voice almost hid his keen interest.

"A Bastinado didn't need it anymore, so I confiscated it."

He laid it on the table beside the magazine. "Ever used it?"

Oh, boy. How did I answer a cop's question about that? "Only in self-defense."

Flynn laid the gun beside the magazine. "It's heavy. Are you a good shot?"

"Yes."

I'd spent hours at the target range, and every couple of years I go to one of those survival schools where I learn to shoot moving targets and fire from any position. He didn't need that information right now, though. His face held a neutral expression usually indicative of heavy thought.

I stood. I needed another shower. The stink of the Goblin Den clung to me like a thin, disgusting oil. "I'm going to clean up. You can have the bathroom when I'm done."

Suddenly weary, I rubbed the back of my neck. I had

to give him a way out and hope he'd take it. "Flynn, if you want to leave, I'll understand. I won't tell your mother, and I'll find Selene."

He nodded. Then he turned back to face the girls and Horus. I trusted them not to bite him unless he did something incredibly foolish. Unlike myself, I'd bet Detective Flynn rarely made the leap into imprudent acts. I studied him for a moment. Flynn was a man with rough edges but seemingly strong principles. Though he claimed he was acting on his mother's wishes by staying with me, I knew he was really there because he cared about his sister. He would endure venomous snakes—and a lot more—to get her back home. And he was attractive as hell. In some ways, I wished we'd met under different circumstances.

I took my time in the bathroom, showered, shaved my legs, rubbed on lotion, and dried my hair. Weariness settled in. Since eight o'clock that morning, when Detective Flynn had pounded on my door, I'd been beaten up, healed, faced temptation in the form of gorgeous Michael, and given an enemy one more reason to hate me. I dressed in a shirt that came down to my knees and put on panties, something I didn't usually wear to bed. I didn't need thoughts of the hot cop to complicate things even more.

When I went back into the bedroom, I heard no sound from the living room, so I figured he was gone. I hoped he'd gone. What was the Mother thinking? How could a rational man like Flynn understand the mystical? Horus, Nefertiti, and Nirah weren't the most exotic of what I knew in Mother's secret world and her war with what lay in the Barrows.

I walked back into the living room.

Flynn sat at the table, intently watching Horus, Nefertiti, and Nirah eating something in saucers.

"What are you doing?" I asked.

"I thought they might be hungry," he said. "All I could find was a jar of caviar in the fridge."

"That's the caviar my cousin sent me." I'd never eaten caviar, and had left the stuff in the refrigerator until I could get up the nerve to try it.

I sat in a chair and watched them polish off the fish eggs. Horus finished his, walked over to Flynn, and patted his hand with one paw. Nirah joined Horus. She bumped Flynn's fingers with her small head. Great Mother! He'd formed a bond with them. As far as I knew, only Abby had ever done that. I found myself both dismayed and pleased at the same time. How was I going to get rid of him now? Did I even really want to be rid of him? He'd shown some compassion for my injuries and complimented me on my hair, but many people do that. If he'd given me any indication that he liked me as a woman, I'd missed it.

"You're welcome," Flynn said. I was afraid he'd try to pet Horus, which would've been a mistake, but he didn't.

Flynn grinned at me, his eyes bright with mischief. "How long since you've had a boyfriend?" he asked abruptly.

"A few months." I lied. No woman wants to admit to a sexless year—or two.

"What happened to him?" He leaned back and his grin grew wider. "He didn't like snakes?"

"They made him uncomfortable." I bit my lip to hold back a laugh. "Man had no sense of humor. He woke up one morning with Nefertiti coiled on his chest. Ran out the door, naked and screaming. She only wanted to be friends. I mailed him his clothes."

Flynn chuckled. "So where do I sleep?"

"Floor or couch. Take your pick. I'll leave the bedroom door open so you can get to the bathroom. Put the seat back down."

Not long after that, I heard him go into the bathroom

and close the door. The day had wrung me out like a damp towel, so sleep claimed me instantly. So much for the sharp-eyed, always-on-guard Huntress. A strange man in my apartment and I crash. Nirah, Nefertiti, and Horus had accepted him, though, and that gave me some degree of security.

I woke during the night and realized someone was in the bed with me. I rose up on one elbow and punched Flynn in the arm.

"What?" He grumbled, his voice heavy with sleep.

"You're not supposed to be here. Sleeping bag. Couch. Living room."

"Not comfortable. Need to rest." He rolled over and turned his back to me.

I sighed. At least he was dressed—khaki shorts—and I had a queen-sized bed. How odd. I should've been terribly uncomfortable with him beside me. Why hadn't I woken up when he'd lain down?

Clearly, this guy had the ability to lull me into deadly complacency. In some ways, that made him more dangerous than all the monsters lurking in the Barrows.

I'd had guys in my bed before. Some were fantastic lovers. I had even asked Nirah and Nefertiti to keep their distance, and they complied. Eventually, though, the guys would leave. But it wasn't just the snakes. It would take a special, persistent man to accept a woman who jumps up in the middle of terrific sex and rushes out because of a phone call from someone she won't identify. In the past, some nice men just wanted a night of sex and left the next day. A few of them really liked me and wanted to stay. But my strangeness, my inability to get close, show them my world—it just didn't work for them. There were no happy endings in those relationships, only pain and loss. I fought to remain aloof, telling myself my duty filled my life and I didn't have time for a man.

I held my hand over his bare shoulder, close, but I didn't touch him. He radiated warmth that had nothing to do with the temperature. My mind formed a fantasy vision of snuggling up to him. He might make love to me if I wanted him to.

Get a grip, Cassandra.

To get involved with a man, particularly this man, would lead to disaster. I drifted off to sleep and didn't wake again until morning.

I rose first, grabbed my clothes, and went to the bathroom. I didn't want to be tempted to actually touch him. He was still asleep when I came out. I stood and watched him, his steady breath, that kissable mouth. A cop. The man. Authority figure. I went to make coffee. Today would be a long day.

chapter 9

"This wreck doesn't even have air-conditioning." Flynn had griped about my car since we left the apartment. He didn't seem genuinely irritated, but he significantly contributed to my foul mood. The blast-furnace heat didn't help.

"There's air coming through the window," I said. "Pretend it's cool. Are you a stoic cop or a wuss?"

Not that he'd had a good morning. He woke up with Horus sitting on his face. Nefertiti lay coiled in his clothes, and when he picked up his shoe, Nirah fell out. Then I told him he'd have to buy a case of caviar. I also bitched at him for getting in my bed uninvited. He told me I snored, which is an absolute lie.

I stopped the car at a light. A Duivel PD patrol car pulled up beside us and Flynn hunched down in the seat. I slugged him in the shoulder. "You ass, you're ashamed to be seen with me."

"I'm ashamed to be seen in this rolling disaster." Disgust etched lines in his face.

I waved at the patrol car, then pointed at Flynn. I could see them laughing. Made me feel a lot better.

The day's egg-frying heat cooked both of us, even

though the sun had barely reached its noon height. Actually, my car does have an operable AC, but with so many holes, it uses too much gas to lower the temperature even a few degrees. For the price of a tank of gas, I could sweat a little—or a lot.

I wore the lightest clothes I had, jeans and a cotton shirt. Flynn wore a T-shirt, jeans, and a light leather vest that partially covered his gun. I left my gun at home.

"Where are we going?" Flynn asked.

"Avondale Manor."

"The asylum? You're checking in? Excellent move." He chuckled. "I'll feed your snakes and water your plants if you like."

"I want to talk to someone." Might as well make use of him if I had to drag him along. Maybe I could have a flat tire. Make him change it. "You got your badge with you, right?"

"Yeah, but I'm not going to play the bully cop for you."

We'd developed a relationship of mutual mistrust. "Even for Selene?"

He sighed and stared straight ahead. "Who are we going to see?"

"Elise Ramekin."

"And she is?"

"Michael's mother."

Flynn frowned but didn't say anything. I turned down Twenty-fifth Street. I didn't know what to expect of Michael's mother, but he wanted me to meet her. Of course, he'd made me curious.

"Tell me about Michael's record," I said. I remembered Flynn's accusations.

"Rape, murder, and aggravated assault," he said. "Five years ago. Arrested, but his expensive lawyer got him off. Not enough evidence. He owns major property. A warehouse on the river, and ..."

"And what?"

"Half interest in the Goblin Den."

Now that was a stunner. I managed to keep the surprise out of my voice. "Who owns the other half?"

"Pericles Theron."

I gritted my teeth. Michael had lied. Now I'd have to go see him and try to kick his pretty ass. Rape, murder, assault? I'd seen his instant violent reaction at the Goblin Den the evening before. Whatever his actual crimes, he'd concealed them well. He left only rumor as evidence. Evidently, the police had the same problem. If I could point to one event of particular evil, I'd probably be angrier. Being lied to was personal.

The hiss and rumble of traffic eased as Twenty-fifth Street morphed into a residential haven of spacious lots. I'd driven by Avondale a few times, but I'd never been inside the ten-foot white block wall surrounding the place. No guard at the black iron gate, but there was a call box. As we arrived, the automatic gate slid open to allow a plumbing repair truck to enter. I hit the gas, closed the distance, and followed the truck inside the wall.

"You don't think they'll let you in if you ask?" Flynn said.

"Maybe. But this saves time."

"Wonder why they don't have a guard at the gate." He studied the place with a cop's eyes.

"Don't know." I was grateful for no guard. I'm not one for overanalyzing a situation, but this one seemed unusual.

I followed the truck until it turned at the sign marked SERVICE ENTRANCE. Gravel crunched under the tires like a giant eating stones as I drove into an empty area marked VISITOR PARKING. The drive had led us more than a quarter mile from the main road.

Flynn made me open the trunk so he could leave his gun behind. An asylum for criminals probably wasn't the best place to carry one. I used the key and didn't tell him that his gun storage locker would open with a good hard smack. It often popped up when I hit a bump in the road.

I had to shade my eyes against the sun reflecting from three stories of blinding white brick as we climbed the steps to the front door. Decorative metal grills covered every window, and created a cage with elaborate bars.

Flynn stopped before we entered. He stared back across the expansive stretch of green lawn. "No wonder they don't have a guard. High-tech ground security," he said. "See the little spikes. Sound, probably motion sensors, too. They know we're here."

This cop's eyes had seen what I'd missed.

We walked inside and had to stand blind for a few moments while our pupils dilated. The vestibule contained a single spare desk, and an equally spare woman sitting behind it. Her long, bony fingers clutched a phone receiver and she radiated an unwholesome air, almost like someone worn down by a chronic illness.

"May I help you?" she asked. Her lips barely moved. "I didn't get a call from security to—"

"We're here to see Elise Ramekin." I stepped up to the desk and spoke with as much authority as I could muster. She wasn't a big woman, and that put me in the superior position of towering over her.

She hesitated, so I rushed on. "I'm a friend of her son, Michael."

"May I see some identification?" She lifted her hand from the phone.

I dug out a driver's license and Flynn flashed his badge and ID. Her eyes slid over my license, but lingered on Flynn's. Flynn's charm wasn't like Michael's. He had no hypnotic thing saying, *Adore me, worship me.* Flynn made a connection on a human level. He asked for nothing more than goodwill and, in this case, seemed to receive goodwill as requested.

"We don't permit weapons—"

"None." Flynn smiled. He drew back his vest to show he was unarmed. He gave her a dazzling smile. "Social visit."

The woman almost smiled back. *I probably should have let him sweet-talk her in the first place instead of playing a bully. Damn it! I'm in charge here.* I glared at him and he winked. I resisted the urge to punch him.

Her eyes lingered on him as she spoke into the phone. "Mrs. Ramekin has visitors."

A lock clicked and a door to my right opened. Two doors actually, one wood and the other behind it steel bars. A mouse-faced woman with a tag clipped to her white nurse's uniform entered.

The receptionist waved her hand in our direction. "This nurse will escort you." She did smile at Flynn this time.

The mouse-faced nurse, so low in the pecking order that even a receptionist didn't introduce her by name, stepped back and motioned us to enter. She closed and locked the door behind us, and we followed her down a silent hall. Her spine was so rigid it allowed only a bare hint of movement in her hips, but practical, thick-soled oxford shoes squeaked faintly with each step on the polished wood floor.

We went through a metal detector and another barred gate. A few people walked the halls here, nurses, a janitor mopping the floor, a maintenance man with a ladder. After we passed the last checkpoint, the close halls stood empty and silent except for the squeak and shuffle of our shoes.

"This is the sun room," Mouse Face said. Her voice carried a nasal whine. "That's her." She pointed at a smallish woman sitting at a table beside a vast wall of barred windows. Some designer or architect must have decided that natural light gave the illusion of freedom, but it only illuminated the cage. The nurse walked away, but not far. She stood at attention like a soldier in a milk white uniform, guarding the door we entered.

The high-ceilinged room had a number of chairs and tables, but Elise was the only occupant. She seemed like a frail child, alone in a sparse lunchroom, ostracized by her schoolmates.

I approached cautiously, not knowing what to expect. The chairs appeared to be solid blocks of foam. The tables with rounded corners were bolted to the floor, as if prepared for an act of violence.

Elise's short hair was a cap of pure snow in the sunlight. She wore slippers and a dull green cotton dress that matched the room's walls. It gave the illusion that she might disappear if she stood against one. The papers on the table in front of her had her undivided attention. She bent over them with unwavering intensity. As we moved close, I could see soft charcoal drawings.

"Elise," I said softly. I didn't think it wise to startle someone who seemed so fragile.

She didn't look up.

"Elise."

Still nothing.

Flynn laid a hand on my arm and said, "Elise?"

Elise raised her head and stared at us. She responded to his deeper, masculine voice. So did I. Kindness and warmth filled it, making a sinfully rich sound. Except for a few furrows on her forehead, Elise's face was smooth as a woman no more than thirty. Her eyes held uncertainty, but cleared when she focused on Flynn. She immediately stood, laid her tiny piece of charcoal aside, and practically leaped into his arms.

She surprised him, but he seemed to have the rare ability to discern emotional need and respond immediately. He gently embraced her.

"How are you today, Elise?" His hand stroked her cap of white hair.

Elise laughed in a musical voice that sounded so much like a feminine version of Michael's.

"I'm so happy you came." She cocked her head as she studied him. "Ah, the wolf. The Guardian. Yes. Oh, you *are* a fine one." True joy filled her voice.

Flynn drew a quick breath, but he didn't falter. I bit my lip and kept my face straight. The Guardian. The Earth Mother had called him that. It surprised me, but why did it surprise him?

Flynn guided Elise back to her chair, had her sit, then knelt close beside her. She ignored me.

"Elise," Flynn said. He held her hand. He spoke with care, as if to a child. "My friend Cass wants to ask you some questions. She's—"

"The Huntress." Elise sounded a bit annoyed. "The great holy whore's bitch dog."

I sighed. *Holy whore.* I'd heard that before, or at least read it in Abby's history books. The Mother reigned over man- and womankind for thousands of years until the coming of the male sky gods, the gods of anarchy and war. Then mankind repudiated her and turned her daughters into possessions rather than helpmates. They also applied the vile names they gave her to those daughters, too.

So I could be on her level, too, I stepped around to kneel at her other side. As I did, I saw her drawings. All were excellent pictures of Michael. One a very young Michael, maybe ten or eleven, but he already had that compelling face that begged women to desire him. I wanted to pick one up for a closer look, but since they and the piece of charcoal appeared to be her only possessions, I left them be. Unstable people often clung to certain objects to solidify their lives.

Bitch dog, she'd called me. I'd bet Elise had far more functioning brain cells than everyone believed—or was I just in a snit because she called me a nasty name?

"Those are nice pictures of Michael." I gestured at the drawings. "Does he visit you often?"

"Often enough. He looks so much like his wonderful father." Elise answered the question without looking at me. She raised a thin hand and stroked Flynn's cheek. The hand showed her age even if the face did not. How old? Sixty? Seventy? Surely not.

"I tried to save him," she said. "My beautiful boy. My Michael. I tried to give him the greatest gift. To be with his father." Her mouth turned down and anger filled her voice. "But that woman came and took my little angel away." She held out her arm. Small arc-shaped scars decorated her skin from wrist to elbow. "I bit down hard. I didn't scream. He hurt me, but I didn't scream. No one should know." She glanced around as if to see who was listening, then whispered, "I was so quiet." Elise caught Flynn's hand with her own. "But when he came out, he cried. I tried, but I couldn't stop him."

She huddled closer to Flynn and said, "I have a secret. The child you seek. Your moon child." She stared over his shoulder. "You must . . ."

Two women marched across the room toward us. One wore pale blue nurse's scrubs and the other a gray suit so tailored it could be armor. The one in scrubs had a needle in her hand and she hurried toward Elise.

We stood to face the armor suit. The woman had drawn her hair so tight into a bun that it stretched pale skin across her cheekbones and narrowed her eyes to dark slits. The female guardians of this hellhole had an unwholesome lack of grace and humanity. I wondered if they were that way when they came, or if the place leached the warmth out of them over time.

The ID badge pinned to the suit gave her name as ANITA COHEN, DIRECTOR.

"Get out." Cohen's hands curled into fists. "You do not have permission—"

In a surprising move, Flynn offered her his badge. He stood tall and straight. He mastered intimidation on a cold, forceful level I couldn't match.

"That does not impress me," Cohen snarled.

"I'm not here to impress you, Director Cohen. I'm following leads in an active investigation and I *will* go where they take me. Hindering that investigation is a felony." Flynn pocketed his badge. "And since you've incapacitated the person I was interviewing—" He nodded at Elise. The nurse in scrubs was withdrawing the needle from her arm.

"Leads? This patient?" She sneered at Elise. "They locked her in here twenty years ago. She could not possibly have any information for you. I'm going to file a complaint with your superiors and—"

"Hey!" I said the word with a little more force than I'd intended. "This patient? This woman is a human being, not an animal."

The anger in Cohen's face faded, replaced by a neutral mask. "Technically, you're quite right. She's not an animal. But I doubt if you could make the parents of the infants she strangled in their cribs believe it." She stared at Flynn. "You're the cop. How many were there before they caught her?"

I started to speak, then gave up. There was nothing to say.

"I want to see her records." Flynn's hands clenched into fists.

"Get a warrant." Cohen called his bluff.

Two men arrived, men so bulky you knew they did some serious bodybuilding.

"Show Detective Flynn and Ms. Archer out," Cohen ordered. She crossed her arms over her chest and glared at us.

"Elise?" She watched me with vacant eyes. Hopeless. I knelt beside her. "I'll talk to Michael. Maybe he can fix it so we can see you again."

Flynn and I left, escorted by the two steroid boys. Neither of us spoke until the car moved onto the street and the wind blowing through the windows cooled it down to a hundred and ten.

"Wow." I'd never had an experience like that one.

"Bullshit!" Flynn spit out the word. "You think I wouldn't have heard of strangled babies? I know guys who have been on the force over twenty-five years. They're always ready to lay a crime story on anyone who will listen."

"Money buys silence. How much money to keep parents quiet? A million? Two million? I hear it costs a quarter to half a mil a year to keep someone in Avondale, and she's been here a long time. Someone is paying her keepers not to let her talk about what happened."

Flynn slapped his hand on the dash and instantly snatched it back. The plastic had almost reached the meltdown stage.

I reached in my pocket, pulled out the small leather case, and tossed it at him. He opened it. "This driver's license has your picture, but . . ." He frowned. "Who's Mary Ann Halstead?"

"No one. At least no one I know. Fake ID."

"Jesus, Cass, that's—"

"Yeah, yeah, illegal. But guess what. That's the ID I used when we entered the forbidden halls of Avondale. When we left, Battleship Cohen called me Ms. Archer."

"How did she know who you were?"

"I don't know."

"Why use fake ID?" He closed the leather case.

"Habit. Makes it easier to get information at times."

Flynn stared out the window for a moment, then said, "Elise called me the *wolf*. My first name is Phelan. It means wolf. How could she know that?"

"Phelan?" I grinned.

"If you call me that, the next time I find this car illegally parked, I will have it towed to the junkyard and crushed." He pocketed my fake ID.

I laughed. He probably wasn't serious about the car. The fake ID? Not a problem. A graphic artist whose kid I brought home made me as many as I needed.

"Are you going to talk about what else she said? I think I should know."

His hand tugged at the seat belt as if it chafed him. "Selene's name means moon. We called her 'Moon Child.' Just a nickname. She made us stop when she was eleven. It embarrassed her." He paused. "Is there anything I should know?" I knew he was still pissed about Michael. "What's the connection to Michael?"

"Selene is in the Barrows. Michael belongs to the Barrows. I asked him to help me and he asked me to visit his mother. That's all I know right now. Something's happening, things are connected, but I'm not sure how— yet. I know it's confusing. I'm sorry I can't figure things immediately."

"Drop me off at the station," Flynn said. "I want to do some research. I'll take a cab and meet you back at your apartment. Right now I'm going to ignore the commandment to stay with you for the sake of information."

"Okay. I need to go talk to a friend down at the mission. See if he knows anything. Sometimes kids show up there."

The Lost Lamb Mission was a long shot in this case, but I didn't have any other leads. I also wanted to have a serious chat with Michael about his mother—and the Goblin Den. I didn't want Flynn around.

I had to admire Flynn, though. He'd had a lot dumped on him. Sentient snakes and a cat with a serious attitude, and now Elise's pronouncements. He'd absorbed it and was proceeding with a good degree of calm. And he was impressive at Avondale, despite Cohen's iron bitch attitude and Elise's odd pronouncements naming him the Guardian and me the Huntress. He had faced the receptionist with mildly friendly flirtation, Elise with kindness and compassion, and Cohen with the firmness of the detective on the case. While I had some sympathy for Elise, my combative nature would have caused me grief before I even got to see her.

I made sure Flynn had my cell phone number and dropped him off a block from the station. Cell phones didn't work deep in the ruins, but they did okay on River Street. The ass still didn't want anyone else to see him with me. I headed for the Barrows, but on the way I stopped at the apartment and strapped on my gun.

chapter 10

A young, pretty blonde with a forced smile and narrowed eyes greeted me as I entered the Archangel a little after eleven o'clock in the morning. She wore a thin, stretchy, flesh-colored garment with a neckline cut almost to the perky nipples of her firm, perfect breasts. Her brightly manicured fingers motioned for me to follow her. When she turned, her ass, covered with the same thin, stretchy material, appeared as perfect and rounded as her tits. Definitely a surgeon-sculpted body. In fact, all of Michael's attendants seemed to be the perfect type. What did he see in me, a woman with an ordinary body and a shitty attitude—an especially shitty attitude when it came to him? My sparkling personality? My weapons?

The girl led me across the main floor and through a door to a hall. The hall ended at an elevator. She pushed a single button on the wall, the door opened, and she walked away without a word. Michael's bouncers gave me smug leers occasionally, but his female employees hated me as if I'd cheated them of something they desperately desired.

I stepped in the elevator, a small box that could hold three people max. Only one button, so I pushed it. The door slid shut with a gentle whisper that gave way to a hum as the car started up. I loosened my gun in my holster, let it slide back, and checked my knife. I was going to confront a dangerous man who had lied to me by omission of certain facts. Is that what made him so desirable? The danger? The challenge? If so, it made him perfect for an action junkie like me. The elevator door opened into a small vestibule, and a few feet away a regular door stood open. When I stepped through, I expected another entrance to Michael's office, but instead walked into an apartment that made mine look like a shipping crate with plumbing.

Decorated straight out of an Oriental harem movie set, brass lamps cast a warm glow on floor cushions of crimson and gold silk and furniture draped with shiny fabric the color of new copper pennies. The floor was patterned tile punctuated with an occasional cream-colored rug. My mind went blank as I stared at the sheer opulence. A scent filled the air . . . Incense? No, something more personal, more indefinable.

"Do you like my home?" Michael spoke from behind me.

He'd come into the room through a door on my left. He wore nothing but a pair of loose, silky pants. The muscles on his chest and arms glistened with moisture in the soft, warm light, and his hair, usually so perfectly groomed, was mussed as if some woman had run her fingers through it while he made passionate love to her.

"I like your home." *And you*, my traitorous mind whispered. "It doesn't look like your style, though."

Michael shrugged. "You don't know my style. You don't know *me*, Huntress."

True. He had shadowy places inside that I had no desire to explore—and other places that tempted me.

"Did I interrupt something?" I tried to sound cool and aloof.

"Just a workout. I have my own private gym in the next room." He walked over to the door I'd entered and closed it.

Michael moved closer and I caught the scent of sandalwood drifting from his perfect golden skin. Oh, shit, hadn't I sworn I'd never let myself get in a dangerous situation with him?

With my senses overwhelmed, I had only one feeble defense. I closed my eyes. Yes, I could smell him and feel his presence close, so close, but I regained some control. I opened my eyes. Michael laughed, soft and low. He moved in. I backed up—until I hit the wall by the door I'd entered.

I could draw my gun. Or was that overreacting? Or should I . . . ? He pinned me to the wall and his mouth came down on mine, hot and savage as a branding iron. His hands slid around my back and he jerked me toward him, gripping me tight against that magnificent body.

Do something, my mind screamed. *Fight him.* But my body, in a blatant act of treason, responded to his kiss. My hands locked into that wonderful hair and I kissed him back. The room spun in a riot of red and gold color and the taste of his mouth was a drug, an addiction.

Addiction, obsession, then denial: something shattered inside my soul. If I let him have me, he would own me. He could bend me to his will with desire and I would never be free again. Suddenly I thought of Flynn. *Why did I think of Flynn?* Flynn, with his dark eyes, kindness, compassion, and grudging acceptance of the small part of my world he'd seen. Flynn, whose steady, solid image, his absolute human nature made me see the flaws in Michael and beat down the fire of passion within me to nothing but an ember.

Michael's formidable body trembled against mine and then I could feel something besides my own need. A terrible fierceness that surged through him—not like his cold anger at the Goblin Den, but a hunger, violence, that suddenly terrified me. Terror ripped away desire. I jerked my mouth away from his.

"No!"

I jammed my hands against his shoulder and pushed. Strong as I am, I couldn't move him. I gasped as he released me and staggered away. I wrapped my arms around myself and held tight.

Michael straightened and backed away from me, his face cold and desolate as a beach in winter. He clenched his fists at his sides, as if he, too, had to hold them to keep from reaching for me. "Forgive me, Huntress. I promised I would be patient and wait for you to choose the time."

I drew a deep breath and released it, then swallowed, trying to regain my voice. "I shouldn't have come here."

"Why did you?" Michael's expression suddenly changed and he gave me his usual pleasant mask with the smooth, disinterested half smile he usually gave strangers. The real Michael went back into hiding behind his facade. Or was this the real Michael? I didn't want to find out.

"I came to—" I bit my lip. Had I forgotten? No. I came here for a reason. Two reasons. "I went to see your mother."

Michael raised an eyebrow, obviously interested. "And what did you learn?"

"She's obsessed with you. She said you look like your father."

"Perhaps." He shrugged. "I've never met my father."

"Your mother also has an excellent guard. Mom started to talk, whisper secrets, and then Cohen and the storm troopers arrived and drugged her."

"I should have made arrangements." He appeared annoyed. "Forgive me, but I didn't think you would go." He frowned. "Tell me about Detective Flynn. I understand how desirable you are. But I want to know why *he* so obviously appeals to *you*."

Appeal to me? How had he come to that conclusion? In one brief meeting, had he imagined something between me and the cop?

"Flynn's not the subject here. And he doesn't appeal to me. I want to know about you owning half of the Goblin Den." I remembered my anger. I straightened. "Do you get half the profit on Theron's kiddie porn?"

"No. I've owned part of the Den for less than a year. Theron had a funding problem. I didn't learn that particular side of his other business until a month ago. I told him I'd kill him if he didn't stop. Something else is going on with him, though. I don't know what, but I will." Michael spoke as if his words explained everything.

"You broke his arm, forced him to talk to me. What's that going to do to your *partnership*?" My hands clenched into fists.

"When the time comes, Cassandra, I'll kill him if I have to. For your own sake, you don't need to know anything. Just trust me to take care of it."

"Trust you? And your record? Assault? Attempted murder? That I can imagine. But rape?"

Michael laughed, but his voice dripped of irony, not mirth. "You stand, Huntress, proof of the fact that I can't charm *every* woman I meet. I see Detective Flynn has apprised you of some of my sins. Some overzealous law enforcement officers were frustrated a few years ago because they couldn't convict me for something else."

"Something else. You mean the assault and what? Murder?"

"Ah, yes." Michael smiled and held out his arms, palms up. "I had my reasons, Huntress. Do you plan to throw stones?"

He had me. I was willing to kill Theron, or at a minimum cut him. I had killed in self-defense. I had injured others for no greater reason than the fact that they'd hurt children and deserved it. I doubted his reasons were as righteous as I believed mine to be, but I didn't know.

I shook my head.

Michael came closer to me, but not close enough to touch. "You see, Huntress, as I told you last night, you and I are much alike."

"Sure we are. How many kids did your mother kill?"

A shadow crossed his face. He stared at me, raw emotion in his eyes. I'd hurt him, made him think of things he'd rather forget. What did he expect from his invitation to meet her? What ever it was, thanks to Cohen's intervention, I'd missed it.

"I was ten years old when it happened. I don't know."

"Why did she kill them?" A personal question, but he asked me to go. He teased me with information, gave me a puzzle. "What does it have to do with the kids I'm looking for?"

"Her particular brand of insanity, I suppose. It doesn't matter now. She's safely locked away. You should go." He walked out of the room through the door he'd entered and closed it behind him.

What was I going to do? Michael, beautiful, ethereal Michael, full of secrets and violence, a dark angel if ever one haunted the Earth Mother's world. The clues mounted and intuition, that raw gut feeling that often guided me, told me that Michael and his mother were part of my hunt for Selene and Richard.

My years in the Barrows had taught me the subtle differences between bad men—mere criminals—and evil men, the servants of the Darkness. I could see Michael as a criminal, but I couldn't see him serving *anyone*, not even a malevolent spirit like the Darkness. Still, if he owned the Den, did he also own Pericles Theron? Too many questions and no good answers. This dark moon hunt would not be an easy one.

chapter 11

Heavy traffic lurching along in stops and starts slowed me down, so I didn't get into the Barrows and to the Lost Lamb Mission until after two o'clock. The Lamb's director, Reverend Victor Payton, has helped me find a few kids. He's different from Father Jacob, the elderly priest who ran the mission until he died last year. Jacob was a friendly, hands-on kind of guy. He'd dish up soup, make beds, do laundry, things Reverend Victor wouldn't touch.

Victor is nice, but coldly efficient at times, unless he's with the children. He sits with them, reads them stories, and really listens when they talk. They listen to him, eyes glowing with absolute trust. He is a master of organization.

The Lamb distributes bag lunches at noon and serves one hot meal a day, dinner at five thirty p.m. Not many people would be there now, in the middle of the afternoon. When I opened the door, my nose wrinkled at the faint antiseptic smell lingering where the staff had scrubbed the floor and walls to their gray, bare bones.

I reminded myself of the good things Victor had done in the year he'd been in charge. Father Jacob welcomed everybody and often the undeserving benefited. Victor rigorously screened those he helped. No bums or druggies allowed. In spite of the fact that he said he was always short of money, Victor's staff sorted out those in need of medical care and carried them uptown to the clinic. Women with kids could always have beds for the night. The new clean and efficient Lamb served its charitable purpose, even if it no longer had a warm, fuzzy feel.

The woman behind the reception desk puffed up and frowned when I entered. She was ready to order me out since they didn't allow clients to hang around between meals. When she recognized me, she didn't speak, but her disapproving stare followed me across the room and up the stairs to Victor's office. I'd had more than my share of unpleasant women for the day.

The office door stood open and Victor sat at a utilitarian desk with a notepad and a couple of pens in front of him. Multiple file cabinets stretched along one wall. Father Jacob's bookkeeping and supply system consisting of hundred of piles of paper didn't fit the Lamb's new director and his obsession with organization.

"Cassandra." Victor gave me the briefest of smiles and gestured at the chair sitting by the desk. A slim, lanky man, his well-worn clothes came from the thrift shop up the street and matched his equally worn face. Stealthy gray had crept into his dark hair. In another year, it would take over.

"Hi, Vic." I sat in the uncomfortable chair. I handed him the photos of Selene and Richard.

He stared for a moment, then shook his head and laid the photos on the desk. "I'm sorry, my dear, but I haven't seen them." Sadness filled his voice.

"Something wrong?"

"You mean other than this godforsaken place? The Barrows. Eating at our young, using them, tossing them aside." He spoke through clenched teeth. A surprise, since he rarely displayed emotion.

"Whoa, Vic. Talk to me. I'll do something if I can."

He relaxed and a sad smile crossed his face. "Dear Cassandra, our Barrows version of the knight in shining armor."

I waited to see if he had more to say.

"I'm sorry, Cass." He rubbed his hands over his face and straightened. "Last week, I had a young girl, fourteen, come to me, beg me to help her. She'd hooked up with a Bastinado, one of the Butcher Boys, and he beat her. She wanted to go home. The Lamb isn't a fortress. I called her parents. No answer. I called the police. No one came. We are low on the priority list, it seems. Before I could do anything else, the place was full of those filthy Bastinado monsters who think they're still human." Utter defeat filled his voice. "She went with them, rather than having them tear the place apart and maybe hurt someone."

I'd heard his story before in different versions from different people over the years. Pericles Theron's thugs had done the same thing to Father Jacob with a twelve-year-old boy. I arrived shortly after that violence, though, went in, found and retrieved the boy, thereby putting another notch by my name on Theron's shit list.

I bit my lip and didn't express my irritation. Victor had called the police and the girl's parents, but he hadn't called me. Oh, well, I'd do what I could. "See if you can find where the Butchers are hanging now. I'll see if I can find her."

"If she's alive," he said softly.

"I hope she is, but it won't make a difference in how I deal with them."

Victor nodded. "Lady Justice."

"No. Only a woman with a pissy attitude. And a gun."

"Yes. And, God forgive me, this time I hope you get to use it."

Something new. Victor, like Abby, had always discouraged me from using weapons.

"Has anybody said anything to you about the dark moon?" I asked.

Victor frowned. "Dark moon? New moon. It happens every month."

Father Jacob, like so many others, had had the usual stranger's blind eye of disbelief turned on the Barrows, even though he lived there. Most who live in the Barrows know, but never speak of it. I don't know why. Maybe Jacob's faith kept him from seeing all but what he considered his own life's purpose. Victor is a far more practical man. I'd bet he forced himself to explore. It had occurred to me, more than once, that he might be a little . . . disturbed. He wouldn't be the first one who's mind has slipped from reality because of the bizarre life he leads here.

"There's supposed to be some sort of conjunction," I said. "Stars, planets. Really spooky shit."

Victor smiled. "Spooky shit. How eloquent."

"You know Michael? The Archangel? He says—"

"I presume you mean the owner of that decadent exercise studio." Victor's eyes narrowed. When he spoke, it was with the same cold rage he'd spoken of the Bastinados. "In the Barrows, Cassandra, there are hideous monsters with fangs and claws that feed on human flesh. And there are beautiful monsters with smiles and gentle hands that feed on human souls. Which do you prefer?"

"The ones I can kill."

"Will you kill Michael or give him your soul? Do not get too close to him. I know him. He'll destroy you." Victor's thin shoulders slumped, making his rummage sale clothes look like they were still on the hanger. "What will happen to the children, Cassandra, if evil takes you and you become what you most abhor?"

He'd touched on a sensitive point for me. "The Earth Mother would sucker some other adolescent girl into living her life for the cause."

I'd discussed my beliefs about the Earth Mother with him, but he accepted them without comment. He was not a person given to casual conversation. I don't know if he believed me or not. No surprise. I picked up the pictures and returned them to my pocket. "I can't see Michael as a monster."

"That's the problem." He grasped my hand.

I stood and he released me. "Try to find the Butcher Boys' hangout for me," I said. Bastinados were not that hard to deal with under certain circumstances. "Okay? I'll check on your girl."

He nodded and I started out the door.

"Cassandra?"

I turned back to him.

"Dark Moon, your Earth Mother, monsters above and below the streets—how do such things survive in the modern world?"

"Don't know. It's a way of life for me."

"I'm a Christian, and I shouldn't even acknowledge such things. But please be careful. That dangerous Michael, and the dark moon . . . I would miss you so much if something happened."

I grinned at him and headed down the stairs.

I'd lied. I could see Michael as a monster. Not the filthy Bastinado kind, but one far worse. Michael would be beautiful and terrible, and those who did his bidding would love him, even as he destroyed us.

It pissed me off that Reverend Vic had no faith in my ability to resist Michael's charm. My anger was pure, irrational hypocrisy, of course.

chapter 12

Flynn called me as I stepped out the Lost Lamb's door. I flipped open my phone.

"Where are you?" he asked.

"The Lamb, on Twentieth, half a block from River Street."

"Stay there. I'm on my way."

Since there was minimal cooling inside, I went back, sat at a table in the dining room, and watched the local news on the television mounted on the wall. Another day of record heat, power outages, too many air conditioners, and not enough electricity to go around. An attractive woman in a blue suit came on the screen. She droned on. High pressure covered the Midwest and promised no rain until September. I'd bet a drop of sweat wouldn't dare form on her perfect alabaster forehead. She finished and the station cut to a commercial when Flynn walked in.

He sat with me at the table.

"Find anything?" I asked.

"Sealed records. None of the old-timers would talk, but I went to old Abraham. He told me a lot."

"Abraham?"

"Janitor. Been at the station for at least fifty years. I don't know what we'll do if he ever retires. Institutional memory is a powerful thing."

"I know that kind. They'll probably have to bury him with his mop and broom."

"Yeah." Flynn grinned. "Anyway, he says thirty years ago, back when more people lived in the Barrows, there was a string of baby murders. More than four. Some kidnapped, some murdered in their cribs. Ten years later there was another incident."

My stomach knotted and I swallowed hard. "You couldn't get into sealed records, but Cohen at Avondale dumped us with information? She must've been pissed. I'm not sure where to go with this."

"Me, either. I'm following you, remember?"

"Tragically, I do."

We exited the Lamb and emerged into a concrete and asphalt oven. Three in the afternoon and it hurt to breathe. I'd left the windows open to stave off complete interior meltdown in the car, and I had some rags in the backseat. I used them to open the door and hold on to the steering wheel. At least the seats were cloth.

All I could do at this point was check out some of my other information sources in the Barrows.

"I need to talk to some people. You sure you want to tag along?" I asked Flynn.

"You don't want me to come with you?"

"I might not get anything with a cop in tow." Abby and the Mother needed to stop micromanaging my job.

"I'm sure you'll overcome that obstacle," Flynn said.

"Maybe. Depends on how fast you are with a pair of handcuffs. Do you think you can refrain from arresting criminals for minor infractions?"

"How minor?"

"Anything less than murder."

"That stretches the definition of minor. I'll ignore small drug deals. But armed robbery? No."

He wasn't budging, so I'd have to make the best of it. Flynn had taken in a lot this morning. Aside from the nagging fear I know he was carrying for Selene, I'd bet my *So what* attitude concerning Michael's criminal record didn't make him happy. I did care, but running through the Barrows had taught me expediency. I used the tools at hand. Michael was a tool. Or so I thought. Or was Michael using me for some reason?

Elise was far less a mystery to me than Michael. She seemed like a witch, or at least a strong psychic. Most likely one who delved too deep into mysteries best left alone. One delving journey must've stripped her mind bare and seared her soul. Abby told me of such things, a grave danger for those who worked with magic.

I wasn't prepared to rush to judgment on Michael, in spite of Theron and the Goblin Den, especially since I knew so little. Michael was right. My less than sterling character didn't allow me to throw stones. I could, however, make good use of master criminal Carlos Dacardi.

We rode farther south on River Street. First stop would be Holey Joe's.

Flynn scowled as I parked out front. "This is a strip bar. You don't think—?"

"I'm looking for information. I saved Joe's oversexed ass from a bunch of Bastinados one night. It's been a while since I reminded him of my bravery on his behalf."

Flynn raised an eyebrow at my assertion, but didn't argue.

Joseph P. Holey used his entrepreneurial skills to poke greedy fingers into more than one unsavory trade. He didn't deal in kids, though. That put him a notch above the other scum.

Flynn followed me through an alley to the back door since the front wouldn't open for business until after dark. The day's suffocating blanket of heat morphed to a thick, stinking pool in the close confines between buildings. An unidentifiable dead animal lay next to an overflowing Dumpster, and arrogant rats dined on the carcass. The little bastards didn't bother to look up as we passed.

"Try not to breathe too deep," I told Flynn.

A single *H* painted on the wall marked Joe's place. The steel-barred outer door stood open, but the solid door behind remained closed.

I pounded on the door. "It's Cass. I need to see Joe."

The lock clicked and the door swung open. I walked in and immediately went on alert. Hector, Joe's bouncer, stood across the room. A beefy giant with a walnut-sized brain, he'd backed up to give himself room to maneuver. Hector lumbered toward me. I stepped aside, hooked his ankle with my foot, and tripped him. I forgot about Flynn behind me.

Hector slammed Flynn and they both went down, Hector on top. Flynn's breath went out in a sharp gasp. Shit! This was all I needed.

Hector, enraged beyond reason, locked his hands around Flynn's throat. I grabbed Hector by his hair and jerked his head back so far I could stare into his eyes. I only wanted to get his attention.

Flynn punched his fist straight up into Hector's exposed jaw. A short jab, but it connected with the crack of a tree branch snapping under the weight of winter ice. Damn impressive.

Hector collapsed.

I was rolling him off Flynn when Sho Yi, Joe's bartender, arrived.

"Did it again, didn't you?" Sho said. "Now I got to rent a bouncer for tonight."

"He started it, Sho."

Sho didn't seem genuinely upset. Hector was the kind of guy you really didn't miss when he was away.

"Is Joe here?" I asked.

"Barroom." Sho nodded at the door. He glanced at Flynn. He hesitated, then said, "Dancer audition."

I helped Flynn to his feet. He swayed a few times, then seemed okay, except that I could tell by the way he glared he was pissed at me. It's not as if I'd intentionally set him up. I smoothed his clothes and dusted off some small pieces of trash. Oh, those muscles felt fine.

"You were supposed to jump out of the way," I said, trying to sound apologetic.

"Is that what we came here for?" Flynn's voice would have chilled the scorching pavement outside. He rubbed his hand across the fist he'd used to crack Hector's jaw. No blood, but it had to hurt.

More words might've made things worse, so I turned and went into the dark hallway that led to the main barroom.

Holey Joe's was a copy of most strip clubs, complete with tables and a wide U-shaped bar with a pole where patrons could ogle and pay to feel the girls as they danced. Though infinitely cooler than the alley, the air reeked of old beer and stale cigarette smoke.

Joe sat at one of the tables, his eyes locked on a naked girl standing a few feet away. She made no eye contact with him, and her face had that rigid, I'm-not-really-here expression of a much older woman doing something she hated.

"Turn around—now that's my girl," Joe said. His voice was laced with anticipation. Her long dark hair fell to her waist and the light played across her small, slender body, a body that nevertheless curved in the right places. She had the look of a young virgin prepared for sacrifice.

Flynn stood at my back and had his hand on my waist. It felt good—steady and reassuring—but his fingers tightened. He was, without a doubt, projecting the image of his sister onto the girl. I gently jabbed him with my elbow. "Please not now," I begged. I felt him relax, but only a little.

Joe is a self-described voyeur. Only watches—or so he says. I don't care as long as what he's watching is willing and at least eighteen.

Joe jerked when I dragged out a chair and sat across from him. His eyes slid over me and focused on Flynn, who stood behind me. Flynn probably gave him his grim-faced, narrow-eyed, bad-assed cop expression. He'd have a hand close to his gun. Scary stuff, even to me.

"Don't sweat it, Joe." I gave him my best smile. "Unless—" I nodded at the girl.

"She's got a birth certificate." Joe shoved a piece of paper across the table.

I picked it up and did a bit of calculation on the date. "And she's thirty-eight years old?"

Joe leaned over, snatched the paper out of my hand, and held it inches from his face. The man had good distance vision, but refused to wear glasses to read. He studied the paper, then laid it down.

"Okay, honey," he said. "Get dressed and come back next year. Don't need no trouble from her." He jerked his head at me. Regret filled his voice, but no ill will. She'd given him a show, so it wasn't a waste. He pulled a wad of hundred-dollar bills out of his shirt pocket, peeled off two, and tossed them on the table. "That's for your time."

The girl shook her head. She quickly dressed, but when she reached for the birth certificate lying on the table, I snatched it away. "You steal this?"

Her eyes met mine straight on. Being dressed made her feel less vulnerable.

"It's my mom's." A bit of defiance hummed in her voice. Some desperate situation must have driven her here.

I winced, but I handed the certificate to her. "You should take Joe's money if you need it. He has plenty."

She glanced at Joe, then back at me. She scooped up the bills and walked away.

Joe frowned at me. "Did you hurt Hector again? I had to pay for a week in the hospital last time."

"He'll be okay." Maybe. If he didn't have a broken jaw.

I laid Selene's and Richard's photos on the table.

Joe stared at them and shook his head. His mouth twisted down at the corners. "Girl's pretty."

Flynn laid his hand on my shoulder as if he needed me to steady him.

"You know Hammer?" I watched Joe closely. He had a small eye tic that fluttered when he lied.

Joe shrugged. "Met him. Heard he was a runner. Made deliveries, not girls. Or boys."

He was telling the truth.

"You call me if you see him—or these kids. You got my cell."

"What's with the cop?" He eyed Flynn.

"He's my bodyguard."

Joe laughed, a good-natured sound bouncing around the empty barroom. "You need a bodyguard like Hector needs more thick muscles between his ears."

I made Joe let us out the front door because I didn't want to run into Hector again—if he'd come to, that is. The sun had dropped midway in the west, but the sidewalk baked. A heavy truck rumbled by, headed for the docks, leaving a roiling cloud of stinking, eye-burning smoke behind.

"Who's Hammer?" Flynn demanded.

"A delivery boy mostly, petty thief, pickpocket. He seems to have developed aspirations of greater things if he's moving children around instead of drugs. I see him around occasionally. As long as it doesn't involve children, I ignore him."

"And the kid? The one in the other photo."

I hadn't told Flynn about Richard, mostly because I didn't want to explain Dacardi. "Name's Richard. I found out Hammer had him and Selene a few days ago."

His eyes widened and he grabbed my arm. "Hammer. First name? Last name? I can call it in and find—"

"Absolutely nothing. The Duivel Police could have a name, address, DNA sample, photo. None of it would do any good in the Barrows."

"Don't give me that shit. If you're holding back—" He squeezed my arm tighter.

"Let me go. Now!"

He released me and drew a breath, probably to threaten me again. He stopped at the sound of a small scream. It came from the foul-smelling alley.

I stepped to the corner of the building and peered around. Flynn stood at my back. A couple of Bastinados had the girl Joe had sent away backed up to a wall. Her blouse lay in rags at her feet and her arms crossed her chest as she huddled in terror. The girl who pretended to be a woman for Joe wasn't so grown up now.

"Let me do this," I said softly to Flynn. "I need to show you something. If you interfere, I won't let you come play with me in the Barrows again." Time for another lesson in the Huntress's world.

"I should stand and watch you get killed?" Flynn's voice carried a dangerous note.

I laid my hand on his chest. "Please. I know what I'm doing."

Another big truck passed and covered the sound of my footsteps. I moved in fast. The sadistic bastards had their backs to me, and while they wore their colored scarves, chains, and knives, they'd stripped to T-shirts in the heat. No guns exposed, but that didn't mean they weren't armed. I'd have to take them out fast. One was my height and the other was six or seven inches taller.

I balled up my fist, drew back, and punched the taller one in the kidney. Hit him so hard I felt and heard the lowest rib break under my knuckles and slice into his body. He staggered forward and slammed into the Dumpster, sending rats scattering across the alley.

The shorter one whirled and I slugged him right between the eyes—almost. His nose caved in as I'd intended, but I hit a little low and smashed his teeth. They broke rather nicely—and tore the skin across my knuckles. Sharp pain shot up my arm. I'm super strong, but not invulnerable.

The Bastinado fell to his knees, arms limp at his sides.

I held out my bleeding hand. "Son of a bitch. Look what you did."

He stared at me with wide, shocked eyes. His mouth gaped open and blood streamed over broken teeth to stain his shirt in a crimson bib. I kicked him in the stomach. He made a gurgling sound, doubled over, and smacked facedown on the pavement.

I heard a shoe scrape and turned to see the one I'd punched in the kidney miraculously on his feet, gun drawn and pointed at me. Before I could move, Flynn jumped between us.

He caught the Bastinado by the wrist and jerked his arm away. The gun fired once, loud as a lightning bolt in the alley's narrow space. The Bastinado screamed as Flynn twisted his arm behind his back and relieved him of the gun. When Flynn released him, his body jerked once, then went limp.

Flynn gave me a level stare. "I want to hear that part again. About how you know what you're doing."

I sighed. I'd been showing off and screwed up big-time.

Flynn stripped off his vest and handed it to the girl. "Come on, we'll take you home."

She quickly slipped the vest on. She pointed at the Bastinados sprawled on the asphalt. "What about them?"

I shrugged. "I guess we could call nine-one-one."

Flynn said nothing. He knew the Bastinado rules. He'd probably seen the torn, bloody bodies, the young girls raped, then cut to pieces. He was a cop who believed in the law, and a man who believed in justice. At times like this, the conflict must tear him apart.

He walked away. He carried the Bastinado's gun with him.

I believe in justice, too. No moral conflict for me, only a little larceny. After he left, I did a quick search of the downed gang members and relieved them of their cash. The kidney guy had only a couple of twenties. The one with the smashed face carried a small roll of hundreds.

"Here." I offered the roll to the girl. "Go buy yourself a new blouse. Don't tell anyone. And stay out of the Barrows."

She shoved it in her pocket. "Thanks. Mortgage payment. Mom's been sick."

When we exited the alley, Flynn was talking on his cell phone, giving directions to Joe's.

"Yeah, the alley. Couple of Bastos fighting. Think they did each other. Send an ambulance if you feel like it." He chuckled. "Of course, you should be careful, Linda. Wouldn't want you to break a fingernail dialing for help." He closed his phone and gave me a level stare. The corners of his mouth twitched, but he turned away before I could see if he smiled. Would the smile be for me or the fact that he'd found an orderly thing to do in a messy situation? I didn't know.

We drove the girl home to a lower-middle-class neighborhood and she insisted that Flynn go in with her to retrieve his vest once she had dressed. Minutes later, she came to the front door with him as he left. She smiled, said something, and Flynn laughed.

"What did she say?" I asked when he climbed back in the car.

"She said my girlfriend and I were really cool, but we better not piss each other off. We'd probably both end up in the hospital." He studied me. Picturing me as a girlfriend? Not likely, even though he'd impressed me enough that I'd consider it. "Joe said he didn't want trouble from you. Why?"

I shrugged. "I've been known to break things—and people—when I find a kid being exploited or hurt."

He lifted my hand and studied the scrapes on my knuckles. "I've seen women hit that hard in the movies."

"But never in real life?"

"Never in real life. I heard his rib snap from twenty feet. I don't think I can break bones with my fists."

I started to remind him of Hector's jaw, but decided the moment wasn't right. "I don't have superpowers, Flynn, but I'm a lot stronger than most women."

I let out a long breath. Now that he'd seen me fight, it was time to let him in and explain a few things.

I drove and parked under a tree with a little shade. I told Flynn exactly how the Mother came for me when I was eighteen, and the vow I made that night. A few tales of my more successful and less violent rescues filled out the accurate, but somewhat vague, picture I painted. I left out the monsters in the sewers. That, I'd definitely have to prove to him.

"What can I say?" Flynn asked when I finished.

"Well, you either believe me, which is great, or you don't. If you don't, I'll show you and say 'I told you so.' I believe in God and the Earth Mother. I believe that there is a plan for this world and humankind. My work with the Mother and Abby is a part of that."

"This is a religious thing for you? A holy mission? I guess questioning your belief is like me telling you your precious psychic Abby is a fraud."

"Abby could teach you not to call her names, but she's not a show-off."

He sighed. "Are there any other surprises?" He sounded resigned, like he already knew the answer to the question.

"Yeah, Flynn. Lots of them. Brace yourself. We'll get to them in time."

chapter 13

My phone rang and I flipped it open.

"How is your search going?" Abby asked.

"The usual. Shitty. Why?"

"Bring Detective Flynn over here for supper."

"Abby, we have a kid to find."

"You won't do that tonight. And you have to eat anyway." She spoke with a surety I found uncomfortable. The Earth Mother's High Priestess, like her boss lady, always knew more than she told me.

"Okay. Be there in a while." I closed the phone.

"What was that?" Flynn asked.

"We have to go to Abby's. She says for supper, but I'll bet there's more to it."

There was. Flynn's red truck sat parked at the curb. Company for dinner in the form of Flynn's mother. He mumbled under his breath as I parked, but fell silent as we walked around the house to the back door.

The room smelled heavenly as it usually did, and had the feel of a country kitchen where a family gathered. Flynn's mother sat at the table, but she stood when we entered. She gave us a brilliant smile. A tall, rawboned woman with jet-black hair, she seemed far too young to have a son thirty years old. Only a few wrinkles around her eyes and mouth made her look older than him.

Most of her attention went to me. Curious, I suppose. She'd sent her son to live with a strange woman based upon faith and Abby's word alone. She'd also dropped her daughter's life in that woman's hands.

"Hello, Cassandra," she said. "I'm Amanda Flynn."

To my surprise, she suddenly embraced me in strong arms. "I know you'll find her. I know you will." She spoke the words in a soft but passionate voice.

I hated it. What if I failed? I'm human. I do fail.

"Thank you, Mrs. Flynn." That was all I could say.

"Mother," Flynn spoke. "I'd like to talk to you— alone."

When Flynn's mother released me, he carefully grasped her arm and led her outside to the edge of the woods. I could see them through the screen door, standing forty feet away under the shade of the massive oak tree that was only an acorn when the first white man set foot in America.

I sat at the table, and Abby, who hadn't moved from her place by the stove, came to sit beside me. She placed her finger against her lips and shook her head when I started to speak.

The room grew silent. Then came the sound of voices, Flynn and his mother. We shouldn't have been able to hear their conversation, but obviously the Earth Mother wanted us to.

"She's a criminal," Flynn said. He pointed toward the house. "You know what I did today? I let her play might-makes-right and beat the shit out of—maybe even kill—two Bastinados. They—"

"Earned it, didn't they?"

"Yes, Mother, but—"

"I was married to a cop, lived with a cop, long before you were born. You think your father didn't want to create his own law at times? Do you think he never did?"

Flynn sighed and raked his hand through his hair. "I can't reason with you."

"Listen to me, Phelan. Has anyone investigating this found a single clue?"

"No." He stared into the woods. Then his loving mother sent him on a spiraling journey into the convoluted realm of guilt. All mothers are good at that, including my own.

She laid a hand on his chest. "Every day, your father was forced to look away from some crime because he had to deal with greater crimes. I'm asking you—begging you—to do the same. You know where the line can be drawn, the things you won't do. You always have."

Flynn rubbed the back of his neck as if he could massage away his frustration. "But there are better ways to find Selene, Mother. I can't keep running up and down River Street following some pagan gunslinger."

"Whoa!" I said to Abby. "Pagan gunslinger. Bet Mom loves that."

"Hush," Abby said. "We're hearing this for a reason."

Flynn's mother wrapped her arms around him and began her final assault. He didn't stand a chance.

"When your father died, you gave up being a little boy. You had to grow into a man. You worked and went to school, and then on to the academy. You don't date women—"

"It's not like I'm a virgin, Mother—you know that." Flynn made a weak effort to fight back. "You also know the trouble I had with one woman in particular."

"That's because you focused so much time and energy on Selene and me. I threatened you the other day. To leave and never come back. It frightened you. I was wrong. Now I'm begging you. I know perfectly well that the odds are good that she might be dead and—"

"Don't say that. Cass thinks—" He stopped when he

realized his blunder. He'd come perilously close to ad-
mitting I'd given him some hope. "All right, Mother. You
win."

She hugged him tighter. "Abigail says Cassandra *will*
find her. Try to be patient."

Flynn stroked her hair with his hand, much as he had
Elise earlier in the day. "Patient. Okay. I can tolerate
her—and the snakes. She's . . . okay. Sometimes. But if
that cat sits on my face again, I'll probably toss him out
the window."

"Detective Flynn likes you," Abby said to me as their
voices faded.

"He does not."

"And you like him." She reached over and squeezed
my hand.

"I do not." I pulled my hand away. Abby heard my lie
and smiled.

"Okay, yes, I like him. He's attractive, Abby, but
there's a lot he doesn't know."

"Well, hurry up and enlighten him." Abby stood as
Flynn and his mother started back toward the house.
Flynn walked with sure steps, strong, vital, appealing in
every way a man could be to a woman. Or did he just
appeal to me? I was curious now, though. What woman
gave Flynn so much trouble he had become wary of any
relationship?

"You told him about the Mother, didn't you?" Abby
asked.

"Yes. He still doesn't believe me. He's met Horus and
the girls and has seen how strong I am, but he's a long
way from accepting everything."

"He'll come around."

"Why is she so adamant that he stay with me?" I
scowled at her, suddenly uncomfortable, almost embarrassed, a rare feeling for me.

Abby was silent for a moment. She sighed. "I suppose it's my fault. I expressed concern about you being around that man, the one they call the Archangel. He is dangerous. She apparently agreed. She can see into the Barrows, I think, even if she cannot go there. I suspect she thinks Detective Flynn a better match for you."

"That's bullshit." I rubbed my gun-hand callus, reminding myself who I was and what I did. Michael was . . . Michael. Somehow, I'd placed him in a separate class from the rest of them. "Everyone tells me that he's evil, but when I press for specifics, I receive nothing. Flynn is the only person who has pointed out crimes, but even he admits there's no real evidence."

Michael had admitted he wasn't perfect, but he'd suggested that his motives were what he considered acceptable. "Is Michael dangerous because he's not one of hers? Or dangerous because she thinks he'll seduce me away from her?"

"I have no idea, but, Cass, there's more to it. In the years that I've known you . . . never have I seen— Your aura, and Flynn's, which I can see quite well, are in harmony. They fit together like a complex puzzle. They're different, vastly different, but incredibly close to a perfect pattern."

The aura thing was a mystery to me, but, yes, it felt like he fit, like he belonged in my life. But what did he feel? I'd had few signals from him. He'd expressed a little admiration, but not enough to make me think it went beyond casual compliments to ease tension. And he irritated the shit out of me a lot. Not the most auspicious beginning to a great love affair of soul mates.

The meal went well. Good food and no talk of the problem we all faced. A charming woman, Amanda Flynn. When she left, Flynn followed her out to his truck. We didn't get to hear that conversation. When Flynn came back, he thanked Abby. Polite, but not overly friendly. She accepted his words, giving him a warm smile I certainly didn't think he deserved.

It was nine o'clock and full dark when we left Abby's house.

"What now?" Flynn asked.

"I need to go home and feed Horus. He gets cranky when he doesn't get his dinner on time. I don't like going into the Barrows after dark unless I have a sure target. Too dangerous. We won't help anyone if we get killed." The look on his face made me want to reassure him. "I'm not finished, Flynn. I have a lot more area to cover."

There was also a lot less time to cover it. If I thought of one thing I could do down there, I'd have gone. The whole situation had the feel of a well-choreographed dance. I also had a feeling it would come to the dark moon night and a final raging battle. The Mother made plans and let me in on them at her convenience, not mine. But bad things could happen to Selene and Richard before then. If I could end things before that, I would.

Flynn didn't speak as we rode—the steaming air didn't encourage conversation, but I was very aware of his presence. It was much like last night, when I woke to find him sleeping beside me. Even then, he'd provoked powerful emotions in me.

When I reached my apartment house, the lot was full and I had to park by the Dumpster. That meant my car would be incredibly fragrant in the morning.

Horus and the girls waited expectantly as we walked in the door.

To my complete surprise, Flynn produced two jars of caviar from his pocket and handed them to me. I mixed it with tuna. Yum!

"So, what do you usually do at night?" Flynn asked as I set the saucers of fishy mixture on the table. He glanced around the room. "No TV."

"Cable costs too much. I read." I pointed at the book-case. "There're some magazines. Help yourself."

He walked to the bookcase and pawed through them. "*Gun Digest, Herpetology Today*." He held up one. "*Farmer's Almanac with Moon Signs*. No mysteries? No romance novels? You don't even have Tolkien."

"No Tolkien. Fantasy is the real thing for me. Mystery, too. I don't want to read it." I plopped down on the couch. I avoided staring at him, even though I wanted to. "And I don't do romance." I'd read Tolkien in high school, happily unaware that, someday, I'd meet the Barrows version of his Orcs.

Flynn came to sit beside me. Close enough to be inti-mate, but not close enough to make me uncomfortable. In fact, it felt quite good. I'm a woman who had snakes and a demanding, hardscrabble cat for friends. Unable to articulate my bizarre life to a stranger, I'd always pre-ferred being alone most of the time.

"I don't do romance, either," he said. His voice was heavy with unspoken words. "Must be something wrong with us." He shifted his body off the miserable cushion he'd had to sit on because I knew enough to pick the good one. "Now I remember why I didn't sleep here last night."

"Yeah, well, my decorator is happy."

Flynn grinned at me. Oh, that smile—so provocative, so delightful. "Your decorator is salesman of the month at the Salvation Army thrift store."

With no effort at all, he was drawing me in, making me feel things I had no right to feel. In my mind, Flynn was just as dangerous as Michael. *I don't do romance*, he had said. Great. He could take me and eventually reject me. I stood. "If all you're going to do is insult my furni-ture, I'm going to take a shower."

I stuck my nose in the air and marched away. I went into the bathroom, showered, and dressed in a T-shirt. This time I put some stretchy leggings on instead of my panties. Just in case. I mean, he probably wouldn't get in bed with me again. Probably.

I went back into the living room and found Flynn reading a copy of *Gun Digest*. His long legs were stretched out, and one of the dark curls of his hair had fallen on his forehead. He had a soft smile on his face, as if something in the magazine amused him. Nefertiti had draped herself over his shoulders. I'd told the girls and Horus that he was one of us. They accepted him, but it seemed odd that he would accept them.

"You actually like snakes?" I asked.

"No." He frowned. "I like this one, though."

He gently lifted Nefertiti from his shoulders, laid her on the couch cushion. She slid down onto the floor, crawled up the coffee table leg, and into her aquarium home.

"Why don't you do romance?" Flynn asked. I saw no mockery on his face, nor did I hear it in his voice. "It can't be only the snakes."

"True. But all my romances end the same. I usually say, 'Don't mind the gun and knives, darling. I almost never use them. And, yes, I need to go out alone at midnight . . . You be sure you close the door on your way out.' I'm told I'm too belligerent, too pushy." My eyes narrowed at him. "What about you? No romance, either?" I was curious. Maybe he would tell me about the woman that had caused him so many problems, he'd sworn off relationships.

"The career. I work a lot. Living with a cop is hard on a woman. My mother's proof of that. I watched her sit and stare out the window some nights when dad was late. I knew she was afraid someone would come to tell her he'd been injured or killed. And then one night . . . He'd walked in on a robbery. Never had a chance."

"Didn't your mother object when you wanted to become a cop?"

"Oh, yeah. But she knew it was what I really wanted to do. What I had always wanted to do." He moved his arm and winced as he did.

"You're hurt?"

"Old shoulder wound. I tried to disarm some distraught teenager rather than shoot him. He was acting out his frustrations with society by robbing a convenience store."

I grinned. I lifted my sleeve and exposed the now almost invisible puncture wounds on my left shoulder. "This hurts sometimes, too, but Abby gave me something for it." I went back to the bathroom and retrieved my jar of salve from the medicine cabinet. I wanted to know about romance and he talked career.

I went back to the living room. "Take your shirt off. This will help."

He remained seated but stripped off the shirt. I sat beside him.

Oh, shit. Oh, damn. What had I done? Such a fine body. I opened the jar and hesitated only a fraction of a second, but . . . he smiled. Damn it. He knew he was getting to me. He told his mother I was *okay,* but that wasn't an *okay* smile. I smeared the salve on his shoulder, rubbing it into the thick muscle. Abby had added sandalwood to the mixture and the sweet fragrance filled the air. A thin scar ran down his arm. I turned sideways, and as I did, he laid a hand on my knee, cupping it gently.

I swallowed hard. My mind screamed *Stop!* but my body almost vibrated in desire. I forced it away. He wasn't for me. He'd called me a pagan gunslinger, after all.

"How strong are you?" he asked. He stared intently at me. His hand was still on my knee.

Was that a challenge? I could deal with that. "Stronger than you. Faster, too."

"Prove it." He cocked his head and gave me a sexy,

playful smile. No man smiled at me like that. *Playful* described only one man in my life, and that relationship ended in tragedy years ago.

"Prove it? Okay." Once I beat him, his masculine pride would send him sulking away. And, no, that was not bitterness I felt. It was practicality. If I didn't stay practical, this man would break my heart. "Let's go."

"Where?" He raised an eyebrow and sounded surprised that I'd accepted the challenge.

"A place where you won't get hurt again."

I led him out of the apartment and up the stairs to the apartment house's flat roof. It was late enough on a weekday night that we would be alone. Last year, I had joined the other tenants in purchasing a large weatherproof cushioned mat for the kids to play on when the weather was nice. It measured twenty feet by twenty feet and we rolled it up and stuck it in the basement during the winter. My contribution to the cause came under the heading of self-defense. It meant that at least part of the year, I wouldn't have yard apes running up and down the hall screaming at the top of their lungs.

The roof soaked up the day's heat and now released it in vast humid waves. Sweat instantly formed on my skin as my body tried to compensate. We'd both be soaked in seconds. A single lightbulb over the stairwell door cast a sickly yellow glow that barely reached the safety railing around the roof edges. Thunder rumbled in the distance, the promise of a storm teasing the parched city.

Flynn hadn't put his shirt back on and he stood there, his skin shining and wet. Great Mother! I wiped my mouth to be sure I wasn't drooling. Okay, but any desire would go away as soon as I pissed him off by beating him in a fight.

I planted my bare feet firmly on the mat. "Take me down."

"You're kidding." He walked closer, moving with effortless grace.

"Not kidding. Take me down."

He stood within reach now. "No. I don't fight women."

Sexist bastard. My competitive spirit rose in me. "Hah! Afraid you'll lose?"

He stepped closer and I circled. I spun and kicked out at him, knowing I wouldn't reach him, but backing him up just the same.

Flynn charged.

The force of his attack sent me peddling back, but I ducked low and caught his ankle and jerked it out. He went down. Shocked, I'd bet, but he gracefully rolled and jumped to his feet. He charged again. I pivoted and danced out of the way. I swallowed. Excitement rose in me, so much I had to force myself not to shove my hand between my legs and ease the fire.

"This is fun," he said. He laughed low and sexy, taunting me. "But how does it prove you're stronger?" He held his arms out. "Come and get me."

He didn't take me seriously, of course. He didn't even move when I caught his arm and jammed my shoulder into him midbody. But then I rolled him over my shoulder, straightened, lifted him, and tossed him ten feet across the mat. He landed on his back and a great whoosh of air burst from his lungs. Not easy, that move, even for me, but I was motivated. This is, of course, what drove men from my bed. Not the snakes or the gun, but my need to win, to be the alpha.

Flynn lay there for a moment, breathing deeply. Oh, shit. Had I hurt him?

"You okay?" I went and knelt by his side. I squeezed my hands into fists, trying not to touch him.

"Yes." He sounded a little breathy. "How did you do that?"

"Magic. Same as the snakes."

"Bullshit."

"Tell Nirah and Nefertiti. Flynn, you accepted them. Can't you accept that I'm different? That I might be telling you the truth. That there are some things in this world you don't understand?" He groaned. I leaned closer. Had I hurt him?

Stupid. He grabbed me and rolled. I was on my back with him straddling my hips. He captured my wrists in a firm but not crushing grip.

"You're heavy," I said. Not really, but, damn, he looked good leaning over me. He drew a deep breath, his face flushed, but his dark eyes focused on me. He wasn't exactly handsome, but he was perfect. I'd lost the fight. I freed indomitable, repressed desire and let it flow through me. I'd pay the price eventually, but I had to have him now.

"You tossed me across this mat like a kid." He grinned. "What kind of vitamins do you take, the cavemen or the little dinosaurs?"

"No vitamins. Nutritious meals. The basic food groups—pizza, burgers, and cheesecake. If I make it to my feet—"

"You can't."

I could. I wouldn't. We were playing a delicious game and I didn't want it to end too soon. Every inch of my body demanded that he never let me go. So greedy. I wanted more.

"Tell you what." He released my right wrist. "You can have one hand. How's that?"

"I can do a lot with one hand, Flynn."

"Such as?" His laugh came deep, low, and seductive. Great Mother, let him want me as much as I wanted him.

I grabbed the hem of my T-shirt and jerked it up to expose my breasts.

chapter 14

Flynn gasped. Ah, the power of the unexpected.

I arched my back and tossed him off. He landed hard and rolled, but I was after him. Then I straddled him as he had me and held his wrists as he had held mine. He struggled, but couldn't break my grip. I wiggled against him. How totally gratifying. He was big and hard between my legs, rubbing me just right. Once I got our clothes off, got him inside me . . .

Flynn laughed. "I concede. Can I look at them again?"

"What? I should reward a loser?"

"Only if you want to."

"Okay." I released him, but I didn't move.

He laid his hands on my thighs and slid them up across my waist and under my shirt. He cupped my breasts and rubbed his thumbs against the nipples. Great Mother, they sent shock waves of pleasure down my body. My hands closed into fists.

"They're hard," he said.

"So is something else." I gently moved my hips against him.

"It hurts, too. Maybe you could rub some of that cream on it."

"And make it go numb?"

"Ah, on second thought, not a good idea."

Sweat glistened on that sleek, magnificent body. I relaxed my hands and laid them flat on his chest. His heart hammered under them. His scent, his own personal odor, rolled off him as his body released moisture to compensate for temperature and exertion. I leaned forward and licked his skin. His body tasted salty and quite wonderful.

"I've never met anyone like you," he said. Flynn's fingers slipped through my sweat-soaked hair. "I shouldn't even like you."

I rubbed my cheek against his and spoke softly in his ear. "Nefertiti, Nirah, and Horus are nice. Busting Bastinados is fun. But you haven't even touched the Barrows and the Darkness, Flynn. You'll get your turn to despise me."

"That's my decision," he said. He spoke with determination. "How about another round?"

"How about a shower and a bed?"

I pushed myself to my feet and walked toward the stairs. He followed me. No matter what he said, the time would come when he would look at me and ask if I was worth the strangeness he'd seen in and around me.

But not tonight.

He had my shirt off the moment the door to my apartment closed behind us. I shivered as the cooler air played across my skin, but then my heart rate rose to compensate. He grasped my face in his hands and gave me the kiss of a lifetime. So warm at first, then savage. His arms wrapped around me and he maneuvered me backward toward the bedroom, toward the bed. There was an animal in him, primitive and dangerous.

Into the bedroom, to the bed, he pushed me down so I lay on my back. He stood over me. Not a hint of this deeper wildness had crept into the controlled personality he'd shown me before.

"The pants. Take them off." His voice was deep and rough.

I slipped my thumbs in the waistband and pushed the fabric down over my hips. He grabbed them and pulled them off my legs.

I'd made love, passionate love, before, but I always controlled things—when, where, and how.

But not tonight.

I am a fighter, rough and hard, a warrior, a stealthy predator, all things that could be male or female. Never had I felt so much desire, been so willing to let go of cherished personas of power that had ruled my life.

The only light came from a small lamp across the room, enough light to glitter in his eyes as he gazed down at me. Enough light to cast a glow over his body. I wanted what I'd never wanted before. To belong to a man. Not a casual lover, but a man who could match me in violence—should he choose to do so. I wanted him to ravish me.

He shuddered.

"Your turn," I said.

He popped the button on his pants and unzipped them, then stripped.

The Earth Mother had given this son everything, from that beautiful face and powerful muscles to his rigid cock. How could I bear it when he eventually left me? He wouldn't just run away, not this one. Not his nature. He'd politely thank me and close the door.

But not tonight.

He placed one knee on the bed and bent over me. His finger traced my mouth, down my throat, and circled my nipple. He pinched and gently tugged.

I whimpered. All my nerve endings stood at attention, pleading for more.

His fingers trailed on down and he pushed his hand between my legs.

"You're wet," he said.

I tried to say yes, but I choked on the word. I twisted

under his hands, under his caresses. A powerful yearning filled me, the desire to connect with this man both physically and emotionally. Every part of his body appealed to me, tortured me with a longing I'd never felt before— the curve of muscles, strong legs, gentle hands, and that wonderful mouth.

"Please." I reached for him and pulled him down on the bed beside me. His hand never left the damp hollow between my legs. His fingers probed deeper and spread ripples of delight racing up my body. I touched him, everywhere except where I wanted to. So hard and swollen, I was afraid I'd make him come too soon. But thanks to his magic hand, my own body was close to where I needed to be.

"Now," I said. "Oh, please now."

"Cass." His breath came out ragged. "I wanted— I forgot. I don't have any protection with me. It's been so long."

"I won't get pregnant, Flynn." There was no point in telling him I hadn't had a period since I was eighteen and accepted the Earth Mother's call to service. Let him believe I used birth control.

His hands roamed over my body and the heat of his skin against mine burned like the sun had on the asphalt outside. I loved the taste of him and his scent that drove me beyond anything I believed possible. I had to move, or I'd be the one coming too soon. I had to slow down. I pushed his hand away and rose up so I could touch him. I traced his mouth with my fingers, his nipples, that flat stomach, but I stopped short of where I wanted to go. I teased it with a brief kiss. He groaned and I felt like I'd won some great prize.

He suddenly grabbed me, rolled me over, and was on top again.

His lips closed over mine for a long, sweet time. My nerves danced everywhere he touched me with his mouth or hands. My fingers played along his skin. He raised himself and I spread my legs to welcome him.

I cried out when he slid inside me, not in pain, but in the sheer joy of having him. I writhed, but he held me tight and steady against him.

When I breathed, I drew in his scent, until the world consisted of the power of his presence stroking my ecstatic nerves. In his embrace, I could feel my heart pounding, something the greatest of my fears had never produced.

"You are so beautiful." He slowed his movement, prolonging my agony—and ecstasy.

When I could no longer hold out, I crashed, rolling down into pure delight. Delicious pleasure burned my nerves. He moaned and shuddered. The world disappeared around us, leaving only two people lost in each other's arms.

"Wow," I said when I could catch my breath.

He rolled off me and dragged me on top of him. He lay warm and solid under me.

"I suppose we should take a shower," he said.

"Suppose we should." I fought the urge to giggle.

"Ladies first."

"That generally leaves me out."

We rested and made love again and he continued to surprise me. Gentle, at times, then rough, we explored each other's bodies, laughing softly as we did. We'd get close to the edge, then pull back and explore more sensations. Like saying *One, two, three, go!* ten times before you finally get the nerve to leap off a high diving board— and drowning when you hit the water.

When I finally surfaced and my muscles stopped quivering, I found myself lying on damp sheets, as if we'd brought the steaming outside air in with us and the air-conditioning had failed. He lay beside me, breathing softly in my ear.

We didn't shower. We simply clung together and caressed each other until sleep dragged us down. Before sleep came, I realized what was missing from my life, or at least that part of my life. Joy. Pure joy at being with someone. It would end badly, but the joy I would keep and cherish forever.

I woke during the night. The lamp was off and the room dark. I reached for Flynn and found his place empty. He stood across the room, his shape outlined against the window. I had a good idea what he was thinking.

"Flynn, we *will* find her," I said.

He came back to the bed. He sat beside me and laced his fingers in mine. "She was six the year I graduated from the academy. When everyone stood to applaud, Selene jumped on her chair so she could see over the crowd and wave at me. Her face was shining so bright."

He lay beside me again and I stretched out against him. My mind, operating on sensory overload, kept banging thoughts together like Ping-Pong balls in a bucket. One thought screamed, *Fool, don't get in too deep!* Another cried that this man was what I'd wanted and needed all my life. Another taunted me with my rough Huntress persona and farm girl upbringing. What would he want with me, this cool, educated man who had given his life to protecting not only his family, but strangers on the streets of Duivel. I lay beside him while he slept, touching him occasionally, listening to him breathe, until the sky grew lighter and another day began.

chapter 15

August 7—9:00 a.m.

"Where do we go today?" Flynn asked.

"Couple of people I need to talk to. I call them the spectators. Don't have a life or a job, so they watch everything." We'd snuggled in bed until eight. Great Mother, how nice to have him with me. I knew he'd probably leave eventually, and that made me sad, but right now things were fine.

When I headed down River Street, I passed the 1760 building. I didn't think of it much these days, but Flynn in my bed last night stirred memories of lost love.

"You smiled," Flynn said. "Why?"

"Just thought of something."

"An old boyfriend?"

Oh, so he'd been thinking, too. "In a way."

"Tell me."

I chewed on my lip a moment. Traffic had us stopped like cookies lined up baking in an oven. I supposed it wouldn't hurt. "When I first came to the Barrows, I was eighteen and I needed to know my way around. Abby could show me only so much. I came down here looking for a job. I figured that would give me a better picture. Not much money, so I had to ride the bus to her house and back."

My mind traveled back to my early days in Duivel. I couldn't say I missed them. At eighteen, the world of the Barrows seemed much larger to me and I was still ignorant of so many evil things . . .

Winter had settled in, and the bus was late. I'd tugged my jacket closer around me, but the wind from the Bog roared down River Street. It cut through cloth seams like frozen scissors. The plaid flannel shirt that had served me well on my family's Southern farm seemed like sheer cotton here. I hunched my shoulders and endured. I'd walked twenty blocks, asking for work at any place that looked like they had something I could do. The guy at the pet store wanted to hire me because of my experience with animals, but he didn't have the money.

Then I noticed the sign in a second-floor window across the street: FILE CLERK NEEDED. I could do that. I'd taken business classes as electives in high school. I made a mad dash between the cars and trucks and crossed to the building.

The aging wooden stairs rising to the second floor creaked under my feet. One groaned like it was going to give way. I grabbed the rail and the beast rewarded me with a splinter. It wasn't much warmer than outside, either. The air carried an aged musty smell that told me my search in this place was as hopeless as the structure itself.

Two doors at the top, one with a padlock on the outside and the other a sign.

E. DURBIN, PRIVATE INVESTIGATOR.

I opened that door and walked in.

The windowless outer office had a desk, a chair, and a sagging couch piled with boxes. A fine coat of dust skimmed the desk, and the tracks of a tiny four-footed creature made a wavy path across the surface. Cinnamon-colored water stains from a mighty roof leak bloomed like flowers across the ceiling. The smell . . . I drew shallow breaths.

The floor still complained at my steps, in spite of a rug that looked like a million souls had wiped their feet on it on their way to heaven or hell.

"Go away," said a rough voice from another room.

I walked to an open door. A man sat behind the desk. He looked lean and hard, like someone who spent hours at labor in the sun. He might have been forty, but it was hard to tell. Dark hair with a skim of gray, gray eyes, handsome in youth, still handsome now, but . . . worn. Worn as the shabby room around him. A half-full glass and half-empty bottle of bourbon graced the desk at his right hand.

"I said . . ." His voice trailed off when he saw me. The frown, the obvious irritation on his face, faded. He raised an eyebrow. The corner of his mouth twitched like he felt like smiling but didn't want to. "You come straight from the farm, Bo Peep?"

"Don't worry. I scraped the shit off my shoes." Damn, I had to get some new clothes.

"What do you want?" His deep voice sounded only slightly interested.

"A job. I saw the sign. I can type and file." I glanced at the window, but it was covered with stacked boxes. It had probably been covered for months. Maybe years.

"Forget about that." He eyed me, as if speculating. "You can do better than this place."

I shrugged. "Maybe later. I'm fresh off the farm, remember? No one wants to take a chance on me." It was worse than that. Most of them laughed at me.

He drew a breath, then hesitated. His mouth twitched in a half smile. "Okay. Part-time, twenty hours a week, minimum wage."

"Sounds good."

"It's shit. Let me guess. You want to learn the trade. Be a PI like in the movies."

"You mean so I can be successful like you?" I gave him a rather superior grin. I liked this man.

He laughed, but it sounded more like a bark. "You got a point, Bo. Listen, I don't have time for the usual paperwork. Okay if I pay you cash?"

"For now. Mr. Durbin, I—"

"Eddie."

"Eddie. I'm Cass."

"Cass?"

"Cassandra."

"Unusual name." He wrapped his hand around the glass of amber liquid on the desk.

"Actually, I'm blessed. My aunt's name is Cassiopeia. They call her Pete."

Eddie shifted in his chair. In what had to be a well-practiced move, he lifted and drained the glass.

I reminded myself I really needed a job.

Eddie plunked the glass down and stared at me for a moment. Then he smiled. Oh, that was nice. Made him look ten years younger. "Be here at eight in the morning. I'll find you a key. You can use the desk out front."

I glanced over my shoulder. A pile of stuff—scraps of cloth, bits of stuffing from an upholstered couch— formed a football-sized wad on the chair. I knew a rat's nest when I saw one. "You going to fumigate, or shall I bring my own supplies?"

Eddie picked up the bottle to pour another drink. "Don't talk about fumigation. You'll upset my clients."

"Both of them?"

The traffic started moving again. "And that's how I wound up as a PI. I learned the Barrows and made him the money to keep the place going. Eddie . . ." Ah, may as well say it. "He'd had bad things happen in his life. His son died, wife left him. Eddie was my first lover. I was a virgin and I fell really hard. I loved him so much. He even cut down on the drinking. We were great together. But when he was killed—" I choked.

"Killed?"

"He came in one morning and surprised a thief. Just a kid, but he ran and knocked Eddie down the stairs."

It occurred to me that Flynn looked a little like Eddie. A younger, healthier version, but his smile was just as warm.

"What about you? No lost love?"

"One. When I was eighteen." Flynn left it at that. Of course, getting a man to talk about a *lost love* wasn't easy—it was next to impossible.

We didn't talk much after that, and I shoved the memories to the back of my mind and locked them in a box. I drove on down to River Street and parked in a public lot not far from Holey Joe's. I jumped the curb to beat a truck to the last spot left under a tree. I'd just turned the engine off when my cell phone rang. Before I could get it, Flynn picked it up and flipped it open.

"Flynn." He sat silent for a moment, then asked softly, "When you say 'bitch,' are you referring to the owner of this phone?"

Uh-oh. I had a good idea who it was. I held out my hand. "Gimme."

He handed me the phone. I kept my eyes on the road so I wouldn't see the expression on his face.

"What do you want, Dacardi?"

"What the fuck are you doing screwing around—?"

"Screwing? I wish. Did you get what I asked you for?"

"Said I would, didn't I? Still working on bronze ammo."

"Okay." I hadn't wanted to ask him, but I knew he had resources I couldn't touch. "Need you to find someone. Carefully. Don't run him underground. Name's Hammer. Sometimes they call him—"

"Sledge. Yeah, yeah. Does runner work for me occasionally. He know something?"

"Maybe. Do *not* let your goons hurt him. I need to talk to him." Abby could supply me with some nice drugs to encourage more stimulating conversation.

"He'll talk to me." Dacardi wasn't interested in stimulating conversation.

"That'll depend."

"On what?"

"On what he's most afraid of. You or what's in the Barrows. Remember, Dacardi, I get him first."

Dacardi grunted.

I flipped the phone shut and laid it on the console.

"Carlos Dacardi." Flynn's voice sounded so cold it made me ache. All the warmth of last night froze in me.

"The boy in the other picture is his son."

"Cass, Carlos Dacardi is—"

"A man who loves his kid. Loves him as much as you and your mother love Selene. Flynn, I've given my life to finding kids in the Barrows and I use whatever tools the Mother gives me. Carlos Dacardi is a criminal son of a bitch, probably no better than a Bastinado. He doesn't want to rely on *me* any more than you do. But I *will* find his son. I *will* find Selene. Sorry. That's the way it has to be."

Oh, Mother, I shouldn't have made love to him. Things were getting complicated. I knew better. Why did I want him so much?

Flynn locked his fingers together and misery radiated from him as he stared out the window. A good man, a good cop, stuck with a woman who bent the law to serve her own ends. Granted, a woman who'd actually found a single lead on his sister, something the entire Duivel Police Department hadn't been able to do. He could ignore a couple of downed Bastinados, vicious animals, but the cold, calculated nature of crime boss Dacardi moved events to a different level. Unfortunately, it was a new game for me, too. Using Dacardi and his weapons might be like using nitroglycerine to solve a termite problem.

"I'm with you, Cass," he said suddenly. "I don't care anymore. Do what you need to do. Just find her." He did care, though; I could hear it in his voice.

I drove down River Street, trying the usual places. The bars where they'd let me in—I'm considered a troublemaker—the Abundant Savior homeless shelter near the docks, and the few street people who would talk to me with Flynn around. I've always worked alone, and my search slowed to a crawl with him along. Many of my sources wouldn't show their criminal faces to a cop. Worse than that was the hope I saw in Flynn's eyes when someone hesitated over the photos. Hope crushed in an instant with a shake of a head. At one o'clock, I finally located one of my best sources sitting in the shade of an oak tree in the trash-littered area that had once been a city park.

Wheelchair Harry is generally a happy man. He rolls up and down River Street's sidewalks like a gray-bearded, indigent Santa Claus. I liked him, but I always tried to stand upwind because he rarely bathed, never shaved, and had tiny, unidentifiable things living in his beard. People often gave him money to go away.

I discovered his secret one night when I came on him robbing one of his homeless brothers as the man slept. Harry can walk. When I confronted him, he told me he used the wheelchair because he had a college degree and people kept telling him to get a job.

Harry gave me a grin as I approached. He wore a T-shirt with the sleeves torn out, and when he wiped his hand over his sweaty forehead, he flashed underarm hair long, thick, and curly as a poodle's coat.

Flynn wrinkled his nose and gave me a *You have to be kidding* look.

"How's it going, Harry?"

"Wheels keep turning, Cass. Looks like you got someone to keep yours greased." He winked at me.

"Oh, yeah." I laughed at his crude joke.

Flynn's jaw tightened as he clamped his teeth shut. I drew out the pictures of Selene and Richard. Harry suddenly wouldn't meet my eyes.

"What's wrong, Harry? You've seen them? Give me a name. No one will know."

Harry grumbled. "It isn't fair."

"What's not fair?"

Harry sighed. "Doesn't matter, I guess. I don't have a rat's chance with everyone searching." He dug in his pocket, drew out a sheet of paper, and handed it to me. A photocopy of Richard's and Selene's photos.

"What in the hell? Where'd you get this?"

"That pretty man who drives the Jag went around handing them out late last night. Bastinado, street whores, we all got one."

The words printed below the photos said everything. A promise of a hundred thousand dollars for information on their location, and two hundred if both kids were delivered unharmed to the Archangel. People would keep information close in hopes of collecting mega dollars. I would get nothing in the Barrows.

"Shit, shit, shit!" I screamed as I climbed into the car. Flynn slumped in his seat and wouldn't look at me. He understood the situation. I cranked the engine and headed for the Archangel.

chapter 16

At least we didn't have to fight for a parking place at one p.m. Good thing, because I was pissed enough to crash through the glass doors and into the lobby. I parked by the building, directly under the neon angel still beating its electric wings, even though the brilliant summer sun had reduced it to a feeble flash and hum.

The receptionist sitting behind the desk inside the door stood when we entered. She gave Flynn a dazzling smile. "Mr. Michael sent word he was in his office," she said, her eyes never leaving him. Michael was expecting me. He had to know I'd learn about the flyers sooner or later.

Flynn muttered something under his breath as we marched up the stairs.

Michael opened the door before I reached it. With a graceful sweep of his hand, he invited us to enter. He closed the door behind us.

I fought for calm, but my voice sounded ragged. "What the fuck have you done?"

Michael, not at all disturbed by my rage, said, "I'm trying to save your life, Cass. That's why I took you to the Goblin Den myself. You can't—"

"Son of a bitch!" I shouted. My body brimmed with fury racing along my nerves, ready to spill out and cut down anything in its path. I did my damnedest to rein in all emotion.

No need to overreact.

But damn him. I had a right to overreact.

Flynn faced Michael. "This is insane." His arms hung at his sides, but his hands clenched into fists so rigid his fingernails might slice into his palms.

Michael shrugged. "I want Cass alive. Money is nothing. She's important. If she keeps digging around in the Barrows . . ."

Flynn's body relaxed slightly as he, too, regained control. The sharp-eyed cop returned. "So money buys lives. Children's lives." His voice stripped the words down to a naked truth.

Michael nodded. "As anywhere else, greed and perversion are powerful in the Barrows."

An emotional war suddenly flashed across Flynn's face. Torn with conflicting desires, the brother wanted his sister at any cost; the cop didn't want to owe anything to anyone, especially a criminal like Michael. The brother won. "I can't ever pay you back, not that much money."

Flynn had more faith in Michael's money than in me. Not surprising, but it hurt. I hid it with a sneer and a warning. "He isn't doing it for you, Flynn."

Flynn must have heard the pain and anger in my voice. Did he know me so well, so soon? "No, he's doing it for *you*. Cass, what have we done the last two days? Visit an asylum? Beat up a couple of Bastinados? How are we closer to finding her?"

I kept my voice low and even, in spite of my churning insides. "Ten years. Ten years digging around in the Barrows and—" I'd never convince him with words. I started for the door. "Okay, Flynn, you and Michael can have this fucking hunt and be damned."

Flynn reached for me, but I jerked away.

I couldn't dodge Michael. He grabbed me by the shoulders.

I snarled like an attack dog. I couldn't twist out of his hands.

"Listen to me." Michael gave me a mild shake like a parent trying to force his will on a child.

I kicked at his balls. He jumped back and released me, so I missed.

Flynn stepped between us. "Stop it, Cass. Please." He held his hands out, but didn't touch me. His troubled eyes and grim face held all of his desperation. So frayed, so uncertain of what to do next.

"You don't know the Barrows, Flynn. You don't know me. But you've already decided I'm incompetent and some rich asshole's money is a better way." I stared straight into Michael's eyes. I cocked my head and put as much contempt as I could in my voice. "You've bought my hunt. And that's *all* you'll get."

Michael turned his face away.

Over the years, I'd seen so much. Alone, always alone. No matter how painful for me, I understood Flynn's faith in money, a real and tangible power. He barely knew me. Obviously what we shared last night didn't matter. Nothing new—men have always felt that way when they start getting to know me, but it felt so different this time. I had hoped—

"I have faith in you, Cass," Michael spoke from across the room. His voice carried a plea. "I've seen what you can do. But this dark moon . . . Time's running out." He came closer, but kept Flynn between us. "Let me do what I told you I would do. Find your children."

"Do I have a choice?"

"No. And furious as you are, that is my intention. Tell me, what are you planning? Lead Flynn into the Barrows one night, yell *Surprise!* and hope nothing eats him? He's carrying a gun. Does it have bronze? Can you protect him *and* yourself?" He glanced at Flynn. "Has he ever seen what lives there?"

I hated it, but he was right. Perhaps I'd deliberately held back. Flynn had drawn me in from our first meeting. I didn't want him to bolt when he saw what I dealt with every day. He watched me with intense and unhappy eyes. What was he thinking? I went to him and laid my hand on his cheek.

"He's right. You need a lesson in Barrows 101," I said softly. "If *he* finds Selene, fine. I swear to you, though, I'm not finished yet." I might lose whatever personal relationship we had by giving him the grand tour, but there was no other way. Flynn had to know what he faced.

Michael had seen my intimate gesture toward Flynn and understood. For the briefest moment, a look of dismay passed across his face. It quickly returned to its usual slightly amused expression.

"So you'll show him?" Michael suddenly asked.

I faced him. "You think the real Barrows will drive him away."

"Maybe." Michael, seeing my rage had passed, moved closer. "But regardless, I want you alive. Please."

That last word cost him. Michael wasn't accustomed to asking for anything.

Flynn had sized up the situation between me and Michael, too. He slipped an arm around my waist, a possessive arm that claimed me for his own. Great Mother, let him feel the same way after our trip through the Barrows.

The phone rang, a shrill, strident sound that shrieked down my nerves.

Michael made a sharp turn and hurried to it. "Wait." He held up a hand to us.

"Archangel," he answered. He listened. "Hundred. Yes. Cash. Of course." He listened longer, his face intent as if he tried to squeeze more meaning out of the words coming from the other end. "Half an hour. I'll be there." He hung up the phone and gazed at us. "This is a line I set up for information. We have an informant."

"So." My fury had drained away, but a deep, abiding anger remained. "That's your hunt. Not mine, Mr. Moneyman."

"Very well. But why don't you and Detective Flynn join me? He didn't say to come alone. It's probably bogus. I've had a number of those."

I glanced at Flynn. He was looking at me. "Okay, but where?"

Michael gave me a brilliant smile. "Behind River Street about six blocks in. Too deep for me not to be suspicious. There are many more suitable sites around, all less dangerous. I'll send for my car." He reached for the phone again.

"No. We should go in mine. That fancy Jag will attract too much attention. I take the POS in a lot. No one will be suspicious . . . I hope."

Michael nodded. "You're right."

Before we left the office, Michael walked behind the bar, drew out a knife in a leather sheath. He also picked up a briefcase. A hundred thousand dollars? Like pocket change? The action wasn't lost on Flynn, either, because he turned a thoughtful gaze at me. I shrugged. "Money doesn't buy the things I need, Flynn. And that was a mighty damn convenient phone call."

"Seems that way," Flynn said. "But over the years, I've seen more coincidences than you would believe. Suspicious, but sometimes they happen."

I'm sure he had, but I think his thought process might have been skewed on this one.

Michael handed the knife to Flynn. "Take this. It's the only bronze I have."

To my surprise, Flynn accepted the knife. Of course,

he'd done so carefully, not touching the handle. The damned thing would be under a microscope and in a police evidence locker somewhere soon.

Michael shrugged. He had to have known, but he also knew the value of bronze in the Barrows. A puny defense, a single knife, but better than nothing.

We trooped downstairs and out into the parking lot. The day's furnace had passed its peak temperature, but the asphalt radiated accumulated heat in intense waves.

Michael opened the back door of my car and slid in as graceful as a ballet dancer. He would make any vehicle, even my POS, seem like a Jaguar.

Michael's instructions were easy to follow. To my surprise, it was to the place Abby had brought me on my first day in Duivel. She said she wanted to show me what I'd face occasionally, and this was a great classroom.

"Why bronze?" Flynn asked as I started the car. "What's it for?"

"Bullets, usually," I said. "Some things are hard to kill."

"Things?"

"Things." I sounded grumpy, but I wasn't a patient teacher and I had no way of truly explaining what he needed to see for himself.

After we turned off River Street and, into the ruins, Flynn watched the passing blight, actually seeing it for the first time. His expression was one of a man who found something appalling in his closet or under his bed. I understood. If I'd gone uptown and picked up an ordinary citizen and brought them here, it would be the same. However, that knowledge would most likely pass away as soon as the ordinary citizen left the invisible boundary of the Earth Mother's spell. Because of his involvement with me, I think Flynn would remember.

I carefully steered the car through the desolation across cracked pavement, around potholes, and past abandoned buildings with gaping black holes where windows once protected humans who called it home. Rusted and burned-out cars sat in empty lots, wastelands where even weeds wouldn't grow. The side wall of one building had a single graffito word painted in black: UNCLEAN.

When we reached our destination, I parked, climbed out, and opened the trunk to retrieve the glass bottle of blood Abby had preserved for me. Blood worked great as a distraction. I could always break the glass. Monsters naturally gravitated toward it as food. If Michael's weasel didn't show, I'd use it to teach Flynn what we faced.

"This was a school." Flynn climbed out of the car. He nodded at a chunk of granite with the figures P.S. 112 carved in the stone.

Michael came to stand beside us. "This part of Duivel was once almost the entire city. Its decline began in 1900, and it was systematically erased from the history books. The larger part to the south lasted until the early 1960s."

"That's been a real bitch for me," I said. "All I can find is bits and pieces of information. No street maps, nothing to help me." My sense of direction didn't need maps, but one would be nice occasionally when I scouted out Bastinado hideouts.

Flynn waved his hand at the blight around him. "This is irrational. Crazy. I never saw past River Street and the docks. No one looks past River Street. Why? And who would—or could—go in and erase history?"

"It's cursed," Michael said, his voice hard as the broken stone around us. "The ground, the air, the Barrows. It's an evil place." His voice had lost that perfect musical tone. Michael's face was no less handsome in the bright sunlight, but it appeared harsh and very human.

Flynn frowned. I'd bet it jarred him, Michael's sudden personality shift from rich business owner to a mystic speaking of curses and evil.

Flynn's eyes met mine, and he spoke with what I knew would be short-lived surety. "Places aren't evil. Only what lives there."

I remembered my own shock at the Barrows' desolation and the way people ignored it. "What's that?" Flynn pointed at my glass bottle.

"Blood."

"Whose blood?"

"I don't know. It was buy one get one free at the Barrows Jiffy Mart."

Flynn started to argue with me, but Michael interrupted.

"Let's get this over with. I expect it's a false call anyway. There were a couple of Bastinados last night who thought alone meant helpless."

"You think this is a trap?" I slid my hand over my gun and loosened it a bit.

Michael smiled. He'd stuffed the briefcase under the car seat. "We'll wait a while on that."

The brick building was a single story, an oddity here. Those that weren't warehouses or factories were usually two or three. Interior floor coverings, ceilings, and walls were long gone, making one enormous room with a concrete floor. Holes pocked the roof, creating an eerie, dappled light. It grew darker, deeper in the building, and the shadows suddenly weighed on me like a black soul, unable to pass beyond the prison of the living world. I glanced at Michael and Flynn and knew they felt the same.

"Whoa," I said as we approached a gaping black crater in the concrete floor twelve feet in diameter. "It's gotten bigger."

A crude crosshatch of bronze rods, held together by thin wire, covered the hole. Time had chewed its edges, so the bronze grid balanced precariously over the darkness. I didn't know who'd laid the prison bars down, but

I knew why. The creatures below wouldn't risk passing by the bronze except under extreme conditions.

I didn't need my bottle of blood. An appalling liquid sheet of red smeared across the concrete floor toward the pit's crumbling edge. "Is that your weasel, Michael?" I pointed at a male body, drained of vital fluids, that lay faceup in a pool of thickening red fluid. The gruesome clean slice across his throat looked as if someone held him while he bled out. Fresh, very fresh, cut only minutes earlier.

"It would appear so," Michael said, his voice tight and definitely unmusical this time. He knelt by the dead man. Flynn simply stared. My hardened cop appeared to be on sensory overload. Up close and personal in the Barrows can do that to a person. I was used to it. I'd seen worse. And I saw it for what it was—a trap.

"There's nothing here. Let's go, Michael."

"No." Flynn suddenly remembered he was a cop. "I have to get someone down here. Identify him. This is a crime scene."

"They won't come, Flynn. There's no phone service this deep in the Barrows. Even cell phones won't work here. And I keep telling you this place doesn't exist uptown."

I heard the sound then, the frenzy of small things that came from the hole. Little creatures with their ratlike squeaks and chatters, small harmless horrors scrabbling around, crawling over each other, seeking drops of blood. My mind pictured the little creatures now chattering over the blood drained into the hole, an incredibly ugly mixture, some spiderlike, others shaped like giant toads or turtles.

I understood the nature of the trap now. Simple, nothing sophisticated. The clamor would attract a larger predator. Whoever did this thought Michael would come alone, maybe in the Jag. And if he happened to have the money in the Jag . . . yeah, definitely worth it. They would back him against the hole where he couldn't escape and toss his body in when they finished.

Men's shapes appeared in the doorway we'd entered. The sudden rattle of Bastinado chains signaled they were headed into battle. As a rule, Bastinados aren't very bright. Except for an occasional leader, they are locked into their rules and rituals and would follow them to hell. Rattling chains equal a battle cry.

A thick grunt came from below.

The bronze crosshatch suddenly popped up like a champagne cork. The crosshatch toppled over and landed with a screech and clatter on the concrete floor, where the thin wire holding it together broke and it collapsed into a pile of bronze sticks. Above that racket came an undulating foghorn howl of a very large beast.

The Bastinados raced out the door. They'd wait outside for the monster to get us. We'd have to go out shooting. "Run!" I shouted. "Get into the light."

Even as we turned, I knew it was too late. The grizzly bear–sized monster huffed, rumbled, and clawed its way out. Like an obscene rhino, gray hide armor plated its body and its four long legs ended in big cat claws. Its elongated head had a mouth with multiple rows of teeth, and the bulbous eyes of a creature that hunted below the street in eternal night.

As we scrambled away, I drew and fired one round. The bronze bullet hit midchest, directly under its jaw. It bellowed in pain and staggered, but it kept coming. Shallow penetration in tough hide. The predators I'd encountered before would never have touched the bronze barrier over the hole. Did that tough-looking hide make this one less sensitive? It should have gone for the easy meat, too, the body on the edge of the pit.

Because I'd turned to shoot, it caught me first.

It slung one clawed leg.

Too close. The claws missed. Its leg slammed me on the hip and sent me flying. I hit the concrete with bone-rattling impact. Then it was on top of me. I stared straight up into a mouth of razor teeth. Bloody slobber sprayed over me.

Great Mother! Its breath smelled like its guts had died and rotted and its animal brain didn't know it yet.

I've learned to hang on to my gun, though, no matter the circumstances. I pulled the trigger and shot straight into that gaping maw. One. Two. At the third shot the thing jumped straight up and away. It choked and vomited blood. I didn't kill it, though. This kind appeared damn near indestructible. I needed an eye and brain shot.

I didn't know Flynn's or Michael's location, so I couldn't risk dangerous random fire. The three shots had hammered my eardrums. I couldn't hear them, either.

I spotted Michael to my right. The creature charged him. He swiftly and gracefully danced out of the way. Where was Flynn?

As I scrambled to my feet, the barbaric creature charged again. It had a knife hilt sticking out of its neck. Great Mother, the knife Michael had given Flynn. Had Flynn jumped on the thing's back?

I shot again. Solid in the body but missed its head. An agonized roar vibrated even my abused ears.

Flynn suddenly stepped between me and the creature. Oh! He'd remembered my words. He hadn't drawn his gun with its useless bullets. A bronze rod from the shattered crosshatch shield poised over his shoulder like a baseball bat. He gripped the rod tense and steady, like a pro baseball player who knows he's facing an incompetent pitcher. His mouth tight with determination, his dark eyes focused on the bizarre creature rushing toward him. The man who'd walked into a nightmare of epic proportions now stood between me and death.

Flynn swung the rod with enough force to hit a home run way past center field. The bronze rod smacked straight across the eyes. They popped, spraying sulfur yellow slime everywhere. I dropped the magazine from my gun and quickly shoved in another.

The thing still stood, blind, head swaying.

Flynn stood watching ten feet to my right. Michael on my left. Relief. Both men lived.

I closed in for a kill. Careful aim . . . one of the damaged eyes . . . I pulled the trigger. A direct hit. The creature flung itself up, whirled around, coughing and clawing at the concrete floor. It collapsed and died. As it did, it slammed into Flynn and knocked him backward into the monster-filled sewer.

chapter 17

I raced for the hole, but Michael beat me to it. He snatched one of the bronze rods on the run and, without hesitation, jumped in, feetfirst. I made it to the hole and, by all logic and reason, should have stayed there to help them get out.

Fate isn't logical. The unstable edge crumbled under me. I'm quite sure Michael landed on his feet in a graceful upright position like a gymnast. I landed on my ass.

Many of the storm sewers under the Barrows still function. During a rainstorm, deadly walls of water rush through them and out to the river, cleaning them to a degree. It hadn't rained in three months, so at least a foot of monster shit cushioned my fall. I held my gun high and kept it clean at least. I straightened and the stuff oozed over my legs. Great Mother, what a stink.

Flynn, also slimy, crouched next to a wall near me, puking his stomach out, just as I had the first time I went below the streets. Michael stood guard over him, bronze rod poised to fend off larger predators. Sure enough, the shit reached only to his knees. A medium-sized predator, one certainly big enough to kill a man, lay to the side, its head a bloody mass. It would have taken Flynn if Michael hadn't guarded him.

All the little horrors had scrambled away in terror, so

we were alone—for the moment. This sewer wasn't the largest I'd been in, ten feet high and ten wide. To my right, it tunneled into darkness, black and thick as roofing tar. To my left, the faint glow of lichens marked a funnel deeper into the Barrows.

I managed to get to my feet without using my hands, but filth coated me from the boobs down. I went and crouched by Flynn. "You hurt?"

"No." He choked on the word and retched again.

"You're doing good," I told him. "My first time down here I couldn't talk for a couple of hours."

Clinging to the wall, Flynn forced himself to his feet. With shallow breaths, I could see him fight for control. I wanted to wrap my arms around him.

But first we had to get out. "If one of you gentlemen could give me a boost, there's a rope in my trunk."

"We don't have time for that." Michael nodded to the sewer hole behind me.

At least four hulking predators stood at the edge of the pool of dim light, and there might've been more behind them. Not as big as the one who climbed out, but still dangerous.

I'm not sure what they were waiting on, unless they could sense the bronze rod in Michael's hand. The monster that dumped us into this mess had ignored the bronze hatch. If they charged en masse, they'd overwhelm us in an instant. Why hadn't they charged? All Michael had was a single piece of bronze. They almost seemed to be waiting on something, some signal to attack.

I glanced the other way. Nothing, and the faint lichen glow meant we wouldn't be completely blind.

"Okay," I said. "I've done this before. They eat anything organic. I'll take one of them down, and we leave while the others have dinner. They'll follow, but it'll buy us time."

Michael nodded.

The predators staring at us walked upright on two legs and had arms that ended in clawed hands. A couple of them had porcupine quills down their backs like some I'd seen before, but the others were a new . . . breed? Species? And when did there get to be so many of them? A year ago, I could walk these tunnels for a mile or more and never encounter one.

They twisted and shuffled as they watched us with glowing eyes. I have an affinity for Earth Mother's animals, even those that are not special like Nirah and Nefertiti. These strange creatures did not belong to her.

I aimed for an eye of the one that appeared the softest. "You guys head the other way. I'll catch up with you. Shouldn't be too far to a manhole or grate." I pulled the trigger.

Good shot. The bronze hit the eye and sheared off the top of its head. Before it hit the floor, the others pounced on their meal. One more shot and another went down.

A storm sewer, like an enclosed building, isn't a good place to shoot a high-powered gun. The blast slapped my already sensitive eardrums again. I didn't want to hear the feeding frenzy anyway. Too many beasts and not enough food. If I'd had an extra magazine, I'd have killed more, but I had to save the precious bronze for whatever lay ahead. I hurried after Flynn and Michael.

The lichens' faint glow showed only the silhouettes of the two men ahead of me. Michael led the way and Flynn staggered along. When I caught up with them, I could see that with each step, though, he grew stronger. He'd glance at me occasionally, but I couldn't read him. I prayed the memory of what we shared last night would override the impromptu lesson I'd thrown at him like a grenade.

Flynn cleared his throat. "Doesn't this terrify you?" His voice came out with the texture of a rasp.

"Yes, but . . ." I tried to find a way he would understand. "Aren't you frightened when you bust some bad guys? When you go into a place where you know they're going to be shooting back?"

"Yes, but I'm trained to put it aside. You—"

"Oh, I've been trained. By experience. By focusing on the job to be done. Knowing what happens to children in this place."

Fear. It coursed through me as we spoke. Mostly fear for him. Michael and I knew how to take care of ourselves. Our odds? Fairly good, given that knowledge. Flynn didn't belong. I didn't like the thought.

Then he touched me. Just a brief hand on my shoulder. How idiotic. One touch and I felt desire rise. Not so much for sex as for the sheer pleasure of him at my side. Great Mother, what was I going to do?

The sewer grew lighter here, more glowing lichens and less monster shit covering the floor. Occasionally we'd pass a storm grate, where wonderful sunlight poured down, but all were too high to reach. Getting out required a manhole.

We moved along quickly, until we came to an intersection where four tunnels joined.

"Now what?" Michael spoke softly.

I went to the first corner, drew my knife, and scraped lichen from an area four feet up on the stone. Nothing. The same at the next corner. The third gave me what I was looking for, a series of numbers and letters.

"There's a system," I told them. I pointed down one tunnel. "If it's open, there should be a manhole, about fifteen hundred yards."

"You come down here often?" Flynn asked.

"Only when I have to." There wasn't enough light to see his expression.

"What if it's blocked?" Michael asked.

"We come back and go another way." I hoped it was

open, because the other way led deeper into the Barrows toward the Zombie. I headed into the tunnel.

Fewer lichens grew here, and walking was treacherous where rushing water had loosened stones on the floor. Flynn went to his knees once and even graceful Michael staggered.

We trudged on, occasionally sloshing through a seemingly endless tube.

"How long have they been here?" Flynn asked. His voice sounded almost normal. "These . . . things. What are they?"

"They were there when I was a boy," Michael spoke softly. "Only a few, though. There is no name for them. We always believed they came from the Bog. They came out on dark nights and fed. It was a terrible time to live in the Barrows."

"I'm still having trouble with why all of this is ignored." Flynn had moved closer to me. I wanted to hug him, shit and all.

"I asked my questions when I first came and Abby said—" I hesitated, expecting his reaction to the mention of Abby.

"What? Just say it. I'll believe. Or at least I'll accept it." Resignation filled his voice.

"Abby says there's a spell, cast by Mother, to keep people out. But it clouds people's minds. The longer they stay here, the less susceptible they are, but they become more accepting. Like Joe Holey, at the strip bar. He knows what's here, but he stays away and plays ignorant."

Flynn said nothing, but I'd bet he had heavy thoughts on the matter, or had pushed all thoughts away rather than deal with them right now.

The tunnel grew brighter. It could be light from a hole like the one that dumped us here.

As we approached, we could see it was indeed a hole,

one with sloped sides that led into a rough basement. The basement wall had collapsed into the sewer. The structural integrity of the building above concerned me, but not enough to pass up the chance to get out. From the looks of the debris, it hadn't been open long. This, unfortunately, wasn't unusual. One of my great fears was that I'd be running for my life and be trapped against a cave-in.

The light came from a single bulb hanging from a cord, welcome as a lighthouse warning ships away from the rocks. We'd actually come out of the Barrows and into one of the periphery buildings, one with electricity.

Boxes, cartons, and assorted scrap metal lay scattered across the room, much of it directly below a set of wooden stairs leading up to a door. Flynn grabbed a rag he found on the floor and cleaned his hands as much as possible. Then he wiped down his gun. Our clothes and shoes were a total loss.

We climbed the stairs and easily opened the door at the top.

I kept my gun drawn as Flynn opened the door. He had his in his hand, too.

Silence greeted us as we entered a large warehouse; then came a sound I'd heard before. The faint jingle of the metal chains Bastinados wore around their necks to show their particular affiliation. They weren't close, but if we could hear them, they could hear us—or smell us.

We couldn't see anything because of a mountain of wooden crates stacked between the sound and us. High windows near the roof gave dim, dirty light. The boxes had markings, some Oriental, others English letters and numbers, and none specifying the exact nature of the contents.

Flynn nodded and I followed him as we eased toward the sound. Michael came silently behind us. It didn't take long to locate the source.

Two Bastinados sat in plastic chairs near a door in the building's metal-clad side. Both had plugs stuck in their ears, plugs connected by wire to something in their pockets. One sat motionless, but the other rocked back and forth in his chair in time to a rhythm only he could hear. Both had their eyes closed.

I glanced at Flynn to tell him I'd take one and he could have the other, but Flynn wasn't looking at me. His attention focused on the contents of a box with the lid pried off. Lying on blocks of foam were rows of automatic rifles. Flynn carefully lifted one. He gazed at it, then at the boxes around us.

So did I, but my eyes stopped at eight four-by-four shrink-wrapped pallets set along the wall. I carefully walked toward them and used my knife to slice the wrap open a foot or so. Inside were brick-sized cubes of what looked like individually wrapped gray modeling clay.

Flynn drew a sharp breath. Michael merely stared, his face grim.

It had to be C-4. I'm not an explosive expert, but I knew it was relatively stable, requiring a detonator or blasting cap to set it off. Flynn had said that the Bastinados on Exeter Street had plastic. The idiots must have tried to use it, or maybe they already had some made up, ready to go and set it off.

To my surprise, Flynn turned to Michael.

Michael had left his bronze rod behind. He stood, loose and relaxed, with his hands at his sides.

"Are these yours?" Flynn spoke softly, mouthing the words.

Michael shook his head. I believed him.

Flynn leaned close, whispered in my ear, "You take the one on the right. I'll do the left. Probably shouldn't do any shooting in here."

My heart did a little flop. *You take the one on the right.* He'd acknowledged my skill as a fighter. Did this mean he wasn't too ticked off at me for having him dumped into a hellhole sewer? Or was it the fact that we were now in a place, a situation that he moderately understood?

I agreed with the no-shooting rule. We had no idea if more men waited outside. Of course, it all went to hell the minute we started toward the Bastinados. Mine glanced up as we started our charge. He was on his feet by the time I reached him. I already had my fist balled up to punch him but came within danger of impalement. A ten-inch knife suddenly appeared in his hand.

I dropped back, but my feet didn't get the message in time. I landed on my ass and slid into his legs. He came down on top of me. In a tangle of legs and arms, I focused on the most important thing. Where the hell was the knife?

I saw it in the corner of my eye as it arced toward me. I caught the Bastinado's knife hand by the wrist. A look of surprise crossed his face when he realized my strength. I could hold the knife back, but he had a free hand. He locked the hand on my throat and dug his fingers in with enough force to crush my windpipe. Each finger gouged in and his fingernails cut into tender skin. I had a free hand, too. I jammed my forefinger into his eye. The eye popped and gooey stuff gushed over my hand.

He forgot the knife and my throat. He rolled off me, howling as he went. I hadn't had time to get short of breath, but my throat hurt like I'd swallowed fire.

The Bastinado writhed across the floor, holding his hands over his face, wailing like a child. I staggered to my feet and drew my gun. If there were more outside, I'd need a weapon. The Bastinado's strident cries abruptly stopped. I guess he fainted.

Flynn stood over the other Bastinado, who lay silent on the floor. Michael stood not far away, shaking his head.

"What?" My voice croaked like my POS on cold winter mornings.

"I could have distracted them for you," Michael said. He sounded irritated. "But you and Flynn were in such a hurry, you left me behind."

"Fuck you, Michael," I said. Or at least tried to say. My voice came out as a whistle. A very painful whistle.

"What was that, Cassandra?" Michael smiled.

"She said, 'Fuck you,'" Flynn volunteered. He picked his phone out of his vest pocket, where the leather had kept it shitless. He would have phone service since we'd come to the Barrows' northern edge. "I'm calling this in. It can't be legal. Bastinados, heavy weapons, explosives." He glanced at Michael. "You'd better go. Might be a few questions asked that you don't have answers for."

Michael nodded. He reached out and laid a hand on my shoulder. "Are you all right?"

"Yes. Thank you," I whispered. "For saving him. If you hadn't gone into that hole after him, those things would have taken him."

"You'd hate me forever if he died," he said softly. "I'd never have a chance to prove that I'm better for you." He kissed me on the forehead.

"Go by my car and check on your money. It's probably gone, though."

"I brought no money. Only a briefcase."

Michael went to the door and opened it. No point in looking outside. If there had been any more Bastinados outside, we would have known it by now.

"Michael," Flynn said.

Michael turned back, his face once again calm and beautiful. "Yes?"

"Thank you."

"You're welcome, Flynn. Perhaps you should think of an explanation for how you both came to be in the sewers." He nodded gracefully, then left us, carefully closing the door behind him.

Flynn sighed. "What *are* we going to say?"

"You. Not we. I'll meet you at the car." I didn't want to answer any questions, either. "Can you find it? It's that way." I pointed in the direction of the car.

Flynn came close and suddenly kissed me. Square on the mouth. No gentle brush on the forehead like Michael. With my olfactory nerves on overload, I couldn't smell a thing. His mouth tasted fine.

I leaned against him. "What was that for?"

"I felt like it."

I glanced at the Bastinados and realized I'd almost missed something. I pointed at the one I had taken down. "Hey, that's a Python."

"And that's a Blood Beast." Flynn nodded at the other.

The Bastinado gangs waged savage and deadly turf wars, and if any two tried to join forces, the others slaughtered them. Pythons and Blood Beasts fought so viciously at one time, annihilating their enemies, that both gangs faced extinction.

Flynn gazed around at the guns and ammo. "Bastinado gangs getting together?"

"Shit, that's scary."

I left the warehouse and didn't see Michael, but it was still daylight and he knew his way around. I walked away toward the car. I had gone only a block when a law enforcement convoy swept down the street behind me. The simultaneous arrival of multiple fire trucks, a SWAT team, the bomb squad, and more patrol cars than I believed possible spoke to Flynn's credibility. They didn't send a couple of guys to check it out before they called in the troops. I hoped there wasn't a major criminal event in uptown Duivel, because it seemed as if all the law was here.

I sat in the car and sweated. The only building I could go in was the one with the hole in the floor—the hole now minus its bronze bars.

Less than an hour later, Flynn came strolling toward me. "That was quick," I said. My throat was feeling much better.

He grinned. "Well, there's a bit of a problem. I seem to have significant body odor."

My own clothes had dried in the sun, and they were stiff with caked shit.

Flynn laughed. "They have enough to keep them busy for a while. I'll file a report later." He lifted out his phone again and turned it off. "I've suddenly become unavailable."

We went back to my apartment. When we parked, I left the windows open on the POS and reminded myself I had a case of deodorizer under the kitchen sink. This is the one situation I stayed prepared for.

"What's the plan?" Flynn asked as I pulled into the parking lot. He kicked off his shoes.

"Well, we can go over to the Dumpster, strip naked, and go up the fire escape."

"I will if you will." He wrapped his arm around me.

"Nah, kids live here," I said. "We'll keep enough on to be legal. Someone might call the cops."

"Now that would be embarrassing."

We went to the Dumpster and stripped. He went down to his pants and I had my pants and the thin tank top I used as an undershirt. My boots, his shoes, a total loss, went in, too. Damn, I was down to two pairs of boots. I usually bought them six pairs at a time. My footwear had a high mortality rate. Flynn carried his leather vest, belt, badge, and gun in his hand as I carried my own gun and shoulder holster. I also retrieved my cell phone. Thank the Mother I'd left it in the car, hooked to the charger, so it remained shitless, too.

Flynn stared at my chest and grinned.

"What? So I got boobs and nipples. I seem to remember that you examined them quite thoroughly last night and this morning."

"Yeah." He laughed. "Nice rack."

"Ass." I started for the building.

Mr. Blackstein, the neighbor across the hall from me, stood in the building's shade by the back door and smoked one of the five cigarettes his wife permitted him to consume daily. He stared at my chest. "Nice rack." He winked at me.

chapter 18

As we entered the apartment, my cell phone rang.

"Got Hammer." Dacardi's voice came across the distance, cold and clear.

"Where?"

"Columbia Stores warehouse by the river. North door."

"Be there in an hour, maybe an hour and a half. You remember—"

"Yeah, yeah." He sounded justifiably frustrated. "You get him first."

I closed the phone. "Dacardi has Hammer. I really think you should stay at the apartment, or maybe go file your report at the station. You don't want to get dirty hanging out with a crime boss."

"No, I'm going with you." He looked at me hard. "Do you trust him?"

"Dacardi? I trust him until I get what he wants."

He shook his head. "Michael."

"What about him?"

"Do you trust Michael?"

"What do you want me to say about Michael, Flynn?"

"Try the truth. What's he to you?"

I gave him a look of my own. "Okay. You asked. The truth is, Michael is a desirable man and I've known that since the day we met. I'm not immune to his . . . attributes.

His charm? Whatever it is, I'll never accept him for reasons I don't want to talk about right now. There are other truths that are more important. I want you. I want you in my bed and in my life. You called me weird, and—"

"I meant different, not bad."

"I know. But you're the one who's different, especially in the Barrows. Michael is a lot more like me than you are. And, no, I'm not going to give up and trust him to find Selene. Michael's too mysterious to be trusted. If I trusted him, you and I would go screw each other's brains out in the shower, and again on the bed, not spend the evening with a bloody gangster."

Flynn didn't say anything, but after a while he grasped my hand and locked his fingers in mine. "Forget the cop. Let the man who cares for you and his sister go with you."

He released my hand and lifted the case containing his badge and his ID, opened a kitchen drawer, and placed them inside.

I've always classified people I deal with as an ally or an enemy. No neutrals existed in my world. I don't have time for them. But Flynn and Michael had no neat little labels. I guess life would grow boring if I lived it in black and white all the time.

Flynn and I had admitted caring for each other. That was enough for now. Each day that passed would solidify our relationship like cement, or force it to crumble like the Barrows buildings.

We showered and dressed in clean clothes. And deodorant. Lots of deodorant. Our remaining soiled clothes I packed in a plastic bag to carry out to the Dumpster. Flynn did manage to clean his leather vest, and I gave him my gun-cleaning kit for his pistol. Fortunately, he had a pair of athletic shoes with his things.

Things were happening fast, so I loaded Nirah and Nefertiti in the basket I sometimes used to carry them. No matter what, they would be safer at Abby's house.

Horus followed us out and jumped in the car. And jumped back out. I had to go back for a can of deodorant spray before he would ride with me.

It was late afternoon when I drove into Abby's driveway, parked, and led Flynn to her back door. Nefertiti and Nirah slid out of the basket and headed for the garden. Horus raced after them.

"No birds, Horus," I called after him. "Remember the rules."

We approached the back porch, where a terra-cotta jar sat on the top doorstep.

"Go cleanse yourselves," Abby called from inside.

"Aw, shit," I grumbled. I snatched up the pot. "Come on."

Every time I had to go into the sewers, Abby made me use her cleansing potion before I could come back into her house. She wouldn't make an exception because of Flynn.

I led a curious Flynn back to the front sidewalk so whatever we washed off wouldn't contaminate the soil. "This won't hurt, but it will feel funny."

I dumped half the jar of clear liquid on his head.

He gasped and shivered. "What the—"

"Magic bath." I poured the rest over me. The familiar sideways shift of the world overcame me, but instantly passed.

"I was happy with soap and water." Flynn brushed at his clothes and hair. The potion evaporated almost instantly, though, and his hands came away dry. His puzzled expression gave way to resignation.

"Sorry, Flynn. Rules is rules, especially Abby's."

Abby stood at the stove stirring a pot when we went in. The table was set for three. A heavenly aroma filled the air, but I couldn't stop now.

"I need something to make a man talk to me," I said.

Abby raised an eyebrow and pursed her lips. "Good

evening to you, too, Cassandra." She gave Flynn a warm smile. "Detective Flynn, welcome. I have supper ready. I hope you like vegetables."

"Come on, Abby. I'm on the trail now." I said it without much force since the odor of food caught me like a love potion and drew me in.

"I can tell." Abby gestured at the table. "Sit down, please."

She removed a vase of red and gold flowers from the middle of the table and replaced them with a trivet and the pot from the stove.

My insides twisted. "We don't have time—"

"Yes, you do. I want an explanation before I start dispensing drugs."

"Why? You never have before."

Abby's face had that *I'm going to send you to your room, you smart-mouthed little girl* look. No argument would work here. I sat down and filled her in on what had happened. While I was doing that, I consumed two bowls of vegetable soup, a couple of glasses of iced tea, and several slices of golden brown homemade bread with butter. My throat hurt, but that didn't stop me from eating or talking.

Flynn ate, too, and just listened to us talk. I guess he was hungry after puking his guts out a couple of hours earlier.

"That's it so far." I leaned back, feeling much better than I had all day—except right after Flynn and I had made love that morning.

Abby smiled at Flynn. "And what do you think of all this? The Darkness, the things in the sewer? Magic in general?"

Flynn leaned back. "Cass says the things in the sewer are biological, not magic."

"True enough, but what are they, and how did they get there?"

Flynn shook his head. "I don't know—or care. I have suspended all rational thought until I have my sister home."

Abby smiled at Flynn, but it was a sad smile. She knew, as I did, that he had left the rational world forever. He would never be the same.

Abby stood, went to a dark wood cabinet, opened the doors, and lifted out a tiny blue bottle. She handed it and an eyedropper to me. "To make him talk. Try not to use too much this time." She handed me another bottle, this one green. "To make him forget."

I winced. The last time I used the talking potion, I had a man babbling for two days, and then had to babysit him because I couldn't let him back out on the street. I didn't say anything, but I knew the forgetting potion probably wouldn't be used. I'd try, but Dacardi wasn't likely to let Hammer go free or turn him over to the cops. I'd have to deal with Flynn on that one, too. Maybe I could persuade Dacardi to leave Hammer alone until later, when he was out of Flynn's presence. I stuffed the bottles and dropper in my jeans pocket.

Abby smiled. "Close your eyes."

I did and she laid both hands softly on my face. My skin tingled, warmed, then cooled. I'd bet my face appeared normal now, the remainder of the bruises fading away. My throat felt good, too.

Abby gave a weary sigh and lowered her hands.

"Her face," Flynn said. "What did you do?"

"Flynn, I'm the Earth Mother's High Priestess. She's permitted me to use a bit of her power. I suggest you continue with your plan of suspending rational thought. It will be far less traumatic." Abby gave me an affectionate puppy pat on the head. "Our Huntress is not always rational, reasonable, or consistent. She is, however, loyal and courageous, and she cares for you. Something tells me you would do well to remember that. She will find your sister. Have faith in her."

Flynn mumbled, "Excuse me," then stood and walked out the back door and into the yard.

I started to follow him.

"No," Abby said. "Give him time to think. Remember what you went through. You were predisposed to think the way you do. He's very strong and believes in order, not chaos. He'll come around."

"I know, but everything's gone to hell. Nothing makes sense in the Barrows anymore."

"It makes perfect sense to someone. You seem to be receiving only bits and pieces of information. I've been left out of this, you know. I can only offer you minimal help."

"I figured that. Why? The Mother—"

"Decides what I'm to know and when, and gives me instructions. I have received neither information nor orders in this matter."

"I'm guessing I have something important to do. Something very dangerous. And I think you love me too much. You might hinder me."

Abby laughed. Abby's laugh could make flowers bloom and trees break into leaf in midwinter. "Cassandra, after all our years together, have you finally acquired a little wisdom? Maturity? Will you now actually think before you act?"

"Well, I wouldn't go that far. And if you didn't know, I love you very much, too."

Abby laughed and wrapped her arms around me and gave me a final hug. She held me too tight and too long, and fear radiated from her body. What could so frighten the Earth Mother's most powerful priestess? I figured I'd find out soon enough.

"You and Flynn . . . lovers?" Abby sounded curious, but certainly not disapproving.

"Since last night. It's different. I'm scared. I want him to stay, not—"

"He is not like the others, Cassandra. He is yours. I saw him looking at you."

I stood. "I look at him, too. I'll take it as it comes."

I walked outside and found Flynn standing in the garden.

"Hey," I said. "You okay?"

"Yeah. I think I will be." He wrapped an arm around my shoulders.

All I wanted to do then was make love to him and sleep. Instead, we left the cool oasis of Abby's house and headed for the docks. I squeezed the steering wheel tight as we entered the Barrows. The blazing sun had dropped low on the horizon as I turned off River Street into the industrial district. I glanced over at Flynn and noted his hands clenched into fists.

"Does Dacardi own many legitimate businesses?" I asked Flynn.

"I think so. I don't work that area, but the Feds, mostly IRS, are on him."

"Drugs?"

"Surprisingly, no. He owns a couple of casinos. Probably launders cash. Mostly he deals guns and other weapons. Owns some big things in Mexico. Someone said Interpol had an eye on him, too."

"Hope the stuff in the warehouse today wasn't his," I said. "He's likely to be a bit ugly if he knows what we did."

"It wasn't, though he might have sold them at one time or another. I talked to Perkins at the site. He's with the Feds. Been here since Exeter Street. Did a couple of joint ops with him last year. They were tracking this shipment from China when it disappeared. The Feds don't tell us much, but Perkins says they've known for a year there's a big buyer in the States. Apparently, our find was the first break they've had on it."

"Dacardi might not let you in."

"Then you'll just have to make him, won't you? You

seem pretty good at pushing him around." He reached over and ruffled my hair.

The area consisted mostly of warehouses until you reached the docks. Mostly clean, prosperous places. Farm and manufacturing goods passed through and onto barges bound for the Mississippi. I found the Columbia warehouse easy enough, and the north door. Getting inside proved to be a bit more difficult. As I'd figured, Dacardi's goons didn't want Flynn the cop to pass. I simply told them to tell Dacardi I'd arrived and wasn't coming in unless Flynn came with me. They'd report to Dacardi and he could decide. Five minutes later, one of the goons came out and said we could go in.

"See," I said to Flynn. "Wasn't that easy?"

Of course, the next problem began again when they wanted our guns. We stood back-to-back and refused. The game ended when Dacardi arrived, screaming at everyone involved. To my surprise, he sent the goons away.

Dacardi led us into the deepest part of the warehouse. We walked down lanes between bales and boxes stacked twenty-five feet high. Only our footsteps broke the silence. He'd probably sent all the legitimate workers home, a substantial financial loss since the docks usually operated twenty-four hours a day.

Hammer sat in a room off the main warehouse. He looked good, considering. Broken nose, a little blood on his shirt, but other than that, okay. Dacardi had him tied to a chair with one goon watching him. He sent the goon away as we entered the room.

A thin, bony man with dark skin, Hammer had eyes as black as puddles of oil on a garage floor. He glanced at me, then jerked his face away.

"Now that's odd, Hammer." I laid a friendly hand on his shoulder. He flinched. "You're dealing kids and you don't seem surprised to see me. Why is that?"

He didn't answer.

Dacardi moved in, fists clenched, teeth bared.

I held up my hand. "I told you, I get to go first."

"Then fucking *do* it." Dacardi's face twisted into a rigid mask and his broad shoulders hunched with solid muscle.

Flynn stood steady, arms crossed in disapproval, but said nothing.

I opened the bottle of talking potion Abby had given me and filled the eyedropper.

"Hold his head," I ordered.

Dacardi grabbed Hammer's hair and twisted his face toward me. Hammer's eyes widened as I pinched his broken nose shut. He opened his mouth to breathe and I squirted the eyedropper's liquid in.

He struggled, fought, and spit. It didn't take long. I barely had time to recap the bottle and stuff it back in my jeans before he grew lethargic. His eyes were a little unfocused, but he stared straight at me.

"Now, Hammer, we need to discuss the boy and girl you had at the Goblin Den the other night. You probably didn't ask their names, but Theron remembered seeing them with you. He told me that after Michael broke his arm."

Hammer's breathing slowed. "Paid."

"Who paid? Where are they now?"

"Gone."

"Dead?" I hated to ask that, but I had to know.

Dacardi growled. Flynn drew a deep breath but didn't interfere.

"Are they dead, Hammer?" I slapped the side of his head, not hard, but I had to get his attention. "The kids. Are they dead?"

"Don't know. Took them." His words came wet and slurred, one side effect of the drug.

"Who took them?" My voice rose to a demand. I wasn't getting the reaction I'd expected. He should have been babbling for the first few minutes before he settled down and talked.

The air suddenly grew tight and close. I actually glanced around to be sure that, like a horror movie, the walls hadn't started closing in to crush us. We were in the Barrows, the realm of the Darkness. This was a mistake. We should have found another place far from here.

Hammer's body jerked. His muscles corded and strained against his bonds before he slumped and let out a long sigh. Then he raised his head. Only it wasn't Hammer. As the Earth Mother had watched me from Abby's eyes, so something gazed at me from Hammer's. Something alien and terrible.

It laughed with a sound like knives cutting the air. Everything inside me recoiled. "Great Mother." I barely breathed the words.

Hammer's face split in a savage, inhuman grin. When he spoke, the words slammed me with power. "Great Mother? You pray to that whore? She whose cunt spawned you? Stupid bitch. I remember you—I watched. You threw your child on the bitch's fire at the stone circle. Sacrificed your babe to her a thousand years ago. Pretty little thing. What was her name?"

My body went cold. A memory slithered into my mind. Was it *my* memory? No, it couldn't have been. But . . .

I hear the chants, see the fire. Astra, my wonderful daughter, clings to me, laughing as I dance with her. Her father died protecting our village. I loved him deeply and she is so precious to me, all that remains of that love. She's seen three summers and is so beautiful they've chosen her to go to the Earth Mother. A sacrifice. Such a great honor. She will bring rain and good crops. Her life will give us good fortune for the next year. Only at the last moment does she realize what is happening. She screams at me, Mother, Mother! with terror in her voice. Her small arms cling to my neck, but they tear them away and . . .

"Cass!" Someone shouted. Something hit me and I reeled across the floor. Then the only thing I heard was sick laughter. Words from Hammer's mouth mocked, "I will see you at the dark moon, Huntress. Watch for me."

I collapsed sobbing on the floor, my mind full of horror and my heart aching with loss. *Is this why I'm the Huntress?* Why I'm compelled to find the children? Guilt for what I had done? The Mother would never ask for that horrifying sacrifice. If I did not believe in her, in her goodness, I would not serve her. Men had made a perverted mockery of her religion as they had so many beliefs. The Darkness was manipulating my mind, as he had manipulated others. I'd thought I was immune, but I was wrong. But that didn't stop me from wondering ... Had I led this past life? Did I have a child? And out of ignorance, did I let them throw her into the fire?

No! No! I wouldn't do that. I could not. I would love and protect my child. I knew.

Flynn helped me to my feet and I clung to the solid mass of his body. Never in my life had I needed someone's strength as I did then.

Dacardi stood beside Hammer. Hammer's mouth and nose gushed blood. His body jerked, muscles straining against the ropes binding him. He died in one final spasm. As he did, the oppressive air cleared and left me feeling very small and vulnerable in the middle of an enormous cavern.

Dacardi's chest heaved. "That . . . *thing*. It has my son?" He held his hands out as if begging for something, anything, to hold on to. He, at least, had understood possession.

I swallowed, but I had to answer him. "His servants do. That was—" The Darkness. This was the Barrows, his place, under his influence, his realm. He had the power to use his servants as the Earth Mother used Abby.

I coughed, hard and dry. "I need some water. I'll try to explain."

Dacardi ran his hands through his hair. His eyes were

cold, hard, and dark. "Take her in there." He looked at Flynn and nodded at a door and glass window in the wall.

Flynn kept his arm around me as he walked me to an office at the side of the warehouse while Dacardi shouted at his men, I presumed to get rid of Hammer's body. Flynn didn't speak, but I knew he had to be doing some heavy thinking.

The utilitarian office contained a gray metal desk and a small table with green folding chairs. I sat on a chair while Flynn dug in a small refrigerator sitting next to the wall. By some miracle, he found a bottle of water. Bottled water always tasted bad to me, but not this time.

Flynn knelt beside me and held my shaking hands. He didn't speak. In this matter he remained silent, giving all authority to me.

"What happened?" I asked him. "What did you see?"

"Hammer raised his head and said something weird ... The Mother and a sacrifice. You froze for a few seconds; then you started screaming and fell." He laid a hand on my knee. "I was afraid you'd hurt yourself."

"What did you see? Did Hammer change? Look different?"

"He looked like ..." Flynn shook his head.

I stroked his cheek and kissed his forehead. "I'm sorry."

"For what? You didn't do—"

"It's not what I did. It's what I am."

I understood that one small piece of the puzzle now. At least I thought I did. I couldn't brush away the feeling that what I had seen was real. But how could I explain it to Flynn?

I laid my hand on his cheek. "I can't rescue all the children who are lost in the Barrows. Sometimes I receive instructions, and sometimes I have to choose. I try to go for the youngest, because as they get older they change, and even if I find them, they won't go home. Something wants me in the Barrows at the dark moon. Selene is old enough that I might have passed her up, if it hadn't been for the Earth Mother, your mother, and Abby. Do you understand?"

Comprehension flashed across Flynn's face, quickly replaced by anger. "The Darkness said he ... it ... would see you on the dark moon. Selene is in the Barrows with those creatures because she's bait. You're the mark, and you're walking into a trap."

"Yeah. It looks that way. But I'm a moving target. And I've had ten years of experience avoiding traps. I don't understand. Why does the Darkness want me? And why the dark moon? I've been in the Barrows for years."

Flynn shook his head. He couldn't possibly have answers. He stayed with the immediate. "And Dacardi's boy?"

"I don't know, but when it comes to things like this, there are no coincidences."

Dacardi walked in. He sat at a chair behind the desk, his face cold and closed. Again, he reminded me of Nefertiti when she readied herself to strike. "Well, what was it?" His voice held no emotion at all.

I had to give him some answers.

"This isn't easy, Dacardi, but at least your grandmother taught you to believe. Flynn's not had that luxury. There are places where the separation between worlds is thin enough to allow an interaction between them. That's the Barrows."

I told him of the Earth Mother and the Darkness, and the Barrows prison, adding the things I hadn't told Flynn, the things he had to see for himself.

Dacardi's face had no expression. "The kids?"

"Are used as servants, soldiers. Probably Hammer was one of them once. The Darkness is a powerful thing, but has to use others, invade their minds. It has no physical manifestation in this world. We, you, me, Flynn—we're all tiny parts in a larger plan."

"Then what do we need the bronze for?"

I spoke of the creatures living in the sewers. How they prowled the deserted streets on nights when they couldn't see the moon. "I don't know what they are, or where they came from, but bronze and fire kills them."

"They exist, Dacardi," Flynn assured him in a steady voice. "I've seen them. Up close."

Dacardi grunted. "I've seen demons before. My granny—evil, damned bitch—called them up in fire. Talked to them."

The criminal was, if nothing else, a practical man. He suddenly turned his attention to Flynn. "You and me going to have a problem? Over Hammer?"

Flynn shrugged. "We're going to have a problem someday, I expect, but not over Hammer. He had my sister, too. And as far as I could see, you—or Cass—didn't kill him."

Dacardi gave a short bark of a laugh. One totally without humor. "She's right. It wasn't Hammer. You saw."

Flynn's fingers tightened on my knee.

"It's okay, Flynn." I reached out and laid my hand on his shoulder. Monsters in the sewers, a tangible thing, were a long way from accepting pure magic like the Mother's passage through the world.

"Now what?" Dacardi demanded. "The thing in Hammer said it would see you under the dark moon. Motherfucker knows we're coming."

"Yeah, but it doesn't know from which direction. Little surprise there, I'll bet."

"Bet? What odds?"

"Not good, but I never let that stop me."

Dacardi nodded, his face bleak. "Me, neither."

chapter 19

Flynn and I left Dacardi at the warehouse and drove back toward Abby's. Night had fallen and I found roads that lay as far from the Barrows as possible. I drove past the run-down strip shopping centers, all-night drugstores, and used-auto dealerships. Behind them were small houses crowded so close to the street you had to look both ways before you stepped off your minuscule porch.

The area between the docks and the shadow of uptown's glass towers reeked of lower-middle-class life, people who lived in modest circumstances. Most would live out their lives never having seen anything other than what lay within the few square miles of Duivel. I suddenly realized I'd never seen great oceans or highest mountains. Farmers like my parents took few vacations. I had locked myself into the Huntress persona and it allowed no time off.

Flynn hadn't spoken for a while. "You okay?" I asked.

"Just thinking. It's only been a couple of days, but it feels right. You and me."

"I know." Amazing. The man actually thought about a relationship. In the middle of chaos he— But wait. How would I deal with this? I wasn't sure I was as capable of juggling this all at once.

"When I saw you in that stupid T-shirt, my first

thought was, 'That's for you, buddy.' It just popped into my head." He leaned back and relaxed.

Sure it did. Mom had laid her manipulating hand on him, too. "I don't know why," I said. "Let's face it. I'm not beautiful. Some malcontents say I have the personality of a pit bull."

"Malcontents? So it must be true."

"I'm not really a prize catch among women."

"Prize catch?" Flynn laughed. "I had one of those. Three years ago. She was rich enough for me to take care of Mama and Selene. I made my plans. Even rehearsed my proposal. Certainly my chosen bride was ready. Selene heard me and told my mother. Let's just say it was not a nice scene. Mother believes in marrying for love."

"Glad to hear that. *Do* you have a problem with what happened to Hammer? I mean, he's dead and Dacardi is going to dispose of the body."

"Your involvement with Dacardi and what it might lead to troubles me. Hammer, no. We didn't kill him. Did we?" He hesitated on that one.

"The stuff I fed him didn't. Abby doesn't do poison."

"There are some things I won't do to find Selene." He shifted uneasily in the seat.

"I know. That's why it might be best if you let me get her by myself."

"You're saying you're willing to do things I won't." Flynn's voice hardened around the words.

"Some. I'm not a psychopath, but I've been known to play judge and jury."

"That's comforting."

I heard bitterness, but I couldn't afford to be nice to him now. His sister's life could depend on my actions over the next couple of days.

Flynn asked me to take him to the station house so he could write his report on the weapons. We stopped by my apartment so he could retrieve his badge. He said he'd take a cab and meet me at Abby's later. He was quiet, so I figured he needed time away from me to think.

Dacardi had said, "Motherfucker knows *we're* coming." That meant he intended to come along for the ride. His son, his guns, I guess he had the right. Unlike my guerrilla attacks, that kind of strike force would need streets to travel and there wasn't a map anywhere.

I called Thor, my computer geek.

"Static resistance rules," Thor answered.

"Hey, circuit man."

"Cass." Thor sounded delighted to hear from me, which was weird because I owed him money.

"You get a machine to search for me this week?"

"Oh, yeah." He laughed. "And when I told the guy your previous balance, he—"

"Tossed money at you. Great. I need something. Can you find me any aerial photos of the city? And print them out if you do?"

"You're kidding, right?" He sounded indignant, as if I had challenged his superior intelligence. "How close you want?"

"Close enough to show buildings and roads."

"Come get it."

"Don't you ever sleep?" I asked.

"Sleep? Waste all that time?"

I hung up.

Thor leased a narrow storefront in a strip shopping center that had seen better days. Half the glass-front shops stood empty, and those occupied ranged from the Hallowed Church of the Steadfast Savior to Clara's Thrift Shop and Harmon's Used Appliances. He ignored city codes and lived in the shop's back room to guard his merchandise. A single geek didn't need much space.

I drove to the murky, shadow-filled delivery alley behind the strip and parked near the ten-foot concrete block wall that buffered houses on the other side from the commercial center. A door painted with a bright yellow hammer and lightning bolt marked Thor's place. I stood in front of the peephole, punched the buzzer, and beat on the door with my fist. Getting Thor's attention required a bit of effort at times.

Finally, he opened the door. "Greetings," he said. "You're early."

"Sorry. I'm on a mission." I gave him my best smile.

Thor barely reached five-four and weighed a hundred and ten pounds. A disadvantage in many places, but in a world run by computers, he could cut anyone down in a heartbeat—or a few clicks of a key.

I followed him into his workroom, where a myriad of machines lined the walls. Such gadgets were beyond me. My highest level of technical ability involved a simple cell phone and an ATM machine.

"You find anything on that boy's machine I had someone bring to you?"

"Nothing you usually look for. Kid was into creepy stuff. Hard drive full of really sick music, too."

A subjective opinion since Thor, unlike many of his kind, preferred classical symphonies to rock and roll.

Thor led me to a computer with a coffee table–sized screen. He sat in the chair facing it and motioned for me to drag up another. His baggy clothes made him look like a boy ready to play a game. He hunched over the keyboard and his fingers danced along them like a pianist at a grand piano. "This is the latest satellite the Ruskies sent up. Better than their usual crap."

"You read Russian?"

"I read computer." He tapped a few more keys. "Here's Duivel."

The main uptown plaza stood out at the city's center, with the spikes of multistoried glass-walled buildings surrounding it.

"Great, Thor, but I want the Barrows. Southwest, between the plaza and the docks."

He scrolled the picture to show the docks, but went too far west and cut off the Barrows in favor of the green-and-brown morass of Misfortune Swamp across the river.

"Thor, move the picture a half mile to the northeast. Can you do that?"

He moved it, but skipped over the Barrows again and picked up small towns outside the city. Amazing. The Mother's *You won't notice me—I'm not here* spell had grown to exert its influence miles beyond its borders to catch even Thor.

The screen went blank. Thor sat staring, his fingers poised above the keys.

"Mother help me," I muttered. I leaned close and spoke into his ear. "You are the best, Thor. There is no place in the world you can't go. Are you going to let this beat you?"

"No!" He gritted his teeth and punched the keys. In seconds, we had the city in view.

"Show me how to move the picture," I said.

He passed me the mouse. "Hold the left button down and slide it around."

"Close your eyes," I ordered.

With a bit of clumsy mouse maneuvering, the Barrows came into view. "I'm too close. How do I back out a little?"

Thor opened his eyes. He drew a sharp breath. "What the . . . ?"

"That's the Barrows, circuit man." The spell broke once he actually saw it.

For ten years, I'd walked the Barrows, and with the exception of the Zombie Zone, I thought I knew it well. No matter where, underground or above, the compass points are burned into my brain like animal migration instinct. I don't get lost. From its place in the high, cold reaches of space, the satellite's camera gave me a perfect view of the Barrows' street grid. I sat with my mouth open, staring at the screen, until Thor's voice cut through my shock.

"Hey!" He bumped me with his elbow. "You okay?"

"Oh, yes."

I'd noticed that the streets met at odd angles in places, but from the ground I had no idea they formed a perfect giant pentagram with the Zombie at its heart. The points of the star were marked with buildings constructed at cross-angles, and the lines were the widest streets.

My skin prickled and I shivered. I knew where I had to be on the dark moon. The magical convergence of planets and stars, the thinning of barriers that Abby and the Earth Mother spoke of, would remain a mystery. I had no grasp of such arcane matters. But I would go where I had to go to get the job done. I reached out and laid my finger on the screen. "I need this printed. Can you do that?"

"Sure." Thor's voice was soft. "I never saw it before."

"You've seen it; you just never paid attention."

Discomfort flickered across Thor's face. Like most scientific types, he didn't like mystery or mysticism. For him, magic was a sword-and-sorcerer video game. His eyes narrowed and his mind focused on something *he* considered more logical. "You're not the FBI or something, are you?"

I had to laugh. "Come on, buddy. If I were a cop, I'd have busted you in June when you had your back room full of new laptops. You can classify me as an 'or something.' Gotta go."

Not being a techno person, I'd never thought of an aerial view until now. Might have saved me time and kept me from some dangerous situations. I knew the big storm sewers followed the street grid, so they made the same pentagram belowground. Thor printed the picture on an eleven-by-seventeen page, which I folded and stuffed in my pocket.

"Thanks, Thor. I owe you big-time," I said as I walked to the back door.

"I take cash," he called after me as I stepped outside.

Exultation at my find made me careless. The door had no more than closed behind me when a gun barrel jammed into my back.

chapter 20

"Hello, bitch," Pericles Theron's voice said from behind me.

I froze.

"Don't have pretty boy Michael standing between us now, do we?" Theron backed off on the gun. "Search her," he ordered.

One of his goons from the Goblin Den walked around to face me—the one Michael had bounced off the wall last night. He ran his hands down my body and under my jacket. He relieved me of my gun, but I raised my arms to facilitate his search and he missed the knife strapped on my arm under the jacket sleeve. Stupid bastard was more interested in feeling my tits. When he finished, I faced Theron. A cast covered his arm from wrist to elbow.

He shook the cast at me and bared his teeth like a dog threatening to bite. "I fucking ought to beat you to death with this."

"You're going to need more than a cast when Michael—"

"Michael won't know shit. Son of a bitch. I saw him. I saw *you*. Cops took my guns. Three million fucking dollars' worth." His voice rose to a shout.

"Your guns? What are you—?"

"Got me an army, whore." He gave a nasty laugh. "I'm gonna own this town. Dirty little Bastos come together for me. I'm gonna be king of the Barrows."

I could see Theron dealing in guns and explosives, but he didn't have the brains or balls to bring rival Bastinado gangs together. So who did?

"You're gonna be king, Theron? Who's king now?"

Theron grinned. "You don't know shit."

The door to Thor's shop swung open and he stepped out. "Cass, are you—?"

Theron pointed the gun at him.

I grabbed Theron's arm and twisted his gun hand toward his own man. The gun roared, and the blast, amplified by the semienclosed space, hammered my eardrums. The bullet slammed into the goon's shoulder. He crumpled on the pavement.

I had a firm grip on Theron. He wailed as I broke his good arm and twisted the gun from his hand.

His man with the shoulder wound lay flat on his back, but managed to draw. As he pulled the trigger, I shoved Theron between us. The high-powered round slammed into Theron's body. It punched on through his flesh and hit me in the right side.

I fell to my knees and clamped my hands over a wound that burned like someone jammed me full of hot coals. My liver, maybe stomach. Not my heart, but a killing shot anyway. I tried to scream and liquid filled my lungs. For ten years, I'd offered my life in the Earth Mother's name. This time she'd accept the sacrifice.

Thor recovered from his shock and rushed to me. "I'll call—"

"No." I reached out and grabbed his shirt with a bloody hand. More blood bubbled out of my mouth. I was concerned with Theron's goon hurting him, but the man lay unmoving, with Theron's body sprawled over him. He'd probably lost enough blood to take him out.

"Take me to . . ." Blood sprayed with each word. I longed to go to the place where I felt safest. Abby's house. But Thor had no idea where that would be, and no way to get me there.

"Cass!" Thor cried.

His voice came from a distance as I moved on to life's next phase. Pain faded and my limbs went numb. My heart beat wild, frantically, starving for the blood pouring out of my side. As it fluttered for the last time, sight faded in my eyes until only one pinpoint remained—a single star in a midnight sky. I reached for that star, desperately longing for its light. Everything was as it should be in a perfectly ordered and peaceful universe.

She arrived instantly. The Mother had come to take me home.

"Oh, no, Huntress." Her voice shook the darkness like thunder in the night. "I've gone to too much trouble for this."

I returned to my body in an agonizing avalanche. I've had Abby heal me with potions and magic, a gentle thing filled with love. The Earth Mother's healing poured into me like a giant ocean wave of power. Power that picked me up, rolled me over, and slammed me to the ground before it coughed me up on an asphalt beach.

Abby once told me that earth magic was as powerful in a sparrow's wing as it was in the claws of a grizzly bear. The Mother used claws on me. She stitched my torn organs with threads of molten lava and bathed them in an acid antiseptic. Tremendous pressure tightened on my chest, and I choked and spewed scarlet fluid as she cleansed my lungs of blood. My heart beat again and pushed a river of fire through my body.

If I could have found a voice then, they'd have heard me shrieking in uptown Duivel. Shrieking in agony. Shrieking in pure hatred of the power that dragged me back into a world where I no longer belonged.

As suddenly as she arrived, between one heartbeat and the next, the Mother departed. I came back to the world and found myself on my hands and knees, gasping for breath. Pain had receded, but the searing memory would never leave. My body quivered, glowed. My arms shimmered with light, white as a full moon.

Thor sat with his back against the door. His wide-eyed, openmouthed face looked like he'd been struck with the hammer and lightning bolt painted above him.

"Help me," I gasped. If I moved, I'd topple over.

Thor just stared, his mouth open.

Oh, shit. My hands, my arms, glowed with silver light. "Please," I begged.

Thor shook his head, as if he needed to toss out a bad dream. He crawled to me, then reached out a tentative hand to touch the glowing skin on my arm. As he did, the shine faded, leaving me as near normal as I'd ever been.

"You okay?" Thor asked.

"Yeah. It's not as bad as it looks." Strength seeped back into me, but blood soaked my clothes from my shirt to the knees of my jeans.

Thor helped me to my feet. "You were . . . shining. You *shined*."

I swayed, hoping I wouldn't fall on top of him.

"Come on." My voice sounded like I had bronchitis. "We need to clean up this mess." Sirens came in the distance. Someone in the residential area over the wall must have heard the shots and called 911. "There's no way we can explain this to the cops."

I staggered to my car and opened the trunk. A struggle, since I still felt drained. From the look of things, Theron's man had bled out from the shoulder wound. Thor helped me lift and mash him and Theron in, but he had to jump up on the trunk lid to get it closed and latched. Maybe the damned thing wouldn't pop open if I hit a bump. Messy, nasty business. A late-model sedan was parked at the end of the alley, but I couldn't deal with that. I doubted the car would be registered to Theron, and most likely he covered his tracks when it came to such things.

The sirens came closer.

I was, however, curious. "Bodies don't bother you, Thor?"

"Nah. Worked nights in the city morgue in college. Really quiet."

Maybe, but his shoulders hunched and his hands were shaking.

"You have to come with me," I said.

Thor nodded. Then he frowned. "Look." He pointed at the spot where the two men had died. There was no trace of blood. Even the trail leading to my car had disappeared. The Mother had conveniently cleaned up after us. My clothes were sopping and that was fine since I never wanted her to touch me again. If my little journey into a past life were true, she'd allowed me to throw my beloved child into a hideous blaze. When I'd accepted the duties as the Huntress, I'd felt special. I had a mission. Now I knew I was simply being used. A tool. One she tortured to drag back to life and be used again.

I climbed in the car, jammed the key in the ignition, and twisted.

Nothing happened.

"Not again!" I screamed and slammed my fist into the dash. "Lying bastard of a mechanic."

I turned the key again.

The dash lights came on.

Another time.

The engine turned over but didn't catch.

Thor whimpered.

Again.

The engine thumped and chattered like teeth in a blizzard, then smoothed.

I headed out and rolled onto the street as the first patrol car pulled into the strip center's parking lot. Such a fun night, driving a car wearing blood-soaked clothes, carrying a very frightened computer geek as a passenger, and hauling a trunk full of bodies. Things to do: take a bath, get Abby to erase Thor's memory, dispose of bodies. And, oh, yes, try to forget what it felt like to be shot, start to die, and have a power beyond comprehension drag me back. I doubted even Abby could do that for me.

"You okay?" I glanced at Thor. He made a honking sound, stuck his head out the window, and puked for half a mile. He gagged a little when he finished and slumped back down on the seat like a rag doll.

"Hey, buddy, I thought bodies didn't bother you?"

"Don't." His voice wavered and squeaked like a teenage boy with fluctuating hormones. "Bodies in trunk. Police."

"Yeah, that would be inconvenient." And Flynn would be justifiably pissed.

Thor once spent three months in jail for hacking into the Duivel National Bank. He didn't steal any money; it was more of a challenge thing. The jail was minimum security, but it scared him. If they caught us with bodies, the stakes would be higher than a bit of keyboard finger play or a room full of laptops with questionable ownership. Especially since those bodies had bullet holes. I'm sure he imagined himself spending many years in state prison, sharing a cell with Bruiser Big Dog.

"Thor, I know you don't understand, but when we get to my friend's house, I'll explain."

"You were beautiful." Thor sighed. "When you were glowing. Not when you were shot."

I didn't know what to say, so we rode in silence after that. I drove into Abby's driveway and pulled the car around to the back. It would be harder to see. Then I led

Thor inside and sat him at Abby's kitchen table. Only then did I realize how lucky I'd been. Flynn hadn't arrived yet. The instinct that led me to Abby's house had overridden the knowledge that he would be there at any time.

"Thor's had a rough evening," I said to an, as usual, calm and levelheaded Abby.

"Is any of that blood yours?" Abby asked, nodding at my clothes.

"All of it is mine. But I'm okay."

Abby gazed into Thor's eyes as he sat frozen in his chair. When she turned back to me, he stayed lost in his trance. He would remember nothing of the evening.

Before Abby could say anything else, I grabbed her telephone and dialed Dacardi.

"Yeah." He answered on the first ring.

"I need your help, fast. I have some good leads, but there was a problem." I started to speak again, then stopped. "Is this phone . . . ?"

"Not tapped. Guaranteed. How about yours?"

I glanced at Abby. She gave me an insulted look. Of course she would take care of minor things like spelling her phone line for privacy.

I went back to my call. "I have something I need to get rid of."

"What?"

"Bodies. Two of them."

Dacardi chuckled. "I'm getting to like you. Your cop—"

"Doesn't know and doesn't need to." I started to pray to the Mother not to let Flynn find out, then remembered I wasn't speaking to the insufferable hag.

"I'll send a couple of guys," Dacardi said.

"There's another problem."

"What?"

"One of the bodies is Pericles Theron."

Dacardi didn't say anything.

"He tried to kill me!" I yelled.

"Okay, okay," Dacardi grumbled. "Fucker owed me money. Dead men don't pay bills. You'd better find my boy. That witch's house?"

"Yeah."

Dacardi hung up.

I gave Abby a brief description of what had happened.

"She came to you." Abby rubbed her face with her hands. "And healed you. That's not the way. She doesn't . . ."

"I was dying. Then I wasn't." A great deal of physical and emotional upheaval came between those two little sentences, but I needed time before I spoke of the event again.

I heard a vehicle pull in, so I went outside and opened the trunk of my POS. A van backed up the driveway toward me. Two men jumped out. The only light came from the kitchen windows, but it was enough for me to recognize Dacardi's men. They started toward me, then suddenly stopped. I realized that I had drawn my gun—or maybe it was my bloody clothes. The light wasn't that dim.

"Sorry," I said. "I've had a rough night." I walked back toward the house. This was their job, not mine.

"Holy shit!" one of the men behind me exclaimed.

"Damn! I forgot the plastic tarp." The other one wasn't happy, either.

I left them to deal with the disposal problem.

When I walked into the kitchen, Thor sat hypnotized at the kitchen table.

"You go downstairs and clean up," Abby said. "I've called a cab for this young man. We'll talk more tomorrow."

Doors slammed outside and the van drove away. That didn't take long. Experienced corpse handlers, Dacardi's guys.

My body longed for rest, but I had another problem. "My trunk is full of blood. I need to clean it."

"I'll take care of it." She sounded annoyed. "And the next time you have a body to dispose of, talk to me first. I *do* have a fast-acting compost pile."

I choked. The mental image of Theron and his goon buried and rotting in Abby's compost pile was too much for that night.

A horn sounded out front. Thor's cab. Abby beckoned and he followed her. He was going home with a dreamy smile on his face and no memory of the evening's events. Wish I could do the same.

I opened the pantry door, went in, and tugged on the false shelves at the back wall. The rooms downstairs had magical wards that no one could see. They gently brushed my skin as I passed through them. No stranger would enter this place. Anyone searching Abby's house would swear it sat on a slab and had no basement. The basement has a bathroom and the bed where I've spent many hours recovering from injuries. I lifted the paper with the aerial photo out of my jacket pocket. No blood. I sighed. All that trouble for a single piece of paper.

I showered, wrapped myself in a large towel, and lay on the bed for a few moments. It was one o'clock in the morning and I'd been going for eighteen hours straight. If I could lie there for thirty minutes, I'd probably be okay. The bed felt good and I closed my eyes.

Next thing I knew, Abby was gently shaking me.

chapter 21

"How are you, love?" Abby asked. She smoothed a hand over my forehead.

"I'm fine," I lied. My body ached and memories overwhelmed me. Yesterday, I fell in the Barrows' storm sewers with Flynn and Michael, had the Darkness taunt me, Pericles Theron's goon killed me, and the Mother healed me with an iron hand. I shivered.

Abby gripped my face in her gentle hands. "Lie still. You're in pain."

I relaxed and let her touch me. She slowly ran her hands down my body, stopping at my shoulders to knead the joints. Warmth spread as I healed. Abby's power to heal comes from the earth, but she has to make an offering, part of her own life force. I knew what it cost her. In a few moments, I felt much better and even yesterday's terrible events seemed more distant and less traumatizing.

"There," Abby said. "It's all I can do now, but a little tea will help." Her shoulders slumped and dark circles formed under her eyes.

"Thank you, Abby." I sat up and hugged her. "Did Flynn call?"

"He called at seven this morning and asked me not to disturb you if you were sleeping. He said there were more questions and paperwork. He'd be delayed."

A twinge of disappointment must have shown on my face.

"Don't worry, love. He said he'd see you as soon as possible. I heard a great deal of stress in his voice."

Stress? Not surprising. Ten years as the Huntress, I'd never had anything that approached yesterday and last night.

I showered again and dressed. I always kept clothes at Abby's house in case I needed to crash before I went on. She offered to let me live with her, but I'm a loner by nature and I wouldn't want her to know some things. She'd cleaned the blood off my boots and placed them by the bed.

When I went upstairs, I found Abby sitting at the kitchen table staring at a pile of garbage. I sat and glanced at the scattered sticks, bones, rocks, and feathers.

"What are you doing?" I asked.

"Trying to read the future." She almost snarled the words. Obviously, she wasn't having much success. The business of reading objects was way out of her field, but it was better than her venture into pyromancy, when she'd set the kitchen on fire. I'd thought the incident ended her excursions into alternative methods of magic. She'd accept the Mother's gifts and leave the exotic stuff to others.

"See!" She pointed at assorted objects. "It shows a kind of chaotic roller coaster, up and down and—"

"Sounds like my life."

Abby scooped the objects up and dropped them in a leather bag. She handed it to me.

"You cast then."

I reached for the bag with a reluctant hand, rolled it

around, and dumped the contents on the table. With impossible precision, they fell in the exact same configuration as before.

"Oh, dear," Abby said. "That is impossible. They're saying we can't change the future. I don't believe it."

She gathered the things, stuffed them back in the bag, opened a kitchen drawer, and tossed it in. She wiped her hands on her skirt as if she'd dirtied them. Then she went to the sink, covered her palms with soap, and scrubbed under running water. "Now let's get you some breakfast." Abby always liked to feed me.

Flynn called as I was finishing eating.

"Hi," he said. "Did you rest?" His voice sounded cool and empty.

"Yes. Abby gave me some great tea. I'm fine now."

"There are questions about the guns, Cass. And more questions about Exeter Street."

"Who connected me with Exeter Street?"

"I don't know. No one will talk to me."

My world closed down on me. I heard it in his voice and understood, because I'd heard it from men before. The cold, impersonal tone that said he needed to distance himself from me. Men sounded like that when they couldn't deal with my strangeness anymore. I'd dumped an incredible dose of that strangeness on Flynn. I'd never really cared before, but this time I did. This time it mattered.

"I'll call you later," Flynn said. He hung up.

"I'll find Selene," I said to a dead phone.

"Have a little faith in him, love," Abby said from across the room.

I shrugged. After all, or maybe because of all we'd been through, Flynn was drawing away.

I'd gain nothing wallowing in self-pity, so I pushed it aside and decided to head back to the Barrows. My usual sources might not give me information on Richard and Selene because of Michael's offer of a fantastic reward, but who knows what I might stir up if I dug around.

I wore jeans and a loose button-down shirt with an inner pocket originally designed for a traveler's money and papers. I also slipped the small bottle of truth potion in my pocket. Never can tell when you might have to give someone a dose of honesty.

Nirah stretched out on Abby's kitchen window sunning herself, and she didn't object when I picked her up and carefully slid her into the pocket. She squirmed and made herself comfortable. I didn't want to carry a gun in broad daylight since I might have to go somewhere besides the Barrows.

Nefertiti wasn't around, but Horus sat on the back porch staring at the bird feeder, where several warblers, blissfully unaware of possible disaster, pecked at seeds. I bent to scratch his ears and he growled at me. I sympathized with his frustration and left him alone.

A car wreck I couldn't get around had me sitting in a hundred-degree oven for an hour, so by the time I arrived at the Lost Lamb, I found Vic and his helpers finishing their daily handout of bagged lunches and bottled water. He grabbed two bags, led me upstairs, dug around in a small refrigerator stuck in a closet, and brought out two generic-brand colas. We sat at his desk and ate lunch. I wasn't that hungry, but he really seemed to enjoy my company.

"Have you found out where the Butcher Boys have your girl?" I asked.

"Yes. She'd escaped again and gone home."

I breathed an inward sigh of relief. I needed to find Selene and Richard, not take on the Butcher Boys for his missing girl, even though I knew it meant a lot to him.

I'd spent the whole morning trying not to think. An earthshaking event loomed the following night on the dark moon, and I had no idea of what it could be. I felt no responsibility for Pericles Theron's death, but I'd bet his disappearance would have ramifications all through the Barrows eventually.

"Cassandra! Cass!" Vic had his hand on my arm.

"What?" I jumped and reached for my gun, then realized I'd left it at Abby's.

"I've been calling your name. Were you that deep in thought? It's not like you to be so distracted."

"No, but even I think occasionally." I smiled and the concern on his face faded. "Hey, Vic, who do you think is the strongest, Pericles Theron and his bunch, or the Bastinados?" I had to speak in present tense. Right now, very few people knew Theron was dead.

"Theron." Vic's voice was firm. "The Bastinados are vicious, some even intelligent, but they have small minds far more interested in personal power and protecting their turf. Theron is organized."

That wasn't my image of Theron, but I was wrong on a regular basis. "And if someone could organize the Bastinados? Give them terrorist-type weapons?"

Vic shuddered.

"Yeah. That's how I feel."

"I heard the police found a warehouse full of arms yesterday. You think that's what they were for? Someone organizing that particular evil?"

"Maybe," I said. "Maybe wishful thinking, too."

"How much power would it take to organize psychopaths like the Bastinados? Control them. You have to admit it's an intriguing idea."

"Intriguing? No, but it would take more 'power' than you could get from money and guns." I stood. How odd that such a gentle man would think the idea intriguing rather than horrifying. Such a battle would destroy him and his mission.

"Gotta go, Vic. Thanks for lunch."

"Day-old sandwiches and stale cookies? You're quite welcome, my dear." He waved a friendly hand at me. "I know you're tired of me saying it, but please be careful."

I stopped inside the front door and checked on Nirah. "You okay, baby?" I said softly.

Nirah squirmed and stuck her head out of the pouch. It lay right between my breasts. "Okay, little girl, get ready. Next stop won't be as easy as Reverend Vic."

If someone asked me to describe my relationship with the Slum Devil Bastinados, I'd have to say cautious—extremely cautious. My caution, since the gang didn't give a shit. They tolerated me on occasion because, first, they knew I was as vicious and deadly in my own way as they were, and, second, I'd saved Big Devil Snag Shuster's life one night. A bunch of monsters had Snag cornered, and I mistook him for a decent human being and rescued his ass. I have no illusions of his true nature. If I stood between him and something he wanted, he'd turn on me like a shark with a whiff of blood in the water.

The nocturnal Bastinado gangs moved their headquarters often, so I had to give an early-rising prostitute twenty dollars to tell me the location of the Devils' current hangout. They rarely ventured more than two or three blocks from River Street, but that covered a good deal of territory. I had to give her another ten to make sure Snag was still top Devil. I wasn't universally popular with the gang membership, and walking in on a new leader could get me killed.

I parked in front of the building, once a warehouse, and approached with my hands held out to show I didn't have any weapons. I didn't see anyone outside, but the door creaked open ahead of me as I entered. I stood unmoving while my eyes adjusted to the dimmer light streaming through high windows around the building. The stink of beer, urine, and other unsavory odors filled the air, but, thank the Mother, no stash of weapons and explosives appeared.

"Hey, witchy. You too late for the party," Snag called to me from across the room.

Witchy. Ugh. I hated that. I had used one of Abby's repellant potions to rescue Snag from the monsters that night. Using a magic potion made me a witch in his eyes.

Snag sat in a plastic chair with his back to a wall, wearing nothing but extraordinarily worn and dirty jocks. I kept my eyes on his face because part of his equipment peeked out from one stretched-out leg hole in the jocks. Some things I didn't want to see.

Mattresses scattered on the floor held gang members not on guard duty, either alone or with their girls. Most slept, but a few engaged in other, more personal activities.

Snag's dirty blond hair fell in strings down his shoulders and his ribs curved in on one side, making his thin body lopsided. He had a serious limp, too. Not exactly a prime male specimen, but he held the great equalizer, a .357 Magnum, balanced on his thigh. Intelligent, but completely lacking in any sense of morality, he made the perfect Bastinado leader, even if he did have to kill one of his own men occasionally to prove his management skills.

A naked woman sat in another plastic chair next to him. Her tattooed breasts drooped like wilted flowers, a woman old enough to be his mother. Probably wasn't, but the Barrows aged everyone who stayed here too long.

Snag reached over, grabbed her by the hair, and jerked her out of the chair. She slammed to the concrete floor with a single cry of pain. Great Mother help her. She crawled away whimpering.

"Sit down." Snag pointed at the chair he'd forcibly vacated for me. "Someone get her a cold one." He shouted the words to the room in general. He had a raspy, croaking voice, as if he'd been chewing dry crackers and needed water to wash them down.

The last thing I wanted was to sit in that chair. Oh, damn. Such an honor to sit by the Big Devil. I forced my mouth into a fake smile and sat.

Snag silently laughed at me. He'd marked my revulsion.

One of the girls came running over with a cold beer. At least it had a sealed cap.

"You should be my woman," Snag said. He gestured at the gang and chuckled. "All this could be yours, too."

I'd give Snag one thing: he had a wicked sense of humor. He wasn't stupid. Vicious, yes, but not stupid.

I laughed a little at his joke. "You mean you'd share, Snag?"

His gaze ran up and down my body. "I will if you will."

"I'm flattered, Snag, but I already have someone. You understand."

Snag's good humor held. "Yeah, guess you get enough. Hear you doing that pretty boy *and* the cop."

I winked at him. "I am truly blessed these days."

No secrets in the Barrows and no point in letting him know I wasn't "doing" Michael as well as Flynn. No cop scared a Bastinado unless the entire force descended en masse, but I'd always heard that everyone walked wide around Michael.

Snag chuckled. "Got something for you." He waved his hand and one of the gang brought him a wadded-up bloody rag.

"Aw, you shouldn't have." My stomach churned.

Snag unfolded the rag and lifted out a chain with the gang's devil head insignia stamped on a pendant attached to one link. He offered it to me. "Motherfucker don't need it anymore."

I could only assume the said "motherfucker" was dead now. "The Devil chains have to be earned, Snag. I haven't—"

Snag broke out in loud, shrill laughter, exposing a mouthful of blackened teeth. The rest of the gang laughed with him. Forced mirth, but when the Big Devil laughed, they laughed with him. He tossed the chain at me. I caught it and turned it in my hands. At least the blood was dried.

"You did the Slashers, Witchy. Think we wasn't watching the motherfuckers? Took 'em down and blew them to hell in little fucking pieces."

I winced. "An accident, Snag. Only an accident."

"Don't matter. They roach shit now."

"How about you? Nobody's offered *you* guns? Explosives?"

Snag's smile faded. "Who's asking? You or the cop?"

"Me. Exeter Street almost killed me. And there was another, a warehouse."

He nodded. "Heard that. Cops got those. You were there, though. Heard that, too."

"Another accident. Someone's passing out serious shit like a dirty old man handing out candy to little girls. Maybe the Devils should get in on the action. Don't want to be the last kids on the block to get the new toys."

Snag grunted. He stared around at his gang. They stared back with watchful eyes. Communal living left little room for secrets, and every man wanted a chance to be Big Devil. I used to be curious how Snag reached his status, given his physical limitations, but then I began to understand his level of intelligence when it came to the Barrows' streets. Under different circumstances, with an education—and a good doctor for his physical problems—Snag would make a hell of a lawyer or stock-broker.

"Contacted the man," Snag said. "Ain't heard nothing—yet. You keep blowing 'em up and calling the cops, won't be none left."

"If only that were true. Tell me who the *man* is, and maybe I can make sure no one gets any more excess firepower. You get into that kind of war, they'll send in the big boys. National guard has tanks, big guns." I had no earthly idea what the national guard had, and I hoped Snag didn't, either.

"I'll think about it." He reached over and slapped my knee. "Now. Since you're an official Devil, you got to be nish-e-ated."

Damn! That didn't sound good. "Taking out the Slashers wasn't enough?"

"Naw. You got to do three of the boys." He leered and waved his hand in the general direction of the assembled lesser Slum Devils. "You can take your pick."

"Is that how you made it? Was it fun? Which three boys did *you* choose?"

Snag howled with laughter, slinging his head. Thin wet droplets whipped off his hair and hit me in the face. I'd have to scrub my skin raw to get it off.

The gang didn't laugh with him this time. Snag was making a joke at my expense—I hoped—since the usual initiation involved killing and kidnapping.

When he calmed, I asked, "Why don't I break a few bones? Breaking bones is a lot more fun than sex."

More laughter from Snag and dirty looks from the gang. I needed to get out. I'd learned very little for my time and effort, and the longer I hung around, the greater the danger. Eventually someone would challenge me.

Snag's hand tightened on the pistol. His eyes narrowed and he made a barely audible rumble in his throat. A bare-chested bruiser shuffled toward us. Serious tattoos covered his arms and shaved head. He stood at least six-five, and his massive bare beer gut spilled over his belt. He appeared dangerous, but not very smart. The butt of a pistol stuck out his pants pocket.

"What you want, Pogo?" Snag spoke as if asking for the time of day.

Pogo? He had to be kidding.

Pogo pointed at me. "Bitch. I'll teach her some manners."

Snag smiled. "Nah. Too dangerous. Wouldn't want my main man to get hurt."

Pogo sneered.

"Tell you what, Pogo." Snag's eyes had a calculating look. "You take the witch, you can have her, teach her all you want. But I get—" He stared around the room. "Dawn, get your ass over here."

Snag's voice sounded like he wanted to negotiate. I knew better. The Big Devil didn't negotiate anything.

Pogo growled like a bulldog.

A pale, pitifully thin girl in shorts and a torn T-shirt came forward. Part of one breast peeked from a tear in the shirt, but she didn't seem to care. She didn't look over fourteen. Head bowed, eyes on the concrete floor, she locked her bony arms across her stomach, as if those brittle sticks would protect her.

I couldn't afford pity at that moment. I couldn't afford justifiable rage. They make me weak. Calculated justice, though—I could do that.

Snag nodded. "Okay, Pogo. You take the witch, you get an extra twenty percent of the next haul. She takes you, I get Dawn."

Pogo made a chuffing sound I took to be laughter. "She ain't no witch. Just another stinking whore."

Snag spared me a single glance, and that said everything. Pogo was a problem Snag wanted me to remove.

My reaction to Dawn's abuse was a sure thing in his eyes. Getting others to do the dangerous dirty work was one way he stayed Big Devil.

I rubbed my hands together in fake anticipation. "Tell you what, Snag. I take Pogo and *I* get Dawn. I'm thinking of branching out into girls anyway." I flicked my thumb over Nirah's pocket. She had already moved into position.

The woman Snag had thrown out of the chair had crawled around and crouched at his other side. He bopped her on the head with his gun. Hit her hard enough to make her teeth click together. She smiled at him, adoration filling her eyes. "Deal," Snag said. "I don't like 'em that young anyway."

I laid the Devil chain—my Devil chain—on my chair and stood to face Pogo.

"Don't have any guns with me, Pogo. Is it too much to expect a bastard—sorry, Bastinado—to play fair?" Nirah inched up. She had a three-foot strike range, but if she fell on the floor, some overzealous shit might try to shoot her.

Pogo smelled like he'd dabbed eau de Dumpster perfume behind his ears. He obliged me by moving closer and giving me a gap-toothed grin. He stood almost a foot taller than me and outweighed me by at least one hundred and fifty pounds.

I moved my breasts within three inches of him.

He seized the back of my neck and dragged me against his stinking body.

Nirah barely had to move to nip him right in the middle of his chest.

Pogo froze.

I punched up with my left fist and knocked his hand loose from my neck. Then I stepped back. Didn't want him to fall on me. Nirah slipped back down in the pouch, out of sight.

I walked back, casually picked up the Devil chain, and sat beside Snag again.

Snag didn't say anything. He, like everyone in the room, had his eyes on Pogo.

Pogo remained upright. Unusual for someone bitten by Nirah, but he had extensive body mass for the venom to cover. He gasped, hiccupped, and dropped to his knees. His eyes bulged and bloody teardrops formed in the corners. His head bobbed up and down like the little hula doll my grandpa kept on the dash of his pickup truck. Nirah's poison finally completed the circuit and his nervous system shut down, his heart stopped. He toppled over and died.

For today, the Barrows held a little less filth. Guilt would never touch me on this one.

Silence held the room in a taut grip.

"Snag." He jumped when I said his name. "You have any more cold beer?"

Snag nodded and snapped his fingers. One of the girls brought me the beer. She offered the bottle at arm's length, then ran away the instant I had it in my hand.

Now all of the Slum Devils believed I was a witch. Not necessarily a bad thing. Bastinados lived in the Barrows and were, with good reason, a superstitious lot. Pogo's disbelief in my witch's power was foolhardy in their eyes. Certainly, Snag had faith in me, and the intelligence to maneuver me into solving his problem.

"Damn," Snag said softly. "I thought you'd knife him."

"What! And have him bleed all over me?" I wanted no more blood on me, thank you.

"Don't know if I want you a Devil, after all," he said.

"Aw, Snag, you've hurt my feelings."

Snag shrugged. "Don't know who the gunman is, but I'll find out."

"I appreciate that. Hardware like that is expensive. How'd the Slashers pay for it?"

Snag frowned. "Didn't pay. Otto, one of my guys, was on watch. Weird. First, I thought he got high. Drugging on the job. Seeing things. Don't think so now. He followed the Slashers into the Zombie."

"I'd have to be really high to follow a bunch of Bastinados into the Zombie, Snag."

"Me, too. Otto was a good little Devil, but he weren't too smart." He nodded at my Devil chain. Apparently, the dried blood had belonged to Otto. "Anyway, Slashers went together in a circle, made funny noises; then all the fuckers fell in line and kissed each other's asses. Then they got the stuff." Contempt filled Snag's voice. He probably didn't have weapons because whoever passed them out thought him too independent. He wouldn't get in line for anything. He'd described what Abby once described as ritual binding.

"How were they delivered?" I asked.

"Trucks. No markings. What you think, witch?"

"I think you should avoid ass kissing at all costs, Snag. Move to California, maybe. But I'd appreciate it if you'd get me a name first." I drained the beer and set the bottle on the concrete floor. "Let's go, Dawn."

Dawn made tentative steps toward me, but that required her to walk around Pogo's body. She stopped. In a single small gesture of defiance, she found a tiny sliver of courage. She spit on him.

Snag grunted. He pointed at Pogo. "How'd you . . . ?"

"Magic, Snag. Pure magic. Think hard about California."

chapter 22

Dawn didn't protest when we left. For some perverse reason, once some girls made it with a gang, they'd fight to stay there, no matter how brutal their treatment. Snag insisted I accept the gang chain. Big deal. Make the witch who single-handedly blasted the Slashers to hell an honorary Devil. I raised Snag's status in Bastinado land, at the cost of making him a little afraid of me. Maybe he'd come through with the name of the weapons dealer. I stuffed the chain under the seat to throw in the river later.

I tried again to dredge up some concern that I'd become a cold, efficient killer with unorthodox weapons. I couldn't find any remorse, in spite of my effort.

I drove Dawn to Sister Alice May's place, a two-story storefront at the edge of the Barrows. Sister Alice specialized in helping girls brutalized by Bastinados. She had a good success rate—maybe ten percent.

"You'll like Sister Alice," I told Dawn.

Dawn, who hadn't said a word until then, responded with a litany of obscene acts Pogo had forced on her since he'd snatched her leaving the mall one night. She gave no time frame. Maybe a month or even a year ago, but her torment stretched far too long. Her monotone voice sounded thin as her body, but when she reached the part about the "three-way" and "Boston Tea Party," I stopped listening. With great determination, she chewed on her fingernails between words.

How much hurt I could have laid on Pogo if I hadn't been in such a hurry. I should have used a knife—blinded him, cut his balls off, skinned him alive. Then I thought about doing the same to Snag, who richly deserved punishment. He let such things happen.

By the time we reached Sister Alice's place, Dawn had finished her litany. She wiped her bloody fingertips, minus nails, on her pitiful shirt and shorts. I had to help her out of the car and lead her to the shelter.

Sister Alice met us at the door. Her face contorted with rage. "Who did this to her?" She sighed and shook her head when I explained. Her anger softened to resignation. I expected she'd seen worse.

"He won't do it to anyone else, Sister." I offered the information without hesitation. I trusted Sister Alice as I trusted Vic.

She gave me a sad smile. "No, but there are others—though a few less of them, I hear." Half the Barrows probably knew about the Exeter Street explosion. And they believed I was responsible. I hadn't done a damn thing except run through a room followed by a hungry monster. Another day in the life of the Huntress.

Sister Alice found a place for Dawn and began the search for her parents. As I left, the image of Flynn finding Selene in Dawn's condition suddenly popped into my mind.

I checked my cell phone. No messages. I called Abby. Nothing from Flynn, either. Disappointed? Yes. I headed for the Archangel. Maybe Michael had some information.

Michael wasn't at the Archangel, but when I was heading out, his Jag pulled into the parking lot and stopped beside my car.

The passenger window slid down. "Get in," Michael said. "Please," he added when I raised my eyebrows.

"Okay, but you have to promise to behave." I opened the door.

"Oh, I promise." He winked at me.

I climbed in and the window slid closed. Within seconds the AC compensated for the steaming hot air that flooded in.

"Have you learned anything today?" Michael asked.

"Oh, yes. Stale cookies taste nasty. Someone's arming the gangs with heavy weapons. Orgies are a seriously sick way to have sex. Bastinados are *not* immune to snake venom." I shrugged. "That's it."

"Stale cookies—how dreadful. Let me take you to the Lace Curtain for an early dinner. Take your mind off such unsavory cuisine." He turned the Jag down onto Blanding Street and headed uptown. The five-star Lace Curtain, sitting atop the Princess Lily Hotel, charged a cop's monthly salary for a single meal. Like most places, Duivel's priorities sucked. An early dinner suited me, though. Only one problem.

"The Lace Curtain is a pretty fancy place, Michael. Let's hit a drive-through and pretend it's edible. I'm not really dressed and"—I peeked down my shirt—"I have a snake between my boobs."

"The snake is fine, but you're a bit shabby. There's a private dining room."

Flynn had accepted Nefertiti and Nirah, but not with the casual air of Michael, who'd seen far stranger things in the Barrows. If we managed to get through this and find Selene, he'd be gone. I tried to shake off the thought. I had to get out of my own head. Everything would depend on what happened during the dark moon, I supposed, and if I was able to rescue Selene. He'd never want me otherwise, because I'd always remind him of her—and my failure.

"Have you forgiven me for offering the reward?" Michael asked.

"Not forgiven. It takes too much energy to be mad and I've had too many things to do. Have you learned anything?"

"Not much, and I still can't find Hammer. That should have been easy."

"Hammer isn't a problem anymore." I wanted to move the conversation away from Hammer. "How'd you get so rich?" I asked. "Maybe I could invest my pissy little trust fund."

"I'll give you money if you'll take it."

"Shit. I don't want—"

"I know." He laughed. "Sorry. I forgot who I was talking to. Most women would—"

"Fall over and lick your feet."

"But not the Huntress." He reached over and stroked my hair.

"Nope." The only one I wanted to taste was Flynn.

Michael sighed. "To answer your question, my mother was an only child. Her parents were wealthy. They wanted nothing to do with her or me, but they did set up trust funds. I'm good at making money, too. I quadrupled my inheritance before I graduated from college. I had to. The family had locked Mother up at Candlewood. They kept her in a cage the size of a coffin and gave her shock treatments. I couldn't allow that to continue."

"I'm sorry."

Michael then asked me to tell him what happened at Avondale, right down to the smallest detail. He made no comment as I spoke, and offered no explanations when I finished.

"Here we are." He drove into the underground parking lot of the Princess Lily Hotel. "What does the snake like to eat?"

"She prefers live mice."

"Sounds delicious, but I don't know if it's on the menu."

"She'll settle for caviar." I lifted my shirt and peeked down at Nirah. "Won't you, baby? Get that nasty taste out of your mouth."

Michael laughed as the hotel's staff came running to open our doors and escort us to a private elevator for the forty-two-floor ride to the Lace Curtain restaurant—only it wasn't quite a restaurant.

chapter 23

I expected to see the restaurant when the elevator doors slid open. Instead, we exited onto a windowless, ten-square-foot vestibule with pink marble floors, gilded walls, and a single door across from the elevator. The door opened and a sharp-looking man in a gray suit and gold tie greeted us. His eyes played over me, but his face never lost its smiling, servile expression.

"Good afternoon, Mr. Michael," he said with a slight bow.

"Good afternoon." Michael gave the man one of those gracious nods he occasionally bestowed on his followers at the Archangel. "Ms. Archer and I will be dining in."

"Certainly, sir. I'll have the maître d' call, unless you prefer that he come up."

"A call will be fine. The wine . . . ?"

"Is chilled and ready." The man walked out and closed the door soundlessly behind him.

I studied my surroundings. "Hmm, this isn't the Lace Curtain."

Michael went to a sleek black marble bar. "The Curtain is two floors below us. This is my suite."

"Yeah, this looks more like you than the decadent O\ Oriental harem room at the Archangel."

I surveyed the elegant modern room, which screamed of luxury. It was masculine, powerful. A talented decorator had filled it with clean-cut furniture, leather, and brass accessories in a spacious area enclosed by sheets of glass windows. I gazed out the windows to the south, where the Barrows stretched in the distance. Today, a murky dirty brown haze spread over it, like oil skimming over a shallow pond.

"Decadent?" Michael came to stand beside me. "You mean my humble home?"

"Yes, your humble home."

"I come here occasionally. When I have to meet people I can't, or don't want to, take to the Archangel."

"So you rent hotel rooms?" I asked.

"No. This is the owner's suite."

Nirah's head slipped out of her pocket. He held out his hand and she glided onto it and up his arm. She stretched forward and her tongue flicked across his ear. His eyes never left me.

"Huntress, if only you would care for me as the little one does." Nirah kissed him, on the cheek, the lips, then glided across and onto his shoulder. "Was I getting close, before Flynn came along? If he left, would you come to me?"

I shook my head. "No."

That probably wasn't true. I would fight his attraction for the same reason I always had. Michael owned things—and people.

The phone rang.

I kept my face to the window wall as Michael sighed and answered. He told whoever called to send up some caviar immediately. He went back to the bar. "Come here, Cass. I'll behave."

He was on the other side of the bar, so I went to sit on one of the stools. Michael reached under the counter and handed me a bottle of beer. Expensive beer. He poured himself a glass of bloodred wine. Nirah curled on his shoulder, weaving her body in and out of his hair.

"The guns," he said. "Did you learn anything?"

The sudden change of subject caught me by surprise.

"Ah . . . they belonged to your Goblin Den partner, Theron. I talked to him last night. They're for his army of Bastinados. You know anything about an army? Theron said he was going to be the new king of the Barrows. Who's the current king? The one he plans to replace."

Michael frowned. "That can't be. He's hallucinating."

"Yeah, maybe." I sounded skeptical, for good reason. "That happens a lot in the Barrows."

"I'll take care of him, Cass. It's past time."

"Theron is not a problem now."

Michael cocked his head, suddenly interested. He stared at me for a long time. "Is there anything I need to do?"

"Find a new partner to run the Goblin Den." I could see from the expression on his face that he understood. "My, you have been a busy girl, haven't you?"

I shrugged. Neither Hammer nor Theron had died by my hand.

The doorbell chimed softly. Michael lifted Nirah off his shoulder, gently placed her on the bar, and went to answer it. When he returned, he held a shallow, plate-sized dish of slimy black beads. He set the dish on the bar and Nirah dove in, literally headfirst. She rolled and started scooping them up in great gulps. Michael sat on a stool beside me.

"So, Huntress, what do you think? You think I'm arming the Bastinados?"

I bit my lip. "I don't want it to be you. How much was the stuff in the warehouse worth? That many guns . . ."

"Millions. I'm having trouble with the concept of a petty pornographer like Pericles Theron purchasing and delivering that many weapons, even if he had the money. Two months ago, I learned that some of the Bastinado gangs had merged, and someone was arming them. It is not—was not—Theron. He had his fingers in it most likely, but he wasn't a power person."

"Little man with big ideas," I said. I smiled at his use of past tense. *Wasn't.*

"Indeed. Cass, this coming dark moon is—"

"Stop. I have to be in the Barrows tomorrow night. It's not negotiable."

Michael sighed. "Then I'll be with you. You don't know—"

"Right. I don't know. So tell me. I want to hear the words."

"Very well. I love you. I've loved you since the day you came charging into the Archangel's kitchen looking for that girl. You kicked my feet out from under me when I told you to leave."

"Damn! That wasn't what I wanted." I took a step back.

"What did you want?" His eyes sparkled and he laughed softly.

"The truth, Michael. The things I don't know. Who are you? What's your place in the Barrows?"

He stopped smiling. Cool, calm Michael returned, only this time without the usual arrogant amusement. "You once told me you desired me, Huntress, but you couldn't have everything you wanted. You have my love. That's all I can give you now."

Great Mother, what a pain in the ass.

Another phone rang, this time my cell. I stepped away from Michael and turned my back. This was far too intense for me. Flynn spoke when I answered.

"Come down to the Fourteenth Precinct station right away and give a statement on the guns." No greeting, no hello, no warmth touched his voice.

"Why?"

"Because you're going to be arrested for obstruction if you don't."

"Shouldn't we—?"

"Now, Cass. Right now!" He hung up.

Was someone listening to him? We really needed to get our stories straight if we were going to do statements. Something was happening and it wasn't good. But it did allow me to escape.

"I need to go," I said to Michael. "We'll have dinner some other time. They're threatening to arrest me if I don't go in and give a report on the guns."

"They think you're an arms dealer?"

"I don't know. I have a bit of a history with the police."

"It's not Theron?"

"Theron? I told you: forget him and find a new partner. Will you take me to my car, or do I need to catch a bus?"

"Where are you going?"

"Flynn's precinct on Broad Street. The Fourteenth."

Michael asked for five minutes and went into the other room.

Nirah was literally swimming in the caviar dish, her body rolling over and her tail twitching in the air. She was so full, she barely moved when I lifted her out and bathed her with warm water in the bar sink. Her slim body swelled in the middle from her gastronomical orgy and she smelled fishy. I laid her on a towel, dumped the remaining caviar down the drain, washed the bowl, and rinsed it in hot water. No accidentally poisoning anyone if she'd drooled while she was eating.

When Michael returned, he said he'd arranged a ride to the precinct for me. "I'd take you, but it's best you not show up with me," he said.

I agreed.

I lifted Nirah from the bar and slipped her into her pocket.

Michael came to me and laid his hands on my shoulders. "Please believe me when I say I love you."

"I believe you, but—"

The door burst open and Reverend Victor marched in.

I froze and my mouth dropped open.

"Good afternoon, Cassandra." Vic seemed far different from when I'd seen him at the mission. His voice was hard and clipped. "I came to pay my brother a visit. I'm sorry to see you here."

"Brother?" He'd already warned me about Michael, but his *brother*?

"My brother," Victor said. "It's been a while since we've had a little family talk."

"True," Michael said, as calm as if he stood on the Archangel's floor during a very ordinary day. "I've been very fortunate."

"What?" The word popped from my mouth like I'd spit out a piece of sour candy.

"Oh, yes, Cassandra, the Archangel and I have a great deal in common." Victor laughed, again quite satisfied. "I warned you about him, didn't I?"

I swallowed hard. "You told me not to give him my soul, which I hadn't planned on doing anyway, but I don't remember anything about him being a relative."

"How did you think I knew him well enough to warn you?" Victor asked.

"You don't look like brothers." I gazed at them. One tall, blond, and handsome and the other short, slim, and dark; genetics played nasty tricks at times.

"That's because we have different fathers." Victor seemed a bit calmer now.

"Fortunately, we do." Michael almost snarled the words.

"Michael is upset with me because I used the family business profits ministering to the poor," Vic said.

"It's called embezzlement, Victor." Michael's voice seethed with rage. "If I don't sell this damned hotel in the next year, I'll file for bankruptcy and Mother can come and live with you."

"You shouldn't be so bitter, Michael." Vic spoke softly and I heard no anger in his voice, only a deliberate truth. "Mother always loved you best."

"Does that mean she never tried to strangle you?" Michael's hands were clenched into fists.

"No, I wouldn't say that. I was an only child once." Vic sighed.

Elise of Avondale, Elise of the Barrows, crazy Elise— whatever her sons' relationships with each other, life couldn't have been easy. I had missed something, a key piece of the puzzle surrounding her. Maybe the piece Michael had sent me to Avondale to find.

"I need to go." No matter how curious, this wasn't my business.

Michael led me to the door and told me to go to the basement, where someone would be waiting for me. As the door closed, I saw Victor heading for the bar.

Michael said he'd have my car taken from the Archangel to my apartment, but I told him to take it to Abby's instead. He didn't ask for my key, so I figured it was his problem. What other secrets were these two men keeping?

My ride was an unremarkable shuttle van that belonged to the hotel. The nice elderly man driving talked the whole way, mostly trying to elicit information on why he had to chauffeur me to the police station instead of the airport.

Haphazard concrete block additions tacked onto an ancient but graceful brick building housed the Fourteenth Precinct station. Except for the old cinnamon-colored brick part, the structure squatted on the block like a windowless fortress designed by a paranoid architect. Or maybe it was the proximity to the Barrows that made it strange. I'd been here only once before.

I went to the front desk, gave my name, and a uniform escorted me into the pale fluorescent hallways that made up the guts of the building. I rubbed Nirah to reassure her. She was fine. I wished someone would reassure me.

My escort led me into a lounge room with an orange plastic-covered couch and equally orange chairs. An empty snack machine and a drink machine with an OUT OF ORDER sign completed the decor. The uniform stood against the wall when I sat down. Did I actually rate a guard?

The lounge opened wide into the hallway on one side, where a continuous parade of uniforms and other assorted cops went by. They all stared at me. I managed to hide my discomfort with my don't-give-a-shit facade, but the uniform standing watch over me didn't bother to hide anything. He glared at everyone. I guess he wanted to be somewhere else. Another uniform walked by and jerked to a stop. Insky.

I'd retrieved Insky's eight-year-old daughter a couple of years back. His addict ex-wife lost custody, then snatched the girl. She thought she could hide in some crappy apartment house along River Street with her drug-dealing boyfriend. She backed down when I arrived, but the boyfriend was an ass. When I took him down, I kicked him a couple of extra times for Insky, who is a wonderful father and all-around nice guy.

"Cass?" Insky approached. "Everything okay?"

I shrugged. "Don't know. Flynn said I needed to come and give a statement on the guns. I happened to be there when he found them. They don't get around to it soon, I'm going to leave."

I eyed my guard. Sure enough, his body tensed and his hand did an automatic check of his gun. He had orders to keep me from leaving. Insky caught the gesture, too, and his eyes narrowed. He sat in one of the plastic chairs beside me.

"I didn't know you and Flynn were such good friends," Insky said. He lifted an eyebrow, obviously curious, but I didn't want to answer that question, at least not in public.

"Have you seen Flynn?" I asked him.

"He's upstairs yelling at Krause."

I silently groaned. What a pain. Lieutenant Robert Krause was one of the holy rollers who declared war on Duivel's psychics a couple of years ago. He "investigated" Abby—and me—but our clients refused to say we did anything wrong. True to my obstinate nature, I always gave him a hard time. I made a good living as a PI until he came along. Three years ago I gave up my PI license *and* my gun license, which stopped some of the harassment.

Robert's crusade crashed on the rocks of political expediency when he set up a sting and "accidentally" arrested a city council member as she visited her own private and very masculine fortune-teller. Abby, confident and serene, always cooperated, so Robert reserved the greatest portion of his loathing for me.

"I thought they sent Righteous Robert to purgatory in the records department," I said.

"Election." Insky gave an exaggerated sigh. "New mayor goes to Robert's church. Robert promised to be good and they gave him his halo back."

I laughed and even my guard smiled.

Of course, if I were in Robert's place, I'd be suspicious of me, too. While I might be honorable in my own way, I am not a virtuous person by modern cultural standards. *Virtuous person* is Flynn's province. I knew that's what made everything about me so hard for him.

The sound of voices, loud voices, coming toward us made us all sit up.

"I'll do what's necessary, Detective." That was Robert, snarling to put a junior officer in his place.

"You're twisting facts to create evidence for your crazy theories." Junior officer Flynn wasn't buying. He kept his voice calm and reasonable. Smart. Left on his own, Robert would eventually trip over his own zealous feet. I'd move that event along if I could.

Robert stopped when he saw me. A short, chunky man dressed in beige polyester, he filled the stereotype of a used-car salesman. His face turned red and he balled up his fists. "What's *she* doing here?" he shouted. "I said *interrogation*."

Flynn stepped forward. "She came to make a statement on the weapons. Not be interrogated." He still sounded calm, but I detected an edge.

Robert glared at me. "Get her in a room."

He whirled and marched off down the hall.

I stood. Flynn laid a hand on my shoulder. "Cass, please."

I shrugged his hand off, even though I wanted it to stay. If I broke down, I might do something foolish like ask him not to reject me.

"Please what, Flynn? They aren't my guns."

"He knows that. He's trying to pin something, anything on you."

"Well, I can—"

"Hey!" Another uniform marched down the hall. "Fuck off, Flynn."

Great Mother, if you put him in filthy clothes and shaved his head, he could be the late Bastinado Pogo's twin brother, even if his name tag did say BRUNNER.

Flynn whirled to face him.

"What did you say?" Flynn's voice iced the room and Brunner stopped. The Barrows might be mine, but Flynn carried some weight in this place.

"Krause don't want you two swapping stories," Brunner said, but he kept his distance.

Flynn stood motionless for a few seconds, then sighed. "Come on. I'll walk you. Officer Brunner can follow and make sure we don't swap anything."

I grinned at Brunner. "Good doggie. Heel."

Flynn gripped my elbow, a little too hard, and guided me down the barren hall. Insky followed at a discreet distance. We stopped at a door and Flynn reached for the doorknob.

"I'll be okay," I said. I winked at him. "I know what I'm doing."

Flynn sighed. I guess he'd heard that before. He knew me better than ever now, and would be worried about what I might say—or do. Good reasons to get me out of his life as soon as possible, I imagined.

Flynn opened the door and gestured for me to enter. Robert stood waiting. Flynn gave Robert a good, long stare before Brunner followed me in and closed the door behind him. Flynn the detective threatening a superior—because of me. My heart soared. But what did it mean? That he still cared for me—or that he disliked what was obviously an unfair situation?

I'd been in the interrogation rooms uptown at Central numerous times over the years. It wasn't bad there: windows, modern equipment, cameras, and tape recorders. The Fourteenth Precinct room looked like something straight out of the Barrows. Industrial gray walls, torn linoleum flooring, a rickety table, and two folding chairs, all coated with the faint scent of chlorine bleach. No cameras, no mirror, no tape recorder, only Righteous Robert, Brunner, and little old me—and strictly against police procedure as I understood it.

"Sit." Robert pointed at a chair.

Brunner grinned.

Let the battle begin. "I gotta go pee."

"Tough shit." Robert smirked and hiked his pants up. Polyester didn't do well with a heavy gun on the belt. He'd have been better off with a shoulder holster.

I shrugged. "No shit. Just pee. But it's okay, I guess. If I wet the floor, you can send Bummer for a mop."

Robert bared his clenched teeth. "Take her across the hall," he ordered Brunner.

I went into the bathroom and Brunner stood outside the door. No windows, so he knew I couldn't escape. When I came out, Flynn and Insky stood at the end of the hall, and I waved at them. I also nodded cheerfully at Brunner. "Thanks, Bruno."

He drew a breath through clenched teeth. My potty break killed ten minutes, though I didn't know why I felt it was important to stall. Rescue wasn't likely.

I sat across the table from Robert in a chair that tilted to one side. Uncomfortable, because it made me constantly compensate for being off balance. Brunner stood against the wall as Robert sat across from me.

Robert leaned back and his chair creaked. If he landed on his ass, he'd probably blame me for that, too.

"So." Robert gave me his smug bastard smile. "Tell me about the guns."

"Whole warehouse full. Pretty cool, if you like that sort of thing."

"Where'd they come from?"

"The gun fairy? It's too early for Santa Claus."

"You know, I'm trying to be nice to you." Robert didn't look nice. He didn't even look smug anymore. His mouth was thin and tight, and his eyes narrow with deep wrinkles etched across his face. Such an angry, bitter man.

"What's the problem, Robert? Other than the fact that I'm an unwashed heathen female. Or is it pagan? I get my prejudices mixed up sometimes."

"The Lord could turn your heart if you ask him to."

He relaxed, leaned forward, and laid his hands flat on the table as if he was ready to slap them together in prayer if given a sign. Calm, patient, saintly Robert, ready for the sermon.

Nice. We could have a theological discussion instead of a loud conversation on guns.

I laid my hands on my thighs and kept them out of sight under the table. "I'm satisfied with my religion."

"Worshiping the devil."

"Oh, for—" Now that pissed me off. "What makes you think I'm into devil worship? You had me followed for weeks. You bugged my apartment, illegally—"

"I was doing the Lord's work. Witches, sacrifices—I know you." He lowered his voice. A muscle in his cheek twitched. "I've seen. The Bible says, 'Yea, they sacrificed their sons and their daughters unto devils.'"

Oops! Righteous Robert must have been snooping in the Barrows and something scared the shit out of him. He neared the line between reality and its opposite. Brunner squirmed as if he wanted to be somewhere—anywhere—else but in the room with Robert and me.

"Describe it," I said. "What did you see?"

"Evil demons. You consort with them."

"Which ones? The four-legged ones with rhino skin or the ape boys with the balls that hang down to their knees?"

Robert's face turned as gray and pasty as overcooked oatmeal. A little drool ran from the corner of his mouth. Brunner inched toward the door.

We all face God eventually, each in our own way. I'd studied his Bible and respected his beliefs. I didn't respect him. Robert Krause used the police power of the state to force his values on everyone.

Robert slowly stood, jammed his fists on the table, and leaned forward. I slipped my hand into my jeans pocket and found my only reasonable defense: the bottle of potion Abby had given me to make Hammer talk.

"Get out, Brunner," Robert ordered.

No cameras, no one-way glass, no witnesses. I thumbed the cork off the bottle.

"But I'm supposed to stay." Brunner, for all his stupidity, knew where the line was drawn.

"Get out!" Robert shouted.

Brunner raced to the door, opened it, and rushed out. I had only a few seconds before someone realized something bad was going to happen and maybe they should intervene. I nudged Nirah. I wouldn't let her bite him, of course. He was a scummy excuse for a human being, but he stood five stories above Pogo or Snag.

"Here's one for you, Robert. Psalm 140, Verse 3: 'They have sharpened their tongues like a serpent; adders' poison is under their lips.'" I flipped the bottle's contents at him with a quick snap of my wrist—a direct hit in the face.

Robert's eyes popped open. He jerked back, gasped, and sucked the liquid in. Nirah surged up from the pouch in my shirt, so I stood and leaned forward as she swayed inches from his face. She hissed and bared her fangs. Little snake made a lot of noise.

Robert froze. His body trembled as if she'd actually bitten him.

Nirah slid back into her pocket and I stuffed the potion bottle back into mine. I scooted back from the table and jammed myself into the corner. I tried for a horrified but innocent expression as the door burst open and Flynn rushed in, followed by Insky. Brunner hovered in the hallway.

Robert straightened. He gazed around him like a sinner surprised to find himself in heaven. Abby brewed the potion to persuade Hammer to talk, but as with any medicine, each individual could have a different reaction.

Robert hiccupped twice. The corners of his mouth twisted up in a sappy grin. He cocked his head and stared at me. "Your hair's red."

"Yep." Great Mother, what a show.

Robert frowned. "She had red hair, too. I didn't mean to, but it was so nice. She wanted . . ."

Whoa! This was great. I grinned at him. "What did she want, Robert?"

Robert's face clouded with a dreamy expression. "She wanted me to kiss her down there. It was red there, too."

Oh, boy. The bastard had made Abby's life hell for almost two months, hauling her downtown for "questioning" once a week. I had had the honor of a ride downtown for what seemed like every other day. Vengeance stood before me.

"Who's 'she'?" I asked.

"Cass!" Flynn threw his hands up in dismay.

Insky laughed—loud.

"What?" I laughed, too. "I want to know the brave female who had the guts to want his mouth on her," I said to Flynn.

"She kissed me down there, too," Robert offered. He sighed while the silly grin remained pasted on his face.

Flynn grabbed my arm. He lowered his voice. "How long will he be like this?"

I shrugged. "I don't know. Couple of days. He'll be fine."

Flynn sighed. "Insky. Lieutenant Krause seems to have become incapacitated. Will you take him somewhere to recover?"

"Where? Down to Central? They'd get a kick out of this."

"No. Get him out of here before he says too much. Maybe the emergency room."

Flynn dragged me out the door and down the sickly fluorescent-lighted hall.

"Can I see the serpent again?" Robert called after me.

We passed a frowning Brunner, but he didn't try to stop us.

"What about my statement?" I asked.

"Later. He's the only one who wanted it anyway." Flynn urged me on down the hall and out the door into the blast furnace.

"What serpent?" Flynn asked as we left the building.

I pulled my shirt out and peeked inside. "You did good, baby."

Nirah stuck her head out of the pocket and flicked her tongue at Flynn.

"Oh, shit, Cass. What am I going to do with you?"

I didn't want to know the answer to that question.

"Where's your junker?" Flynn asked. He kept a good three feet of distance between us.

"Probably at Abby's by now. I left it at the Archangel and Michael said he'd have it moved. Michael was going to take me to the Lace Curtain for supper, only I didn't get to eat because you called. Did you know he owns the Princess Lily, too?"

"No, I didn't know that. If he owns so much real estate, what's he doing in the Barrows?"

"Good question. A short answer would be that the Barrows is his home. I expect the real answer is a bit more complicated." I stepped closer to him and he moved back, a pained expression on his face.

"It's okay, Flynn. I understand. You don't owe me anything. I'll find Selene. What cop needs a girlfriend who consorts with serpents and gangsters, carries an illegal weapon—"

"This cop does." He snarled the words between his teeth. "He just can't show it right here and now. Robert's followers make up half the cops at the Fourteenth. We can't find Selene if we're both under surveillance."

"Oh. Sorry." Damn, damn! Misjudged him again. I had to be careful with my assumptions about the man. He was not predictable. Nice. I would probably never be bored with his company. "Are you coming to Abby's tonight?"

"Yes."

"Good, because if you do, I'll kiss you 'down there.'"

Flynn laughed. "You hold that thought, sweetheart."

Maybe he was getting used to me. Or maybe he didn't want to dig too deeply into the fact that I'd admitted spending the last few hours with Michael. My joy that I hadn't chased him away carried a shadow. What would happen to us once this was all over? He flagged down a cab and paid for my ride to Abby's house.

"What did you do to Robert?"

I explained, "He's the way Hammer should have been."

He nodded. "I'll see you tonight," he said.

When I arrived, I found a shiny silver gray Mercedes sedan in the driveway and Carlos Dacardi sitting at Abby's kitchen table.

chapter 24

Abby didn't seem upset by the presence of Duivel's crime boss in her kitchen. She seemed quite pleased with his company. She sat at the table with a smile on her face while the scent of cambria flower tea filled the air. Maybe it wasn't such a surprise, though, given his affinity for his grandmother and her magic. Not many people understood the nature of such things, and Abby had few peers.

"Where you been?" Dacardi asked.

I sat at the table across from him. "The Barrows, the Princess Lily, Fourteenth Precinct station . . . Hey, Abby, did you know Krause is back in action?"

Abby sighed. "It had to happen eventually. He's not exactly a criminal, just a poor, misguided man." She nodded at Dacardi. "Unlike your new friend."

Dacardi grinned and winked at me. "She must be psychic."

"He's not a friend." I had to object to that one. "He's a client."

"Yeah." Dacardi laughed this time. "Your client wants to show you something. Go for a ride with me." He made it an order, not a request.

Whatever he wanted to show me was relevant, though, if only because he wasn't a man who would waste time on the irrelevant.

A funny growling noise drew my attention as I stood. A plastic pet carrier sat in the corner, Horus glared at me from the cage door. He hooked his impossibly long claws in the wire and growled again.

"Now what?" I resigned myself to a recital of feline bad behavior.

Abby made a wry face in Horus's direction. "He raped Mrs. Cochin's Siamese. A remarkable feat since she—the Siamese, not Mrs. Cochin—has been spayed. And I don't think it was actually rape since she—the Siamese again—followed him when he ran away. Joyce Bulworth's poodle objected to a cat trespassing in his yard and dear Horus chewed off half his ear."

Dacardi chuckled.

"He's a lover and a fighter," I said, not altogether displeased.

"He's also a glutton," Abby said. Her voice now held a note of amusement. "He tore a hole in the Baxleys' screen door, helped himself to a meat loaf, opened the birdcage on Liz Harmon's back porch, and devoured not one but all three of her blue budgies."

Poor Horus. An urban survivalist feline, he remained true to his nature. Forbidden to stalk and kill in Abby's yard, he released his frustration by terrorizing the neighborhood. Abby was an immovable object, though. "I guess you're grounded, cat. Maybe she'll let you out for good behavior in a day or two."

Horus growled again.

I went downstairs and changed. I'd let Nirah loose in the yard, so I didn't need the pocket shirt. This time I'd take my gun and knife. I didn't have a jacket to cover the gun here, so I settled for a thin nylon Windbreaker.

The late-afternoon temperature outside hovered above ninety, but Dacardi had the thermostat in the Mercedes on refrigerate, and I had to draw my jacket tight around me before we'd gone a mile.

"What the fuck is this?" He threw a folded piece of paper at me.

I picked it up, but I knew what it was before I opened it. Michael's reward poster. Michael had seriously screwed up my hunt.

Dacardi probably knew more than he let on, so the truth was in order—at least part of it. "Someone is interfering."

"That fucker at the exercise place." He made it a statement, not a question.

"Yeah, that one."

"Why? He got the hots for you? Or you got something on him?"

"Michael likes me. That's all." I tried to keep my voice even. I didn't want to discuss a complex situation I couldn't understand or control. "I informed him of his error circulating those things."

Dacardi made a smooth turn onto River Street. "I offered a reward for my boy. Got nothing."

"You offered a reward in your world. Michael offered in the Barrows. That's his turf. Big difference."

"You think it'll work?" He steered with one hand. His other, clenched into a fist, beat out a steady rhythm on his thigh. Flynn had been able to release some of his worry for Selene by talking to me. For the crime boss, revealing his true feelings could be deadly for him and his family.

"I don't know. But I don't think anyone is going to deliver the kids to his doorstep."

Dacardi said nothing. He didn't speak again until we turned off River Street and drove into the industrial area along the river. Warehouses with massive unloading docks lined every inch of the riverbank. Crestline Warehouse parking lot. "Too much going on here," he grumbled. He cut the Mercedes's engine. "My wife, she used to go to that place, the . . . Angel?"

"Archangel."

"She talked about him, that man, like . . . like he was a god."

I agreed. "He has that effect on some people."

"But not you."

Damn, I didn't want Michael to be part of the conversation, but I had to give him some answer. "I've been around the Barrows long enough to be wary of everything."

He studied me with dark, steady eyes. "You don't trust him?"

"At this point, everyone in the Barrows is an enemy until he proves he's a friend—and I'll keep a damn close eye on my friends."

Dacardi nodded. "You're like me, bitch, not like that cop. Good man, Flynn. Better watch out for that. I married a good woman. She can't deal with some things."

Relationship counseling from Carlos Dacardi? The bad part? I knew he was right.

"It sucks, Dacardi. But what else is there when you love someone?"

"Yeah. What else?"

Inside the warehouse, the second shift loaded pallets of boxes on trucks. They shouted, laughed, and cursed, trying to force their voices over the noise of industry.

Dacardi led me to a door and into a cool, dark cave illuminated by multiple monitors. Two men sat watching the screens, but both quickly left when he and I entered.

"I own nine warehouses," Dacardi said. "Lease most of them out. Keep two cameras hidden in each building. Like to keep watch on things. Don't usually look at everything, but I was down here the other night and saw this." He pointed at a monitor.

The screen showed nothing more than stacks of boxes on pallets in an empty warehouse.

"There's no one there?" I asked.

"Wharf security checks the outside," he said. "Most stuff is too big to carry out without heavy equipment, so it's not that easy to steal." He chuckled. "But it can be done. Bunch of guards on a single building would make people suspicious anyway." His voice dropped a notch. "Something's strange. Got a good eye for numbers. Numbers on those boxes are the same. Nothing's moved for a month. I charge through the ass for that building. You want to store something a long time, you move it to a cheaper place. What you think?"

"Who's leasing the space?"

"Corporation. Malison Dividend." He bent to study the screen. "Second year, five-year lease."

"So what we see here could have come in a little at a time?"

Dacardi straightened. "Yeah."

"And you think it's guns? Plastic?"

He nodded, his eyes on the screens. "Seen boxes like that before. Same construction. See how the corners are put together? The way the straps are crossed. Maybe coincidence, but it feels wrong."

"Could I get in? Have a look around?"

He lifted a plastic card out of his pocket. "My warehouse. My lease."

The sun had almost set when we arrived at the warehouse. Dacardi kept in phone contact with his men, who in turn followed the wharf security vehicle making its rounds. One of his men drove us to the warehouse in the Mercedes and let us out at the front door. The metal building, one of the larger ones on the block, towered over us like a dirty green temple to the gods of industry. Enormous bay doors on the front allowed big trucks in and out. Equally large doors and a massive lifting apparatus would be on the dock behind for goods loaded and unloaded from barges. A sign mounted on the wall by a small door proclaimed OFFICE. NO SOLICITORS.

Dacardi swiped a plastic card in the lockbox attached to the door. The lock clicked and he jerked it open. We quickly stepped inside.

"Sorry, fuckers," Dacardi said. "Had the codes changed like they didn't think I'd programmed in a master. My property. I come here when I damn well want." He stepped up to a panel with a digital readout and keypad mounted on a wall, punched in some numbers, and all the lights on the pad blinked green.

"I hate fucking computers," Dacardi said. He sneered at me like I was personally responsible for the electronic age. "I hate that bastard who takes care of mine. Have to pay him more a year than I pay my second man."

"What are you going to do if it is weapons?"

"Don't know. Get some men and trucks down here, move 'em . . . Don't know. Gonna take the fall no matter what."

I agreed. Dacardi owned the warehouse, and no matter what happened, no one would believe he didn't own the guns.

The office had an empty water cooler and a clean desk, a room not used in some time. It fit with Dacardi's assertion of inactivity.

We entered the hushed confines of the main warehouse. Though we were the only living beings in this steel cave, menace hung in the air like the ghost of violence. Dacardi carried a powerful flashlight. Nothing but numbers marked the crates, stacked five high, two by two in rows. They reached the metal ceiling far above us. None were open like the one at yesterday's site. "I don't know, Dacardi. Look for pallets set apart, away from the crates."

"You mean like those?" He flashed his light between two rows. Sure enough, five pallets sat near the back wall like tombstones clothed in shrink-wrap. More C-4.

We approached cautiously.

"What do you think?" Dacardi spoke like he knew the answer to his own question.

"I think we should probably leave here now."

"Yeah. Too many for me to get them out without somebody seeing. I'll call my lawyer, then be a Good Samaritan and call the cops."

"Best you can do, I guess. Don't tell them I was here, or you'll need more than lawyers."

"You been a bad girl, huh?"

"No. Guilt by association. Like a crime boss owning a warehouse full of guns that aren't his. I've blown up one cache and found another. My credibility level is in the basement."

"Your cop?"

"I think he likes me. And believes me. But he's only one man."

Dacardi grunted. "Crime boss. You know how hard I worked to get rid of that—"

The sound came, soft, the opening of a door, a slight change in air pressure, then the sliding of a shoe on concrete. Someone had come in the front. Someone with a key and all the codes. I glanced at Dacardi. He switched off the flashlight. As he did, the main warehouse lights flashed on. Ten men moved toward us across a hundred and fifty feet of open space. They'd spread out. One wore a security guard uniform, but the others looked like dockworkers. I doubted they'd be dumb and drugged like the Bastinados.

I was sure they'd be armed. Would they shoot? The guns and ammo really weren't much of a danger, but the four pallets had the potential to blow us all to hell. Overwhelming us with numbers would be their best bet.

"Is there a back door?" I asked.

" 'Bout fifteen feet behind us."

"Will your card—?"

"Back door should open."

"You carrying?" I asked.

Dacardi nodded. "Little .38 in my pocket."

I drew my gun. "Let's go. I'll hold them back while you open the door."

We quickly backed away to the door. The men coming toward us slowed when they saw my gun. They jerked to a stop when I pointed it at the four pallets, confirming my suspicions of their contents. C-4 wouldn't likely explode from a single bullet, but they obviously didn't know that. Or it was something more volatile than C-4.

Dacardi cursed from behind me where he worked at the door.

"Got it," he said as the door opened.

We rushed out the door and onto the docks. Our only escape was the river. I could swim, but the Sullen ran deep and cold here. And it was at least thirty feet down to the water.

Dacardi slammed the door. The lock clicked shut, but would probably open from the inside unless . . . I scanned the area. The docks themselves were clean and clear except for the winches and other loading equipment, but six-foot strips of heavy angle iron lay piled near the building. I grabbed a couple and wedged them against the door.

"How are we going to—?"

"Swim. You swim, right?"

"Yeah, but I'm not much on diving." Not thirty feet anyway.

"Don't know much, do you?"

"Not about docks."

He grinned. Great Mother, the crime boss was having fun.

We ran to the end of the dock, where a ladder dropped to a smaller floating platform.

I jumped at the whir of the big bay doors on the back of the building opening.

Dacardi had already started down the ladder.

I turned back. Our pursuers, crouched low, hurried toward us. I couldn't shoot and climb a ladder, so I holstered the gun and started down. I made six feet when one of the men pounded across the dock. I glanced up. The barrel of a pistol pointed straight down at me.

Out of the blue, two shots cracked into the night. The gunman standing over me collapsed as the top of his head popped off. A splash of warm blood hit me and ran over the dock's edge. His weapon, released by nerveless fingers, hit the river below with a small splash.

I hurried on down the ladder. Blood and brains? No problem. I needed a bath anyway.

The last rays of sunset painted the sky, and the automatic security lights flashed on.

I jammed my gun into my holster as tight as it would go. As one, Dacardi and I made a running dive into the black water of the Sullen River. Water closed over my head as I entered a cold, silent midnight envelope.

Too quiet. They should have been shooting at us by now.

I stroked as far and fast as I could underwater, trying to reach the current in the main channel and ride downstream. Finally, I had to surface. When I did, my eyes burned with the dirty, petroleum-filled water. I had to fight to stay up. My boots dragged me down. If I had shoes, I could kick them off, but I'd laced the boots tight, all the way above my ankles.

"Dacardi," I yelled, gulping a mouthful.

He surfaced beside me, spit out some water. "Swim!" he shouted. He surged ahead of me.

We struggled on. Still no shots followed us. I glanced back.

The dock suddenly flashed with fire. Not an accident, I'd bet. Someone would rather burn the warehouse than have the weapons taken by the police.

I swam harder without making much headway. I called on all the strength the Mother gave me, pumped my arms, and willed my heavy-weighted feet to kick faster. My legs felt like tree branches loaded with ice in a sudden storm.

Dacardi fell back to swim beside me, though only the Mother knows why. He'd been wearing shoes and had probably long since shed them. Sirens sounded in the distance—the far distance, I hoped. No one needed to be close, not as close as we were.

Flames lit the night now. They had spread to sheet the warehouse's back wall. I jerked at an explosion. A small one. Probably a fuel tank or something. We'd finally caught the current, and the Sullen dragged us downstream—but not fast enough.

The warehouse exploded with a catastrophic blast louder than anything ever heard in Duivel. Someone had detonated the C-4. Dacardi's hand seized the back of my neck. He made a powerful dive for the river's bottom. We plunged down into the cold, dark depths filled with death.

chapter 25

When I was a kid in school, they told us not to tap on the aquarium tank because it hurt the little fishes' ears. They suspended me for beating the shit out of a boy who kept pecking at the glass with a ruler. Now I played the fish.

Sound, incredible sound, more felt than heard, vibrated my bones. The river convulsed in a great shock wave. Caught in the throes of its giant spasm, I tumbled and rolled like a surfer losing a battle with a mighty wave. For a brief moment it tossed me high out of the water. I caught a glimpse of an inferno burning like the mouth of hell before gravity plunged me back into the roiling river.

I gulped one breath before water closed over my head again. The river churned around me like a giant washing machine. Light blazed as the river, the oily surface, caught fire. A flash, only seconds, but it warmed the water around me. Darkness enveloped me again.

My lungs burned. Just a few moments and . . . maybe it would be quick. Like going to sleep, I'd read once. Like the person who wrote those words knew.

My body jerked. Something seized my arm and dragged me through the darkness. I should help . . . should kick my feet . . . My head popped out of the water. I gasped and sucked in some water, but it had air mixed in it. I coughed, choked . . . My head went under again, and was immediately jerked back, this time by my hair.

"Come on, bitch," Dacardi shouted in my ear. He had my arm, and he slung it over a white foam cylinder, the kind they use to keep boats from hitting the dock. Thank the Mother. I locked onto it. My boots tugged at my legs, but I clung tighter.

Dacardi moved us toward the shore. Pieces of burning debris and other unidentifiable objects floated around us. We'd been pushed out of the main channel. If not, we'd be on our way to the Mississippi. Blood seeped from a cut in his forehead, and with each breath, he gave a small gasp of pain. I kicked with my iron-weighted feet. My legs protested by sending tremors of fire through the muscles.

The inferno upriver lighted the sky like a second sunset. Occasional smaller explosions cracked now and then. That was probably the ammunition. The blast and the surge of water, combined with the river current, had taken us a quarter mile downstream.

My feet touched bottom. Soft, mushy stuff clung to my boots like a giant bowl of toxic pudding. The bank, only a small place between warehouses, made a short, slick incline. They built no docks here because the channel cut to the river's other side and it wasn't deep enough to bring the barges this far.

I clawed through onto a lovely patch of scraggly yellow grass and wonderful semidry earth. I rolled onto my back and stared up into clouds of smoke. If the fog came before dawn, the docks and the Barrows would reek of a great burning.

Oxygen deprivation has a terrible effect on the human body, even one sustained by the Mother's strength and will. Arms and legs that burned moments earlier now felt numb and hard as ice cubes.

Much as I wanted to lie and rest, I knew we had to get

out of there. If someone saw us, we'd probably both spend the night in jail, or at the minimum an interrogation room. I probably wouldn't have to fake anything to get them to take me to the emergency room, though.

I had to try twice, but I finally sat up. I felt for my gun, miraculously still wedged in the holster, and my knife, in the arm sheath. Feeling slowly returned, bringing the sensation of . . . Oh, damn. Something moved inside my muck-coated pants. I popped the button, tore open the zipper, and shoved them down. Several unidentifiable crawling things dropped out.

Dacardi laughed, a slow, frayed sound.

I laughed, too. We were alive, not something I'd have bet on fifteen minutes earlier. I pulled my pants back up, used my knife to cut the laces on my boots, and shucked them off. Dacardi had crawled to one of the buildings and used it as a climbing wall to get to his feet. I did the same, whimpering the whole way. Then I had to bend over and pick up my boots. Tempting as it was to leave them or even throw them in the river as retaliation for almost killing me, I wanted to leave nothing behind.

Clinging to the wall, we carefully limped our way toward the street.

My strength returned faster than Dacardi's, and I could walk using the building for balance, not as a lifeline. I couldn't tell how far we'd come, but the fire's light had given way to the flash and shadow of emergency lights down the street. We stayed in the shadows, not wanting to be spotted by wharf security, if they weren't all at the fire.

"Wait," Dacardi said. He fished around in his pocket and drew out a cell phone.

"Will that work?" I rubbed my hand across my pocket, where my own was surely beyond resuscitation.

"Damn sure better. Supposed to be waterproof."

The phone did work, and Dacardi's guys came for us,

though they had to walk a quarter mile because of road-
blocks. That meant we had to trudge back that quarter
mile, with only wet socks between the pavement and us.
No way was I putting my feet back in my boots until I'd
dried and fumigated them. Finally, we climbed into the
backseat of the Mercedes, completely ignoring the filth
we were carrying into a car worth more than I'd made in
the last five years. We rolled away from the disaster at
the docks.

"Where to?" the driver asked.

"Home," Dacardi said. "You call the suits?"

The driver nodded. "Soon as I heard the big boom.
Briefcases packed and on their way."

"And you?" Dacardi turned to me.

"Abby's," I said. "Could I use your phone?"

He handed it to me and I called Abby. When she answered, my first words were "I'm okay."

She didn't speak for a moment; then she said, "I know
that. I'm a psychic, remember? Someone else needs to
be reassured."

Flynn spoke. "Tell me you're not at the docks." His
voice came across the line, taut and cold.

"I'm not at the docks." The truth, since we'd left them
behind and were heading north.

"Shit!"

Guess he didn't believe me. "I'll be there in a few
minutes." I hung up, then immediately called the Archangel. Michael wasn't in, so I left a message that I'd survived yet another catastrophe.

"So," Dacardi said. "Every time something blows up,
I should look for you?"

"I guess. You check all your other warehouses?"

He glanced at the driver and the driver nodded his
head.

Dacardi's face was a picture of weariness and worry.
"This is bigger than Richard and Flynn's kid sister."

"Yeah. A lot bigger. Tomorrow night, you going to be ready?"

He nodded. "Said I would, didn't I? But there's something I— I ain't no explosives expert, but I think there was something else in that warehouse."

"Yeah. Think so." I'd seen plastics in the warehouse where Flynn and I had crawled out of the sewer, and I'd bet that's what caused the spectacular blast on Exeter Street that so injured me. "I got connections in munitions manufacturing. I'll see what I can find. Maybe something to bargain with the Feds. They're gonna be all over this."

"Good luck."

Dacardi did make the driver stop by a store and sent him in to buy me another cell phone. Not a megabucks waterproof model, but it worked. It was my carrier, too, and they gave me the same phone number.

Dacardi had received a telephone report on the situation at the docks while we waited. He sighed. "Buildings on either side of mine went up. Men killed. Lot of trouble."

I agreed.

The Mercedes stopped at the curb in front of Abby's house. "Thanks for dragging me out of fire and water, Dacardi. If you hadn't found me that last time I went under, I wouldn't be here."

Dacardi studied me. "What else could I do, bitch? You was shining like a full moon."

Shining? Like last night when I died and the Mother jerked me back to life? What was happening to me? I needed to talk to Abby, but how much help could Abby be on this?

"Well, anyway, that was good shooting on the dock," I said. "Looking up into that gun barrel wasn't as much fun as nearly drowning."

Dacardi slowly shook his head. "I saw. It wasn't me."

"Oh, shit."

"You got it, bitch."

Someone had saved my life. Wish I knew who to thank. Or maybe I didn't.

I closed the door and headed up the driveway to Abby's back door, wet, exhausted, covered with river mud.

Flynn sat on the back doorsteps with Horus at his side. Abby must have adjusted the cat's attitude and placed him on probation. Nefertiti hung from the porch railing, her head swaying in a hypnotic rhythm. The only light came through the back door and the kitchen windows.

Flynn seemed colder, harder, and older. Like Dacardi, he'd come to realized things were bigger than two kidnapped children. He stretched his legs out and leaned back against the porch railing. T-shirt, shoulder holster, jeans, and, as usual, he needed a shave. My weary body stirred at his lean, rugged look.

He studied me for a few seconds, then said, "You look like shit."

"Thank you for your honesty. You look sexy as hell."

He smiled.

I sat beside him. Damp clothes clung to me and my skin itched, probably from pollution or creepy crawlies in the river mud. His nose wrinkled. Yeah, I probably smelled awful, too.

From the set of his mouth to the suspicious look in his eye, I could tell Flynn was on the edge. Before he could ask, I told him the entire story. He deserved the truth. I spoke of everything that happened after I'd left that afternoon, including my encounter with Snag. He accepted it all without question, then called someone named Betty Jean to get information on Malison Dividend.

Flynn stared into the darkness of Abby's garden, maybe searching for some answer to this new world. "Who *are* you? Who is Abby?"

I frowned, then rubbed my thumb between my eyes to

smooth it away. "I told you. Are you ready to believe now? I'm the Earth Mother's Huntress. Abby's her High Priestess, her witch if you want to call it that. I know that's not what you're looking for, but it's the best I can do."

"It's going to take more than words. What is Michael to you?"

"Great Mother, Flynn." Now where did that come from?

"Answer my question."

I sat there, staring at the ground. Flynn, still on the edge, was reassessing everything—my world, our relationship. Again, honesty was best.

"I'm not in love with Michael, if that's what you're asking. I trust Michael with nothing at this point. You . . . I trust you. I trust you with my life. I trust you with my heart." Using the porch railing, I dragged myself to my feet. Like last night, I'd again reached my physical limit.

I laid a hand on Flynn's shoulder. "I'm sorry. I'm doing the best I can. I'll understand if that's not good enough." No way in hell I would, but I had given him a way out if he wanted it.

His hand grasped mine. "I'm dealing with it, Cass. What do you want me to do?"

"Help me inside so I can get a shower. Crawl into my bed, and hold me while I sleep."

He grinned. "That's all?"

"No. But I can't promise I'll stay awake through anything else."

Flynn helped me downstairs, not even commenting on the secret pantry entrance we had to use. He undressed me, showered with me, dried me off, and put me between the sheets. I fell asleep watching him clean river gunk from my gun.

I woke sometime later with him snuggled against my back. A bit of wonder filled me. The man was a bit of a saint for dealing with odors and gunk two nights running.

I rolled to face him and kissed his mouth until he responded. Then I kissed him "down there," to quote Righteous Robert. He groaned and locked his hands in my hair. Good, solid Flynn was solid everywhere my mouth touched. I savored the taste of him, teased him, tortured him, and when I felt he'd had enough, I started back up his body.

"You'd better not fall asleep on me." His voice sounded like a growl. His hand slid between my legs, and he rubbed hard because he knew I liked that, especially if I was good and wet. Glorious sensations spread from that point through my body.

I kissed his face, his eyes, and laid my mouth on his. Everywhere our skin touched tingled as if each nerve was supercharged with electricity.

Flynn shuddered, then released me and drew me on top of him. I stretched my body, raised my arms, and rode him for a while, letting him slide inside me while his fingers roamed across me and caressed my breasts.

Our auras matched, Abby had said. This man had walked into my life and captured me, body and soul. What I feared from Michael—captivity—I would freely give to Flynn.

When I couldn't take anymore, I climbed off him, dragged him on top of me, and wrapped my legs around him. So greedy, I wanted to hold him inside of me as long as I could.

Then, like a coiled spring suddenly released, the orgasm hit me and seared me to the bone. I gasped as spasms racked my body. I forgot everything for those few moments.

I shut my thoughts down at that point. I would deal with tomorrow, with the dark moon, with Flynn, Michael, Dacardi, the children as best I could.

Flynn lay beside me now, breathing deeply. I felt him fall asleep and I drifted off not long after.

chapter 26

I'd slept through the night. At least I hadn't dreamed. I reached for Flynn and found an empty place beside me. When I made it upstairs, he was at Abby's kitchen table, drinking coffee. Much too early. Barely daylight. I am not, nor will I ever be, that irritating creature called a morning person.

Horus, probably still on probation, crouched on the floor, with Nirah across his back. Nefertiti curled up in the kitchen window. I could hear Abby in the front, cleaning her public rooms. She had customers every day. She tried to help them, show them their troubles were mostly of their own making, but I doubt she had much luck.

I went for the coffeepot. "How'd things go with your reports yesterday?"

Flynn shrugged. "Too many questions. Captain's pissed. Everybody's pissed. They're not stupid and they know I'm holding something back. Feds not letting anybody in on the Exeter Street investigation. At least I was at the station when the warehouse blew last night."

I poured a cup of coffee and sat at the table across from him. "You find out anything on the guns?"

"No. The bomb squad says there was something in

that warehouse last night. A lot bigger than guns and ammo."

Abby hurried into the room. "Cass, the television news says Avondale Manor is on fire."

Flynn and I raced out of the house. He called his own precinct, but couldn't get any information.

My POS made good time, but three blocks from the fire, we hit a roadblock of cars. Probably ambulance chasers and other thrill junkies with time on their hands and no life. The police would run them off eventually, but until then . . .

"Shit!" Flynn muttered. "We'll have to walk." He laid his hand on the door handle.

"No, I can do better." I made a quick U-turn before cars stacked up behind me. I headed back and turned right across to the next block. "How close do you want? Simmer, bake, or barbecue?"

"What?" He glanced at me, then back at the street. Apprehension spread over his face.

Oh, was I driving too fast? I laughed. Adrenaline raced along my nerves like electricity. I cut through an alley and made a three-block wrong-way dash down a one-way street. That had us past the roadblock and the fire department barricades. Duivel streets aren't as predictable as the Barrows, but I think the same person designed them. Another alley and we arrived.

Flynn sat pale and rigid, fists clenched in his lap. I think it was because we'd met an eighteen-wheeler on the one-way street. Good thing there was a sidewalk.

"You . . ." Flynn swallowed and breathed deeply and exhaled.

"You're a cop!" I punched him in the arm. "Don't you do high-speed chases?"

"Not if I can help it." His breathing slowed. "And I have lights and a siren. People are supposed to pull over and let me by."

"Well. They pulled over for me. Sort of."

"Only because you— Never mind." He opened the car door and climbed out.

A monumental column of roiling black smoke towered over us when we reached the four-lane boulevard running in front of the manor. The stink of horrific burning rose to mix with another day of three-digit temperatures. Yellowish haze already swirled around the downtown towers.

Michael had arrived first. He'd parked his Jag in the diminishing shade on the west side of a building across the street from the fire. He stood leaning against the car and staring past the flowering shrubs in the landscape median, his face unreadable as the Greek statue he resembled.

"I'll try to get in," Flynn told him. "See what I can find out."

"Thank you." Michael's voice carried no more emotion than the expression on his face.

Flynn hurried away toward the open manor gate. The police stood guard and the fire trucks were inside. Flynn flashed his ID, spoke to the cops, and they let him pass.

I stood beside Michael. "Maybe she's okay." I thought of all the locked steel gates Flynn and I had to pass before we reached Elise. "They have to have an escape plan."

Though Michael had encouraged me to visit Elise and obviously wanted me to learn something from her, he'd given me no clue as to how he felt about her. Kids have a tendency to love their parents, no matter how evil the parents are.

Michael moved, not much more than shifting his weight. "I was nine, the first time I ever saw her." He smiled at the memory. "I thought she was the most beautiful creature on earth. Apparently they had locked her up because she'd tried to kill me. They discharged her from the hospital into a halfway house and allowed me to visit. I begged to go every time possible. Victor went, too, at first. She ignored him and doted on me. I felt so sorry for him. It wasn't long, though, before she stopped taking her medication and the babies went missing. Little boys. They found the bodies under her bed." His voice broke. "She said they were her sons and she named all of them Michael. I sent you to her, hoping you would see the humanity in me, since you seem to prize it so much. I was wrong."

I didn't know what to say or do. As for Michael's humanity, knowing Flynn and how much I wanted him now, it wouldn't have mattered. Michael could be completely human, but he would still try to own me. Something Flynn wouldn't do.

We did the only thing we could do: we stood and watched. I jumped when an explosion came. Not a large one, but I'd been close to such blasts recently.

Flynn hurried back across the street toward us, stopping for a moment in the median to allow more fire trucks to pass. His grim expression said a lot, but when he spoke to Michael, he did so with his neutral cop-bearing-bad-news voice.

"Your mother's missing. The entire smoke detector system failed. Sprinklers came on, but it was too late. Staff, patients. It's bad. It's going to be a couple of days before they identify everyone. I'm sorry."

"Thank you." Michael didn't sound thankful—or sad, or anything for that matter. He'd regained control of himself. He bent and kissed my cheek, then opened the Jag's door, climbed in, and started the engine. "I'll call you later."

Flynn and I watched him drive away.

"There is another thing," he said. "They found Avondale's director."

"Cohen?" An image of the sere, acid woman dressed in an armor gray suit popped up in my mind.

Flynn nodded. "Lying in her office with a broken neck. No fire there. Signs of a struggle, though. She fought—hard. This is getting too complicated. Too many mysteries."

"What about Selene? You've given up on her?"

"No, but isn't there any other way?" He grasped my upper arms and shook me, not hard, but with passion. "If Michael does find something, I can—"

"I don't need Michael, Flynn. I don't know where they are, but I have a good idea where they'll be tonight. And we're going to be there, too."

His arms circled me and held me tight, as if he could somehow squeeze some personal comfort from my body.

I wished I could say something to comfort him. Fate and duty ruled this day, and the inevitable dark moon the night.

Over Flynn's shoulder, I was surprised to see Reverend Victor staggering across the street toward us. Flynn released me at the sound of footsteps.

Victor stumbled and fell to his knees on the pavement. Flynn and I ran to him. We grasped his arms, lifted him, and led him out of the street. He didn't make any noise, but his thin body shook and his breath came in short gasps. Tears mixed with soot smeared his face. Finally, he calmed and breathed easier.

"Thank you." In a sudden move, he hugged me, then quickly released me.

"What happened, Vic?"

Vic glanced at Flynn and I introduced them.

"I went to visit." Vic stared at Avondale as Michael had minutes earlier. "The fire started. I tried to help. The doors wouldn't open." He shook his head. "Two of the orderlies, big guys, managed to get one door open. But the patients, they were so afraid." He sobbed. "What few we could find panicked and ran from us, some straight into the fire, and those locked in their rooms never had a chance." He didn't mention Elise by name. His mother. Michael's mother.

"They didn't have an escape plan," Flynn said, his voice hard and cold.

"That much money should buy the best." Vic rubbed his face with his hands.

Yes, but it didn't always buy safety. Had a monumental failure of a critical system doomed patients and staff at Avondale? Flynn gave me a level stare. Or was the fire meant to cover murder? He was right. The mystery deepened. But how was it connected to Richard and Selene?

"I'm sorry, Reverend," Flynn said. "The fire marshal will investigate. Did you leave your name and number? There will be questions."

"Yes." Vic sounded more in control now.

There were always questions, and many of them were mine.

We drove Vic back to the Lamb. He'd parked his car inside the wall at Avondale and wouldn't be able to retrieve it for a while. I didn't ask him about Michael, but I did tell Flynn about their relationship on the way back to Abby's. He listened without comment.

When we reached Abby's, Flynn went to walk in the woods. I let him go, knowing he needed to think about things. Nefertiti had followed him and he'd carefully held the screen door open for her. Maybe he'd find some peace.

Abby called me into her parlor and closed the door. "Do you need to talk, Cass?"

I nodded.

I sat on her couch and let the comfort of the room surround me. It smelled of citrus at times, then lavender or sandalwood. She sat beside me and I leaned against her solid shoulder, trying to draw from her strength.

I told Abby exactly what my near-death and return to life did to me. "Abby, I'm sorry, but I think I hate her. It's not that I wanted to die to begin with, but once I was on my way, she should have let me go. It feels so wrong. I'm not supposed to be here."

Abby reached out and wiped tears from my eyes. I hadn't cried in years.

"Cass, you have every right to hate her. I've hated

her, too. The Huntress before you died in my arms, so injured I couldn't possibly save her." Abby's hands clenched into fists. With visible effort, she relaxed.

What had happened to those who came before me? How many had Abby buried? How many had gone into the Barrows and never returned? I didn't ask. I figured it would hurt her. She had told me that each Huntress had a different task. She wouldn't talk about that, either.

Then I told Abby about Hammer and the vision. "She was so beautiful, my daughter. Could I have done that?" I touched my fingers to my eyes and felt tears again.

"The Earth Mother never *required* any worship. She is not God. The ancients perverted her name. First they sacrificed animals to her, then their enemies, and, finally, their own children." Abby reached out and grasped my face with both hands. She peered into my eyes. "Cassandra, Earth Mother's Huntress, you would not harm your own child—for any reason. Why would you believe the lies of the demon Darkness?"

She was right. The memory, true or false, had made me dangerously weak.

"Now," Abby said in her practical earth witch voice. "Do you have a plan? How can I help you?"

"No plan. Just a location." I drew the aerial photo out of my pocket and gave it to her.

Abby's eyes widened as she grasped its meaning, just as I had. "Sacrifice. They're going to sacrifice children on the dark moon. This dark moon. The conjunction. Oh, Mother, what's going to happen? You can't go—"

"I have to. Don't ask me why or how, but all my life has come down to this day—to this night. If you want me to live, tell me what I don't know about sacrifice."

Abby nodded. "In the lore, the oldest myths, there are three kinds of so-called sacrifices. The powerful enemy, the innocent, and the self, supposedly in that order. The myths are horribly wrong. The only true sacrifice is the self. There is great power in giving up your-self for the good of others. I think you've done that in your service to the children." Abby drew herself up. "You don't have to lecture me on fate. You will have guns. With bronze, they will serve you well for the mon-sters. But I'll make a few things you may take with you."

"Weapons? Abby, using earth magic to create weap-ons is—"

"Black magic." She stood and smoothed her skirt. "Something new for me. Why don't you go find your man? Make love to him. Then both of you should rest."

She walked out. Well, that was the best advice I'd had all day.

I headed out to the garden, walking by the cultivated vegetable rows and into the miniature forest, where a tiny spring bubbled from the ground. The water trickled over a stone bed and ran deeper into the woods. Abby's little patch of forest was at least fifteen degrees cooler than the world outside, but it was still hot enough Flynn had stripped off his shirt. He sat on a patch of grass where trees shaded the ground with dappled sunlight.

I sat beside him. "Hey. You okay?"

"Yeah. Just thinking."

"Too much think. Not enough action." I jumped Flynn and shoved him down on his back. He laughed and relaxed as I straddled him. Most of him relaxed. One particular part instantly rebelled against relaxation. I kissed his mouth long and hard, and started working my way down to subdue those taut muscles. Then I had a better idea. I jumped up.

"Hey, don't you—?" Flynn protested.

"Oh, yes. Come on." I stepped into the woods, leaving him to follow. I had a special place in mind. When I first came to Duivel, I had to explore Abby's woods. While I am now an urbanite, the farm girl remained. That girl found joy in this particular haven, this special spot I had to share with him.

Deep among the trees is a small hollow with rocky sides. A waterfall, barely above my head, pours out here in a thin stream. Cooler air moved across my skin as I stripped. I stepped down and under the water. A chill at first, then nice. Flynn stripped and joined me.

He hissed as the water first hit him. "This is worse than your apartment."

"Yeah, but we can't both fit in my shower."

He grabbed my butt and jerked me against him. The water warmed, and my skin warmed in response to him. Flynn eased a hunger in me that I hadn't known existed. His mouth locked on mine and his hands did the impossible—they drew me closer, as if his skin and mine were melting together in the heat. I'd never wanted a man as I wanted him. It was as if the Mother—or God—made him by special order, just for me. I belonged to him, with him, and he was mine.

Flynn dragged me away from the waterfall and to a grassy area near the pool's edge. He laid me down and dropped to his knees beside me. His eyes burned with passion as he stared at me.

"Do you know how beautiful you are?" he asked.

"I'm beautiful because at this moment you want me to be."

He laid a hand flat on my stomach, then bent and kissed my navel. I pulled him down on top of me so we could be face-to-face.

He lowered his mouth to mine.

It seemed so unfair. I had no idea what awaited me that night. We might lose each other before the sun rose again. Still, we had now, this moment. A soft breeze ruffled the leaves above us. In the chaos of life, we had made some personal order. Not the end of the story, but a beginning.

chapter 27

Making love to Flynn in the woods energized me. I felt really good until Abby met us on the porch as we returned to the house. Her face seemed troubled as the sky before a great storm. "Flynn, will you excuse us? I need to talk to Cassandra."

Flynn nodded, gave me a kiss, and went inside.

The late-afternoon sun cast odd shadows along the ground, and it seemed as if the incessant heat had penetrated this final oasis with its oppressive air. I don't think I've ever seen Abby's face so grave.

"What's wrong," I asked.

"My power is gone."

"What? The Mother is mad at you? Because of me?"

"No. I can't find her or feel her. I wanted a potion that would cover your scent. I'd hoped the purifier might repel the monsters. I can't make it." She laid her hand over her mouth as if to hold back painful words. Tears ran down her face, the first I'd ever seen on her. "I cannot help you tonight, Huntress." She walked into the garden, her head bowed and arms crossed over her heart.

I hoped she would find some consolation. A nagging thought crept up inside me. She'd built her whole life on her service to an unpredictable and not always benevolent entity. I stared south toward the Barrows. The Earth

Mother gone? Maybe the Darkness would go, too. I suspected the best we humans could hope for was that
they'd both disappear and leave us alone.

Shadows that stretched across the earth faded to black
as the sun descended and the night of the dark moon
began. Flynn sat at Abby's kitchen table, his face blank
and withdrawn. His mother called, crying, and that made
it worse. Had she sensed something?

Abby returned from the garden. Her eyes had the
empty look I'd seen on some children I'd rescued. The
underpinning of their lives, their parents, disappeared in
an instant as they experienced the lonely reality of an
adult world. She walked past us without a word.

Waiting, the worst kind. I'd wanted to be in the Barrows before dark, but Dacardi had called earlier. A
problem with the bronze ammo. He'd sent a truck to St.
Louis, where he'd had it made in a factory he owned. My
ammo guy couldn't make anything like the amount we
needed in time, but he did deliver two hundred rounds,
a hundred for me and a hundred for Flynn's .357. Flynn
grumbled but loaded them anyway.

I slammed my hands down on the kitchen counter.
Shit, what made me think, after ten years, that I needed
an army? I knew the answer to my own question. Shell-
shocked, battle weary, burned out, worn out, and totally
used up. I didn't want to go it alone anymore, even
though I knew it was best. There was more, of course.
Dacardi, his son, and his weapons were not an accident.

When Dacardi called earlier, he sounded excited, not
angry. He saw his son's rescue as one last adventure in
his life, I guess. But what would happen if Richard wasn't
with Selene? Would Dacardi's anger turn to me?

Abby's phone rang. I answered.

"Good evening," Michael said. "I have found your
children, but they're in the Zombie."

Sure they were. Smack in the middle of the biggest known pentagram on earth. "Can you give me directions?" I asked.

"I'll take you there."

"Take me where, Michael?" Shit! I didn't have time for a mystery game.

"It's a three-story building next to what was once the central town plaza."

Sure it was. The plaza and ritual sacrifice under the open sky.

"Any guards?"

"I saw none, but that means nothing. I paid a delivery truck driver to pretend he was lost and take me through the area, but I didn't linger. That one building had signs that someone used it recently. We won't be able to drive up to the front door, but I can probably get us within five blocks. If we arrive early, there shouldn't be too many of the beasts out."

I scanned the aerial photo. Building heights were difficult to determine with aerial photos, but only one looked promising. "The plaza. It's northwest of the Archangel, maybe two miles. The building on the south side?"

The phone was silent.

"Michael? You there?"

"Yes. And, yes, that's where it is. I wasn't aware you knew the Zombie so well."

"I'll meet you in front of the Archangel in two hours."

"Will Flynn be with you?" Michael asked, almost cautiously.

"Yes." I glanced at Flynn. He sat watching me, a little interest in his eyes.

"You can't come now? It would be better if we could go in alone."

"No. It's his sister."

"Very well." Michael sounded resigned. "I'll wait for you."

If Dacardi didn't show in an hour, Flynn and I would go alone.

I'd no more than hung up when the cell phone Dacardi had given me beeped.

"I got the fucking bronze," Dacardi snarled before I could say hello. "And the fucking night goggles, flamethrowers, grenades—"

"Grenades? I didn't say grenades. Flamethrowers? Great Mother!"

"Too bad. Bronze, my ass. I'm on my way."

I didn't have time to argue with him, but he'd better not toss a grenade around in a storm sewer.

"Grenades?" Flynn stared at me in shock after I hung up. "Doesn't it bother you? All the loose ends. Michael, Elise, Avondale, warehouses full of guns and ammunition. A criminal building an army?"

Bother was too mild a word for the shit rolling around in my mind. I'd run out of options, but the gut feeling that I was really screwing things up wouldn't leave me. "Leave if you want to, Flynn. I'll find Selene and Richard, but it's going to get worse."

He shook his head. "It's been getting worse since the day I met you."

That hurt. I guess it showed.

"I'm sorry, Cass. That was stupid."

"It's okay. I know you're worried." I made an excuse for him to cover my pain. I hoped it made him feel better, because it did nothing for me. Making love had brought temporary relief. I needed a bridge. He'd gone from my world back to the ordinary world of being a cop, and then come back to the Earth Mother's magic. He dealt with things adequately, if not gracefully. I had to cut him a break.

I laid out the aerial map and studied it, looking for any possible alternatives to going underground. There were none. Only if the storm sewers had collapsed would I try to sneak in aboveground, as Michael wanted.

Flynn suddenly grabbed my hand and drew me onto his lap, and I snuggled against him. I kissed him, rubbed my cheek against his, and ran my fingers through that dark, curling hair. I'd hold on as long as I could.

"Do you trust Dacardi?" he asked.

"As long as he wants something."

"What does Michael want? You said you didn't trust him."

"I trust him . . . marginally. I don't know what Michael wants." Not exactly true. I knew one thing Michael wanted. Me. "I've always worked alone, taken care of myself and whatever kid I was after. Michael has helped me find kids. He saved your life after I'd put it in danger, showing off the Barrows."

"He did that for you, not me. You'd go alone? Tonight?"

"If I had my way, yes. But I don't have my way. I don't think I've been making many of my own decisions since you showed me Selene's photo. We're pawns on the game board."

"Can't we do better than that? Let's call ourselves knights at least."

That made up for his earlier remarks and earned him a kiss. He squeezed me too tight and shuddered. We held on to each other until we heard vehicles pull up out front.

Two long, black steel boxes stood at the curb. At first, I thought they might be those gas-guzzling things referred to as Hummers. A closer look and I realized they were different. Bigger, stronger, maybe armor-plated tanks disguised as street vehicles, vibrating with the grumble of diesel engines. Maybe I shouldn't have told Dacardi I'd be willing to go to war. I meant a small assault force, not an all-out invasion.

Nefertiti nestled in the basket I was carrying. She had come from the sewers and she would be my guide. I placed Selene's stuffed rabbit and Richard's dirty jocks in with her so she'd know their scent.

Flynn and I climbed in the wide, leather-covered back-seat bench. Dacardi rode shotgun in one of the bucket seats up front. The driver was not one of his usual goons, but a sharper man, more alert. Odd instruments gleamed on the van's dash and filled the interior with a green glow; gear covered the area behind us, probably the guns and ammo. Dacardi had raised the stakes far beyond anything I'd thought of. I was suitably impressed.

"Damn, Dacardi, nice wheels. What are they?"

"*Perros bomberos*—Fire Dogs. Backup. Men, guns. Just in case." Dacardi chuckled, but it sounded dry and flat.

"Won't the army miss them?"

"The army wishes." Pride filled his voice. "Own a factory south of here. I might sell the Feds one or two if they talk nice to me—and stop poking around in my business." He held out a small instrument. "Satellite positioning," he said. "When we're ready, my men can find us, get us out."

Good. He knew we couldn't take too many men with us. Carlos Dacardi: more than a city crime boss, maybe an international arms dealer, a man whose grandmother taught him about magic. A man who loved his son enough to risk everything. I glanced at Flynn. As usual, his straight face gave little hint to his emotions, or to the conflict that had to be raging in him now.

Nefertiti poked her head out of the basket I'd set between my feet. She stretched toward Dacardi, her tongue flickering at lightning speed as she explored her surroundings.

Dacardi stared at her.

"She won't hurt you," I said.

"Hello, snake," he said softly. He held out his hand. Nefertiti bumped it with her head and coiled around his

wrist for a moment before withdrawing into the basket.
She accepted him. I guess one deadly creature knows
another.

"I called my mama today," Dacardi said. "Hadn't
done that in a couple of years. My mama doesn't like me
much. But I asked about my grandmother. She died last
year. Had to have her cremated 'cause they wouldn't let
her be buried on church ground. Parish priest tried to
get her to confess before she went, but she wouldn't
have none of that. Bet she'd have burned his ears off.
Old witch was a hundred and five."

I smiled. I didn't know if his grandmother served the
Mother or some other entity, but I could imagine some
priest trying to cajole Abby into confession.

Who could I count on tonight? Flynn, loyal and at my
back. Nefertiti, swift and deadly. They would have to do.
Dacardi would probably be with me, at least until he
found his son. The big unknown was, of course, Michael.
I had to make a decision. Should I leave the Archangel
behind? He'd cared enough to personally take me to the
Goblin Den, where he knew I'd get hurt or killed if I
went alone. He wanted me. He'd saved Flynn's life.
When the monster knocked Flynn down in the sewers,
he had only to wait a few seconds and it would have
been over.

"Stop at the Archangel," I ordered the driver as we
entered the Barrows' dark ruins.

chapter 28

Michael stood in the Archangel's parking lot when we arrived. An almost empty parking lot. How rare. Had the patrons felt the dangerous pall cast by the dark moon?

Michael had dressed his fine muscled body in black and wore a black cap over that silky blond hair. He frowned and straightened, suddenly on alert at the appearance of two thinly disguised war machines. If I hadn't been expecting Dacardi at Abby's house, I'd have done the same.

Michael's frown turned to shock when the Fire Dog stopped and I opened the door.

"Come on, Archangel," I called to him. "Let's roll."

Michael walked to the open door. "What are you doing? We can't go in the Barrows with—"

"Yes, we can. And we are."

Michael didn't hesitate. He climbed in. "You are the damnedest woman I have ever met in my life," he said.

I'd expected a fight. "That's why you like me so good, huh?"

"Where did you get this military strike force?" Michael asked.

Dacardi turned and grinned at him between the seats.

Michael's mouth twisted in distaste. "Carlos. I might have known."

Dacardi sneered. "Don't push it, pretty boy. I know you, too."

Michael shrugged, then said, "Tell me something, Detective Flynn. Cass, Dacardi, and I all have something in common. Do you know what it is?"

Flynn's voice sounded strained. "You're all criminals. You tell *me* something, Michael. Dacardi is here for his son. I want my sister. Cass is on a holy mission. What do you want?"

"There wasn't anything good on television tonight." Michael laughed, but it sounded brittle, like crushing aluminum foil. "And I love the absurd dark comedy."

Nobody said anything to that. So Flynn considered me a criminal. Just because I carried an illegal gun and a few pieces of fake ID. Well, I did ask Dacardi to kidnap Hammer, but it wasn't my fault Hammer died. And I probably killed that Bastinado whose ribs I'd punched in. Killing Pogo the Slum Devil didn't count, and Flynn didn't know about Theron, which was self-defense anyway. I let out a mental sigh and gave in. *Okay, I'm a criminal.* Yet he accepted me anyway . . .

We rolled down River Street toward the docks—an empty River Street. No prostitutes, no strutting Bastinados; animal instinct must have told them this wasn't a night for ordinary evil. I leaned forward and told Dacardi's driver to turn left into the Zombie.

"No!" Michael's hand suddenly shot out and caught the back of my neck. He squeezed. "There's another way!"

"Let me go." I twisted, trying to break his grip.

With the faint whisper of metal sliding over leather, Flynn suddenly had a knife at Michael's throat, under his ear. "It's not bronze," he said, his voice quiet and steady. "Let's see if it cuts anyway."

Michael froze.

So did I. Flynn's words carried deadly intent. Flynn would kill to protect me. Flynn loved me. I'd seen the signs, but my own emotional roller coaster got in the way. The moment I realized it, the warmth and love I felt when I rescued a child was nothing compared to the joy gliding through me then. And I loved him. The thing, the ball of fire that rolled during our lovemaking; his steadiness when I, a very strong person, needed it—how could I not love him? But this wasn't the time or place to dwell on it.

Michael released me with a sigh, leaned back, and crossed his arms.

Flynn relaxed, but he kept the knife out and ready.

I turned to Flynn, but he stared out the window at the rolling dark. My ten-year private battle with the servants of the Darkness had gone to hell in two days. If I survived the night, I'd have a poster printed to hang on my wall next to Murphy's Law: CHAOS RULES!

The Zombie's streets were often blocked and debris crunched under the tires. We had to make detours twice, once around a massive crack in the pavement and another where a building had collapsed into the street. I'd memorized the aerial photo and guided the driver. Two creatures dashed away from the headlights, humanlike, but one dragged a tail behind it.

Dacardi hissed, but he held steady. His driver simply drove. Had he seen these things before?

"They run from the light, Dacardi," I tried to reassure him. "We really didn't even need this much backup."

"Bastinados got guns, too, you know," he said.

I started to say that they didn't have much firepower compared to us, but given Big Devil Snag's story of arms, I knew I might be wrong.

Flynn draped his arm across my shoulder and dragged me closer against his solid body. When he did, he swiped the knife past Michael's face. Michael didn't blink, but it must have reminded him of his earlier actions.

"I'm sorry if I hurt you." Michael laid a hand on my arm. "I just think you're making a mistake."

I agreed, but I'd acted on instinct. "Forget it. We're all edgy." Edgy? We were damn near insane. Rescuing kids used to be as easy as a quick snatch and run. Me, the Huntress. Alone. How did I wind up dragging armed, dangerous men with me? Men who despised each other at that.

The Fire Dog slowly made its way deeper into the Zombie, the headlights cutting the claustrophobic dark and creating odd, menacing shadows in eerie urban ruins. No sound penetrated the Fire Dog other than the soft grumble of the engine.

"Stop here," I ordered.

"Cassandra, what are you doing?" Michael demanded.

"Exactly what she wants to do," Flynn said. Resignation weighed like granite stone in his voice, but determination lay there, too.

"Damn it, Cass." Michael grabbed my hand, then, with a glance at Flynn, released it. "I told you we can—"

"No. Michael, you've lied to me, directly and by omission. Theron and the Goblin Den, Victor—you give me hints like I'm supposed to be a sleuth in a mystery novel. I can't trust you."

"But you're bringing me along."

"Yes, I am. You're right. I want to know where you are. All the time."

Michael said nothing, and he wouldn't meet my eyes. Not angry, but elusive and evasive as ever.

Dacardi grumbled from the front seat. "My men—" He nodded his head toward the other Fire Dog. "They can take him somewhere else."

"No. Let's go get this disaster over with."

Flynn squeezed me tight one last time as we climbed out of the van.

I convinced Dacardi not to bring the flamethrowers. Excellent weapons they might be, but not in a tunnel, where a back draft could incinerate us all.

The Fire Dogs remained, lights off, while we used flashlights to check our weapons. Dacardi thought of everything right down to plastic bags for his electronic gadgets. He wore multipocketed coveralls like those you see in hunting magazines. He and the two men he'd chosen to accompany him carried automatic rifles, and Flynn accepted one when offered. Dacardi wanted to bring four men, but didn't argue too much when I said no. Dacardi grumbled about how much the bronze ammo cost.

I stuck with my pistol. Michael refused all weapons. I guess he thought he was indestructible. We were all loaded down with ammo, and we had brilliant, but unlit, halogen lights attached to our bodies, so our hands were free.

"This is great," I said as I adjusted the light harness so my gun wasn't covered. "For once I'll be able to see really well."

"You've never used lights?" Dacardi asked.

"No. I never go below unless necessary."

"It's not necessary now," Michael said. I jumped because he spoke from behind me. I hadn't seen him move. Sneaky bastard. I ignored him.

My night vision and sense of direction were excellent, and with the glowing lichens, I could find my way. I doubted I could guide them in that manner. The drastic increase in the number of monsters was problematic, too.

"This one." I pointed at a manhole cover. Dacardi's men lifted it off with their bare hands and exposed a three-foot black circle into hell.

I gave the signal and the Fire Dogs left us standing alone in the street. I realized my mistake when grunts and groans filled the night air. The vehicles should have stayed until we went down. At least Dacardi remembered to bring the ladder I'd asked for.

Once the manhole cover came off, I made Dacardi and his men take a good whiff so they could get their puking over with before we went down. Dacardi gagged, but he held. His men grumbled, but had no other reaction. Where had they been that such a powerful stench left them unmoved?

"I'm going down first," I said. "Michael, you and Dacardi come after me. You two"—I pointed at Dacardi's men—"come next. Flynn comes last." I laid a hand on Flynn's chest. "Watch out—when you're alone, they may charge. Try not to shoot if you don't have to. We're more than a mile from where we need to be, but we should keep the noise down."

"I'm ready," he said. "You be careful going down."

Most manholes have climbing rungs set into the walls of the tube, but they aren't always stable. They might hold me, but the bigger, heavier men could break one loose and fall. We'd use a ladder here. I lifted Nefertiti out of her basket and draped her around my neck. She coiled and made herself comfortable, her head close to my ear. Somehow, the weight on my shoulders comforted me.

I started down, carrying another of the powerful halogen lights Dacardi provided. Most predators would run from that much light, at least temporarily.

The last thing I heard before I went down was the rumble of distant thunder. It hadn't rained in three months, and a half-inch shower over the Barrows would send walls of water crashing through the storm sewers. The Earth Mother ruled the weather, though, and if she wanted this job done, she'd send any rain far from here.

As soon as my head went below the road surface, I turned on the lights. Nothing greeted me when I reached the tunnel floor and, better yet, only an inch or so of shit covered my boots. That meant fewer monsters in this section. Of course, one is too many. I lifted Nefertiti off my neck and laid her on the floor. She rolled to wet her body in the slime much as Nirah had rolled in caviar at the hotel.

Michael followed right behind me.

"You sure you don't want a gun?" I asked when he stood beside me.

"No. I'll depend on yours. I place my trust in you, even if you have less faith in me."

"Trust is earned. I'm predictable."

"Oh, if only that were so, Huntress."

Dacardi lumbered down the ladder. He gagged but, again, didn't lose his dinner. His two bruisers followed him. Flynn suddenly dropped, clinging to the rungs to break his fall. The ladder gave a violent jerk as he released it.

I stepped under the manhole and fired two shots straight up. The ladder stopped moving. The explosion of shots in the sewer's confines left us deaf and our faces pinched with pain. Dacardi bent over holding his ears. I motioned everyone to stand close while our hearing returned. When it did, I said, "That's why we don't shoot unless necessary." I eyed Dacardi. "And we don't use grenades unless we want to bring the roof down. Everyone stay in the light."

Dacardi sneered, but he'd lost confidence, so it quickly faded.

The sewer was square here, and brick, at least fifteen feet wide and almost that tall. The walls and floor appeared to be in good condition. We'd entered almost a mile from the pentagram's center, and we'd have a long walk to the first cross point.

I pointed at Dacardi's men. "You two come last. Take turns, but keep a light shining behind us at all times."

The pair looked at Dacardi for confirmation of my orders.

I made an instant decision. "These two don't go. They're not listening to me."

Again, they glanced at Dacardi for direction.

"You got your men. I got mine." Dacardi lifted his rifle in outright defiance.

"Okay." I threw my hands up. "I'll leave. You can go

on, go back, or go to hell. Your choice." I snatched the
map out of my shirt pocket and offered it to him. "Just
follow the lines."

Flynn moved quickly to me. So did Michael.

"Bitch!" Dacardi spit out the word.

"Yep, that's me. First class. Look, Dacardi, I appreciate what you did for me last night in the river." I ignored
the fact that if he hadn't taken me to the warehouse in
the first place, I wouldn't have required saving. "And I
appreciate the badass weapons. But it's *my* hunt. Either
they take orders from me or I leave."

We stood in a semicircle, in a brilliant pool of light.
One of Dacardi's men suddenly lifted his gun and pointed
it at us. As he did, he backed up, too close to the pool's
edge. A clawed arm flew out of the darkness, snagged him,
and dragged him back. He didn't even have time to scream
before the snarls and the flesh-ripping, bone-popping
clamor began. The smell of fresh blood filled the air.

Everyone but me stood stunned. I swept the brilliant
flare of my light toward the hideous sound. Three large,
slimy predators writhed and tore at something on the
tunnel floor. I drew my pistol and fired three shots into
one. In spite of the light, the monsters never slowed
their feast. The one I shot went down, and I hoped the
other two would start on him when they finished their
human dinner. We needed time to get away. I sent a silent *Thank you* to the Mother that they were in the opposite direction we needed to go.

I waved my arms to get everyone's attention, since
we were all deaf again.

Nefertiti slid in front of us as they followed me down
the tunnel, leaving the banquet behind. When we'd gone
a short way, I fixed one light on the back harness of Dacardi's remaining man so it would shine behind us. He
didn't object.

Dacardi hadn't spoken since his man had gone down,

but he drew a breath, coughed, and said, "Those things . . . if someone got them uptown . . ."

"Not uptown. The Mother keeps them here in the Barrows. River Street, maybe, if there was a complete blackout."

Dacardi didn't say anything to that.

I'd seen no evidence of the larger predators since we left the manhole entry, though we did come across a few bones now and then. The thin stream of water that sloshed under our feet wasn't clean, but also not as foul as that behind us.

In that environment, in the heavy darkness that had probably not seen light since construction early in the twentieth century, time became indeterminable and indefinite. Maybe we were down an hour, and maybe five minutes. A long, lonely journey filled with heavy silence broken only by the echo of breathing and the slosh of water at our footsteps. We came to a crossroads where the tunnel diverged in two other directions. We'd reached a place where the pentagram lines met, and we weren't far from our goal. I had to decide: find a place to go up, or see if I could get closer by using one of the smaller feeder lines?

"Cass." Tension suddenly rippled through Michael's voice. "Can you hear . . . ?"

I did. Rain. The blessed sound people prayed for over the long summer; the deadly sound of a swelling wall of water. A drip, a trickle, then finally a rushing deluge to sweep human and monster away without prejudice or discretion.

We had to get out. Already, a small surge sloshed over our feet. Nefertiti whipped her body in a large splash and rushed away down a side tunnel.

"Come on," I said. I followed my snake.

We had no choice really. None of our flashing lights showed a single manhole. Once we passed a street grate, far too small for us to get through. The sound of rain

hissed on the pavement above, so we picked up the pace.
Nefertiti waited at a smaller tunnel to our left, then entered as we reached her. I started after her.

Flynn grabbed my arm. "Cass, if we get trapped in there—"

I pulled away. "I follow Nefertiti. Michael?"

"Yes, Cassandra."

"You can say 'I told you so' anytime you want."

"I'd love to, if I weren't down here with you."

We headed down the side tunnel, barely wide enough to walk single file. We'd gone no more than a hundred feet when it suddenly ended at face level. At my feet was a three-foot-diameter concrete tube. I stooped down and shined my light in the hole. I couldn't see the end, only Nefertiti, who had stopped again, waiting on me. She writhed and I could feel her agitation. I dropped to my hands and knees.

Flynn crouched beside me. "You're not going in there!"

"Yes, I am. No one has to go with me, but—" The sound of rushing water came closer. "Sorry, guys. I should have gone in alone."

Should have—Cassandra's famous last words.

I started in. I did hurry, but by the time I'd crawled twenty feet, four inches of water sloshed under me. The poor condition of the concrete pipe became more evident with every foot. Cracks cut into my palms and knees like I crawled over broken rock.

How absolutely fucking miserable. I couldn't die of a nice noble gunshot. I couldn't even drown in the river after a massive explosion. I had to drown in a tube of shitty water. Worse, I had dragged the man I loved and three others behind me. There was nothing to do but go on. I could feel a faint brush of cool air on my face, but if the pipe completely filled . . .

"Nefertiti," I yelled. "Where are you?"

The water rose to my forearms. Nefertiti whipped her

body in front of my face. The light I'd secured to me burned bright, but it couldn't penetrate water murky and thick as sludge from a clogged drain. It covered my elbows and sloshed against my stomach. I crawled faster.

All our weapons were wet. They should fire, but I had always had some doubts about the integrity of ammunition manipulated to add the bronze. Two things I left to the experts—my ammunition and my car. Point them in the right direction, pull the trigger or step on the gas, and life was good—if they worked. I hoped my ammo man was more competent than my mechanic.

Damn. I was going to drown and all I could think of was my water-soaked weapons.

The water had risen to my chest. Numbing winter cold, cold as the depths of the Sullen. The dark sewers leached every bit of warmth it might have gained passing over steaming asphalt above. I had to drag my heavy, soaked clothes with me.

"Cass?" Flynn gasped from behind me.

"Keep moving," I yelled.

The pressure came from behind, which meant the main sewers had filled and forced the water up this tubular death trap. Why had the Mother let it rain now? Had she abandoned me as she'd abandoned Abby?

Water splashed up and filled my mouth and nose. I choked and blew the filth out. I crawled in the complete darkness of what would be my tomb.

Nefertiti's body hit my face. She writhed weakly, a reptile dying in the frigid water. I opened my mouth and liquid filth poured in. I grasped Nefertiti in my teeth as gently as I could and forged on. We probably had less than a minute before the tube filled completely and we all drowned. My hands clawed at the pipe, scrabbling and scratching for momentum, and found . . . nothing.

I fell forward into the gap and my head went underwater.

chapter 29

The water's force shoved me from behind, rolled me, slapped me against concrete, and flung my body out onto open, level ground. Water spewed from the opening and covered me in a dirty waterfall. My lungs heaved and gasped for air, but my light, free from water, returned the gift of sight. I coughed and gagged, spitting and sputtering to get the filth out of my mouth.

Nefertiti flopped weakly in a small pool beside me. The gushing torrent spread out on the flatter surface and started to drag her away, so I grabbed her.

Like the basement under the warehouse where we'd found the weapons, a part of a wall had collapsed into the storm sewers. The gaping crack spewed a torrential flood.

Flynn surged out next. In an instant, though, he scrambled back to the opening, shoved his body in, grabbed Dacardi, and dragged him out. Michael came next. The water gushed harder. Flynn stuck his arms in, feeling for Dacardi's man. He drew a breath and shoved his upper body in. Finally, he pulled back gasping. "I can't find him."

"I'm sorry, Dacardi," I said.

Dacardi shrugged. "Don't think he followed us in. I didn't hear him. I guess he ran."

While the others sat coughing and trying to shake off the effect of the cold, I moved away from the pipe. I managed to stand, not an easy task with an armful of snake.

My light flashed on our surroundings.

"Where are we?" Flynn stood beside me.

I swung the light to the floor. A set of rails, twisted and broken, ran into the darkness in both directions. "A subway tunnel."

Nefertiti was limp as a length of rope in my hands. Shit! I had to get her warmed. Dacardi was wearing the most clothes. I went to him. "She needs close body heat."

"Goddamn, bitch." He unzipped his coveralls. "Better a snake around my neck than following you." He ripped his shirt open so she could lie against his skin.

"She likes you, too," I said to Dacardi. I coiled her as best I could and deposited her in his coveralls.

To my amazement, one of Dacardi's coverall pockets produced a plastic bag with dry cloths. What an incredibly complex man.

We had no way to dry anything else, but we cleaned up the weapons as best we could. Water from the hole in the tunnel wall still gushed, but quickly drained away in the vastness of the subway tunnel. That particular danger seemed to be over. I relaxed and oriented myself. The pipe we'd crawled through felt straight enough; that would put the pentagram's center a hundred yards to the southeast.

"This way." My little band of warriors followed me. Not that they had a choice at this point.

Water had slicked Michael's hair back. He'd lost the cap he'd worn earlier, but his wonderful face and graceful body gave no hint of discomfort, even though he was as wet as the rest of us.

Dacardi stared around, interested in his surroundings, on his great adventure to rescue his son. He fared the best of all, I think. His coveralls didn't keep him dry, but they kept him warm. Flynn, like me, seemed to be concentrating on putting one foot in front of the other.

We hadn't gone far when we reached a platform where passengers once waited for the trains. "Anybody know how long it's been since the Barrows had an operating subway?" I asked.

Michael answered me. "It's never had one. It was close to completion in 1948, the year the sixty percent of the Barrows' infrastructure collapsed. They'd built the subway and were going to link it uptown. Those tracks have never had a train roll over them. An old man who worked at the clinic told me about it. I was curious, but not brave enough to go into the monster's lair and explore."

"What caused the collapse?" In a few sentences, he'd given me more information than I'd ever been able to find.

"He didn't know. The electricity stopped working and regular sewers failed."

"Not surprising." Not given the total aberration of the place we called the Barrows. Those aberrations extended far beyond the ruins and to the people who lived here. I climbed onto the platform and the others followed me.

"How's Nefertiti?" I asked Dacardi.

"She's moving better now. She led us here?"

"It appears so. Let's search the general area and see what we find."

We crossed the platform. The stairs going up to the street had collapsed into a pile of rubble, so no escape there. I wasn't looking for escape, though.

Dacardi grunted and Nefertiti's head popped out of his coveralls. She squirmed and stretched her body out a foot. I rubbed my thumb under her chin. "Which way, baby?"

She twisted to my right. Debris piled against the wall, partly from the falling stairs. "Go closer," I told Dacardi.

He walked slowly toward the pile. Behind it, I could see a steel door. Where would that lead? Thirty minutes later, with a minimum of grumbling, we had the frame cleared. The opening revealed a closet full of wires hanging in mad disarray, an electrical closet that once served the subway.

I wasn't willing to let matters go so quickly. I shoved myself into the closet. "Bring Nefertiti here."

Dacardi came to me, Nefertiti slid out of his coveralls into my arms, and I laid her on the floor. His body heat had revived her and she moved normally now. I worried, though. She immediately crawled through the clump of wires and disappeared.

I dropped to my knees and the remaining floor debris cut into my jeans. "Nefertiti, we can't go that way." She didn't return. I bent down to dig through the wires and they parted as easily as spaghetti in my hands. I found what she wanted me to see. Behind the wires was a three-foot-square box that led into what had probably been a service passage.

"Okay, guys. Help me get some of these wires out of the way."

They let out a few sighs, but gave in. What else could they do? Call a cab and go home? I stood back while Michael and Dacardi tore at the wires so they wouldn't tangle in any equipment we carried.

Flynn stood beside me. "Cass, if we can't find Selene, I'll understand."

"Why shouldn't we find her?" I laid a hand on his chest and felt the steady beat of his heart. "Nefertiti is on the trail."

"You were right, though. I should have had faith in you." His lips brushed across my forehead. "We didn't need Michael or his money."

"No, we didn't need Michael or his money. But I think he's here with us for a reason."

"Not a good one."

"Don't let your prejudice make good guys into bad guys." I said *prejudice* when I meant *jealousy*.

"And Michael's a good guy?" Flynn's voice sounded tight. He didn't believe that.

"Michael is Michael."

"And Dacardi?"

"Dacardi is a criminal, but I like him, too. Bare-ass courage made him what he is. He'll stand with us. Remember the knights on the chessboard. We'll see what he's made of soon."

"The same could be said for all of us, Cass."

He was right. I drew a breath to speak, to say the words, tell him how I felt when a scrape came from behind me. Claws on concrete. I knew that sound. One of the rhinolike predators I'd killed the day we'd fallen into the sewer was scrabbling and clawing its way onto the platform. Ungainly, slow, and lumbering, probably injured by the storm sewer flood. I drew my gun but hesitated. I'd be shouting *Here I am!* by blasting monsters this close.

"That's it," Michael called from the closet. "We're in."

Nefertiti suddenly raced past me. She coiled and struck the predator in one smooth movement. Her fangs caught the thing in the softer-looking tissue around its lips. The thing froze and she struck again, this time under its eye. Then she calmly glided back toward us.

The monster stood rigid. It gave one long, mournful cry that stretched away down the long tunnel and into the darkness beyond. With a heavy, wet smack, it toppled over onto the concrete platform. The gray hide quivered and jerked. One final sigh escaped its lungs like air from a balloon.

"Damn," Dacardi said from behind me. "She's good."

Nefertiti crawled to him and stopped at his feet. He crouched in front of her. Then he held out his hand and she crawled up his arm to nuzzle his ear. I went first, a bit of a squeeze, but no more than the pipe that dumped us here. At least it was dry. As I suspected, a duct carried electrical wires serving the subway. Twenty feet down, it opened up into a narrow passageway that let us stand. Still more wires to shove aside, but easier this time.

"These wires are copper," Dacardi said. "A million dollars in salvage here."

"Probably." I had to agree. "There's a lot in the Barrows that's salvageable."

"Who owns it?" Flynn asked. "They pay taxes, don't they?"

"Yes," Michael said. "I do." His words weighed heavy with irony.

"All of it?" I stopped to turn back and stare at him.

"No. A large portion, the Zombie and the areas close to the docks."

"You own the Zombie? How did you manage that?"

"Abandoned property. Tax sales. I purchased it from the city. They were happy to sell. Taxes are pennies a square block until I redevelop. I'd begun the redevelopment process near the docks when I suddenly ran out of money."

Oh, yes, brother Vic had helped himself to the cookie jar. That semi-explained why Michael tolerated Theron. He needed the money.

We came to another metal door, but this one cocked to the side and hung from one hinge. We emerged into an underground parking garage.

This was ideal territory for monsters, but there was no sign or smell. Only one level below the street, but I could hear water seeping in the lower end, lapping at the pavement like a dog slurping from a toilet. The roll of thunder thudded through the building. Now relatively safe, I prayed that the Mother would send a biblical flood to cleanse the nightmare under the streets—and I wondered why she didn't do it before we went down. Abby said she controlled the weather. I assumed she controlled the weather. So how did we go wrong here?

Nefertiti slid down Dacardi's arm and headed across the garage to the high end, where a set of twisted steel stairs led up into the building itself. She waited for us. I picked her up when I reached her and draped her over my shoulders. I knew she could climb, but I still worried. She'd taken a horrible chill for a snake.

We climbed the stairs one person at a time to distribute our weight, but they creaked and groaned. We gathered on a more solid landing.

"This is too easy," I said softly. "Nothing I do is this easy."

"Don't borrow trouble, Cass," Flynn whispered in my ear.

"Dim the lights," I said as I gripped the metal door handle. *Great Mother, don't let it be jammed.* The door opened with the perfect ease and oiled silence of something used often. Disturbing. Were we expected? Most likely. The hallway we entered was clear of debris. An easy path to the interior and another set of stairs leading up to the next floor.

Our feet made little sound on the steps as we climbed. Shreds of ancient rotted carpet clung to the steps—at the outside edges, not the middle. Someone used this path often enough to wear the threads away. The air smelled different here. Not like habitation, but not the tomblike atmosphere of a truly abandoned building. The signs of use ended at a door. I signaled for them to cut off the lights and we walked into a dark, silent hallway. In the distance, I could see a faint glow and hear the soft sound of voices.

Nefertiti writhed and slid down my body to the floor and headed for the light.

The men fanned out on either side of me as we crept down the hall. I had them turn off their lights and let their eyes become accustomed to the dimmer illumination.

Then a child's voice, a little girl's, said, "Oh, look, the snake is back."

"No, that's a different one. The other one was bigger." A boy spoke this time, his young voice pitched high with fear. "Don't go over there, Kimmy. It might bite you."

Soft light spilled from a room on my left. An open, steel-barred cage door stood in place of a regular one. I faced my troops and held up my hands, palms out, trying to make them not rush into a trap.

"Careful." I mouthed the words. Still too easy.

I peeked around the door's edge. Several kids—I couldn't tell how many—sat huddled together on mattresses on the floor. The light came from a few battery lamps scattered around the room. Cookie and candy wrappers littered the area, along with empty water bottles. At least the scum who locked them up fed them. A couple of portable toilets sat in the corner, but in spite of that, the room smelled of sewage. Long-term planning by someone who kept children as sacrificial lambs.

Dacardi surged forward and I blocked him with my body. Had he heard Richard's voice? "Wait," I said. "It could be—"

"What was that?" another girl said. This one sounded older.

Flynn drew a sharp breath. Selene's voice, most likely.

I stared straight ahead down the hall, still looking for a trap. I saw nothing but darkness.

"Who's there?" a boy called. Fear came with his words, but anger, too.

Dacardi jerked again. Richard for sure.

I stepped in front of the door so they could see me. They all stood now, huddled in a group. Selene was there, as was Richard. Teenagers, they stood tall above four other children, two boys and two girls. The older pair stepped in front of the smaller children.

"Hi," I said softly. "Richard—quick—are there guards?"

He shook his head. "No. At least not close. Men come at daylight and bring food." He didn't talk loud, hadn't moved, and held the others back. Healthy suspicion resonated in his voice.

"Stand still and be quiet. Okay?"

Richard nodded.

"Michael, give me a hand here." His strength, combined with mine, should've let us remove the door.

Michael came forward. "Stand back."

He wrapped his hands around the barred door and jerked up and out. It cracked with the sound of a demolition crew at work as it popped loose at the lock and tore out half the doorjamb.

Dacardi rushed into the room. Flynn followed him. I couldn't blame them.

"See!" Selene cried as she flung herself into Flynn's arms. "I told you my brother would come. I told you!" Flynn didn't say anything. He cried. So did Dacardi.

"We need to go," Michael said. "Now."

The other children had come forward, but they huddled together, despair on their faces.

"Can we go, too?" one little girl asked. Her voice quavered and tears glittered in her eyes. No one had come for them.

"Of course you can." I reached out to reassure them, but Michael stepped forward first.

He crouched down to be on their level and gave them that beneficent smile. "You can come with me."

One of the girls, a lovely child, reached out to touch him, then drew her hand back. "Are you an angel?"

"No, but I'm someone who will help you," he said. This was a Michael I'd never seen. Man, human, or something else, he had a complexity I did not understand.

They'd been psychologically wounded, these young ones, probably traumatized to the deepest places in their hearts. I hoped they would recover. Maybe Abby would help with a potion or two—if she could.

I went back and checked both directions in the hallway. Nothing.

I didn't want to go back the way we came in, but we were in the heart of the Zombie Zone, and nothing good lay outside. The rain had stopped, and I'd bet the storm sewers were moderately clean by now.

"Nefertiti," I called softly. Damn, where was she? "Nefertiti, come on, snake."

"Maybe she went with the other snake," Richard said. "The big one that looks like her."

"Oh, yes," Selene chimed in. "One of the men came back after they fed us one morning. He came in and said I was a big girl and he wanted to play with me." She sneered. She knew how he wanted to play. "The snake came and bit him. He fell over and died." Her eyes glittered, even in the soft light. "It came and stayed with us sometimes. We weren't scared when it was here."

"He'd locked the door behind him before he died, so we couldn't get out," Richard said. "But I took this and hid it before the others came and found him." He held up a stunner. "Batteries are good." He had a dark streak near his eye. He'd fought somewhere along the way.

"And I got this." Selene drew a bronze-bladed knife out of her pocket. She grinned and I could see so much of Flynn in her.

These two had been willing to fight, not surprising, given their relatives. I didn't know of a big snake, but Nefertiti knew her way around. This was where I'd found her and maybe she called it home. Others like her might live here. I certainly couldn't go hunting for her.

"You ready?" Dacardi held a cell phone to his ear, and his little GPS thing glowed in his hand. "Good.

Track us. Hurry. Blast your way in if you have to. There's an extra hundred thou for all of you."

"Damn, Dacardi. That's big-time." I couldn't hide my shock.

"Ain't going back in those sewers." He stuffed the instruments in the plastic bag and shoved it back in his pocket.

We made our way down to the first floor using one dim, shaded light. There were no windows or doors left there, and no sign of monsters.

"Still too easy," I muttered.

I peered outside and tried to get my bearings. The plaza, the center of the pentagram and the last place I wanted to be, was behind us on the other side of the building. Lightning flickered across the sky and skirted the tattered edges of boiling clouds. Not crashing bolts, but what my mother called God's lace. A precise scientific name, I'm sure. The street was empty but the night had a heavy silence, as if greater things were ready to fall upon us.

Flynn wrapped an arm around me and kissed my ear. He was shaking and he couldn't talk. We made a three-way clump, since Selene wouldn't let go of him.

"Thank you," he whispered, as Selene finally broke the embrace to talk to Richard.

I had to say it. I grabbed his shirt and held on. "I want to tell you . . . I . . ."

"I know. My love, my life, I know." He rubbed his face against mine.

For once, I had no words.

Richard comforted the younger children. A born leader, that boy. I could feel the power in him and Selene. That was the thing that caused the Mother to send me after some children. These were the ones the Darkness desired. The others, while still precious, were simply children. I always rescued them when I could and I hoped that somewhere there was someone to love them, joyful to have them returned.

Michael stood silent, his eyes on the street.

Michael turned to me. I couldn't see his eyes, but I felt the weight of his gaze. Had he proven himself this night? I wanted to think so. I wanted to think that Dacardi's men would arrive and we'd all go safely home.

Dacardi was whispering in his phone again and the mechanical sound of approaching vehicles came. Then the sound of gunfire. "Use the big ones," Dacardi ordered, his voice rising. "Use the fucking flamethrowers." He shouted the last words.

Light, brilliant as a high summer morning, filled the streets a block away. Howls and screams filled the night, then roars of rage. The battle had begun—and since the vehicles hadn't slowed, I'd bet humans and their guns were winning—for now. When they moved closer, their light filled the street before us. I had a bit different perspective.

I'd seen the monsters in the sewers, an increase in the numbers over the years, but now at least a hundred milled in the street. They must have climbed aboveground at the first sign of rain. Now they poured out of buildings and threw themselves in front of what looked like a couple of Fire Dogs on steroids. Men sat on top of one and suddenly sent out a thirty-foot slash of fire. That fire sent dozens of blazing monsters running away screaming. Other men with automatic rifles fired indiscriminately through the throngs and mowed the creatures down.

"Dacardi," I screamed over the deafening chaos of battle. "How did you know we'd need this much firepower?"

Dacardi was laughing. "My granny told me. I dreamed about her two nights ago. Paid attention for a change."

I saw no reason for the humor, because more creatures were pouring out of the buildings around us, packing the streets with fangs and claws. Why were there none in the building that held the children? Because, of course, we'd walked into a trap. I didn't think the person or thing setting the trap had counted on Dacardi's army getting us out. They had expected me to come alone, I realized. I was supposed to go in, unchallenged, until someone snapped the jaws shut around me. Maybe I had done something right, asking for help.

The roar of battle buffeted us: screams, donkeylike brays, the firecracker chatter of guns, and the racing engines of the Steroid Dogs. The vehicles had made their way to within sixty feet of us and stopped where the street ended in a series of cracks they couldn't cross. We'd have to weave our way between those cracks— and we'd have to fight.

I drew my gun and heard the others ready theirs.

"Richard, Selene, you keep the little ones together," I shouted above the screams and gunfire. "Stay in the middle and let us fight."

They did as I asked, their faces solidified with determination. After weeks of fear and captivity, these two brave children wanted to take a stand.

Dacardi yelled final orders into his phone. "Get down," he said. He pulled something out of his pocket. He threw it outside. Oh, damn. We all dropped. The grenade exploded, sending monster parts flying everywhere, even onto us. We surged out of the building and onto the street. We made it a good way over the pavement before the beasts realized we were running among them. Only forty feet to go.

Flynn and Dacardi were the only ones with rifles. They mowed quite a few down. I had to be more selective. I'm a good shot, and every time I pulled the trigger, every time the gun slammed against my palm, one went down. The brilliance of the lights on the vehicles helped. The creatures frantically shook their heads in an attempt to keep from staring into it straight on.

Then they surrounded us and our forward motion slowed. Another searing blast of fire came close—too close. The biggest problem was the monsters between the vehicles and us. We couldn't shoot in that direction and the men couldn't shoot in ours. I moved to the front, where my shots—individual, precisely placed—were more effective. I dropped a magazine and loaded another. The men on the vehicle shot them, too.

Another fifteen feet. With horrified faces and wide, bulging eyes, the younger children screamed, but those small cries were lost in the clamor of battle. Richard and Selene had them by the arms and dragged them on.

Sometimes an idea, a bit of knowledge, a realization comes to you, but you shove it aside when faced with major distractions. In the back of my mind, I knew something was wrong. The monsters weren't attacking us. They thrashed around, slashing and screaming, they threw themselves at the war machines, but they didn't attack the humans moving among them. They only used their solid bodies to hinder us. *Control.* What could possibly be controlling them?

We made it to the Dog by climbing over the hideous carcasses we and Dacardi's men had killed. The doors popped open and Michael loaded the kids. Dacardi, Flynn, and I fired into the press of beasts. The troops on top of the vehicle could fire over our heads now. They beat them back until the living had to crawl over the dead. And crawl over they did.

Dacardi climbed in the Dog, then Flynn and Michael. The beasts froze. I wasn't sure anyone noticed but me, since the troops on top of the vehicle continued to fire. The change came in a chill whisper that echoed in my head, not my ears. As one, the monsters surged, throwing their bodies, shoving me backward, separating me from the others. One of them barreled into me from behind.

Stunned, I staggered forward. Another of the apelike beasts caught me in its arms. The thing was three times my size. With five-inch claws—claws that never touched me— it scooped me up like a child and carried me away. Up and over the dead, down the street. No one would shoot for fear of hitting me—if they even saw what happened.

Gunfire ratcheted up behind me as the attack on the Dog resumed. I bounced in painful slaps against the beast's rough hide as it made heavy, galloping leaps across the pavement. It grunted with each step and blew foul carrion breath over me. I finally got over my shock and realized I still had my gun. I shoved the barrel under the beast's chin and pulled the trigger. It died instantly as the bronze blasted out the top of its head, but forward momentum carried it on—and if it fell on me, I'd be lucky to get off with broken bones. Another creature grabbed me as the first collapsed.

Animals! Who controlled animals—monsters—the way I controlled Nirah and Nefertiti? I was in deep shit. I shot the second beast, same as the first. As it fell, I twisted away, but I landed hard on the pavement. I kept my head up, but my hip and one elbow flared like someone drove a nail in them.

Stunned, I couldn't tell how far I'd gone. Not too far, because light glowed from fairly close by. I heard gunfire, though, and I could go in that direction. Or even back into the storm sewer, which had to be free of monsters because they were all up on the street.

I rolled and tried to push myself up. Liquid splashed in my face. I gasped as Robert had when I'd hit him with the truth potion, and, of course, I sucked it into my lungs. My body instantly went limp. Fingers, not claws, tore the gun from my hand. My eyes burned like an acid bath and a corrosive taste filled my mouth.

Someone bent over me. I couldn't see, but I knew the voice.

"I'm sorry, Huntress." Reverend Victor, benevolent director of the Lost Lamb, a man I trusted. I had seen not a single hint of betrayal.

"No! Victor!" Michael shouted from a distance. He had come for me, but I knew he was too far away.

Vic laughed with a high, hysterical cackle. "You're too late, little brother! You had your chance. Now I get mine."

"Victor, stop! Madness is her province, not yours." Michael was closer now. Much closer.

I fought a useless battle to regain control of my limp body. Whatever he used had turned my muscles to mush.

Victor shouted, "Kill him!"

Some of the sewer monsters milled around. I couldn't tell how many, but they all suddenly marched in the same direction. Consciousness slipped away.

chapter 30

I woke lying on something soft. Disoriented, I kept my eyes closed, trying to get things together.

"You're breathing faster now, Cassandra. I know you're awake." Vic swabbed a wet cloth on my mouth and I sucked a little moisture and worked up some saliva in my parched mouth.

I opened my eyes and focused on his face above me. Damn, I wanted to smash it, to break bones. My hands clenched into fists, but he'd tied my arms to what felt like a camping cot. Tied so tight my fingers throbbed, desperate for life-giving blood.

I spat at him.

Vic jumped a little but, other than that, didn't react. He had a ridiculous smile and tears ran from his eyes. For whom was he crying?

He sat in a chair beside me. His shoulders slumped and he twisted the rag in his hands.

My head and body ached, but not in the raging pain of broken bones or other serious injuries. I studied the room around me. A couple of battery lanterns cast dim light on what had once been an office. It had a dusty aura of disuse, a battered desk, and old file cabinets with missing drawers. Two bottles of water sat on the desk, but the cot I was lying on was the only actual sign of habitation.

Vic didn't look happy. No *Ha ha, I won* gloating.

"Come on, Vic. Let me loose and give me my gun. I'll save you."

A peal of shrill, penetrating laughter filled the room. Elise Ramekin came into view. She'd aged twenty years since I'd met her at the asylum. A decrepit old woman walked toward me. Her eyes were sunken deep into her face. She wore a long black robe with a bunch of peculiar designs woven into the fabric. It was far too long; she had to hold it up to walk. Even so, it trailed behind her like a giant dust rag, gathering all manner of filth. She'd pushed the sleeves back to reveal heavily bandaged arms.

I sneered at her. "What happened, bitch—get too close to the fire?"

Elise strutted up to us. Vic's head bowed, but his face was a mask of pure, blind hatred. Mother had indeed loved one of her sons more, and it wasn't him.

Elise raised her nose in arrogance and smiled. "Minor burns. I couldn't leave without saying good-bye to dear Anita. My relentless guard for so many years. Victor held her while I gave her my parting gift, so I suppose he is good for something."

A parting gift—a broken neck. Vic kept his face averted so Elise couldn't see his expression. "My older son is not beautiful like my Michael," she said. "But he's useful at times."

"Useful?" Victor hissed the words between clenched teeth. He still wouldn't look at her. "Who came to visit you every week, Mother? Who remembered holidays and birthdays?"

Elise sneered. She held up her bandaged arms. "Who was so incompetent he had to burn the whole asylum down to get me out?"

"Why did you try to kill Michael when he was born?" I asked Elise.

Elise laughed again. This time the sound filled the room, a strident crowing, dried to the bone and completely mad. Drool ran from her mouth and she swiped at it with a bandaged arm.

I suddenly knew the answer to my questions. Abby's words came to mind and I said them aloud before I realized I was speaking. "The power of sacrifice."

"Yes," Elise agreed. "I would have sacrificed him. That whore, that so-called nurse, she stopped me and took my beautiful baby away. Kathy, they called her." She sneered. "*She* had me locked up."

"And then they let you loose. You killed more kids, right?"

She frowned. Her eyes clouded. Did she not remember? As suddenly as she drifted away, she returned, but I doubt she remembered what she'd heard.

"He is my beautiful son," she crooned in an ecstatic voice. "My Michael. His father is a god. Can't you tell?"

Elise suddenly stepped forward and slapped Vic across the head. It sounded vicious, like a rock smashing a melon. "Not like this one."

Vic kept his face down, but he snarled in rage. She hit him again. His body rocked and he almost fell off his chair.

I didn't want to watch anymore. "A god?" I shouted the words. "What god? Elise, I know you're seriously cracked, but even you—"

"No!" she screamed. The sound expanded to fill the room. "You stupid cow." Elise bent over me raging, her feverish face twisted into something altogether inhuman. "I went to his world, my master's world, and I lay with him, the wonderful creature you misname the Darkness, and conceived a child." More drool slid from her mouth. She didn't bother to wipe it. "When this dark moon is over, it will be different. I will stand by Michael and his father will give us power to rule this world."

Vic growled like a dangerous mongrel backed into a corner.

Elise ignored him. She whirled and marched out of the room, dragging yards of filthy fabric behind her.

I jerked at my bonds and twisted my body, but all I received for my effort was burning pain at my wrists that compounded my other aches. I was limp as a pair of dirty jeans in the laundry basket.

Victor stared at the door where Elise exited. He licked his lips. "I'll reward my mother for her kindness very soon. She's needed—for now."

"So Mom doesn't know you sent the monsters to kill Michael."

"I had to do it. I didn't want to, but I couldn't let him stop me now. Why couldn't he understand?"

I glanced at the bottles of water. Vic saw my look, retrieved one, and held my head while I drank. I didn't spit at him this time. The water revived me some, but did nothing to stimulate my body, nothing to make me stronger. The ache in my fingers ceased to trouble me as they went numb.

Michael? The Darkness has a body? And a son? Nothing about this was good.

I had one other angle to work on. "So Mom loves pretty Michael best."

"She's obsessed with him." Vic returned to his chair. He laid a hand on my arm. To comfort me? Or himself?

"Uh, is he really . . . ?"

"Yes. The Darkness has a physical shape and, apparently, that shape is male. She did go to his world and conceive Michael—and it drove her insane. She was so beautiful before. I was only a child, but I remember the night she returned. Her hair had gone completely white. Lying with a god? She smelled like she'd fucked a rotting corpse." He sobbed and his face twisted in agony.

"Does Michael know?"

"About his father? Yes. What's happening here and my part in it? No, he didn't know. He bought the Reverend Victor, Lost Lamb thing like you did, though I think he was suspicious at times. I stole money from him. But when he was little, I protected him. Michael is dead now, and I loved him."

Michael? Dead? A deep ache welled up inside me, but I pushed it aside to deal with the immediate problem—survival. "How? You control the monsters? The Bastinados?"

Vic shrugged slightly. "My master, your Darkness, talks to me and gives me great power—his power. The Barrows creatures respond to me. I bring the Bastinados here and show them his power. Then they obey me. I am what Michael could have been. The Bastinados are human. Humans will sell their souls for the simplest of things. Pericles Theron was a partner of sorts, but he seems to have disappeared."

In all my life, I had never made such a gross misjudgment of a person as I had with Vic. "Michael's daddy won't be upset that you killed him?"

"Why should he be? Michael has lived his life torn between two worlds. He's never committed himself to anything. I've given everything."

I could agree with that. Michael was a neutral in many ways, both good and, if rumor was to be believed, evil. Someone who watched and waited. Waited for what? The dark moon?

"Vic, I may not be the best judge of character but, you . . ."

Vic sighed and lowered his head. "I enjoyed the Lost Lamb, helping people, and I'll do it again when this is over. What's lost here is a small sacrifice."

"Fuck!" I screamed. "That's because you're the one holding the knife."

"No, you don't understand. A few lives here are nothing compared to those I can save, when I have the power. I have you to thank for that."

"What did I do?"

"Only Michael could have stopped me. Michael fell in love with the Huntress. If he hadn't, he'd have made a choice. You've seen him. The young god and his adoring followers. If he'd accepted his proper place as his father's heir, he could rule the world. Now it will be me. I will be a kind master, Cassandra. I promise."

Michael owned the Goblin Den, supported Pericles Theron, and was probably guilty of the criminal acts Flynn said he'd committed. But some innate humanity existed in him. At least I liked to think so. I doubt it was love for me that kept him from overwhelming evil. Michael remained a mystery, even in death. "It's all about sacrifice, isn't it?"

"Yes. You are one of the Earth Mother's Huntresses. The powerful enemy. There are many, but none so attuned to this place they call the Barrows. By your own power and will, you belong. I knew it the minute I met you." He sounded so joyful. Of course, no one was going to kill him. He twisted his hands together, as if trying to wring something from them. "This dark moon, along with the astral conjunction, weakens the barriers between worlds. We had to have you here at this particular time. Your life is going to open a door, a permanent door to his world, and allow my master inconceivable power. He will not come here. Mother wants him, too, but he would be weaker here. He will give me strength to destroy your Earth Mother and rule this world—through me."

"Bullshit! Absolute bullshit!" I could see everything quite clearly in the face of imminent doom. "There's only one sacrifice: yourself. Oh, you can kill me. You can kill children. But you won't gain anything—certainly not power.

"And the kids?" I continued. "How do they fit in?"

"I'm very proud of my network of spies. They watch people for me. Flynn's sister was taken to draw you in. Because his mother worshipped your precious Abby, we knew she'd send you for her. The others happened to be in the same place at the same time. We would have used them if we couldn't get you."

Whoa! Just happened to be? Nothing unintentional happens when you're on the chessboard of two incredibly powerful supernatural entities. Something, someone put Dacardi's son with Selene. Why? So I'd have access to his weapons?

"So you bought the guns and explosives? With money you'd embezzled."

Vic nodded. Dirty light played across his face. He had more malfunctioning brain cells than Elise. It probably never occurred to him that he might have waited until yesterday, and hired goons to kidnap me like Dacardi did. No. Too simple and direct a plan for a sick, twisted mind. That's the thing with prophets and, yes, fortune-tellers. Everything is part of some mystical, but unarticulated, scheme. I suspected some reluctance on Vic's part, too. Did he secretly hope it would fail? Somewhere, deep in his twisted soul, had he complicated things to the point it would all come crashing down?

"Give me a break here, Vic. A couple hundred scaly monsters who avoid sunlight and stupid, unreliable Bastinados against heavily armed soldiers? You've been watching too much television. If you unleashed them on the world, all you'd do is call attention to something best left alone."

"It doesn't matter. You destroyed too many of my weapons, at least for now. I had to burn my own guns down by the river and set detonators on the C-4." He didn't sound pissed, only matter-of-fact.

Vic continued to babble. "I held Anita down and

Mother grabbed her head—twisted . . . the sound . . . a pencil snap . . . and she died."

He smiled and squeezed my arm tighter. "I shot him. At the river wharf. His head came off. Did you see? The man was going to kill you on the dock. I told them not to shoot, but he didn't listen." He giggled and I could almost see pieces of his mind jittering and breaking apart. Reverend Victor was as cracked as his mother. "I had to save you for tonight."

"Victor!" Elise screamed from another room. "Bring her."

Vic's face changed. In an instant he went from a babbling idiot to a calm, cold psychopath. He stood. "Come, Huntress. It's time."

chapter 31

I fought, but the drug I'd inhaled was coursing through my system. He released me, retied my hands behind my back with a strong nylon cord, and hauled me to my feet. The room swayed, then righted. Strength flowed back into my muscles. Not enough to break the binding on my wrists, but I stalled by pretending to be weaker, forcing him to drag me inexorably through a series of rooms out onto the main plaza, the center of the Zombie's pentagram.

Flaming torches created a nice mystic touch and cast a hundred-foot circle of light in the plaza's center—gas patio torches, made in China, just for ye olde ritual sacrifice. The taller building loomed over us, but open sky had appeared above. A few stars twinkled. A draft of cooler air drifted between the buildings after the drought-breaking rain, sweeter and cleaner than I'd ever smelled in the Zombie.

We splashed through potholes in the pavement to an altar, a crude affair of stacked concrete blocks that stood in the middle of yet another pentagram drawn in—Great Mother—blood. Gallons of blood.

Elise stood grinning at me. She carried a plastic bucket that dripped red. Blood covered her hands and soaked the bandages on her arms. She flung the bucket away and it landed on the bound and stacked bodies of a woman and three men. I didn't recognize the men, but the woman was the one who'd greeted me at the Lamb yesterday.

Vic's breath hissed through his teeth as he struggled to propel me forward.

"You kill your own people, Vic?" I twisted hard and braced my feet. "Really sucks as an employee benefit. Makes recruiting tough, I'll bet."

"I had to!" Desperation and guilt filled his voice. "We needed blood. I had to bring them here last night and lock them up. They begged . . . You were supposed to come alone. *You always work alone!*"

The man was a bundle of raw, lashing emotion. I'd bet it ran around his mind like a wild animal in a cage. He heaved a great sigh. "I'm glad you freed the little ones, the children. I don't know if I could have killed them. I do like children."

"Fucking insane hypocrite." I jerked and almost tore myself from his hands. "Worried about a few kids when you plan to turn monsters loose on the city?"

"Hurry up!" Elise screeched. "It's almost time."

She whirled and marched to the altar, gathering up the robe and taking a delicate step over the line of the pentagram drawn in blood.

A large, plastic battery-operated clock sat propped on a barrel not far from the altar. The barrel had a skull and crossbones painted in white on the side, along with the words CAUTION, POISON and a long, multisyllabic chemical name. Ancient things in a modern world, a perfect definition of the Darkness and the Earth Mother. I expected no help from the Mother. She could not enter the Barrows without breaking her own spell that kept the Darkness contained.

Vic dragged me toward the altar, where Elise stood with a knife—a relatively sharp-looking steel knife, not bronze. Apparently, they considered me easier to kill than the monsters.

"Hurry," Elise demanded again. Her body rocked as she lifted her arm and pantomimed stabbing with the knife. She drooled in full force now and panted like a dog in midsummer heat.

Strength continued to rise in me, but not enough to break the cord holding my wrists. I thrashed my legs. Vic had to fight to get me on the altar. Grunting and straining, he finally rolled, lifted, and slammed me on my back. I outweighed him by at least thirty pounds, but it was like fighting a gorilla. My body weight jammed my hands, tied behind me, into the rough concrete. It dug in and scraped the skin like sandpaper. I barely felt it or my other pains. By now, my adrenaline level had climbed to astronomical levels.

Elise bent over me. "Only a minute now."

Her breath smelled foul and tainted as if she'd been eating carrion along with the sewer monsters. Vic's face was grim—and determined.

Only a minute.

Time, the conjunction. I, who never had a purely psychic thought, could suddenly sense the universe around us. My grandfather repaired watches, not digital, but the old mechanical kind. Once he showed me the gears and how they inched along, larger, smaller, all meshing together to make a tiny, well-ordered machine. Like the watch, the universe, the stars, the multitude of worlds—all aligned, moved in time on a scale beyond belief. How amazing. Were I not in such a desperate situation, I might've enjoyed it.

There would be no rescue. Flynn didn't know where I was. Michael might've known, but he was most likely dead. Dacardi had his son and he would be long gone.

The plaza lay silent except for the hiss of the gas torches and the grim sound of physical stress as I struggled against Vic and he held me down.

I wasn't afraid, at least not for myself. I'd already died once; maybe this time it wouldn't hurt as much. *Flynn ...*

Ah, best not think of him. My time with him, so sweet, had passed. I still had to fight. It is not in my nature to surrender to the inevitable.

Vic held me down with his arm across my chest. I twisted against him.

"Hold her head." Elise stared down at me. Her crazy eyes narrowed and a look of stunning rapture came over her face.

Vic slapped one hand on my forehead, but he kept my chest pinned down.

Elise glanced toward the clock. She leaned forward. Couldn't she see it? Maybe her eyes were bad. The timing had to be precise, I'd bet. Why did *she* need the clock? If I could feel the movement of time, the precision of the moment, a witch should have been able to sense the same. Whatever power she'd had, I'd bet her trip to conceive Michael had drained it away. They'd kill me, but if I could slow things down, get past that optimal time, I might change the outcome of this monstrous event.

The clock on its barrel was at my feet, which Vic stupidly hadn't tied. Elise walked past my knees, my ankles. She peered, squinty-eyed, at the clock. She turned back.

As she did, I used Vic's arm across my chest as leverage, jerked one leg back hard and fast, and slammed my foot into her chest. A good, solid hit that I prayed had broken something. It would have if I'd had my full strength. She went flying back out of my sight.

Vic jammed his arm over my chest and his other arm twisted and wrenched my hair. I lashed back up at him with my knee, but he easily evaded it.

Elise was on her feet. Howling like a wolf, she raced toward me with the knife upraised.

Stupid woman. She took the same path.

I kicked her in the face.

When I did, Vic's grip loosened. I brought my knee up against the side of his head. He barely winced.

Elise returned. Blood ran from her nose and mouth, and she bared broken teeth—but she avoided my feet.

Gunfire, heavy caliber, and the roar of engines sounded in the distance. The clamor echoed from the hollow, abandoned buildings and danced away down the deserted streets. The cavalry to the rescue—but they would never arrive in time.

Elise raised the knife. Slow motion, like in the movies. The blade started down.

A single shot cut the night. A crack, a whine overhead, so close—some hero was racing ahead of the main battle. Elise suddenly froze, the knife suspended above me. She twisted. Her eyes wildly searched the area around her.

Vic straightened to look, too. The idiot released some of the unremitting pressure on my body. I whipped my legs up, caught one around his neck at the knee. I used the other for a scissor lock on his head. He staggered backward, his hands clawing at my legs. I had him tight and wasn't going to let go. Damn! Little rat stayed on his feet.

I hung upside down, my head banging on his knees. If I had been in his position, I would have dropped to the pavement, which might have loosened my grip. I would have leaned forward, grabbed my captive by the hair, and banged her head against the concrete block altar.

Not Vic. Vic the weasel, Vic the traitor wasn't a warrior. He kept staggering backward across the pavement, out of the pentagram, hands desperately trying to tear my legs loose. He tripped over something, a pothole or curb, and we both crashed down. I immediately released him and rolled away toward the black edges of the plaza. I was beyond pain at that point. Across the damp pavement were water-filled potholes—better a monster eat me than this.

Vic seized me by the hair. I screamed and cursed as he hauled me back. I'd left a good layer of exposed skin on the asphalt.

"You won't ruin this for me, Cassandra. Not after all I've done." Vic snarled the words through rigid, clenched teeth. I kicked at him again, trying to trip him, but I'd taught them both to be wary of my legs. He dragged me through the bloody pentagram to the altar.

"On the altar!" Elise screamed.

"Damn the altar," Vic shouted back. "She's in the pentagram—that's all he needs."

He rolled me over on my stomach, jammed his knee into my back, and pinned me tight. He caught my hair again and jerked my head back so she could slit my throat.

A movement caught my eye. Nefertiti! She slithered across the plaza at incredible speed, over the asphalt, and through the bloody pentagram line.

Vic saw her, too.

His first reaction was the usual human reaction to a snake. He jumped up, desperately backpedaled. He tripped and fell, then scrambled to rise. He froze on his knees. His eyes bulged and his hands waved as if that would stop her. Nefertiti coiled. Her head darted forward. Fangs snapped into his cheek.

Vic howled a high-pitched wail of pain and terror.

Nefertiti drew back and struck again. She nailed his throat.

This time, he acted. He caught her body in one hand, her head in the other. With the strength given a terrorized, dying man, he tore her head from her body.

I gasped. He'd just killed my friend, my protector. He'd cut a part out of my soul. I felt her die. Her presence in my mind, the power that let me communicate with her, faded as she returned to the Mother. Loss and sorrow consumed me, so powerful was that pain that I couldn't find a way to give it voice.

I might have wallowed in silent agony and allowed Elise to cut my throat then, but words echoed in my head: *Nefertiti's sacrifice, you fool. Don't waste it.*

I forced myself to roll out of the pentagram again until a curb stopped me. I couldn't go on. I could barely raise my head to look back.

Vic still knelt, his eyes bulging. Nefertiti's body twisted and whipped in death spasms beside him. He held her head in his hand and lifted it near his face. His mouth worked as if speaking to his killer. Elise had stopped to stare at him. Her face had a look of total incomprehension.

Like the monster in the subway tunnel, he gave one cry. His body jerked and shivered as he vomited blood across the pavement, a red stream that appeared black in the torchlight. He stiffened and toppled over.

The distant chatter of gunfire and roar of engines came closer.

Did I dare hope for rescue? Would they come soon enough?

Elise suddenly had me by my shirt. She dragged me back into the pentagram.

"Get away from her!" The shout came from across the plaza. Flynn! Flynn had come for me.

Elise stared at him. Flynn rushed to me, pistol pointed straight at her. At this distance he couldn't miss.

"Drop the knife." He used his cop voice, filled with command.

Elise hesitated. She glanced down at me, then back at him.

"The knife," Flynn demanded again.

Elise straightened, but didn't let go of the knife. She stepped away, lifted her arms. "You wouldn't shoot an old woman. Not the Wolf, the Guardian." She moved farther, too far to strike me. Slowly, step by step.

He kept the gun trained on her, but he knelt by me.

What was she up to? Her face was pinched and calculating.

Elise bolted. She rushed to the altar.

"Flynn, stop her!" I screamed, but it was too late,

even if he had been capable of shooting a woman he didn't perceive as a danger to anyone.

The planets, the stars, the gears of the universe clicked into place like my grandfather's watch.

Elise bent over the concrete blocks.

"Mother!" Michael suddenly raced into the plaza. I heard a child's desperate cry in his voice. "*Please, no!*"

She didn't hear him. No hesitation. She jerked the knife up and slit her own throat.

Her eyes popped open and her lungs drew one last, choking breath. She collapsed facedown as her desperately beating heart pumped great spurts of blood across the concrete block. She'd completed the ceremony. She'd made a powerful offering on the moonless night, at the appropriate time. What would happen now?

Flynn holstered his gun, then grabbed me, lifted me, and held me in his arms. His breath was ragged in my ear as he said my name. A bleak-faced Michael used his knife to cut the cord holding my completely numb hands. He hadn't gone to Elise. There was nothing to be done for her. To my surprise, Dacardi stood, too, his rifle ready. He stared at Nefertiti's still writhing body.

I wanted to cling to Flynn, but my fingers wouldn't work. I cried, mostly in physical pain, but more in gratitude that all three were there with me. I tried to form words to say *Thank you*, and to Flynn, *I love you*, but my tongue didn't work, either.

Michael stared at the body of his mother sprawled across the crude altar. "I tried so hard," he said softly. "I thought she was safe at Avondale."

A sound came, a whooshing noise, as if someone had flipped on a giant vacuum cleaner. A jet-black cloud formed over Elise's body and the bloodstained concrete block. The cloud hummed and flickered with red lightning. Still closely attuned to the workings of the universe, I knew what was happening.

The door between worlds opened into a great cavern of space where indefinable, sentient things lived. The stars disappeared and the midnight sky swirled with a prism of color. Images, shapes, some humanlike, others horrific ... *Mother ... God ... help me.* They were aware of me—and were curious. Curious about me, about this world. These things were beyond conception.

Terrified, I swallowed the nausea that suddenly twisted my stomach, but my skin crawled. They faded away. I am the Earth Mother's child. Things, creatures beyond this world should never be seen by mortals, humans like me.

The cloud over Elise remained. Lightning that cut like sharp knives grew brighter and a foul, stinking wind burned our eyes.

A scream began. It sounded far away at first, but grew ever closer, undulating and filled with incredible fury. The cry grew louder, as if someone was falling from a great distance.

The black cloud disappeared and a man dropped on the altar, seemingly from nowhere. He bounced hard in a wet slap of Elise's blood and rolled off onto the plaza pavement. That fall would have killed a human.

We stood frozen in fascination.

The man lay on the pavement for a few seconds, moving slowly. He stiffly forced himself to his feet. Man? A loose description, but I had no other words. He was naked, with burnt gold skin and incredible hair—hair not blond like Michael's, but red as my own. He stood, smeared with the blood of sacrifice, tall, powerful, and fantastically masculine.

He had Michael's wonderful face, but his eyes burned bright, filled with deadly rage.

The Darkness had entered the Barrows in person.

chapter 32

The Darkness stared at Elise's body on the altar. She was gone, though, free of his dominion. He turned to us—to me. That gaze bore down like a speeding car.

"Huntress." His voice was far more compelling than Michael's. "There are windows in my world and I've watched you." The Darkness raised his hand and beckoned me. "You've cleaved your way through my servants, stealing away children who would grow strong for me. You've left me with a madwoman and her equally mad son to do my bidding. Come, Huntress. I won't let you live."

I stepped toward him, my body willing to obey that command and my mind shrieking at me to stop. Flynn grabbed my arm and yanked me behind him. I started to jerk away when Michael stepped in front of both of us.

"No." Michael stood firm.

The Darkness laughed, laughter filled with irony and mockery, not humor. "Ah, my imperfect son. If you had half the Huntress's courage. You cannot stop me. I will kill all of you."

And he could. Somehow, I doubted our precious bronze would work on him.

A dreadful, gut-wrenching force suddenly roiled inside of me. Something akin to electricity flashed across my eyes. I crashed to the pavement on my hands and knees. Pain consumed me, suffocated me. I shrieked as white-hot fire blazed along every nerve in my body.

The Darkness was killing me.

No, this was something different, something more familiar. This torment had a name.

Flynn grabbed me, but I flung myself away, beating him with my hands. How much more pain could I take without going as crazy as Elise? Finally, that hideous, corroding agony burst out of me like Elise's sacrificial lifeblood had spurted over the makeshift altar.

I lay choking and convulsing on the pavement as the night filled with the brilliance of a full moon. Michael, Flynn, and Dacardi hovered over me, but kept their eyes averted from her radiance.

"What's happening?" Flynn asked.

"The Mother," I moaned. "She's here."

Every inch of my body quivered and protested the abuse. I had a good idea what she'd done, though. The Earth Mother had hidden inside of me to enter the Barrows and confront the Darkness. Something she couldn't do on her own without breaking the ward that she held to keep the Barrows a prison. Shit, I hated her.

Michael and Flynn lifted me to my feet again. I clung to them, unable to stand on my own. Some of the Mother's light had faded, so we stood and watched as two demigods faced each other. A little tingle of common sense, never one of my strong points, said we should be running like hell. But I was her Huntress. By my own vows, I belonged to her. I had to bear witness to this world-altering event.

The Darkness laughed again. Still no true humor there. "Innana," he said. "How wonderful to see you again."

"Aiakós." The Earth Mother, still robed in light, nodded her head. She stepped toward him.

He stepped back.

Innana? Was that her name? And the Darkness was called Aiakós?

This was the first time I'd ever seen the Mother's face. She'd hidden it from me when she'd approached me ten years ago and spoken to me through Abby or directly into my mind. A goddess version of a young Abby, she matched the Darkness perfectly—and was his opposite at the same time. One incredible difference marked them. The Darkness had a physical body and the Mother shimmered like a ghostly specter.

"Beautiful Innana." The Darkness bowed low to the Mother. "I have missed you, my love."

The Mother's silver grew brighter and the Darkness averted his eyes. "Your love, Aiakós? I am nothing of yours. Be assured of that. The conjunction has come and gone. You are still caged, only now you lack the power to corrupt so many minds at a distance as you did before. You'll have to face them one at a time." The Mother laughed, and it seemed as if flowers would suddenly bloom in the Zombie Zone, where nothing of hers had lived in over half a century. Elise and her son had tried to give him more power. Instead, the power of her self-sacrifice had brought him here in person.

Aiakós stared at her. If he was reacting to her words, I couldn't tell it by his alien face. He suddenly turned to Michael. "I claim my son, though. I can make good use of him."

"No!" I grabbed Michael.

"No." The Mother echoed my words. "He is torn between us, Aiakós. You may not have him yet." She nodded at Michael. "You have only postponed your time of choosing, Archangel. Have care. You may yet fall."

The Mother turned to me.

"So I screwed up," I grumbled. I wanted to stand straight, but had to cling to Flynn.

"No, Huntress. You have fulfilled your duty. I am pleased."

"But he's *here*."

The Mother laughed and Aiakós snarled like a caged cat.

"And so, my dear, am I, since you so graciously brought me in. Leave Aiakós and me to discuss our affairs." She glanced at him. "I will keep him from you until you're gone. Go now."

"And Nefertiti?" I nodded at my friend's torn body.

"She served us well and will be rewarded."

The Earth Mother dismissed my sorrow. She didn't understand. Abby once said that, to the Mother, life and death were the same things, only a different passage through her world.

Michael stepped forward. "I want my mother."

Aiakós studied him for a moment, then walked away from the altar. Michael approached and carefully wrapped Elise's body in her robe. He lifted her gently in his arms.

A movement to my right caught my eye. Dacardi had torn Victor's jacket off his body and was carefully gathering the pieces of Nefertiti's body.

"I did not summon your mother to my world, my son," Aiakós said to Michael. "She was once a powerful witch and made her own to me. I did not ask her to sacrifice you in my name. It would have given me nothing, and she paid a terrible price."

Michael refused to look at him.

The monsters would take care of Vic's body. I should have hated him, that traitor, but the only thing I could find was pity—and maybe a bit of kinship. I am the Earth Mother's servant. He served another. We both had the dubious honor of being human pawns for powerful beings.

Flynn wrapped his arm around my shoulder and steadied me as we left the plaza. As we passed out of the circle of torches, out of the pentagram, the Darkness—Aiakós—laughed.

"I'll see you again, Michael," he called after us.

The three of us hurried down the empty Barrows streets to one of the Steroid Dogs parked a block away, its engine running. Men stood guard around it, shining the brilliant lights into the crumbling buildings.

"What happened to the monsters?" I asked. We'd seen a multitude of bodies, but not a living thing stirred at our passage.

"They probably sensed the disturbance when the dark moon reached its place in the conjunction," Michael said. "Unlike us, they did the wise thing and went into hiding."

Dacardi had his man open a back hatch and Michael laid Elise's body inside. Dacardi placed Nefertiti beside her.

We climbed in and the Dog slowly made its way out of the Barrows. Dacardi was on the phone again, arranging another pickup.

I wrapped my arms around Flynn and hugged him and kissed him and—

"Hey!" Michael gently elbowed me. "He wasn't the only one there."

"You're right." So I hugged him, too. He didn't get any kisses. "I thought you were dead."

"I would have been," Michael said. "Flynn saved me. Vic threw something at me. It made me sick. Flynn arrived before the monsters killed me, but it took time to recover enough to tell him where you were. Or where you had to be. I know the Zombie."

"You know the Zombie. You knew other things. Why didn't you tell me?" My voice had a hard note in it, and Flynn stirred as if preparing for violence again.

Michael didn't speak for a moment. "I'm sorry, Cass. I didn't want you to hate me. You already doubted my humanity. I swear, I didn't know where the children were until yesterday. I wanted . . ."

He'd wanted to be a hero. He'd wanted me to love him.

I changed the subject. "Do you have any control over the monsters? Like Vic did? You seemed pretty confident in the sewers, facing them with only a bronze stick."

"I have a little. I didn't know Victor had any. That's why I wanted you and me to go alone—aboveground."

"Michael, I had a path to follow."

"I know. One you didn't create and couldn't control." His voice tightened. "They used us, your Mother and . . . Aiakós."

I couldn't disagree. Many things in this dark moon night had been suspended over a chasm of chances—a split-second decision to move to the left or right, take action or choose inaction.

Dacardi was riding shotgun again. Nefertiti's basket sat between the seats. I reached forward and laid a hand on it. Tears came to my eyes. I'd miss her for a long time.

I turned to Michael. His eyes narrowed with weariness and sorrow. "So tell me, Michael. This Aiakós, he's your dad?"

"Mother said he was—she described him, but she was . . . disturbed. If *he* says so, too, I won't argue. When I would go to visit her, she told me things. Some I believed, some I did not. I don't know what she told Victor."

I believed pressure from the Darkness, Elise's denial of love, and her obsession with Michael had destroyed Victor.

"I never suspected Vic," I said.

"Neither did I," Michael said. "He started to change about ten years ago. I knew he'd taken over the Lost Lamb. He came to curse me occasionally for being evil, the son of the Darkness. The money he took? I didn't know he was using it to amass weapons. I thought he was stealing it and giving it away to charities. That's what he told me. It all started to come together after he visited me that day at the hotel, but it was too late. Even then, I hoped for the best. Vanity on my part—I thought I could handle him."

Michael's face darkened. "I was born forty years ago on a dark moon conjunction. When I visited Mother once, she said she'd tried to sacrifice me at birth because she believed it would solidify a connection between this world and his and increase his power here. I don't think he was actually supposed to come here in person."

If Michael did choose to serve Aiakós in the future, he would be a far more potent enemy than Elise and Victor.

"You're forty?"

"Yes. I don't seem to age like others."

I heard sadness. Sadness not necessarily because he was or was not human, but because he was something in between. I grasped his hand. "Elise made the most powerful sacrifice—the only sacrifice that would work. She offered her own life."

"Yes." Michael sighed. "It opened the door and dragged him through, physically."

"So what does that mean?"

"It means he's here, he's powerful—but no more powerful than his . . . rival."

That didn't sound good. "Why'd you hesitate before you said 'rival'?"

"I received the impression he and your Earth Mother weren't always enemies."

"Yeah. He called her 'my love.' That's scary."

The vehicles rolled out of the Zombie and into a Barrows street where two semitrucks with ramps waited. In minutes, the Steroid Dogs, Fire Dogs, and their mercenary crews were loaded and away. We transferred to one of Dacardi's Escalades. Again, Elise's and Nefertiti's bodies went in the back.

As we left the Barrows, I had to ask, "So you have your own army, Dacardi?"

"I got shit. What happened here tonight stays with us."

"Okay." I was relieved. "Same as always for me."

"What about you?" Dacardi asked Flynn.

Flynn nodded in agreement, but his face was close and grim. "Tonight in the Barrows is done. Tomorrow? Walk slow and careful uptown, Dacardi."

"Fair enough," Dacardi said. "You want me to bury Nefertiti?"

"No, I'll take her to Abby's."

Michael had Dacardi drop him at the back door of the Archangel. He carried Elise's body inside.

We each had our own version of events to ponder. I knew more about Michael and Dacardi, but both remained a mystery. I had too many questions. I figured I'd learn more in time.

"What about the other four kids?" I asked.

"Sent 'em to my house with Richard," Dacardi answered. "I'll find their parents, give 'em money not to talk." He turned to Flynn. "I'll send you their names. I figure you'll want to check on them. Make sure they're okay."

On the surface, these men seemed ready to settle back into their ordinary lives. I doubted that would happen. We'd all been changed by the last few days, even me. I had carried a powerful being inside me, and something had to come from that.

Dacardi drove Flynn to his mother's house, where they had taken Selene. All the lights blazed. "I'll see you soon." He kissed me long and hard.

Special children, Selene and Richard. Both would grow powerful in their own way. I hoped for the good.

Just before we arrived at Abby's, Dacardi said, "You did okay, bitch. I owe you."

Abby came rushing out when we drove into her driveway. She threw her arms around me and squeezed so tight, I gasped. Didn't think she was that strong. Dacardi went to the back and brought me Nefertiti.

"You're hurt." Abby touched my face.

After rolling over what seemed like a mile of pavement, being dragged by my hair, almost drowning, nearly having my throat cut, I thought I was in pretty good shape. "I'm alive, Abby. Some didn't make it through the night."

Dacardi handed me the jacket carrying my snake. I accepted it. She wasn't heavy.

"What am I going to do, Abby?" I wanted to scream. "I've lost Nefertiti."

"Oh, love." Abby wrapped an arm around me and led me toward the house.

Dacardi didn't speak as he climbed back in the Escalade and drove away. I guess he had some heavy thinking to do about his own life and future.

When we reached the back porch, Abby took Nefertiti's body from me. "I'll take care of her," she said. "You go in."

When I walked into Abby's kitchen, Horus crouched in the middle of the table, with Nirah coiled beside him. Should I tell them I'd lost Nefertiti, or did they already know? When I sat heavily in one of the chairs, Horus came to me and patted my face with his paw. Nirah nuzzled my hand.

"I'm so sorry," I said. "She saved my life and I couldn't do anything to help her."

They stayed close as I put my face in my hands and sobbed. Abby came in and cried, too. I knew the Mother's dogma. Death and rebirth, the earth's cycle, but I wanted my snake back here and now.

"I buried Nefertiti by the spring," Abby said through her tears. "You go clean up. We can talk later."

I showered and she dressed my scrapes and cuts. She put me to bed, not downstairs, but in her spare bedroom. That suited me. Time would pass before this Huntress went underground again. Abby sat beside me while I told her of the evening's events.

"She hid inside of you to enter the Barrows?"

"Yes."

"Can she get out of the Barrows on her own?"

"She didn't seem concerned."

Abby's face remained grave. "I went into the woods last week, before all this started. I accused her of using you up like a bottle of floor cleaner." She smoothed the hair from my forehead. "She seemed confused. I told her she had my life from birth to death, and I asked if it wasn't enough. I gave up men, marriage, children for her. I don't regret it. Never have. You, however, were raised to look to a different life."

I didn't know what to say. I knew what I wanted to ask. "You've always been hers? How long?"

Abby smiled. "I am the descendant of a long line of priestesses. My mothers, grandmothers have served her, kept her word sacred. I can trace my direct lineage back over a thousand years. The gifts she gave me were knowledge, use of the earth's power—" She hesitated. "And a very long life. I was born in 1765, on a prison ship. My mother had been sentenced into bondage for pagan worship. When we reached the shores of North Carolina, she ran away and joined the native tribes. They lived with the land, not perched upon it like vultures." Sadness filled her eyes. "It's been a good life. We have served well, you and I. We have made the sacrifice."

The phone in the kitchen rang. Abby kissed me on my forehead. "Sleep."

So I slept, slept without pain. Healing sleep, contented sleep. Tomorrow? Flynn. I wanted Flynn tomorrow and all the tomorrows.

chapter 33

August 10—10:00 a.m.

I was asleep, but I woke when Flynn came into the bedroom and lay beside me. His face was serious. I snuggled against him and he held me tight.

"Will you marry me?" he asked.

"No. I can't." I tried to push away, but he wouldn't release me. I relaxed. I was where I wanted to be.

"Why not?"

"I love you so much, but we've only known each other for days. Not weeks or months. We have a relationship built on danger. On high drama. Like living in a movie."

"Cass, a mortal's relationship with *life* is built on danger. The past few days would make a good movie, I suppose. If we could ever tell anyone about it."

I stroked his cheek with my hand. I told him something I rarely acknowledged. "I'm terrified. I don't think I'm biologically suited to being a cop's wife. Or any man's wife. *Wife* means doing important things with a family. Not just returning a child. What if we have children?"

"Then they will have a mother who has the ability to protect them in a dangerous world."

He kissed me, long and sweet. When he finished, he said, "No, you're not suited to being anything but what you are. That's who I want. We'll make it, Cass. There's no one else for me. Only you. Please."

How could I resist that? "Okay, I'll marry you. But we have to wait at least six months. Maybe a year."

"Fine. I love you, Huntress."

"And the Huntress . . . no. Just Cassandra. Cassandra loves you."

Flynn glanced at his watch, then drew away from me and sat up. "Damn. Another meeting. I slept for a few hours; then the chief called. They gave me a promotion for finding the guns. More work to do. And I've been appointed to the mayor's task force on organized crime."

"That should be easy. Call Dacardi and ask him to fill you in on the details."

"Very funny." Flynn took my hand and squeezed. "Bunch of pompous asses in city hall. I'm a cop, not a bureaucrat."

"Any discussion of the Barrows? What happened last night? No one heard the noise? Saw the lights?"

"Not a word. As far as I'm concerned, it's like Dacardi said—what happened in the Barrows will not be on the afternoon news." He brushed my hair from my face.

"Would you like to stay with me?" I asked. "Since we're engaged. At the apartment? I'll give you a key."

"I'd like to, Cass. And I'll take that key. I'll be there as much as I can. But I'm going to have to stay close to Mama for a while. She's scared something will happen to Selene again."

"Something has happened to Selene. She'll never be the same." I sat up and rubbed my cheek against his. He smelled clean and wonderful.

"Selene wants to talk to you. You seem to have impressed her."

"Abby would be best to do that."

His body tensed, and I knew the reason.

"Selene is not a Huntress, Flynn. Abby might teach her some serious shit, but I won't ever let her run through the sewers. I promise."

I hesitated to bring up the next thing, but I required a little honesty from the man I'd agreed to marry. "Does Selene know you're her father and not her brother?"

"How did—?" He drew a breath, then slowly let it out. "No. I was eighteen. There was a girl. She was older. I loved her, wanted her—and knew it was a mistake a week after we were married. I thought she was on the pill." He bowed his head. "She didn't want Selene. I managed to keep her from having an abortion by giving her money. She left the day after Selene was born. Mama took over raising her. Couple of years later, I divorced her. She hasn't returned and I haven't looked for her. I should have told you, that first night when we made love."

"I'm not the one you need to tell. Why keep it a secret?"

"Mama was afraid it would hurt my career. I think she wanted to pretend Selene really was hers—and my dad's. She missed him so much. I didn't care—then. I had Selene, could watch her grow, be with her."

"You'd better talk to her, Flynn. Soon. She's going to feel betrayed no matter what you do, but she'll recover. She loves you."

"How did you know about her?"

"Math. You're thirty-one. You said she was six when you graduated from the academy. It would've been difficult for your mom to have her. Took me a while, but I think about you a lot."

Flynn relaxed. "You're on my mind constantly, too. You're going back to your apartment?"

"I'll be there tonight. I do want to marry you, Flynn."

He suddenly grabbed me and held me tight. I gave him a serious kiss.

"Oh, how's Robert?" I asked.

Flynn laughed. "Insky took him to the emergency room and they gave him some valium. Didn't have any place to go, so Insky took him to his house. He said Robert confessed to a lot of shit, cried, begged Insky to help him 'make things right,' and fell asleep. When he woke up, Robert *said* he couldn't remember anything, but he was muttering something about a serpent when he left."

"Damn. I was hoping to get my PI license back so I could make some money. You think Robert will try to stop me?"

"No. Insky said we shouldn't worry. He has enough dirt on old Robert to last a few years, at least. You think you need the license? It caused so much trouble before."

"No, it didn't. Robert caused the trouble. I was fine. I was fine. Oh, did you ask Selene about the Goblin Den card in her room? It set me on a good path."

"A friend of hers gave it to her. She'd never been there. Apparently it's some sort of preteen fantasy to get in the Den."

"Sure." He laughed, then kissed me long and hard.

After he left, I rose, dressed, and went to the kitchen, where Abby insisted on fixing me breakfast.

"Carlos called last night while you were sleeping. I went to Riverside and smoothed out some memories."

"The four kids?"

"Yes. Two were in foster care. Parents were on the way to get the others. Richard's insisting that the two in foster care stay with him, and his father has enough money to make it happen. He's a fine young man, that Richard." Abby set a plate piled high with a two-day supply of food in front of me.

"Richard has guts. Like his father." I picked up my

fork and my mouth watered. On second thought, maybe the food would last only until supper.

"Did you tell Flynn that the kids were okay?" I asked. "That a couple are staying with Dacardi?"

"Yes. He seemed to accept everything without concern."

Later, filled with Abby's tea, toast, cheese, and fruit, I walked out to the woods and sat on the grass beside the spring. I smoothed my hand over the spot of fresh earth that marked Nefertiti's grave. Last night's rain left everything fresh and green. Maybe the heat wave had broken.

"Are you here?" I spoke to the air.

"Were you worried?" The Mother stood across the spring in the woods. Sunlight sparkled in her hair, blond as Michael's this morning. I could have sworn it was much darker last night.

"No. I guess you can take care of yourself. Why haven't you shown yourself to me like this before?"

"There was no need. I don't want my ... people ... to depend on me too much." She gave me a radiant smile. All the birds in the garden suddenly broke into song.

"I hate you," I said, but I spoke without any real passion.

"That is your right. Do you still wish to serve me?"

"What else would I do? What about Abby? She needs her power back."

"She never lost it. Her power comes from the earth, but not directly from me. When she could no longer sense my presence, she'd lost faith in herself."

"And Dacardi calls *me* a bitch."

"It's a term of endearment—for him. You're a bit more honest with me." She tilted her head and the birds sang. "What do you think of him? Your Warlord."

"My Warlord? He's made of better stuff than I thought." I leaned back and stretched out my legs. "Did you have Selene kidnapped?"

"No. Once it happened, I saw the possibilities."

"Such as having Richard in the same place so I could use Dacardi."

"I whispered in a few ears." The Mother laughed again and I'd swear the garden, the trees, the grass and flowers stood straighter and taller. "It is complex. And truly, it did not end as I had planned. I trusted you, Huntress, to know and do what was right. Even if it cost your life."

"You manipulated, is what you did. Playing chess with us. With our lives. With children's lives." I knew she didn't understand.

"I gave you Flynn. Do you really want to know the details?"

"No. It's done—for now." I had one thing I desperately wanted to know. "My vision when the Darkness spoke through Hammer. It happened in the Barrows, but—"

"I have access to your memories, Cassandra."

"Did I throw my daughter, my child, in the fire? Was that really another life, or a demon's trick to weaken me?"

"I never asked for sacrifice." Anger rose in her voice and the garden grew colder. She sighed and things went back to normal. "Huntress, my power—and it *is* great power—lies in the land. I will not control any human. Free will is paramount, a directive from the Great Master. Abby, you and all the others must choose to serve me. That allows me to guide my power to them. I cannot compel you."

She drifted across the spring and onto the grass. Her bare feet made only the slightest impression on the blades. *Innana*, the Darkness had called her. She sat beside me, her body moving with inhuman grace. As the breeze lifted, I caught the scent of flowers, sweeter and cleaner than any I'd ever smelled in Abby's garden.

"When you were dying in that alley, I saw my grand scheme collapsing. As I healed you, I realized you could do what I could not: go into the Barrows. And I could go with you, and not break my own word."

"So you stayed in me. And Aiakós—what's he to you? Your lover?"

"That's not your business, Huntress. Don't you have enough male problems of your own? Will you choose between them? The son of a demigod and the son of humanity? You're my daughter and I'd not think ill of you if you took them both."

Now what did I have to say to that? I laughed and felt better than I had in weeks. "There is no choice. I love Flynn. I care for Michael, but I don't love him. You were in me when I made love to Flynn, here in the garden?"

She smiled. "Yes. He is a fine man. One of my better children. Perhaps I can yet do something for Michael."

"He'd be safer if you left him alone."

"He does not seek safety, any more than you do. You have given me a gift, Huntress. I saw the world through your eyes. Things will be different now. I will"—she laughed—"make arrangements."

"That's pretty scary. Why are you telling me all of this?"

"You have the right to know. You, my Huntress, through the ages, thousands of years, have been constant. Every life you have ever lived, you have served me. Others have served me through one life and tried to destroy me in the next. You are the only human I could have entered as I did." She held out her hand. "I have a gift for you. This is what really happened. Be still. Watch. Believe this is the truth."

I felt the Mother's presence enter my mind, taking me back in time.

The fire looms before me again. The dancing with the drums and flutes, and Astra clings to me, laughing. The

*priests motion me forward and reach to take my baby, to
give her to the Mother. I've been a priestess to the Mother;
it is my duty to serve. I gaze into Astra's smiling face, her
beautiful dark eyes, the trust and love there. Agony fills
me. So close to the fire. Will it hurt her? This is not right,
to kill my child. I cannot. I will not. I whirl and run. If I
weren't carrying Astra, I could escape . . .*

*An arrow tears into my back. I stumble and twist as I
fall. A second arrow punches through Astra and into my
heart. When darkness comes, I know our bodies will go
on the fire, but we will already be gone.*

I cried out as I came back to myself.

"I'm not in charge of souls," the Mother said. "I simply take what's given to me. I use and often reuse it, and
I will, until this ground beneath my feet is dust swirling
again among the stars. I say again, you have every right
to hate me. Some of my other servants do. They see a far
darker image than you. It will change nothing." She disappeared.

Abby came running into the garden. She'd heard my
cry.

She dropped to her knees beside me. "What's wrong?"

I shook my head. I couldn't speak.

"Why are you crying?"

I wiped my eyes. "I'm fine. Abby, go make some potions for me to take home."

Abby shook her head. "I don't know if I—"

"Yes, you can. The wicked witch of the dirt is back.
And your spells damn well better work." I shouted that
last sentence into the fragrant air. The leaves and shrubs
around me shook with laughter—or maybe it was only
the wind.

Abby and I sat in her kitchen and mourned Nefertiti a
little longer. We both cried again. I called my mother
and father, maybe wanting to touch people I loved. Both

were glad to hear from me, and I promised to get home for the equinox celebration. I told them of my engagement to Flynn, and Mom was so joyful, it almost made me feel guilty about not getting married before.

"What are you going to do next, love?" Abby asked.

"I'm going to get my PI license back and go to work. I still have my contacts in the Barrows, and I'm tired of poverty." I was also an honorary member of the Slum Devils, at least as long as that dirty bastard Snag could beat off the competition and stay Big Devil. In the back of my mind I'd always wondered if I couldn't do something to control them and lessen the impact of their evil.

"But not in the sewers." Abby's eyes squinted in strain. "Promise me you'll stay out of the sewers. And the gun, you—"

"Gun's gone, Abby. I lost it last night. And the last thing I *want* to do is go underground again. Especially now."

I grabbed Horus and Nirah and headed home. I went to the Archangel first.

Dacardi called as I pulled into the parking lot. "My boy keeps bugging me about the cop's sister. Wants to go see her. What do you think I should do?"

"Let him see her. You stay away, and it should be okay."

"Yeah. Don't want my boy to be . . ."

"Be what? Like you? Or like me?"

"Bitch, don't want him like either of us. Wouldn't mind him being like your cop. Man's got balls. Me and the pretty boy hadn't gone with him, he'd have gone back after you alone. Bet he keeps his word. He's gonna try to nail me uptown. Should be interesting."

"Well, Flynn's one thing you and I can agree on. Thanks for helping those kids. And taking in those without parents."

"My boy wouldn't let me do anything else, damn it.

Called his mama and got her to come home. Shit and double shit!" He didn't really sound displeased. Dacardi and his wife had managed to raise a good son, so I guess the foster kids could do worse. "You know, that Abby, that witch, she understands . . . Ah, what's the word I'm looking for?"

"*Expediency*. She's practical and does what needs to be done."

"Yeah, that's it. I like her."

I laughed. "Okay, but don't cross her."

"I know better than that, bitch."

"Any trouble about the dock explosion thing?"

"You kidding? Truckload of trouble. The suits say not to sweat it, so I don't. I cover my ass pretty good. Lot of experience. You and me talk later." He hung up.

Yes, Carlos Dacardi would survive, and even prosper in the coming years. And I doubted he'd stay out of my life. He hadn't mentioned the Earth Mother. He saw her as he saw Aiakós. Wonder what he thought of her. We'd have to talk again, Dacardi and I.

The previous night's rain had broken the heat wave, but it was still summer, so when I arrived at the Archangel I tucked Nirah under my collar and carried Horus with me. I wouldn't leave him in the car. The door guard started to object to a cat, but Horus snarled and swiped his claws at him and he wisely let us pass.

When I entered Michael's office, I set Horus on the floor. Michael wrapped me in his arms. I let him, but there was no passion there, at least for me, but there was understanding and a little love. Michael had risked his life for me. I don't forget things like that.

Nirah peeked out from under my collar.

"I don't have any caviar," Michael said.

"It's okay. No point in spoiling her."

"I called Flynn," he said. "I gave him the locations of two more arms caches I found this morning. Self-preservation. I'd rather the Bastinados not accidentally come across a load of antitank missiles."

No wonder Flynn had suddenly become so important.

"Vic must have stolen millions from you," I said.

Michael's mouth twisted in a wry smile. "It'll take me years to recover it. The arms he bought didn't take a third of what's missing. I'm trying to find the rest, but I doubt I will. Its location probably died with Vic."

"What did he think he was going to do? If he'd made it, if everything happened like it was supposed to, the government wouldn't let something like that take over a city."

"Victor was really very intelligent. A wonderful big brother. He watched over me and I loved him. Life was good when it was me, him. When Nurse Kathy rescued me, she accepted him and did a good job of raising us, considering our parentage. After mother came home that one time, Victor lost all sense of proportion and common sense. He told me once, 'She stopped loving me when you were born.'"

"One thing bothers me," I said. "He didn't do it alone. Theron was involved, and such things generally have a functioning network of people, banks, communication. You think there are others with the missing money?"

"I don't know—yet. Let's speak of other things. What are you going to do now?"

"Getting chased by monsters isn't as much fun as it used to be. I'll hunt kids. I'll do things a bit differently, though."

I didn't want him to fall to the Darkness, to his father's world, either, and I'd do my best to prevent it.

"Flynn asked me to marry him. I said I would. With a long engagement."

"Why not now? You love him."

"Yeah, but I'm afraid it won't work. He needs to

think about it. Flynn's smart, educated, has a degree in criminal justice. All I am is a farm girl and—"

"You think you're not worthy of him?" Michael sounded both delighted and incredulous. "That he's too good for you?"

I shrugged. "Not exactly. I think he's going places. He has an aura of importance he didn't have a few days ago. I'd slow him down. He needs a woman to look good and stand behind him, not some scruffy monster chaser." Even as I spoke such noble words, I hated them. I was lying to myself. I'd do anything I could to keep Flynn.

"If that's his choice, then he's not as intelligent as I think." Michael laughed.

Nirah stuck her head out from under my collar again.

"I like her." He brushed her head with his finger.

"She likes you. You give the name *snake charmer* a whole new meaning."

"Obviously I'm not popular with both your pets." Michael's voice hardened. "Your cat has pissed on a five-thousand-dollar leather couch."

"Damn!" I whirled around. Sure enough, Horus stood beside a wet streak running down the leather. I went and grabbed him. He didn't protest, but didn't feel apologetic at all. What did I expect from a cat?

"Get it cleaned," I said. "I'll pay for it."

Michael smiled. "No, I'll get a new one."

I guess five thousand dollars wouldn't mean much to him, in spite of his losses to Victor's scheming.

I laughed. "Michael, my friend. I do so wish you love and happiness." I hugged him again.

Michael was still smiling when he walked me downstairs. In fact, the smile he gave his early-afternoon followers was real this time, not the fake royal beneficence he usually bestowed on them. One woman fainted.

Michael once compared himself to me, hinting that our humanity stood on the same level. We both had supernatural or, as the case may be, abnormal gifts. I realized that, other than his ability to weave a godlike spell over some people, he'd shown me little of himself. He was the son of the Darkness, a demigod who now resided in a physical form a couple of miles from the Archangel—there had to be more to him than a pretty man mesmerizing adoring crowds. I hadn't asked about Elise, but I was sure he'd quietly buried her and would mourn her in the years to come.

Horus hit the ground and disappeared when we arrived at the apartment house parking lot. I trudged upstairs, wondering if I could put off what was probably some heavy-duty housekeeping.

When I opened the fridge to throw out any leftovers that growled at me, I found five thick bundles of hundred-dollar bills wrapped in plastic wrap. From Dacardi? He'd promised me money. I opened one bundle, counted out a thousand dollars, and stuffed the rest in a plastic bag. I wouldn't take the life savings of a hotel maid barely above poverty, like Maxie Fountain's mother. But whoever gave this didn't have a cash flow problem.

Like Abby, I also knew the meaning of *expediency*. Nefertiti's glass aquarium sat on the coffee table, and Nirah had forsaken her own and crawled inside. I dug in the bedding of wood shavings at one end of the aquarium, stuffed the bag of money in, and covered it up.

I'd no more than finished when a knock came at the door.

"FedEx," a male voice called. I opened it and signed for a package with River Street as its return address.

I sat at the kitchen table and tore it open. Inside was my gun, carefully cleaned and oiled and covered in bubble wrap. A note card fell out, too.

Come and see me, Huntress, it said. *I realize now that I saw this world through the flawed eyes of my servants.*

Victor's plan would never have worked. I have banished the creatures under the streets. You may walk freely in the Barrows.

Written in a flowing cursive script, I smiled at the beauty of it. Maybe I should go, I thought. Then I jerked. What was I thinking?

I ran to the kitchen sink and dropped the card. As I did, it burst into flames. I turned on the faucet. The flames didn't die under the steady stream of water until they'd consumed the entire thing. As it disappeared, the sound of laughter—beautiful, seductive laughter—rang in my ears. Tomorrow, I'd have to take the gun to Abby and be sure no spell lay on it. She wouldn't like it, but I wasn't prepared to give it up yet.

Aiakós had apparently found Vic's network, or it had found him. He now had human servants to do his bidding, teach him the ways of this world, including how to send packages by FedEx. To use an old cliché, he'd hit the pavement running. Did he also know where Victor had hidden most of Michael's money? I hoped not.

The heating grate popped up and Horus appeared. He had a single twitching mouse by the tail. A scratching noise came from behind him and a small, furred animal came skittering out of the duct.

"Who's this, Horus?" Horus ignored me and carried the mouse to the aquarium for Nirah. At the sound of my voice, the little creature raced my way, locked onto my jeans, clawed its way up, and tried to bury itself in my shirt. I cupped it in my hand and held it close to my heart. It settled against me, twitching a little, but no longer frantic.

Its little head peeked out from my hand. A ferret? Covered with mink-soft, buff-colored fur with a dark tan ring around its neck, it seemed like one, but I had no way to be sure. When it squirmed, it became obviously male.

"So who are you?" I asked.

A name popped into my mind: *Tau.* Then came the

image of a lion. "You'd better grow a lot if you're going to fit that name," I told him. He chattered again and scrambled up to my shoulder. I found a can of tuna and fed Tau and Horus. I'd go to the pet emporium tomorrow. Ah, caviar. Now that I had some money, I could treat them occasionally. For Tau, we'd start with a ferret diet and go from there.

I relaxed for the rest of the day. Flynn came in later and we walked up the street to the deli for supper. He held my hand. How wonderful to be comfortable doing ordinary things, speaking of ordinary things with him. I could deal with ordinary for a while.

"You're not mad because I want my PI license back so I can go to work?" I asked.

"Cass, I won't order your life. Just promise me you'll keep me in the loop and stay out of the sewers."

"Promise? Big, heavy word."

I sighed and snuggled against him. I could feel his heartbeat, strong and real. This was the thing I'd given up when I came to Duivel. That security that sometimes comes with love. I did not need to be on guard with Flynn, and I never wanted him to leave.

"Okay, Flynn. I won't promise not to go into the Barrows if someone really needs me, but I swear I won't take any unnecessary chances. Is that okay? You understand, don't you? You're a cop. You want to be a cop. You're on the line every day."

"That's not what I wanted to hear from you. I can't change you, though. I wouldn't want to. My mother, Selene—you're all strong women."

"How did Selene take the news? About you being her father?"

"Ungraciously, but she's talking to me again."

Making love that night was a softer, gentler passion that slowly built, relaxed, then soared again. He fell right to sleep, but I understood. His day had been long. He now walked a different path. A powerful enemy now resided in the Barrows and he couldn't completely articulate that danger to his fellow officers.

Something woke me during the night.

Flynn still lay sleeping beside me. Tau had left the bed I'd made for him in a box and come to sleep in my hair. I lay quietly for a while and listened. All I heard was Tau's tiny breaths and Flynn's deeper ones. Horus and Nirah were in the living room, and no danger would come unchallenged from that direction.

I rose, went to the window, and stared in the direction of the Barrows. Lights glowed against the sky in a place where only night ruled since I'd come to Duivel.

The Mother might be pleased he's here, but I think it's dangerous. No one asks my opinion, though. I'm only the Huntress.

When I went back to the bed and tossed the covers aside, I saw it. The dark stain. In the bathroom I confirmed. The Mother had given me my retirement notice. For the first time since I was eighteen, I'd need birth control pills. Or did I? I'd ask Flynn, but . . . yes, it was time. A new Huntress would have to deal with Aiakós the Darkness. Regrets? None. I'd done the best I could. Sadness? A little. Closing a door hurts, even if another opens.

I went back into the bedroom to wake Flynn, to tell him how much I loved him. Today, and all the tomorrows.

Read on for a peek at the
next novel in the Earth Witches series

VENGEANCE MOON

Available from Signet Eclipse
in April 2012.

Sister Eunice tossed me over her head, slammed me on my back, and planted her highly polished size twelve combat boot on my stomach.

I gasped for breath. She pushed harder. Acute agony spread while the malicious bitch mashed my guts around my spine. An evil grin split her rugged face. "Got you now, you nasty little, scar-faced whore."

Sister Eunice is five eleven and weighs two forty. She has the body of a weight lifter and the attitude of a pit bull. I'm five eight, and I barely make one thirty. I'm strong—exceptionally strong—but it would take serious steroids to make me her physical equal.

While she flattened my intestines with one foot, she had the other firmly planted on the floor mat. Grab her ankle and snatch her off her feet? I knew better. That was action movie special effects. I needed more leverage. I made a fist and slammed it into the knee of her straight leg.

She grunted. The knee gave a fraction of an inch, but she shifted her weight to compensate. As she did, I caught the foot jammed on my stomach with both hands and jerked. At the same time, I twisted my body toward her. She went down.

The vinyl mat hissed as she rolled to get on her feet. I'm faster. Blade-sharp pains shot through abused muscles. I ignored them. I leaped up, made a fist, and punched her in the kidneys. She crashed facedown on the mat. Her breath whooshed out, and before she could draw it back in, I caught her right arm at the wrist. I twisted the arm across her back, then stomped my foot on her left hand.

I had her. Sort of. She wore boots and camouflage fatigues. I wore gym sweats and thick practice mat socks. Her fingers clawed at my sock, and in minutes, her nails would tear through fabric. Then she'd rake the skin and flesh off my bare foot, right down to bone.

I couldn't knock her unconscious, despite the fact that she punched me out on such a regular basis that I marked it on my calendar. The Sisters of Justice Correctional College frowned upon lowly students—aka prisoners—beating the crap out of the faculty, even if upon incredibly rare occasions, they could. Secure in her mantel of authority, Sister Eunice—alpha female and consummate she-devil—lived to teach and torture her unfortunate pupils.

I'd beaten her twice. I'd surprised her six years ago when I first came here. Only nineteen, but I'd been in jail long enough to learn a few tricks—and I'd been taking martial arts lessons from Daddy since I was six years old. The second time I beat her, last year, I used the skills she herself taught me. She would never forgive or forget either incident.

Laughter sounded in her ragged breathing. I hadn't beaten her this time either. Unwilling to tear her arm out of its socket and incapacitate her, I was unable to let her go because she would pound the holy shit out of me. Shit pounding me is Sister Eunice's favorite hobby. Shit pounding hurts a lot more than the boot in the stomach.

"Good morning, Madeline," said a sweet voice from behind me. "What are you going to do now, dear?" Sister

Lillian. Dark skinned, petite and graceful, Sister Lillian taught knife fighting. She'd immediately assessed my dilemma.

"Good morning, Sister Lillian. I'm giving serious consideration to releasing Sister Eunice and running away."

"You won't," Sister Eunice said. The mat muffled her words; but she was right. I'd stopped running years ago—and I had nowhere to go that she couldn't find me.

Lillian nodded. "Please release her, Madeline."

I let go and jumped away.

Sister Eunice rolled over, leaped to her feet, and hurtled toward me. I kicked out and planted my foot in her chest. Flesh on flesh, bone against bone. She went down, smack on her ass. She rolled to come at me again. I drew a deep breath, planted my feet, and prepared to meet her. She stopped. She sat on the mat, panting like a winded dog.

Amazing. I'd taken her down. Taken her out.

"Oh, my," Sister Lillian said. "That was well-done."

Sister Lillian's praise meant so much to me. "Thank you, Sister."

"Come with me, Madeline." She turned and I followed her, but I walked sideways to watch behind and in front of me. Sister Eunice staggered to her feet. She glared at me until I left the room. It felt so good to win. She'd make my life hell next week—and the week after. A small price to pay for such a rare and precious victory.

I changed into shoes before I followed Sister Lillian, and pulled a jacket over my lead gray gym uniform. They kept our hair cut short like a man's, so I didn't need a brush. My hair is white as a mid-January snow. That hair, my pale blue eyes, and the scar on my face isolated me long before I arrived here. Sister Eunice wasn't the only one who called me a freak.

I didn't ask where we were going. The Sisters had per-

sistently taught the futility of questions and defiance. I'd
stopped asking questions. Defiance remained a work in
progress.

We walked the brick path through the sculptured
flower gardens to the administration office. Summer approached upstate New York and brought a multitude of
blooms, offering their pretty faces to the afternoon sun.
Sometimes, in my few free hours, I'd come here to lose
myself in the sweet fragrance of the growing season.

The Sisters of Justice Correctional College looked
like a couple of weathered-stone medieval castles with
the incredible English-cottage gardens between. Ivy
covered the walls in some places, and sickly green algae
grew at the foundation in others. I was intimately ac-
quainted with the algae. I spent many hours with bucket
and brushes, scrubbing it, only to have it grow back
within days, sometimes hours. The smaller building
housed the Sisters' apartments and offices, and the
larger building had the dorms, classrooms, and training
rooms.

At first, I had thought the Sisters were nuns. Maybe
they are in a bizarre way. They all wore black robes, except Sister Eunice, who dressed in fatigues like a soldier.
They rarely spoke without imparting some factual information. Some are kind but stern teachers. A few are ill-
tempered hags.

The key word—*correctional*—went by me the first
week. No wall or fence surrounded the grounds, and no
bars covered the windows. No one had ever escaped,
though. I tried twice. Each time, two Sisters met me and
hauled me back before I made it to the property line. I'd
never seen more than thirty young girls here at one time.
Right now, there were only ten. I'd been here longer
than most. The Sisters came and went, too, and it seemed
as if Justice were a sanctuary for them as well as a prison
for us. Only sweet Lillian and brutal Eunice remained

constant here, and for some inexplicable reason, they focused most of their attention on me.

Sister Lillian slowed to walk beside me. I straightened, uneasy at her action. She'd broken a firm rule. Students are supposed to walk behind the Sisters. The hem of her robe brushed the stone path, giving the illusion that she floated rather than walked like a mere mortal.

"Do you remember when you first came here, Madeline?" Her voice usually carried soft laughter, but this time a more serious note crept in.

"I remember." How could I forget? I'd expected state prison when they put me on the transport bus, not to be dropped off at a massive country estate.

"You were so angry." She spoke in a softer voice.

"I'm still angry." I always told Sister Lillian the truth. She never judged me.

"And you learned . . . ?"

"I have a right to be angry." I knew the mantra, the lessons they had pounded into me with complete indifference to my pain. "Bad things may happen. But I can and will control my emotions."

"And why do you control them?"

"Control makes me stronger." Again, recited the mantra. "Control permits intelligent action rather than reckless disaster."

She gave me a wonderful smile, angelic and genuine. I had to smile back. I loved this woman.

"I love you, too, dear." Sister Lillian laid a hand on my arm and squeezed hard. The intensity surprised me. "Madeline, if we could have the scar removed, we would."

"I know, Sister."

The scar—the smooth, flat silver streak across my cheek—had been created by magic, so it was beyond the skill of the finest surgeon to remove. Other than Sister Eunice's occasional taunting, the Sisters ignored it.

I hated it, because it bound my life to a terrible duty. In some ways, though, it was my armor, my shield. My solitary nature and the scar kept my fellow inmates at a distance. I neither wanted nor needed friends. Whatever I endured here, I endured with only occasional comfort or counsel.

I won't say the Sisters broke me, but they came close. For the last six years, they'd beaten me down and raised me up again as a deadly weapon. I don't know why. I was twenty-six years old, and the State of New York had given me a twenty-five-year-to-life prison sentence.